ORACLE OF HELINTHIA

PRAISE FOR ORACLE OF HELINTHIA

"A fast-paced page-turner, the *Oracle of Helinthia* merges the human and the divine, mixing myth and history to deliver **an immersive story bursting with complex heroes**, political intrigue, unexpected twists, and extraordinary world-building. Readers will delight in this fresh peek into ancient Greece."
—**Malayna Evans, author of *Neferura***

"What a ride! **Another gripping story of love, betrayal, and political intrigue** from the author of the *Epic of Helinthia*. Divine motives are unclear, loyalty is in question, and danger lurks in the shadows. Pankey's storytelling will keep you turning pages!
—**Sharon Lynn Fisher, author of *Salt & Broom***

PRAISE FOR EPIC OF HELINTHIA

"**A fantastical adventure** of mortal rebellion and divine games."
—*Historical Novel Society*

"**An amazing debut** filled with gods and goddesses, heroes and villains, love and loss, blood and tears: everything a fantasy novel needs to keep readers turning the page late into the night!"
—**Maria V. Snyder *New York Times* bestselling author of *The Study of Poisons***

"In *Epic of Helinthia*, M.J. Pankey flawlessly combines the magic and mythology of ancient Greece with the richness and scope of the epic fantasy genre. With a fabulous cast of characters, **breathless action** and a driving plot, this adventure is not to be missed!"
—**A.D. Rhine, author of *Horses of Fire***

ORACLE OF HELINTHIA

MJ PANKEY

MUSE AND QUILL
PRESS

Published by Muse and Quill Press
Augusta, Georgia

Edited by Elana A. Mugdan
www.beacons.ai/dragonspleen

Cover design by Sadie Butterworth-Jones
www.luneviewpublishing.co.uk

Interior Cover Design and Character Illustrations by Marina Charalambides
https://www.marinacharalambides.com

Map design by Elana A. Mugdan

ISBN (Special Edition Paperback): 978-1-965752-00-5
ISBN (Special Edition Hardcover): 978-1-965752-90-6
ISBN (Paperback): 979-8-9872521-7-8
ISBN (Large Print): 978-1-965752-01-2
ISBN (eBook): 979-8-9872521-8-5

Library of Congress Control Number: 2025900361

We are not powerless.

CONTENT WARNINGS

This novel contains adult themes and situations that may be triggering to readers. A full list is available at the end of this book.

GLOSSARY

GODS AND OTHERWORLDLY BEINGS

Ajax: Greek warrior who incited Athena's wrath by taking the seeress Cassandra from her temple

Aphrodite: Goddess of love and romance

Apollo: God of the sun and healing

Artemis: Goddess of the hunt and wild animals

Ares: God of war

Atlas: Titan who holds up the sky on his shoulders

Athena: Goddess of wisdom and strategy

Charon: Titan responsible for ferrying souls into the Underworld

Dawn: Titaness who embodies the dawn

Demeter: Goddess of the harvest

Echo: A mountain nymph who was cursed to only repeat the last words of others. The embodiment of an echoing sound

Eileithyia: Goddess of childbearing and motherhood

Eros: Child of Aphrodite and god of love

Fates: Three goddesses responsible for weaving the destinies of humans

Fury/Furies: Demon(s) from the Underworld, often summoned to exact vengeance on mortals who have offended the gods

Gaia: Titaness of the earth, synonymous with Mother Earth

Hades: God of the Underworld

Helinthia: Goddess of the Island of Helinthia, for whom the island is named

Helios: Titan who pulls the sun across the sky behind his chariot

Hera: Goddess of power, Anassa (Queen) of the gods, and Zeus's wife

Hermes: God of stealth and speed, often a messenger of the gods

Hestia: Goddess of the hearth and home

Medusa: A gorgon with snake hair that can turn men to stone with a look, considered a creature of exceptional ugliness

Nymph: Immortal beings who draw power from nature, unlike gods, they can be killed

Ordanus: Demi-god and son of Apollo, the first Anax (King) of Helinthia

Paris: A prince of Troy who proclaimed Aphrodite the most beautiful goddess and was rewarded the mortal woman Helen as his bride

Poseidon: God of the ocean and seas

Zeus: God of justice, hospitality, and Anax of the gods

POSITIONS AND HIERARCHY

Anax/Anassa: King/Queen of Helinthia, rules over the island from the Ninenarn Polis

Archon: Sheriff of a single Polis

Basileus/Basileia: Chieftain/Chieftainess, ruler of a single Polis

Chancellor: Second-in-command to the Anax/Anassakubernai

Doulos/Doula, Douloi: Slave (male)/Slave (female), Slaves (plu)

Kubernao/Kubernia, Kubernai: Governor/Governess, Governors (plu), ruler of a single village in a Polis

Kyrios/Kyria, Kyrioi: Citizen (male)/Citizen (female), Citizens (plu) of a Polis

Strategos: Military Commander, in charge of a Polis's entire military force

ITEMS

Aegis: Shield that bears Medusa's head

Amphora/Amphorae: Jar/Jars (various sizes)

Amphoriskos/Amphoriskoi: Small jar/Small jars (fits in hand)

Chiton: Long tunic worn by both men and women

Drachma/Drachmae: Coin/Coins

Himation: Wrap or cloak

Pelekys: Battle ax

PLACES AND ARCHITECTURE

Agora: Town center or square
Andron: Private sitting room
Atrium: Entrance Hall/Reception area
Bouleuterion: A horseshoe-shaped structure where politicians or council members meet to discuss affairs of polis
Elysium: Where the honorable dead dwell in the Underworld
Gynaikon: A room of a villa dedicated to women and women's work
Khora/Khorai: Surrounding country and provinces belonging to a Polis
Library of Critius: Home of the scholars, the topmost authority in Helinthia for instruction in science, religion, and interpretation of signs from the gods
Olympus: A palace atop Mount Ida, where the gods dwell
Palaistra: A rectangular structure with a large central courtyard that serves as an athletic training ground
Peristyle: Covered porch surrounding an inner courtyard of a villa
Polis/Poleis: City-State/City-States that make up Helinthia (Ninenarn, Shallinath, Thellshun, Golpathia)
Portico: Covered porch over the front entrance of a villa
Styx: The river that separates the Underworld from the land of the living, on which Charon ferries souls of the dead across
Tartarus: The deepest level of the Underworld reserved for disobedient Titans
Triklinion: Dining room
Underworld: Place where the spirits of the dead wander, ruled over by Hades and guarded by Cerberus, the Hound of the Underworld

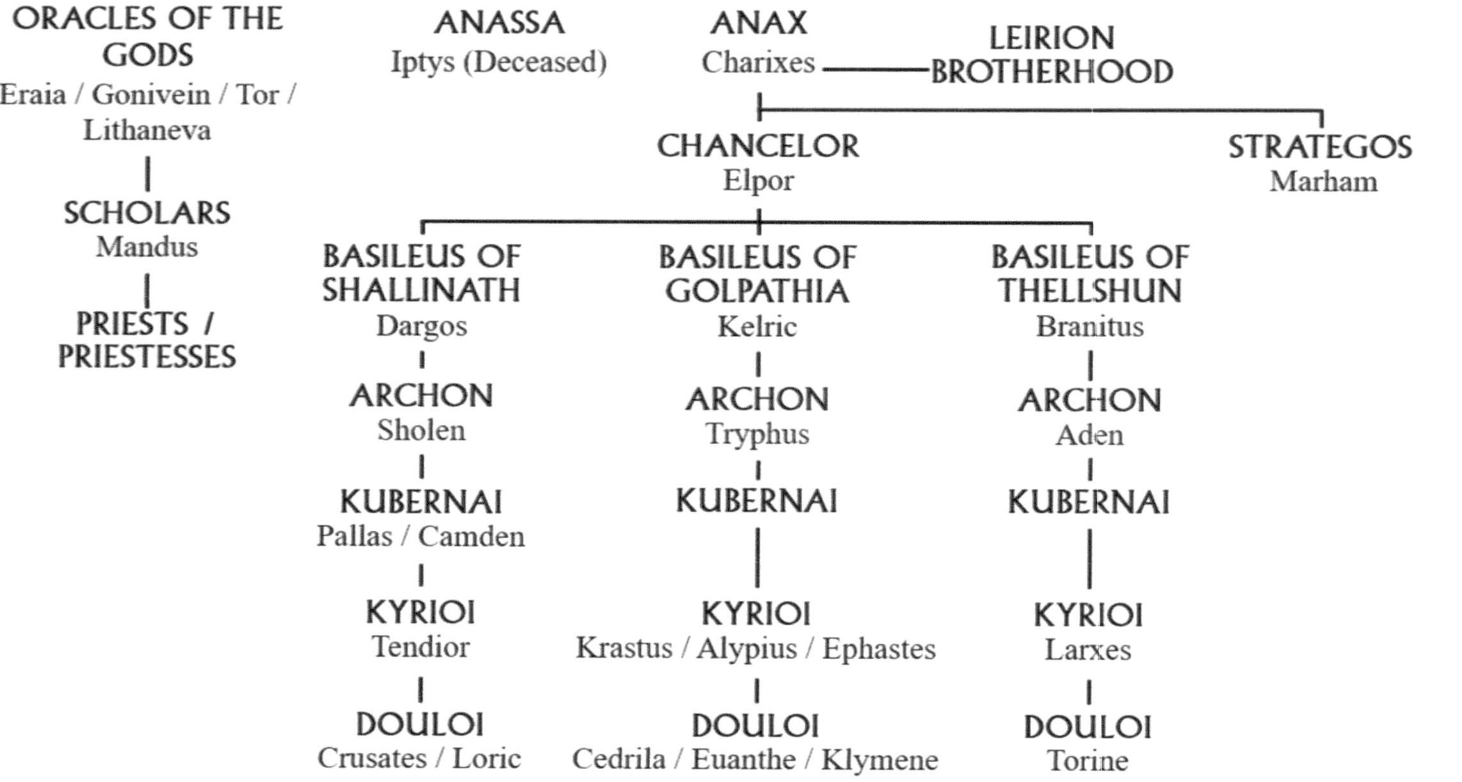

ORACLES OF THE GODS
Eraia / Gonivein / Tor / Lithaneva
SCHOLARS
Mandus
PRIESTS / PRIESTESSES
ANASSA
Iptys (Deceased)
ANAX
Charixes
LEIRION BROTHERHOOD
CHANCELOR
Elpor
STRATEGOS
Marham
BASILEUS OF SHALLINATH
Dargos
ARCHON
Sholen
KUBERNAI
Pallas / Camden
KYRIOI
Tendior
DOULOI
Crusates / Loric
BASILEUS OF GOLPATHIA
Kelric
ARCHON
Tryphus
KUBERNAI
KYRIOI
Krastus / Alypius / Ephastes
DOULOI
Cedrila / Euanthe / Klymene
BASILEUS OF THELLSHUN
Branitus
ARCHON
Aden
KUBERNAI
KYRIOI
Larxes
DOULOI
Torine

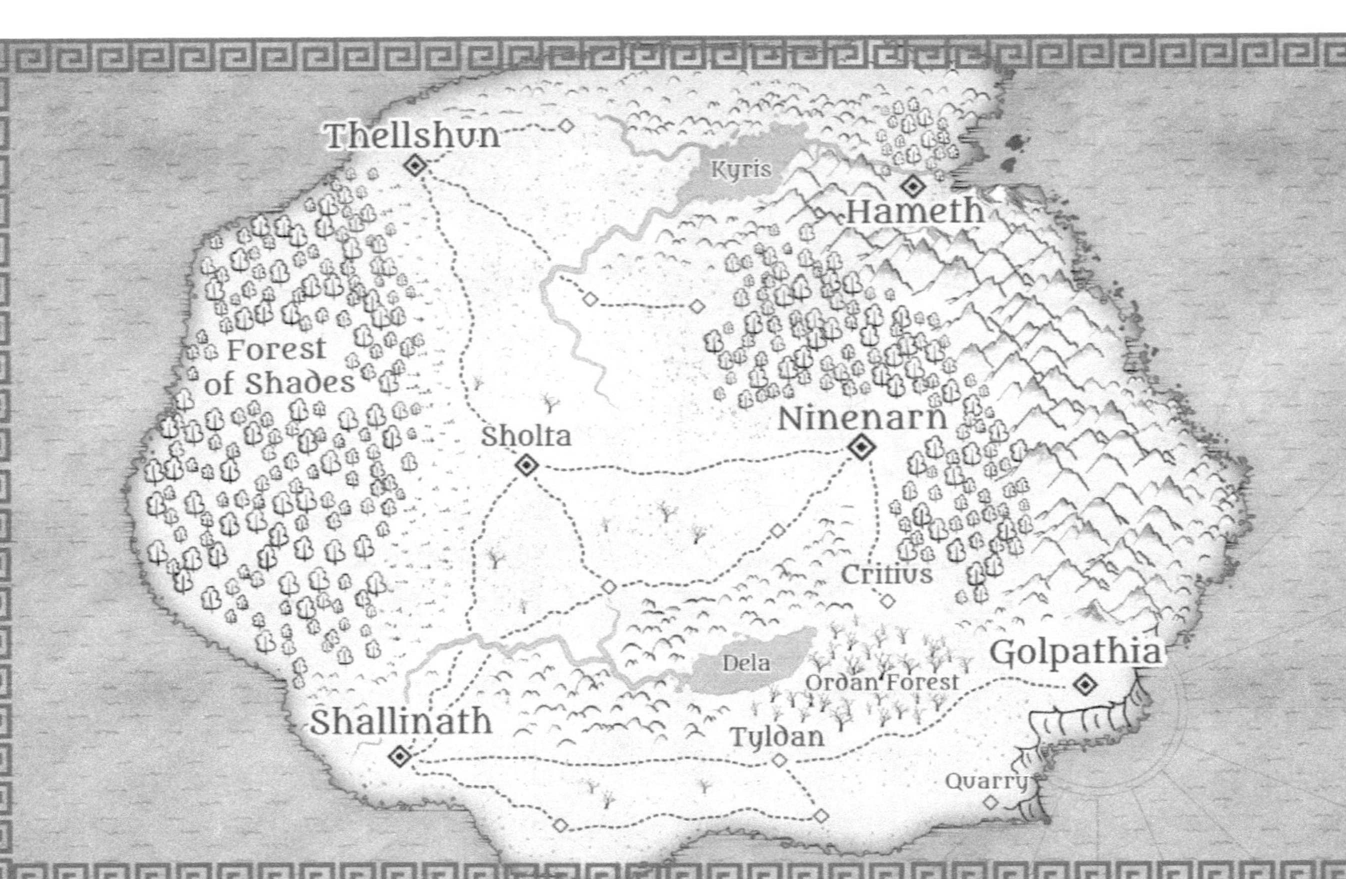

Thellshun
Kyris
Hameth
Forest
of Shades
Sholta
Ninenarn
Critius
Dela
Ordan Forest
Golpathia
Shallinath
Tyldan
Quarry

HELINTHIA

HERA

APOLLO

ARTEMIS

CHARIXES

TOR

A NOTE FROM THE AUTHOR

Thank you so much for reading *Oracle of Helinthia*. I'm thrilled and excited that of all the books available to read, you chose to dive into mine.

Though you are under no obligation to leave a review, I hope you will do so. I'm an indie author, and your recommendation will be the primary way that more readers find my book.

I love connecting with new readers! If you would like to get in touch, please see the ABOUT THE AUTHOR section at the back of the book for all my communication channels.

I hope you enjoy *Oracle of Helinthia*!

ORACLE OF HELINTHIA

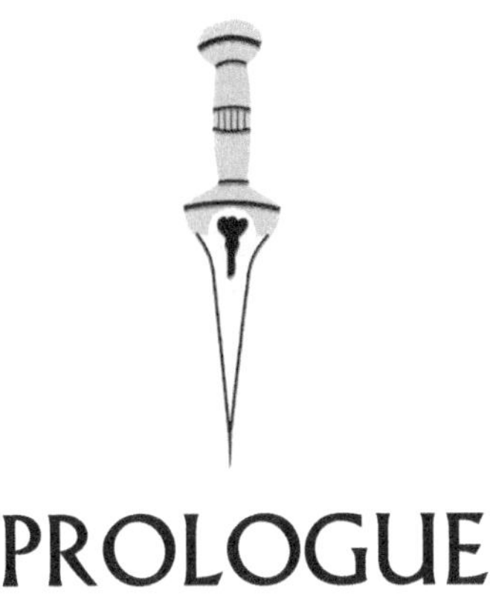

PROLOGUE

FORLUNA

In the fourth year of the reign of Anassa Iptys

"THE *KYRIOI* GROW BOLDER BY the day."

Forluna lowered the scroll she was reading, a surveyor's accounting of land in the northeast corner of the island, and peered at Anassa Iptys lounging on an adjacent couch beneath the window. "Oh?"

Iptys sighed, crumpling the paper she was reading and flicking it away. It bounced on the throne room's tiles and rolled toward Forluna, who snatched it up with a mischievous grin.

Forluna smoothed it out on her leg. "Charixes," she mused, studying the signature. "Isn't he a member of the army?"

Iptys seemed to detect the interest in Forluna's voice because she rolled her eyes. "Yes, a captain."

'My renown and favor grow daily among the ranks. Every victory I dedicate to you. One day, I will be worthy of you.'

Forluna's cheeks warmed at the words. "He sounds smitten. You don't find him intriguing?"

Iptys bounced her foot as she stared out the window at the city of Ninenarn. Her city. "He's too… I don't know. Self-absorbed. 'One day, I will be worthy of you.' Ugh. Then what? That will be enough for me to marry him?"

Forluna shrugged. "Should it not be? Isn't that what men are supposed to do?"

Iptys turned to her. "These men, every one of these kyrioi, are only focused on themselves, their own aspirations, their own 'destiny.' Women are merely the rungs of the ladder they climb to rise higher and higher toward the peak of vain aspirations. Just wait until a man sets his sights on you. He'll say all kinds of honorable things, swear he loves you, does it all for you, but underneath it all, he would forget you if he thought there was nothing to gain from seducing you."

Forluna fingered the corner of the letter. "But you're the *anassa*. There isn't a man in Helinthia who wouldn't gain something by marrying you."

Iptys rested her elbow on the marble sill, the squared edges worn smooth by centuries of royal arms, and plopped her chin into her palm. "I know."

"So, what are you going to do?"

Iptys didn't have the opportunity to answer before a knock on the door interrupted the silence—an assertive knock. The kind that demanded decorum. Iptys rose from her couch and stood with hands clasped. With that, the impassioned young woman transformed into a regal, composed anassa. Forluna followed suit and took her position behind her.

"Enter," Iptys commanded.

The large double-oak doors swung inwards, revealing the intricate carving of Ordanus, son of Apollo and first anax of Helinthia. His eyes seemed to gaze directly at the throne from the wood grains, observing in silent judgment how well the current ruler upheld his legacy.

"Oracle Eraia," Jaxus, the porter, announced. He bowed his head and stepped aside to allow the visitor through.

An ominous feeling settled in Forluna's gut. Why was the oracle of Hera here? It wasn't unusual for representatives of the gods to seek audience with Anassa Iptys, but Forluna couldn't recall a time when word hadn't been sent ahead of their arrival.

Silvery strands had pulled free from Eraia's windblown braids and stuck out in all directions. They created a strange sort of halo in the sunlight filtering in behind her. A layer of dust coated her face, creasing into mud around her neck and elbows. This was not the look of a dignified oracle, more like a harbinger of horror. She stared across the hall at Iptys, eyes wild and forehead furrowed into a determined expression as she hastened around the porter.

Iptys nodded to Jaxus, who bowed again and stepped out, drawing the doors closed behind him. "Oracle Eraia. What brings you here in such… haste?"

"I have a message from Hera." Eraia's voice trembled, her skin pale beneath the dust.

Anxiety writhed up Forluna's spine and lodged in her chest.

"Of course." Iptys strode forward to clasp Eraia's hands. "Shall I order a bath for you, some refreshment? You must be exhaus—"

"There's no time for that. The anassa of gods and mortals demands action," Eraia said. "*Swift* action."

Iptys dropped her hands and fidgeted with her fingers—an early signal of panic. Despite her four years of rule and countless interactions with important figures, she hadn't yet mastered confrontation with the gods' will. Forluna resisted the urge to throw off decorum and stand at her side. Iptys had to carry herself before the oracle.

"Of course. What does she command?" Iptys pretended to smooth her golden hair out of her eyes to hide her fraying nerves. She tossed a tentative glance over her shoulder to Forluna, who nodded back encouragingly.

Eraia took a deep breath, threading her fingers together in front of her so tightly her knuckles turned white. "Helinthia has offended Hera. As recompense, Hera demands that we renounce Helinthia and withhold our sacrifices upon her altar."

Iptys drew back. "What?" She looked at Forluna in earnest now, brown eyes wide as though needing confirmation of what she'd heard.

Eraia focused her attention upon Forluna as well, fierce and demanding. Forluna's true nature—that of a nymph, an immortal, one who should be all too understanding of the wrath the gods could mete—wasn't hidden from Eraia.

The anxiety in Forluna's chest sharpened, bile threatening to rise up her throat. She averted her gaze to the ground, unsure what to say, or if she should say anything. This was Iptys' test.

"That's… unusual." Iptys straightened her spine. "How did Helinthia offend her?"

"My goddess did not say."

Forluna detected a hint of fear in Eraia's whispered tone. Fear of Hera? Or fear that Iptys would not heed her warning? "She said only that Helinthia's conduct was egregious and prideful. To prove that we are not drawn from the same offensive stock, we must renounce her or suffer a famine that will claim the lives of thousands of innocents."

Iptys stepped away from the oracle and walked shakily toward her throne. The cold, hard marble promised little comfort, but she slumped into it anyway. "When did she tell you this?"

"Last night… in the middle of the night. I came immediately."

That explained her haggard appearance.

"How long does she demand we do this?" Iptys said.

Eraia swallowed. "Indefinitely."

Iptys was stone-still for a moment. Forluna wished she could see her face, read what she was thinking. Finally, the anassa spoke, her voice just above a whisper. "How long do I have to decide?"

Eraia stepped forward, tilting her head. "Decide *what*? Whether to let innocent people suffer and die?"

Forluna's gaze jerked up at Eraia's sharpened tone.

Iptys bristled, the skin of her neck flushing red. "Of course not, Eraia. But I can't just renounce Helinthia. She's our goddess! This is *her* island. Surely, something else can be done to appease Hera."

"Hera is the anassa of *Olympus*. What could you possibly offer to assuage her wrath? Nothing. Except obedience." Eraia looked again at Forluna, anger and desperation in the depths of her golden eyes. "You know the gods. Tell her."

Forluna's mouth went dry as she heard Iptys draw a sharp breath. Iptys despised being subverted. Decisions of the throne could not come from the nymph, mentor or not, but Forluna couldn't ignore the dangerous tension taking root, either. She instinctively reached down and squeezed Iptys' shoulder to stop her from saying something rash. Iptys stiffened beneath her touch, then relaxed.

Forluna thanked Hermes that Iptys had withdrawn whatever reaction was poised to fly off her tongue.

"Eraia," Iptys began calmly. "Please do not think I take this lightly. But you have to understand my position. I am the anassa of *Helinthia*—the island as well as the goddess. I am bound to serve her, as are we all. To make a pronouncement such as this, to abandon her? The people will renounce *me*."

Eraia clenched her fists, and Iptys scooted to the edge of her throne, quickly raising a hand in supplication.

"I'm not saying no, but I need time to break this to the *basilei* and the *kubernai*, to seek their counsel in this matter. They have a right to know and offer their perspectives. If I agree to your demands outright, they'll think me foolish and weak, that I'm just bowing to any whim."

Forluna inwardly groaned at Iptys' careless words. A demand of Hera was not 'any whim.' *I still have so much to teach her.*

The oracle had not missed it, either. She drew away in shock and disdain.

Forluna stepped forward, hoping to soften the offense. "You've carried a serious message to us, Oracle Eraia. That's undeniable." She turned to Iptys. "The Oracle of Helinthia should be summoned to give us answers for this slight." She hoped her deflection onto Helinthia's oracle would ease Eraia's temper. But she was wrong.

Eraia's eyes darkened as she shook her head. She scoffed down at the floor, defeated, but still armed with venom. "You *are* foolish and weak, Iptys," she muttered. "As foolish and weak as Helinthia. Your very hesitancy, this idea that you can *bargain* with Hera, is absurd. You will bring ruin on us all." She looked up at Iptys again, eyes brimming with tears. "I came to you because I wanted to believe that Hera was wrong about you, that you are capable of seeing beyond your own pride and self-righteousness to save innocent lives, even at the expense of your own power." Her restraint cracked. "You foolish *child*! It is *Hera* who bestows power upon men, and *Hera* who will take it from you for defying her."

Iptys remained still as a statue, but the reddening hues of her neck and face betrayed the anger boiling underneath.

Forluna's heart pounded in her ears. No one had ever spoken to the anassa like this.

Then she noticed something, *someone*, move from the shadows behind Eraia. Tall and regal. Her breath hitched as the figure came closer. Forluna's mouth opened, but only a raspy wheeze emerged. Eraia bore it no heed. Her voice was rising as she continued her rebuke.

"I should have gone to the Library first. Told the scholars. *They* would have listened. They *will* listen. They have to. The island must know of this."

"Eraia…" Iptys' words were lost as the figure caught her attention. It glided up behind the oracle.

Forluna gasped. *Helinthia.*

Eraia's eyes widened in fear as the goddess' hands circled her neck and lifted her up. The oracle choked, kicking for the ground her toes could no longer reach. She clawed at the hands squeezing her throat.

Iptys grabbed Forluna in terror. Forluna returned the tight embrace. Fear constricted every limb.

With a *snap,* Eraia went limp. She fell, slapping against the tiles in a crumpled heap.

Iptys screamed, nails digging into Forluna's shoulders as they clung to one another.

"You will tell no one what Hera's oracle has said," Helinthia announced, her tone cold, commanding. "And you will *not* abandon my altar."

Frantic voices from outside.

Iptys' scream had been heard.

"Do this, and you will have my favor, Iptys." Helinthia turned and sauntered back into the shadows, fading into obscurity as the doors flew open. Jaxus and two guards rushed in.

Iptys burst into sobs, clinging to Forluna, whose own emotions lodged painfully in her throat. Her knees weakened and she sank to the cold floor, bringing Iptys down with her like a puddle of melted wax.

"What happened here?" Jaxus cried, kneeling to examine Eraia's body as the guards fanned out to search the shadows for an assailant, swords drawn. The porter sank back on his heels, shaking his head. "She awaits the ferry, Anassa."

The guards returned empty-handed, and the porter nodded to them. "Summon the *archon* and the priest of Hermes."

The guards sheathed their swords and sprinted from the room.

Jaxus closed Eraia's lids over her vacant eyes, shaking his head in bewilderment. "What happened?" His low voice was urgent.

Iptys choked down her sobs, rubbing her eyes and nose on the shoulder of her *chiton*. She swallowed and looked at Forluna, stricken. "She came with a prophecy…" Iptys halted as she looked back at the dead oracle. "But…"

"What was the prophecy?" his tone was soothing, but firm.

Forluna's stomach clenched into a painful knot, heart pounding in her ears. Offend Hera, or Helinthia? Could a more impossible choice exist?

Iptys stared into the shadows, where the silhouette of Helinthia lurked, watching.

Calling it a choice was too generous.

Jaxus followed the anassa's gaze curiously, but Forluna knew he couldn't see what she and Iptys saw. Only an immortal, or one with immortal blood, could see the gods. He looked expectantly at his anassa.

Iptys straightened her shoulders and smoothed invisible strands of hair away from her face. "She collapsed before she could give it."

From the shadows, Helinthia smiled.

CHAPTER 1

LITHANEVA

In the eighteenth year of the reign of Anax Charixes

SUNLIGHT TEASED LITHANEVA'S EYES OPEN. The smell of olive blossoms prickled her nose. The cheerful *coo-coo* of a cuckoo on the roof and the screech of some far-off bird of prey carried through the window, borne on the wind rustling through the garden trees.

She filled her lungs with its sweetness, then froze, aware of the body lying beside her and the arm across her stomach. She turned her head slowly, hoping she was the only one awake.

Sensations of the previous night flooded her mind. Long hair tickling her thighs, lips crushing hers, experienced hands coaxing waves of pleasure from every inch of her, beads of sweat gathering from the heat of their bodies and breath.

Lithaneva pressed the plush pillow down with her hand to see her lover's face, and a slow smile tugged her lips.

Helinthia's eyes remained closed, the blanket pulled up to her ears. For a goddess, she seemed a little cold-blooded, unable to sleep if more than her ears were exposed, even on warm nights.

Lithaneva slid her hand beneath the fur blanket to stroke

Helinthia's thigh with the backs of her fingers.

"Mm." The goddess stirred and scooted toward Lithaneva's touch, inching her face closer on the pillow until their noses brushed.

"Good morning, Goddess," Lithaneva whispered, drinking in her perfection. She kissed Helinthia's nose and pecked her lips, dreading the ache that would consume her when this moment was gone.

"It's too early," the goddess pouted, pulling Lithaneva closer until their bodies were pressed together. She buried her face in Lithaneva's dark curls and nipped her ear before growing still, ready to slip back into slumber. Suddenly, her eyes opened wide and she sat up, training her gaze on the window like an eagle spotting a rabbit in the brush. "What is that?"

The blanket slid down Helinthia's shoulders, exposing her lush breasts. If the goddess hadn't seemed so disturbed, Lithaneva would have pulled her back down, captured those provocative lips with her own, and explored her naked skin inch by smooth inch all over again.

"What is what?" She drew her gaze up to study Helinthia's face, still angled toward the window. Lithaneva tilted her head, listening, but all she heard was birdsong. "The cuckoos? They've been stalking a sparrow's nest under the eaves, I think."

Helinthia was still for another breath before she shook herself, as though snapping from a trance. "I've stayed too long," she muttered.

Reluctance writhed in Lithaneva's chest. The goddess was right, of course, and Lithaneva had her own priorities to tackle. "My father arrives today. Branitus expects me to prepare the hospitality."

"Ugh." Helinthia rolled away and stood. "I hate them both. I could just kill them and be rid of them."

Lithaneva giggled as she untangled herself from the sheets and planted her feet on the cold tile floor. "Hera would know we cheated."

Helinthia snatched her chiton from the floor with such aggression Lithaneva was amazed it didn't tear.

Unsure it was safe to show amusement, she hid her face behind her own garment as she threw it over her head and slid her arms through the sleeves, still fastened at the shoulder with the broaches she hadn't had time to unclasp last night. "Besides," she went on, her tone cautious, "Branitus isn't so bad."

Helinthia cut her a glance, eyebrows pinching together as she set her antler crown on her head. "The thought of him touching you makes me want to crash this entire island into Poseidon's domain."

Lithaneva shook her head and closed the distance between them, cupping Helinthia's face in her hands and planting a kiss on her lips. "Branitus has his own conquest. He never wants me."

The memory of catching Branitus in the throes of passion with the dancer from their wedding banquet teased a smile across her face. Branitus was in love, and not with her. She couldn't be more thrilled.

Helinthia swept Lithaneva head to toe with a possessive look that sent a jolt of pleasure down Lithaneva's spine. "He's not pressing you for a child?"

"No," she answered, dreading the very idea. To have a child was to place shackles around a woman's ankles.

That's probably why my father is coming, she thought, sitting on the edge of the bed and slipping her feet into her soft rabbit-skin boots. It was the most unoriginal plan to prevent her from reinserting herself into the politics of Ninenarn, but it would be effective if successful.

Helinthia sat beside her and strapped on her golden sandals, unsatisfied, but willing to let the matter drop.

Lithaneva leaned over and pressed a kiss to Helinthia's forehead. "My father will be watching me closely." She couldn't bear to say the rest: *I can't see you tonight.*

"Hmph." Helinthia's temperament could be fickle, jealous, impatient, angry, even reckless. But that was true of every god, wasn't it?

Biting her lip, Lithaneva slid her finger along the goddess' jaw and turned her face to look into those deep maroon irises. They were bright and fierce as ever, as though on the cusp of unleashing some pent-up fury, but there was something new in their depths that hadn't been there the night before: anxiety, or fear?

She's afraid my father will try to hurt me. And he would certainly try, but no matter how many times Lithaneva reassured Helinthia that her father's callousness no longer cut her, Helinthia didn't seem to believe her. It was no use making another attempt now.

"I love you." She melted her mouth against Helinthia's, gently nipping her bottom lip as she pulled away.

She stood and strode across the room, glancing back when she reached the doorway. She tightened her fingers around the door handle to keep herself from running back.

Helinthia had turned back to the window.

"I'll come to your altar if I can," Lithaneva said. Only the smallest of nods acknowledged she'd said anything at all. She closed the door behind her and hurried from her apartment. Her heart ached at the distance she was creating between her and Helinthia. But love for the goddess propelled her to Branitus' room. She knocked once, then barged in.

Branitus bolted upright, instinctively raising his hand to shield his eyes as Lithaneva threw open the window. Sunlight burst into the room, and Branitus groaned. "Why?"

A second form wiggled beside Branitus, burrowing further under the covers.

Lithaneva lifted a brow. "Have you forgotten what day it is?" She smirked at Branitus' red face, then tilted her head at the lump beside her husband. "Good morning, Larxes."

The cover slowly drew down, and Branitus' handsome lover peeked over the furs. His hazel eyes blinked blearily at her, his black hair a disheveled mess of curls. "Morning, Princess."

Branitus yanked the covers back up over Larxes' head and looked sheepishly at her. He still seemed quite confused as to why she wasn't upset with him over his infidelity. Perhaps he'd heard so many stories about jealous wives that her apparent calmness worried him more than her overt fury might have.

It was thrilling, knowing this simple thing invoked such a reaction in a man known for being brutish. She couldn't help the small smile that lifted her lips.

He saw her amusement and scowled. "I know what day it is, and I'll rise when I'm damned well ready." He slumped back down on the bed and rolled away from her—toward Larxes.

Lithaneva gritted her teeth. If she couldn't be alone one more moment with her lover, she'd be damned to wander the bank of the *Styx* if Branitus did not make the same sacrifice.

"Shall I let my father wake you, then? Oh, but he'll be furious to find you in bed with someone other than his daughter."

Branitus growled in exasperation and threw back the covers, almost leaping to his feet and glaring at her before picking up his tunic from the floor. He slid it up over his shoulders, then reached for his cloak slung haphazardly over a couch. "I thought your father hated you," he snapped, resentment dripping in every syllable.

"He does."

Branitus stopped, then looked at her with narrowed eyes.

She clasped her hands and smiled sweetly at him.

The red in Branitus' face spread down his neck and across his chest as his shoulders began to tremble. He threw back his head and let out a bawdy laugh that seemed to shake the beams on the ceiling. He strode toward her as he tossed his cloak over his shoulders. "How fortunate that my wife isn't as vindictive as her father," he said, bending to plant a kiss on her cheek.

"Not yet," she answered, leaning into the kiss and allowing her voice to don a playful, yet urgent, tone. Though she had no sexual desire for her husband, she couldn't deny a growing affection for him. It was a shame having to mislead him, but she held no delusions that he would support her if he learned of her plans to overthrow her father.

Larxes propped himself up with a sculpted arm to watch their exchange. "Shall I dance tonight?" he asked, a mischievous glint in his eyes.

Branitus grinned and opened his mouth, but Lithaneva spoke first.

"No."

Branitus' thick brows pinched. "Why not? We're having a feast, aren't we? What's a feast without dancing? And for the anax, no less."

Lithaneva rolled her eyes. "If my father sees you ogling Larxes, he'll end our alliance." She knew Branitus took it as a joke, but there was truth behind her words. If there were any doubt that Branitus' attentions lay elsewhere, Charixes might begin to wonder what Lithaneva did with her time. And that might prove bothersome.

"I suppose we should pretend we're husband and wife, then," he grumbled. Her own lip curled at the thought. "Fine. Let's go." He sighed, throwing Larxes a wistful look before focusing his attention on her. "I'll see to the guard. You do the menial wife things."

She patted his shoulder and stepped away to head to the kitchens. Her mind raced with questions. Why was her father coming here? Official business could be conveyed by a courier, or even the chancellor. A personal visit indicated that whatever he had to say couldn't be trusted to another.

She rubbed her hands together and grinned with anticipation. No doubt her father hoped to frighten them with a personal appearance, but she had every intention of disappointing him. He might be able to intimidate most men with a shift of his eyes, but not her, and hopefully not Branitus, either.

She entered the kitchen and instructed the *douloi* on what to prepare for the menu. Charixes hated goat meat, and goose was his favorite, so she instructed the cooks to prepare a roasted swine with boiled barley and carrots—a middle ground to avoid immediate conflict. She slipped a few coins to the *doula*, Torine, to go through the town and command every merchant with a goose to display it in plain view of her father's entourage. Torine eyed her as though she were mad, but didn't question it.

The rest of the morning passed in a blur, her mannerisms and directions to the douloi automatic. Prepare her father's apartment. Wash and dry the linens. Weave fresh laurel crowns. Hang olive blossoms on the windows.

By midday, Lithaneva's blood tingled through her limbs, the unwelcome combination of fatigue and anxiety. The thought of Branitus all over her, even if it was just an act, turned her stomach.

She rubbed her aching neck and rolled her head to the sky. At least she wouldn't have to hide her hatred of her father. He knew full well of her feelings. She straightened her spine. This was for Helinthia.

Helinthia. She needed to see her. Just one more time before she was plunged into a world of misery. Lithaneva's footsteps carried her into the courtyard toward the temple of the goddess. She ached to touch her, feel her warmth under her palm. A drop of her blood, and Helinthia would know she wanted her.

Her body warmed beneath her chiton as her thoughts ran wild with passion. Hunger.

She was almost at the steps of the solitary temple when something dove in front of her. She leapt back, eyes widening at the writhing cloud of feathers and dust before her. A screech, and then a hawk righted itself and stared up at her with a golden eye.

Lithaneva froze. Had the animal fallen, or had it dived on purpose?

The bird fluffed its feathers, blinked at her, then pecked at its underbelly.

Something was on its leg. Something *unnatural*.

She knelt slowly. The hawk raised its head. It didn't fly away. It just stared at her.

Lithaneva squinted at the object, heart beating furiously in her breast. From behind her, she could hear a commotion growing so loud the cuckoos had ceased their songs. Hoofbeats. Cheers. *My father.*

He was early. No doubt hoping to catch them unprepared, but she knew his tricks too well for that. They were ready for him. Branitus would be expecting her presence on the *portico* to greet him as *Basileia* of Thellshun. An urgent shiver raced up her spine.

She eased her hand toward the bird, her breath burning in her lungs. Would it try to strike her? Thrash her with its wings? Her instincts told her to flee. She didn't. The object's existence called to her, practically pulled her fingers toward it.

The hawk blinked its golden orbs. Daring her.

Lithaneva slid her fingertips beneath the hawk's soft belly and grazed the thing around its leg. Paper, tied with a linen thread. *This bird is trained.* It had to be. She leaned forward on her knees to get closer and pulled the string. The scroll came free.

Immediately, the hawk sprang into the air, flinging dust and feathers. The force of its wings nearly knocked her on her rump, but she hardly cared.

Lithaneva unraveled the paper and scrutinized the tiny letters.
We found it.
~G

Air flooded her aching chest. Unprovoked tears stung her eyes. *G... Must be Gadnor. They found the heir!* She turned the paper over, frowning. *But who is it?*

Behind her, the commotion had dimmed. Charixes would be inside the villa now.

No matter. She would learn the heir's identity later. She stood and hurried the rest of the way into the temple and flung the paper onto the coals of Helinthia's altar. Her offering of devotion.

The flames licked it greedily until it was ash.

Lithaneva grinned up at the marble statue of her goddess. The first step of their plan was complete. *The heir is alive.* She resisted the urge to leap for joy and settled on hugging herself tight.

"I will win back your island, my love," she whispered, brushing her fingers along the cold marble toes of Helinthia's image before spinning quickly and bolting toward the villa.

Basileus Dargos and the awkward, lesser-known son of Basileus Raleon of Golpathia had upheld their end of the agreement.

Now it's my turn.

CHAPTER 2

GADNOR

THE TENSION AROUND THE TABLE was becoming an all-too-familiar occurrence. That didn't make it any easier to sit through. If anything, it made it even more challenging to walk into this room meal after meal and day after day and take a seat, pretending everything was fine when it clearly wasn't, not to anyone present.

Especially since Gadnor knew he was the reason for their discontent.

He stared at the grains of the wood table at the center of the room, waiting for the tension to snap. It wouldn't, not yet. But the anticipation made him want to flee.

He chanced a glance up at his five companions, trying to gauge the likelihood that this meal might be different from all the rest of the last week.

Kelric sat with arms folded loosely across his chest, his gaze wandering frequently to Gonivein sitting beside him. She looked as far away as Gadnor wished to be. Her shoulders slumped forward as she stared at her frail hands in her lap. Dargos fidgeted with his thumbs at the far end, and Gadnor could almost see the careful arguments he planned to lay out swirling behind his furrowed brow.

Forluna was just to Dargos' left, watching everyone as intently as Gadnor was. She offered him an encouraging smile when their eyes met.

Gadnor averted his gaze, feeling like a scolded child awaiting his parents' sentencing. Except neither of his parents were alive, and he hadn't done anything wrong. Yet.

The cook, Euanthe, entered from the kitchen with a large platter of roasted chicken and set it down on the table.

No one moved a muscle. The shuffling of her sandals across the tiles and the swish of her chiton as she returned to the kitchen was the only break in the stillness.

She returned a second time carrying a platter in each hand, one with bread and one with roasted potatoes and carrots. She set them down beside the chicken and eyed the ensemble dubiously. Her left eyelid twitched, something that only happened when she was irritated. She turned to Kelric, laying a wrinkled hand on his bare shoulder.

"Shall I fetch anything else, Basileus?" By the sweetness of Euanthe's tone, one would never guess that she was bothered, not unless they'd known her for as long as Gadnor had. She had been their cook since before he could remember.

Kelric smiled up at her and patted her hand affectionately. "No, thank you, Euanthe. You may go."

The fine lines around the woman's eyes crinkled as she beamed down at him. She looked at Gonivein. "I'll prepare your bath, *Kyria*," she said, before sweeping out of the room.

Once she was gone, Kelric immediately tore into the chicken, breaking off a leg and piling two plates high with the variety of food before them. He pushed one plate over to Gonivein.

She offered a weak smile and angled her head at him, but her eyes didn't quite reach Kelric's before they dropped back to her lap. She made no move to touch the food.

"I asked Euanthe to add a pinch of coriander to the dough, just as you like," Kelric said softly.

Gonivein's eyes shifted to the piece of bread before she took a small nibble and set it back on her plate. This seemed to satisfy Kelric enough to turn his attention to his own portion.

"So…" Dargos began, finally ending the silence.

Here it comes, Gadnor thought.

Kelric glared at Dargos, releasing a loud sigh. "Can we have *one* meal where we don't discuss this? I have more important things on my mind today."

Forluna flinched and stuffed a potato into her mouth.

"You know it's too late for that. Your wedding is *tomorrow*," Dargos answered.

"Can't I celebrate one day—a day I've waited five years for—in *peace*? Why must you sabotage everything?"

"This can't wait," Dargos insisted. "You owe Gadnor your answer."

"I've given my answer enough times to bore *Echo* to tears. Gadnor isn't *ready* to take on the responsibility of the *strategos*." Kelric chomped into a bite of meat. "He'll never be."

Dargos' dark eyes flashed beneath a furrowed brow. "Then who? Who will you appoint? If you pick someone else, you risk them overshadowing Gadnor's efforts. You know the strategos gets credit for the battles won."

"And he gets blamed for the losses," Kelric spat. "Trust me, I'm preventing Gadnor from making a colossal fool of himself and leaving our *polis* vulnerable."

"There won't be any losses. You and I will be here to guide him."

Gadnor sank down in his seat, wishing Hermes would throw a cloak of invisibility around his shoulders so he could escape this nightmare. The argument was always the same. Sometimes the words varied, but the outcome never changed. Gadnor doubted a decision would ever be reached about elevating him to strategos, leader of Golpathia's armies, decision maker of battle strategy. It was a title Kelric had held for years as their father's eldest son. Now that Kelric was Basileus, the position was vacant.

Gadnor never wished he had been born someone else more than when he was placed in the middle of this tired argument. He understood Dargos' perspective. To win renown enough to marry a princess required extreme measures, but Kelric wasn't wrong to question his readiness for the role. Gadnor had no experience wielding authority over anything. Dargos' confidence made Gadnor willing to try. If only it would be as simple as Dargos suggested.

Dargos ripped his bread in half, started to take a bite, but then waved both pieces in the air. "Who else would you trust with this?"

"I honestly haven't decided yet," Kelric grumbled. "I've had other things on my mind. As you pointed out, my wedding is tomorrow." He cast a hopeful look at Gonivein, but she was too busy picking at the flakes on her bread to notice his look of desperation, never mind come to his aid.

"The wedding feast is the best time to do it. All your important kyrioi—your councilmen—will be present and in good spirits."

Kelric rolled his eyes and took a big bite of his chicken breast.

Dargos dabbed his bread over the juices on his plate, taking Kelric's silence as encouragement to continue. "Gadnor is your brother. No one will find him taking your place surprising. Some are probably expecting it."

Kelric sneered at Gadnor. "Most of the city doesn't even know who my brother is. Those who do have few kind things to say about him."

Heat rose in Gadnor's cheeks. How he wished he could dispute those facts.

Dargos' vehemence softened. He leaned forward, and a shiver rolled down Gadnor's spine. "Keeping you out of the public eye did its job well. *Too* well. Undoing that is the task before us." His lips curved in a reassuring smile. "Giving you command of Golpathia's armies will put your name on the tip of every tongue in Helinthia."

"And make him the target of every arrow and spear our enemies hurl at us." Kelric flung his bare chicken ribs down on his plate.

Gadnor's heart hammered against his chest as the shapes of food on the table twisted and distorted into a raging army. His entire life, he'd been taught to avoid crowds, punished for drawing attention to himself. The very suggestion of going against this upbringing broke him out in a cold sweat, but since learning he was the heir of Anassa Iptys, he knew he must overcome these anxieties. Recovering his birthright as anax was the only way to restore peace among the gods and prosperity to Helinthia. Though, he'd anticipated having a little more time to do it and a more gradual rise to fame.

His apprehension must have shown on his face. Dargos' smile widened, crinkling the lines around his eyes. "You're more prepared than you give yourself credit, Gadnor."

Dargos looked again at Kelric, who was chewing furiously and glowering at the carrots as though *they* were the ones responsible for this nuisance.

"The hawk has been sent to Lithaneva. Now that she knows we've found the heir, she'll be expecting him to follow through with what we promised her. Making Gadnor your strategos is the best place to begin. And it needs to happen tomorrow, when your entire polis is assembled. We have no time for doubt and rumors. His appointment must be definitive."

Kelric chewed in silence, and Gadnor could see the frustration building in Dargos' expression at his lack of response.

"Perhaps you could assemble the Council after the wedding to discuss this more privately? If your men feel consulted, they may receive this announcement more favorably," Forluna offered.

Hope fluttered in Gadnor's gut as he met her gaze. Her eyes were reserved and calm, yet the way they flickered around at his companions suggested she was trying to hide her fear. She'd spent nearly two decades hiding him from the world, so he wasn't surprised at her hesitation to this plan.

Dargos stopped mid-chew to consider her, a sudden tenderness in his gaze that was impossible to miss. "Normally, I would agree. But I'm concerned about what might happen if we give them an opportunity to object." He sighed. "I wish we had more time to accomplish everything in a way suitable to everyone, but we don't. All we have is what the gods have given us. Golpathia needs a strategos to plan for war. The longer we wait to challenge Charixes, the more *we* are complicit in his atrocities, and, I fear, the less the gods will see fit to give us anything." He glanced down at his plate. "I have plenty of blood on my conscience for not doing enough."

Troubled lines etched into Forluna's ethereal features. She knew more than any of them what a monster Charixes was, had witnessed the destruction he caused more than once. She'd been there the night he sacked the citadel and killed Anassa Iptys, the night she fled with Gadnor in her arms, a helpless babe. Yet she still hesitated to agree with this plan.

Why?

Kelric grabbed his wine goblet, drained it in three gulps, then clunked it down loudly on the tabletop. "The hawk hasn't returned, has it?" He looked pointedly at Gadnor for an answer.

Gadnor shook his head. Tor had expected the hawk to return days ago. So far, the skies had brought no signs of the majestic bird. Tor was on watch for it now.

"See?" Kelric shot Dargos a withering look. "For all we know, someone ate that hawk for dinner and the princess has no idea of anything. That's assuming she hasn't had her motivation plowed out of her by her blubbering new husband."

An awkward silence descended upon the table, and everyone returned to their food. Kelric eyed the last chicken leg on the center platter, and Gadnor reached forward and grabbed it. Kelric glowered and bit a carrot in half.

"What do *you* think, Gadnor?" Forluna asked, looking at him.

Gadnor's blood pumped hard through his veins as every eye studied him. He took a drink of water, trying to quell his nerves and loosen his tongue enough to say something intelligible. He cleared his throat, mustering all his confidence. "I can do it."

Gonivein looked up and stared across the table at him, something in her eyes catching his attention. A flicker of hope, perhaps, some silent plea he wasn't sure how to interpret. It was the most emotion he'd seen in her gaze in a long time.

It unsettled him.

"I'm going to lie down before my bath." Gonivein pressed her weight into her palms and pushed herself to her feet. Her expression scrunched into a grimace of pain as she found her balance.

Forluna rose too. "I'll get you a draught."

"No." Gonivein raised her hand. "My hip isn't bothering me right now."

That was clearly a lie. Her broken hip was on the mend, according to Forluna, but her gait was still a hobble at best, and her face was an almost constant mask of discomfort. Still, there was something to be admired in not wanting to rely on Forluna's medicines all the time.

But Gadnor sensed there was a deeper hurt, one from which Gonivein desired a distraction. Physical pain seemed to fulfill that need. The thought saddened Gadnor. Surely, pain could not heal pain, but he had no alternative to offer.

Kelric stood and helped her maneuver around the table. "I'll carry you to your room," he offered, but she shied away from him, reaching for her crutch leaning against the wall and tucking it under her armpit.

"It's all right, I can manage on my own." Her eyes flickered to Gadnor's before she turned and started for the door that led to the courtyard and her apartment on the far side of it.

Gadnor tucked the chicken leg and the last of his bread into his pocket, then dismissed himself and exited the *triklinion*. Closing the door, he scanned the courtyard for prying eyes.

Splashes from the wash room just to the left of the *atrium* could be heard, along with Euanthe's pleasant singing as she filled the copper tub for Gonivein's prenuptial bath. It would take a while to fill it completely and heat it. Enough time to find out what was troubling Gonivein.

CHAPTER 3

GONIVEIN

GONIVEIN CLOSED THE DOOR TO her room and stood on shaky legs, waiting for her eyes to adjust to the darkness. She thought briefly about opening the windows to let in some light, then brushed the thought aside. She was supposed to be resting, anyway.

She shuffled over to the bed and sank onto the edge of it, wincing as pain throbbed through her fractured hip and shot down her leg. She clenched her jaw. Perhaps she should have accepted Forluna's offer of a potion. The nymph was truly gifted in the healing arts. But the last time she'd drunk the soothing liquid, it had freed her mind to dwell on more than pain. Memories of her past failings had filled the void. She'd ignored Apollo's warnings, and now Loric was dead.

She dragged in a breath, letting it fill her lungs until it burned, and released it slowly. Then repeated. A trick Forluna had taught her to clear her mind. Gradually, the throbbing ebbed, and Gonivein redirected her attention to listening as she stared at the dying fire in the corner of her apartment.

A noisy cricket chirped from somewhere near the door, loud enough, thankfully, to drown out the distant sound of those hateful waves crashing.

She held her breath, straining her ears for the silent *pit-pat* of footsteps. Would he come? Part of her hoped he wouldn't. But she had invited him here. At least, that had been her silent intent, and she was sure he had understood. Creeping into the bedroom of his brother's future wife, however, might be something Gadnor would not abide. Though surely, he wouldn't think she wanted anything inappropriate.

The more she considered how foolish this idea was, the more she wished she hadn't bothered. If he did come, she would have to explain herself. Disclose things she'd kept tamped down in the recesses of her soul. Doubts, fears, regrets. Dredging those up and hurling them into the stillness would bring them to life, force her to face them, battle them.

She wasn't ready. She'd thought—hoped—she might be during the midday meal. Kelric and Dargos backing Gadnor into a corner had stirred something inside of her. She'd been trying to figure out what when she captured Gadnor's gaze, hoping he would see the plea in her eyes.

Now, sitting alone in the cold room, the moments ticking by with no sign of him, the resolve she built up crumbled. *I don't have the strength for this.* What did it matter anyway? *He's not coming.*

She braced herself to lean back and stretch out on the bed, hoping the cricket, at least, would stay and sing her to sleep. If it didn't, the waves would haunt her dreams again, and she would see him there. Loric, wandering the shores of the Styx, mist and *Shades* swirling aimlessly around him. Lost souls denied a peaceful rest.

The cricket fell silent, and Gonivein's heart slowed. Eyes widened on the door. She was focusing so intently that when the knock finally came, she jumped.

She rose and reached for her crutch with trembling fingers.

The soft *tap* against the wood sounded again. She hauled herself up and scrambled toward it. *He came.* A glimmer of hope sparked within her.

What if it's Kelric? Her hand froze on the handle and a shiver slid down her spine. Kelric was no stranger to visiting her in her room at any hour of the day or night, and perhaps he wanted to talk to her about their wedding tomorrow. She let her hand drop and hang limp at her side. If she didn't answer, maybe whoever it was would think she'd fallen asleep and leave. Though she was sure the noise of her crutch thunking against the floorboards eliminated that possibility.

"It's me, Gonivein."

Gadnor. She let out a sigh and opened the door.

There he stood with a sheepish expression worrying his brow, as though she had caught him red handed with honey on his fingers.

She shuffled aside to let him in. He hesitated, glancing over his shoulders, scrutinizing the courtyard, then ducked inside. She closed the door and bolted the latch. When she turned around, Gadnor was poking at the embers in the fireplace and layering on logs.

He blew on the coals until the tongues licked hungrily at the dried wood. It was only then that she noticed the late autumn chill, and she was grateful Gadnor had come. She wouldn't have tended the fire herself, even if she was able to. The sight of lively flames still made her uneasy, and she had no desire to bother Euanthe, either. The old woman had enough to do, and Gonivein was done forcing people to be beholden to her.

Gadnor rocked back on his heels and looked at her as she hobbled to him, then quickly stood and dragged over the couch from underneath the window for her to sit on.

"Thank you," she said, leaning her crutch against the hearth and sinking onto the fur lined cushion. She stretched her palms toward the warmth, willing her racing heart to calm and wondering how she could start this confession. Or… request? What was it, exactly?

"What's this about, Gonie?" Gadnor's soft-spoken question broke into her thoughts.

If only I knew.

"I… wanted to say, I'm sorry." Her own words surprised her, but she realized they were the right ones. She was sorry for so many things. Too many that could never be remedied by words, but she wanted to try.

Gadnor's brows pinched together in confusion, firelight stretching the scar across his cheek into a grotesque shadow. "For what?"

"For never acknowledging your hurt, your humanity." Memories of her laughter encouraging Kelric's teasing and bullying of Gadnor flitted through her mind. How much of his cruelty had been spurred on for her entertainment? *What a silly, stupid girl I was.* Guilt sharpened in her chest. "For not *seeing* you."

Gadnor stiffened. She recognized the impulse to deny his feelings flicker in his eyes, then die on his lips as he opened his mouth and closed it again.

"I wanted to speak to you privately because…" Her throat became dry, and she swallowed. "Because I think you're being forced into this, and I…"

'I've got you.' Loric's words in the aftermath of her brutal attack floated into her mind: a promise that she wasn't alone. She couldn't possibly hope to invoke the same sense of security in Gadnor that Loric had instilled in her. How could she? Loric was brave, strong, soothing. She was cowardly, weak, shuttered. But she owed it to Loric, and Gadnor, to try. "I want you to realize you *can* choose. And no matter what, I… I'm here."

Gadnor blinked and quickly turned away, but not before she saw the tears gathering in his eyes. "Thank you, Gonie. That means a lot."

As the silence between them widened, she realized he wouldn't say more. Disappointment flared within her, but she steeled her resolve. He had no reason to trust her. Why should he? *I've been horrible to him, like I've been horrible to everyone else.* She tried again. "Do you want to be anax?"

He rubbed the long, jagged scars on his arm as he thought. "I want to stop bad things from happening to innocent people. That's what I want," he answered, scooting closer to the fire to grab another log to toss on. "The anax has the power to do that."

She saw his reasoning, but she couldn't help but wonder—no, *feel*—that it wouldn't end how he hoped, how they all hoped. She couldn't explain why, but the fear curling in her gut loosened her tongue. "What if there was another way?"

Gadnor raised his brows. "What way?"

Her mind scrambled, and he offered a kind, resigned smile as the tiniest glimmer of hope faded from his eyes.

"Princess Lithaneva is counting on me to do this, and Dargos. I think Kelric is, too, even though he pretends to hate the idea of me leading anything. But he doesn't have anything better to suggest, which is probably why he's so defensive. And I can't turn my back on what happened to Pallas' village, to his family."

A shudder went through her at the mention of Pallas. Charixes had razed his village, slaughtered his oldest son, and carried away his wife and youngest son as spoils. All because they had given her a bed to sleep in. Their screams still haunted her at night.

Gadnor shook his head, the orange glow of the flames dancing in his golden hair. "When Lithaneva first told us her plan to find the heir and make him a champion worthy of marrying an anassa, I was all too ready to commit to it. Too eager for *someone else* to take that responsibility." He drew in a deep breath and let it out. "Now that I know it's me?" He met her eyes again. "I *can't* back out."

His conviction struck her like a punch in the chest. She found no words to argue, though every fiber of her screamed to convince him of another way.

Gadnor shrugged and looked into the flames again. "What Dargos suggests makes sense. Naming me strategos now will draw less attention, maybe even cause Charixes to underestimate Kelric's judgment." He chuckled a nervous, half-hearted laugh before breathing deep. He nodded decisively, as though talking it through had resolved any lingering doubts.

She couldn't help but admire him, even though her shoulders slumped. She caught him staring at her, and her cheeks warmed.

"Can I ask you a question?"

She swallowed. Gadnor's insight into his predicament suggested he might have a fair amount into her own, or at least good guesses. Part of her dreaded what he might dig up. But another part craved understanding, a confidante. *'I've got you.'*

Loric didn't have her anymore.

"What is it?" she whispered.

"Do you still want to marry my brother?"

Her heart dropped into her stomach, her first instinct one of offense. It quickly fizzled out as the weight of the query sank into her bones. "I… why?"

"Given what you've been through, what you've lost, no one expects you to be the joyful girl we once knew. But there's more at the heart of it, isn't there?"

Sobs began to scurry in her chest. Gadnor was reaching into her very soul, and she could feel it ripping as he scratched at the truth. The truth she wanted to keep tucked away.

"Kelric hurt you, didn't he?"

She considered lying, professing her undying love for Kelric, but she knew Gadnor wouldn't believe it. Kelric had hurt Gadnor far more times than he'd hurt her, and if anyone could recognize those invisible scars, it was him.

Her silence seemed all the answer he needed.

"Why don't you call it off, Gonivein? Dargos gave you the right to break your engagement. Encouraged it ev—"

"That's not a possibility anymore." She dug crescents into her palms. Her sharp tone silenced the cricket, who'd resumed chirping at the door, and heat crept into her neck.

Gadnor waited for her to continue, kindness in his gaze.

She swallowed. "I have no home. Charixes stole that from me, from Dargos, from Pallas, from my people." Her voice began to tremble and she stopped. Took a deep breath. "Alliances have always been made by marriages. That's how it's done."

"That's never been the nature of *your* marriage. Your alliance is not in question," Gadnor pressed gently.

He still thinks the best of Kelric, in spite of everything. She wanted to laugh.

"You think Kelric will still be devoted to me if I refuse him? After what he did to save me? It doesn't matter that he hurt me, that he endangered us both. It's all forgiven now, isn't it?" The bitterness in her tone surprised her. She hadn't fully realized the depth of her resentment. She took another breath, gathering her emotions. "Dargos and I are fugitives, and gods only know what my citizens endure every day from Charixes' occupation."

'*...until they see you return with Basileus Raleon's army to liberate them.*' The last words her archon, Sholen, had spoken to her reverberated in her mind. Just before she'd fled like a coward.

It would be Kelric's army now, with Gadnor leading it, if Dargos got his way. What had Sholen sacrificed in helping her escape? His life? His family? She didn't know, but she wouldn't forsake his hope. She hadn't considered it an oath at the time, but she did now. "My selfish decisions have caused so much pain already, and I can't risk the lives of all my citizens with one more." She wiped rebellious tears from her cheeks and glared into the dying flames. At the tense silence, she met Gadnor's eyes steadily and said, "Kelric protects what is *his*, and if I reject him? Then I am nothing worth protecting, and neither is Dargos."

She could sense Gadnor's desire to say something to set her at ease, give her something to cling to. But as the silence dragged on, she knew the truth of her words had sunk in. The finality of it sucked the air from her lungs.

"Then we are both bound to a fate not of our choosing," Gadnor whispered, his eyes shining with tears as he took her hand. He seemed like he wanted to say more, but he didn't.

She tightened her fingers around his, her own eyes pooling with grief and hopelessness. "We are just playthings for the gods," she bit out, and he scooted closer to her.

"Our choice has been stripped from us, but we are not powerless,

Gonivein," he whispered, then rose. She tightened her grip before he could pull away.

"Do you really believe that?" She hadn't meant for it to come out so condescending, but his soft expression assured her he took no offense.

He squeezed her hands a final time before sliding from her grasp. "I want to."

She nodded at him, then trained her gaze on the flames as he walked away. She waited until she heard the door close behind him before crumpling into sobs.

CHAPTER 4

LITHANEVA

HER FATHER WAS EVERY BIT the imposing figure she remembered. Tall, broad shouldered, some would say handsome, with sculpted arms and legs protruding from his tunic. The only indications of age were the silver veins streaking through his thick head of hair and curly, groomed beard. Charixes and Branitus were already inside the triklinion, ready to take their seats when Lithaneva arrived from her encounter in the garden.

Charixes' eyes fell on her as she made her way across the room, and resentment flared within her. She hadn't seen him since he had sent her away to be married. He hadn't even come to her wedding a month ago. Now he was here, eying her as though she were a pesky branch or thorny bush. An obstacle in his way, rather than his daughter.

But she wasn't going to let him ruin her glorious mood. The heir was alive.

As expected, his face remained unyielding of clues that might betray the dark thoughts she knew swirled behind it. His ability to discover and exploit a person's worst fear was all the intimidation he needed to drive men to their knees and beg for mercy. She had no intention of falling victim to that power, but as she drew nearer, sweat slicked her palms as her fingers curled into fists. *I must be calm.* She forced her hands to relax at her sides.

She straightened her shoulders and stopped before her seat at the table. She met his gaze coolly. "Father."

Charixes' eyes narrowed and swept her up and down. Though she had shaken the dirt from her clothes, his scrutiny made her doubt she had done a good enough job in her haste. Had she left a feather or a dust streak on her knees from where she'd knelt in the dirt to retrieve the message? Her father knew she would never get on her knees for anything. It would be sure to incite his suspicion. She didn't dare look down to check for fear it would draw his eye.

Branitus leapt to her side and planted a wet kiss on her cheek.

Lithaneva tried to jerk away, but Branitus had slipped his arm around her waist, trapping her in his embrace.

"There you are!" Branitus pulled back with the stupidest expression of happiness she had ever seen. It looked wrong. Twisted somehow. His lips were curled upwards into a smile that resembled more of a snarl, and though his eyes were crinkled around the edges, they were wide with fright and frustration.

Charixes smirked. "You're not with child, I see."

Branitus' head jerked to him. "There's plenty of time for that." Her husband sounded more confident than she'd expected as he ushered her into her seat with a sweep of his arm. "I know all too well how motherhood brings an end to a bride's affection. Don't rush that on me, Anax."

Charixes' looked at him with half-lidded eyes. "My daughter loves to be needed, Branitus, and children are needy. If you care about her affection, I suggest you impregnate her as quickly as possible."

Rage burned under Lithaneva's skin. What lies. *Loves to feel needed?* What would he know about what she loved? What would he know about love at all?

Charixes smirked again, satisfied that he had visibly riled her, and took his seat at the table. He reached for the platter in the center and plucked off a slice of swine rump. "Tell me, Branitus, how does my daughter spend her time here?"

"You know, menial wife things. Nothing I care to involve myself in, and why should I?" Branitus shrugged and stuffed a carrot into his mouth.

Charixes narrowed his eyes, and Lithaneva ripped a piece of bread in half.

Great. Now he knows Branitus isn't monitoring me. What suspicions would that spark? She made a point not to look at her father, or he would definitely know she was up to something. Instead, she shot a death glare at Branitus.

"Aren't you going to ask me about the city, Lithie?" Charixes mused.

Lithaneva met his eyes. "Has it fallen into ruin?" she quipped.

"Now, now, Lithie," Branitus chided, and her anger spiked. He was playing this annoying husband role *too* well. Perhaps she *should* let Helinthia kill them both.

Charixes grinned. "On the contrary, Ninenarn is thriving. You should be pleased. The issues you brought to my attention just before you left, they're all resolved now. Morale could not be higher." He sipped his wine, watching her over the goblet's rim.

She nearly choked on her bread. *Remain calm.* Either he was trying to inflict hurt, or else insinuate he had discovered her spies— a network of women scattered throughout the city, women whose lives had been upended when he usurped the throne from Iptys. He hadn't acknowledged their existence then, couldn't fathom the feminine rage his slaughter of so many husbands, brothers, and sons would incite. The women whose lives were ruined by war were rarely factored into the cost to wage it. That was *his* mistake. *I will not make the same.* If he'd found them…

No. That's impossible. There were far too many of them for him to have found them all out, and none of them would have exposed her as their leader if he had. This was all part of his game, and she didn't feel like playing along.

She met his eyes again and flashed him a smile. "Issues? But your rule is flawless, Father. What issues could there be?"

Charixes' smile dimmed somewhat, but the mischievous glint in his eye remained. "There are always those who refuse to adapt to change."

Lithaneva tilted her head as she reached for a slice of meat. "In what way?"

"Since you left, the rumors about an heir of Iptys have increased. I don't take kindly to my legitimacy being questioned. Did you have something to do with this? A last act of rebellion before your own life changed for the better?"

"I imagine they were fueled by your search for him," she snapped. "Perhaps you weren't as secretive as you thought. Something such as that was bound to draw attention, and people do love to share gossip."

Charixes chewed another bite and lifted his wine cup to his lips.

An eerie feeling crept into her gut and curled into a tight knot. She didn't like his calculating gaze. He knew something.

He set his cup back down. "It doesn't matter now; the heir is dead. My *Leirion* made sure of it."

Her heart slammed against her chest. That wasn't right. She bit hard into the slice of meat, forcing her jaw to keep working, to look normal.

"So there really was an heir?" Branitus stopped mid-chew to gape at Charixes. "I was sure that was a myth."

Lithaneva swallowed, the half-chewed lump sliding painfully down her throat. *'We found it.'* Gadnor had said it. But which was more recent, Gadnor's message or the Leirion's? *The heir can't be dead.* Her entire mission depended on his survival!

"Well, who was he?" Branitus asked, taking another bite and waiting attentively.

"Some *doulos* of Dargos', apparently," Charixes answered. "Raised at the Library by a bothersome scholar who smuggled him out of the city. I imagine this heir is why Dargos thought a rebellion might work. Foolish to think anyone would bow to a doulos."

The food blurred before her eyes, her blood racing. It couldn't be true. Dargos hadn't known who the heir was. *Had he?* Had Dargos played her for a fool as she detailed her grand plans to him and Gadnor?

"You look troubled, Lithie," Charixes mused. "Does this news upset you?"

Her face flamed, and she forced a smile. "Only that there was an heir at all. My own status would diminish if he were found. Do you think I would want that?"

Charixes' eyes narrowed as he studied her. "Perhaps not. And yet, I know you hate me—"

"Only as much as you hate *me*."

"Because I'm not your mother?"

"Because I'm not your son?"

Lithaneva's eyes bored into Charixes'. She didn't realize how tightly she was gripping the bread in her hand until Branitus cleared his throat. The sudden noise broke their trance, and she lowered her gaze, relaxing her fingers to reveal the crumpled, ruined loaf. She threw it on her plate.

"What you could have been if you were." Charixes' voice was wistful. "But the gods who determine such things were not on my side. Nor yours. Now I must rule the island alone. And you," he leaned forward, his lip curling into a snarl, "You will produce an heir for Branitus and solidify your place as his basileia. That is the closest you will ever come to wearing a crown, and the only way you can honor *me*, your *anax*. Don't like it? Blame the gods."

Lithaneva bit back the angry retorts gathering on her tongue. *Just you wait, Father. I will become Anassa of Ninenarn, and you will eat those words.*

Charixes took another bite, his cheeks bulging in and out with every crunch of his jaw.

"Well, now that Dargos' plan has been foiled, do you think he will surrender?" Branitus' cheerful tone betrayed his eagerness to change the subject.

A wicked spark entered her father's eye. She knew that look, the signal that an egregiously cruel punishment was imminent. The removal of fingers one by one for writing something he didn't like, or a tongue cut out for saying the wrong thing. After last year's harvest, which was significantly smaller than expected, a mother had dared to complain that the markets were too overpriced to buy food for her children. That wicked spark had flared in Charixes' eyes just before ripping a child from her arms. Lithaneva would never forget the mother's anguished wails as the soldiers disappeared with the little boy.

"It isn't Dargos I'm concerned about anymore, it's Golpathia's new basileus, Raleon's brat son, Kelric. He's harboring Dargos and marrying his sister, I hear. No matter. He'll pay for it." Charixes grinned as he took another bite. Lithaneva couldn't help but think of a wild animal tearing into a carcass as he did.

Branitus' eyes narrowed. "What do you mean?"

"You didn't really think my coming here was to see that my daughter is adjusting to her new life, did you? Come, Branitus." His smile vanished. "I thought you were more intelligent than that."

Branitus' face paled. "I…"

Lithaneva slammed her empty cup down on the table. "Get out with it, Father, we don't have time for your games. What do you want from us?" She squeezed the cup to keep her hands from shaking. Fury roiled inside her, burning her lungs, hammering blood through her limbs. Oh, how she hated him, even more so that he knew it and was pleased that she did.

Branitus' eyes widened in horror at her tone, and Charixes laughed.

"Fine, fine. Assemble your soldiers from the field, get them trained and ready to march on Golpathia by the spring equinox. I need one thousand men."

"One thousand men?" Branitus' mouth flopped open.

"When was your last census, Branitus?" Charixes questioned.

Branitus' just stared, a red flush creeping up his neck.

"Wasn't it completed at the end of the harvest, darling?" she offered. As entertaining as it was to watch Branitus squirm, she was too excited to learn what Charixes had planned not to hurry the conversation along.

"Um, yes, Lithie, darling, it was." Branitus' shoulders relaxed a little in relief.

"And?" Charixes probed, sopping up the fat juices on his plate with his bread.

Lithaneva knew Branitus hadn't even looked at Aden's reports. "I believe the archon reported that there are somewhere around twelve hundred men of fighting age. However, a significant number of these men are douloi and know nothing of warfare. They're farmers."

Charixes wiped his greasy fingers on a napkin and settled back in his chair. "Then train them."

"Pull the douloi from the villages?" Branitus' brow furrowed. "The spring equinox is when we plant our vegetables, and the fields must be furrowed and seeded before then. Women and old men can't do that on their own."

Charixes shrugged. "I need one thousand men. I don't care what you do with the other two hundred. Scatter them if you must. The campaign will last a week, maybe two, and they'll be back with little time lost for planting."

"Two weeks to lay siege to Golpathia?" Branitus drew in a breath to say more, then clamped his jaw tight.

Lithaneva knew what he wanted to say, and she wasn't scared. "That's impossible. Do you take us for fools?"

Charixes' brow furrowed as he leaned forward. "Should I?"

The threat in his tone was clear, and she knew she was pushing her boundaries, boundaries that extended farther than anyone else's because she was his blood.

She evened her tone. "A siege of Golpathia will take months, not weeks. They have an endless supply of food from Poseidon's domain. Our armies will starve before even one of our men can set foot inside their walls. And then *we* will starve, because our fields lie barren. Thellshun is my home now." She glanced at Branitus, who stared at her hopefully, before meeting Charixes' gaze again. "I will not see us brought to ruin by unnecessary risk."

Charixes snatched a handful of raisins from the dessert platter and popped them into his mouth. The annoying rhythm of his chewing made the muscles along her spine grow rigid and spasm.

"What are you planning?" She hated how he made her crave his every word, as though he were some god and she was his supplicant. But these words, she knew, would give her the crown. She could feel it in the marrow of her bones.

"Poseidon's domain will not be bringing them fish, but my fleet of swords and spears."

Lithaneva's knuckles were white. Her fingernails dug painful crescents into her sweaty palms.

Outside, the cuckoo's song, which had cheered her this morning with its rhythmic *coo-coo*s, now seemed shrill. *'Caught you, caught you,'* it mocked.

"We will crush them from both sides, and they will never oppose me again."

CHAPTER 5

KELRIC

KELRIC LEANED HIS SHOULDER ON the arch of the atrium and turned his gaze to the gate house across the front courtyard. He tugged his cloak tighter around his shoulders. "Styx," he cursed. It was colder than Demeter's grief today, and Archon Tryphus was late to give his report. Kelric was anxious, made worse by Dargos' insistent nagging.

Everything had to be ready for the wedding ceremony tomorrow: the streets, the priests and priestesses, the sacrificial animals, the food, and most of all, the new statue of Aphrodite his father had commissioned five years ago after announcing Kelric's engagement.

Kelric had approved the finished product a week ago, and could not be more thrilled with the exquisite craftsmanship. The goddess' resemblance to Gonivein would not be missed by the market goers—a detail previously known only to him and the sculptor. The new marble was supposed to be installed in the center of the *agora* early that morning, replacing the weathered and crumbling one that had stood since the city's beginnings two centuries ago. The transportation of such things came with risks that Kelric was eager to set aside. He'd seen far too many headless, armless, or noseless statues presiding over streets and fountains for comfort.

Kelric breathed into his hands and shifted his feet, his impatience growing. Where was Tryphus?

Movement from the corner of his eye drew his attention inside the villa. A figure moved beneath the *peristyle*, distorted under scattered shadows of the dead palms that towered over the building. Kelric recognized that awkward gait.

Gadnor.

Leaving Gonivein's room?

Kelric's heart thumped as Gadnor disappeared out the back door of the villa. What could they possibly have to discuss? The secrecy bothered him less than it probably should. Even if Gadnor *could* steal Gonivein's affection, Kelric knew he wouldn't. Gadnor wasn't capable of such a betrayal.

But Gonivein's coldness during lunch wormed its way into his mind, dragging a slimy trail of doubt with it. She hadn't spoken more than five words to him in weeks, had hardly let him be near her. He'd thought she might still be processing all she had endured, not letting anyone in.

She let Gadnor in.

And those two had never been close. Jealousy curled inside him, igniting his longing to be near her, to be *wanted* near her. It itched at his palms.

The statue could wait.

He tensed his muscles to move, but Euanthe emerged from the bathing room and started toward Gonivein's door. She noticed him standing there and smiled that endearing smile she reserved just for him. He frowned at his missed opportunity with Gonivein.

"Basileus?"

Kelric whirled around, reaching for an imaginary sword at his belt and balling his fist in frustration.

The owner of the voice jerked backwards, stumbling down the porch steps and out into the bright sunlight.

Tryphus.

Kelric scowled. "Where have you been?"

Tryphus' gaze wandered back to the entrance to the villa. "There's… been a development in the agora."

Panic flared at the strain in Tryphus' tone. "Is it the statue?"

The archon looked visibly uncomfortable, and Kelric feared the worst. "Ah… yes."

Kelric groaned and covered his face with his hand. "It's in a billion pieces, isn't it?"

"Um. No."

Kelric splayed his fingers to scrutinize his archon between them. "Then what? What is wrong with it?"

"Nothing is wrong with it, exactly."

"Was it installed properly in the agora?"

"Yes."

"Then, what is the issue?"

"It's…" Tryphus rubbed the back of his head.

"Out with it, Tryphus!"

"I think you'd better come and see for yourself."

Kelric folded his arms across his chest, his mind lighting on the warm fire burning in his *andron* and the full *amphora* of wine waiting to be poured and consumed. A promise of warmth from the inside out. Kelric would have been more annoyed if he wasn't also a bit curious. And worried.

Kelric growled and stomped down the porch stairs. "Show me," he hissed, flinging gravel in his wake across the courtyard.

The gate guard scrambled to his feet as they approached and hastily opened the gate to let them through, revealing a clear view of the city of Golpathia sprawling down the mountainside before them. Multicolored terracotta, marble, and mud brick mingled together, appearing like a floor mosaic before Kelric's eyes. Lavish two-story homes in the Kyrioi Quarter gave way to more modest dwellings near the center of the city. Bronze statues of gods and goddesses rose above the rooftops, gleaming in the sunshine.

When they were on the other side of the bridge separating the Basileus' villa from the Kyrioi Quarter, Tryphus lengthened his steps and passed Kelric to lead the way, staying just far enough ahead to make conversation difficult.

Kelric focused his attention on the details of the city to keep his anxiety at bay. The dust on the houses was now gone, replaced by the soft white powder of salt from the sea water used to wash them—an effort spanning weeks. He hoped Gonivein would notice to what lengths he'd gone to make Golpathia shine for its new basileia, would take pride in the polis she would rule with him when she saw it from her litter.

The wide archway leading into the agora gleamed, the friezes depicting hydra and dolphins frolicking in the swirling waves freshly painted and vibrant. Kelric followed Tryphus straight to the tiled mall at the center of the agora. The surrounding merchant stalls, though stocked with goods waiting to be sold, were conspicuously empty of customers. A crowd congregated around the tiered platform where officials made public announcements and weary shoppers could find rest on its steps.

Exactly where his new statue of Aphrodite-Gonivein was supposed to be.

There were so many people gawking around it that Kelric couldn't get a glimpse. Packed shoulder to shoulder on every tier of the platform, their animated discussions converged into one annoying buzz in Kelric's head. He could barely form a coherent thought. Didn't these people have money to spend?

"Stand aside," Tryphus ordered, shouldering through the crowd. People turned at the disturbance, nervous tension overtaking them as they spotted Kelric.

As the last of the crowd thinned and parted, the new statue came into view. Shock jolted through Kelric, pinching in his chest and rooting him to the marble step.

Aphrodite, carved in the likeness of Gonivein, stood exactly where she should in the center of the agora. But the deep blues of her gown, and the bright gold of her hair, the lush rouge in her lips, didn't shimmer in the sunshine as Kelric had hoped.

She was covered in filth. Globs of brown and green were splattered across the exquisite curves and fine details of her chiton, in the grooves of her eyes and mouth. Even worse, it smelled offensive.

His rage ignited, shooting into his fingertips and curling them tightly. This statue had been well-anticipated by the entire city for years. Who would have the audacity to do something like this? And why?

Several of Tryphus' guards were posted in a circle around it to keep the crowd back and prevent anyone else from spoiling the statue further. Several conscripted douloi were doing their best to scrub it clean without harming the new paint.

Kelric whirled around, the command to arrest the entire assembly on his lips—but only Tryphus, the guards, and the douloi remained. Everyone else had wisely, and quickly, scattered. The stalls were full now.

"Tell me you arrested the ones responsible for this."

Tryphus shifted his feet, and Kelric was finding it difficult to keep his fist out of his archon's throat.

"Give me one good reason why I shouldn't arrest you for gross negligence of duty."

Tryphus' lips thinned into a hard line. He cast a furtive glance at his guards, who were trying hard not to look interested in the exchange. "Basileus, a private word?"

Without waiting for an answer, he descended the steps and walked out onto the semi-deserted mall, out of earshot of his men and the braver shoppers visiting the fringe stalls.

Kelric followed, brooding. There was nothing Tryphus could say that would excuse this. Any of this. As far as Kelric was concerned, this desecration of his new statue—his gift to the city and his bride— was an act of insurrection against him and an insult to Gonivein.

Tryphus faced him, resting his hands on his hips and inclining his head as though he were trying to help Kelric solve a troublesome mathematical equation rather than a serious threat to his authority.

"By the time the situation was brought to my attention, the damage was already done and the parties responsible were long gone."

Kelric scanned the agora, doubting the culprits had wandered far. They were probably peering out from some tiny hole or crack, watching the chaos of their making and trying not to laugh too loudly and expose themselves to punishment.

"Witnesses say there were about twenty men and women who accosted the statue shortly after it was erected." Tryphus lowered his voice. "From their chanting, this was a demonstration against your marriage."

Anger was so hot in Kelric's veins that he no longer felt the chill in the air. "I want them found, stripped of their citizenship, and sold to the quarries." Golpathia could always use more douloi, and these people had just volunteered.

"Basileus." Tryphus' tone took on a more urgent note. "The smoke rising from Tyldan's destruction casts a long shadow. Arresting twenty people will not put an end to the fear that has gripped the entire polis. Ignoring it will only embolden others who share their concerns."

"So, you're suggesting I ignore this offense?" Kelric couldn't believe what he was hearing. He'd never liked Tryphus. Perhaps it was time he elected a new archon.

"Of course not," Tryphus said. "But this demonstration is only a symptom of a much bigger problem. You've created a delicate situation for us, Basileus. You'd do well to take heed."

Blood pounded in Kelric's ears. "*I* created? Tread carefully, Archon." His fingers curled, itching to put this disloyal leech in his place.

Archon Tryphus' jaw twitched as he chose his next words. "By not extending a wedding invitation to the anax, there's concern it will provoke his anger against Golpathia. That's to say nothing of excluding Basileus Branitus and *Princess* Lithaneva, as well. You're the basileus. This is unheard of."

"The anax evicted my bride from her home and slaughtered her citizens before her very eyes. *Why* would I invite him to our wedding?" Kelric pinched the bridge of his nose in annoyance.

"I understand your reasons, but therein lies the problem. Your marriage to Gonivein is in opposition to the anax by its very nature. Your union all but confirms your intent to war against him."

"Good. One less announcement I need to worry about, then." Kelric honestly couldn't see why he was having this argument. Everything was going exactly as planned, from where he was standing.

Tryphus' brow furrowed, and Kelric could tell he was trying his hardest to keep his voice low. "Your people do not want war. You cannot pretend away their concerns because they interfere with your personal feelings."

Kelric ground his teeth.

"If you continue this path, the unrest will only build," Tryphus said. He reached for the leather bag slung around his shoulders. "Here." He pulled out a scroll and offered it to Kelric. "This is my report from Tetra. The fear outside this city is even worse."

Kelric snatched the scroll and waved it at Tryphus. "My citizens have been supportive of our friendship with Dargos and his criticism against Charixes since my engagement five years ago. Everyone knew this would eventually lead to war."

"That was before Charixes conquered Shallinath in less than a day and made Dargos and Gonivein fugitives." Tryphus shifted his weight, a hint of desperation in his rigid stance. "Your citizens never supported taking on Charixes alone. Look at the report. Please."

The man had a point, which only fueled Kelric's anger. He ignored the scroll. He didn't have time for this. "I need the number of able soldiers in my villages, not a list of whims and whines."

A muscle ticked in Tryphus' jaw. He stepped closer, lowering his voice. "We will not survive a war inside our gates as well as out. Please, do not ignore your people's concerns." His eyes darted to the scroll in Kelric's hand.

"Gonivein will be the Basileia of Golpathia. *Your* Basileia. And the Oracle of Apollo. I think you should focus your attention on how best to keep the people in line and prove your loyalty to her."

Tryphus glanced uncomfortably around the agora to see who was witness to his humiliation. Everyone was keeping their distance. He sighed heavily, resigned. "About that."

Kelric cast him a withering look. "About what?"

"About the Oracle of Apollo."

The scroll's paper crinkled as Kelric crushed it in his palm. He debated if breaking Tryphus' teeth would be more satisfying or his nose. If he dared utter even a hint of skepticism about her claim…

"There is still no sign of the scholars."

"Ferry them all." Kelric was as disappointed in the news as he was in his lack of opportunity to hit someone.

The scholars from the Library of Critius were due to arrive a week ago. Gonivein should be a confirmed oracle by now and, by divine law, above mortal reproach—including by Charixes. Postponing the wedding had been suggested to temper tensions, and now Kelric wondered if he had dismissed the idea a little too hastily.

He shoved the offensive thought away. He wasn't about to let some disgruntled rabble-rousers make him feel guilty. As far as he was concerned, the scholars were to blame for this.

"What if they're not coming?" Tryphus pressed. "It's been years since a new oracle was confirmed. Perhaps they don't believe it."

"Then they're a bunch of old fools, as I always suspected," Kelric snapped. He supposed he couldn't fault them too much if that were true. If he didn't trust Gonivein, he wouldn't believe she was seeing visions from Apollo, either. Nor that Tor, a nothing boy from the Ordan, could speak to animals. But he did trust Gonivein. He'd witnessed firsthand Tor's unique abilities, not the least of which was convincing a wild bird of prey to have a message tied around its foot. Kelric no longer had the luxury of ignorance.

Tryphus wisely decided to let the matter drop.

The statue was nearly clean now, and Kelric was relieved the paint remained vibrant and complete after being scrubbed. The douloi were being reverent in their task, thankfully.

"I want you to station a watch on the statue all night, and double the guards throughout the city tomorrow. Nothing is to interrupt my wedding. And I want these traitors found and punished. Do you understand?"

Tryphus released a defeated sigh. "Yes, Basileus. Perfectly."

Kelric turned on his heel and strode back to the villa. He kept his shoulders straight and even tossed out a few smiles, making sure he appeared confident and collected. Underneath, he was rattled. How dare his own citizens turn on him like this, turn on Gonivein? And for what? Fear of Charixes? Kelric stomped back up to the villa.

Shallinath had always been Golpathia's foremost ally. That hadn't changed simply because the city was conquered. Shouldn't that rally Golpathia to their defense? Clearly, his citizens had no understanding of what an alliance truly meant.

Still, Kelric couldn't shake the feeling that he was missing something. He glanced at the scroll.

Whatever it was, he would figure it out after the wedding.

CHAPTER 6

GADNOR

G ADNOR CLIMBED THE ROCKY SLOPE behind the villa, carefully placing his feet along the path. The tombs of Golpathia's basilei jutted out of the mountainside. An ominous reminder of human mortality. The jagged corners of the sepulchres seemed to crowd the path more than usual today, scraping his biceps and snagging his tunic as he passed. He checked his pocket to make sure the bread and meat he'd saved from dinner were secure.

Hope and anxiety swirled in his gut as his destination neared.

Please be here today.

The hawk.

It had been two weeks since he'd asked Tor to tie the message around the bird's foot. A journey to Thellshun would take four days on horseback. It shouldn't have taken more than two for the hawk.

Every day it failed to arrive added fuel to the contention around the table, and Gadnor was ready for the arguments to end. Ready to embark on the next step to fulfilling his destiny as strategos, as Helinthia's hero, as heir of Anassa Iptys, as Anax of Ninenarn. The thoughts made him lightheaded. A strong breeze pushed against him. Gadnor grasped the ancient, wind-worn stones of one of the tombs to steady himself. *One step at a time.*

Halfway up, the path leveled onto a plateau where a laurel, rumored to have been a sapling when Ordanus landed on Helinthia's shores, stretched its empty branches out over gnarled roots. From this height, the sounds of the city and the crashing waves were subdued, drowned by the wind whistling around the craggy slopes. Gadnor had come here often as a child to escape his father's scrutiny and Kelric's relentless teasing. It was the highest point in Golpathia, and one could see for miles. A place to see without being seen.

As he scanned the flat ground and tree limbs for the hawk, he spotted Xios, Tor's lion cub, pouncing in the grasses, chasing some poor cricket. Tor lay on his back with ankles crossed and arms folded beneath a head of brown curls.

No hawk.

Gadnor's hopes crashed, and his shoulders sagged. What was taking so long? Now that he'd accepted his destiny and all the complexities it entailed, he just wanted to *do* it. To prove himself to the world, to Kelric, to Charixes, to Lithaneva, to *everyone* that Gadnor, son of Raleon—shy, quiet, anxious, awkward Gadnor—could do something worthy of respect rather than ridicule.

Xios noticed him first, forgetting all about the cricket. He hissed, fur bristling along his back, snout crinkling into a snarl and revealing sharp teeth.

Tor raised his head, then smiled in recognition and relaxed again.

Gadnor stepped onto the plateau and approached. "No sign of the hawk?"

"Not yet." Tor studied him beneath a raised brow before chuckling softly. "Relax. He'll come, just give him time."

Gadnor pulled the bread and chicken leg from his pocket and dangled them over Tor's face.

Tor sat up, taking the treats in hand. He took a bite of the bread and held the meat out to the cub. Xios flicked his tail with interest and stalked forward warily, growling in warning at Gadnor. He wasn't the menacing beast he thought he was, but he had grown considerably in the last two weeks. The top of his head was above Tor's knees now.

When Xios was an arm's length away, he crouched and crawled the remaining inches to Tor's outstretched hand. He closed his jaws around the leg and scampered off, leaping behind one of the laurel's roots to devour the meal.

Gadnor stretched out beside Tor. The dead grass crunched under his knuckles as he threaded his fingers behind his head and gazed at the darkening sky. Helios' chariot was nearing the horizon now, leaving streaks of purple, pink, and orange.

Tor took another bite of the loaf and propped himself up on his elbow. "Did Kelric agree to Dargos' plan?" he asked, looking down at Gadnor.

Gadnor's throat was suddenly dry, his tongue thick. He sat up, pulling a blade of coarse grass from the earth and snapping it in two. "No. He doesn't think I'm ready."

"What do *you* think?"

Gadnor flicked the grass pieces into the breeze. "I'm ready to do *something.*"

Tor frowned. "And this is the best plan?"

"It's…" A number of descriptions came to mind: bold, ambitious, Kelric would say foolish.

"Expedient," Gadnor finished lamely. Perhaps too expedient, but he couldn't afford to wait. The island was dying, in dire need of its goddess, and only he could restore her power to make it whole and healthy again. He didn't have a choice. He had to be ready.

"But…?" Tor prompted.

Heat crept up Gadnor's neck. He plucked another blade of grass. As committed as he was, his old anxieties and insecurities were too ingrained into his being, and thus impossible to ignore for long. He sighed, watching his finger turn purple as he wound the grass tighter around it. "No matter what the plan is, I'm afraid I'm going to mess it up. Say the wrong thing. Do the wrong thing. Get innocent people killed. The island is relying on me to set things right, to restore peace. What if I let everyone down? Or what if everything goes exactly to plan, but I'm a terrible anax?"

Was Gonivein right when she said they were just playthings for the gods? What if nothing he did made any difference in the end?

Snap. The grass split and uncoiled from his finger.

Since learning of his lineage, his imagination hadn't stopped conjuring worst case scenarios: being skewered by an enemy spear—or an ally's. War was chaotic.

Even positive scenarios, like leading his army to victory or standing beside Princess Lithaneva before an adoring crowd, were no less exhausting: battlefields drenched in blood, a thousand faces staring up at him with expectations and demands he had no idea how to fulfill, and a princess bride who was completely unaware the heir she agreed to marry was him. What would she say when she found out? It was all too much to think about, really, yet he couldn't stop.

"You're allowed to make mistakes, you know. Every human does," Tor said.

Gadnor released a nervous chuckle. "I'm not entirely human, apparently."

Tor waved his hand. "What god doesn't have at least one regrettable tale?" He gestured at the plains far below and the sprawling city of Golpathia with its twinkling lights—like fireflies in the darkening twilight. "Isn't this drought because Helinthia lost control of her island?"

Gadnor shrugged, conceding. The boughs of the laurel creaked overhead as the breeze picked up, and Gadnor pulled his cloak tighter around his shoulders. As the pause lengthened, he sensed Tor wished to say more and turned to him. Tor stared back. His hazel eyes were a myriad of dark green and gold hues, like a mysterious forest dappled with beams of sunlight. What was Tor thinking behind them? Gadnor found himself wishing he knew.

Tor looked away, resting his arm over his propped knee. His eyes took on a faraway depth. "The hawk will come."

Gadnor sensed that wasn't exactly what Tor had wanted to say, but didn't press him.

"Have the scholars arrived yet?" Tor asked now.

"Not yet." Gadnor studied his friend's face, the furrowed brows, eyes squinting against the setting sun. It struck him that Tor was waiting on the scholars the same way Gadnor was waiting on this hawk.

"Are you nervous about your confirmation as Artemis' oracle?"

Tor shrugged. "A little. But…" He twisted a forelock nervously around his finger.

"But?"

Tor sighed and released the curl. It sprang against his brow, a perfect brown coil. "I've served the goddess a long time. She never required a ceremony from me to prove myself to her. I don't understand why this spectacle is needed. I'm good enough for the goddess. Why isn't that enough for these scholars?"

Gadnor pulled another blade of grass and tested the sharp point against the pad of his finger. He agreed with Tor—what was acceptable to a goddess should be enough for mortals. It never was, though. "They'll say the ceremony is to honor Artemis, but it's really to prove yourself to everyone else, not just the scholars. Right now, you're a boy from the Ordan. Men need a spectacle to believe you're more than that."

"Talking to animals isn't enough spectacle?"

Gadnor shrugged. "It should be."

Tor flopped back against the earth, curling his arm behind his head and closing his eyes.

Gadnor wished he had something noble and eloquent to say to set his friend at ease, but he'd never seen an oracle confirmation before and had no idea what it entailed. So he stayed quiet, enjoying the breeze and peacefulness of the plateau. The laurel's boughs creaked faintly as they swayed overhead.

This might be the last night either of them could truly be themselves.

CHAPTER 7

GONIVEIN

THE CROWDS LINING THE STREET cheered and waved linens in faded blues, pinks, and oranges before the litter. In more prosperous times, onlookers would have thrown flower petals from balconies or waved fresh cut branches loaded with laurel and olive blossoms. Gonivein used to dream of such a wedding. How she would weave through the twisting stone streets on her makeshift throne, breathe in the fragrant scents, and greet her adoring new citizens.

This was not that wedding. There were no sweet scents of flowers, no fresh greenery waving cheerfully. But the linens were still pretty and festive, the crowds still happy to see her—or perhaps they were just excited for an occasion to be happy. The litter that bore her was soft and comfortable. Kelric had spared no luxury to ensure Golpathia's new basileia was honored, drought or no drought.

None of this was the reason this wedding was different from her dreams. In that wedding, she was happy.

In that wedding, she *wanted* to marry Kelric.

The morning was crisp, but the sun shone bright in a cloudless sky. Sweat beaded Gonivein's brow and neck beneath her linen veil.

The threads were woven just thin enough to allow her to see where to safely place her feet while obscuring her features from everyone else. Unfortunately, it hadn't been woven thin enough to let the breeze in. Veils were a leftover element of an era when marriages were arranged between strangers. Back then, veils were considered a safeguard against picky grooms. As though a woman's life being traded to benefit men wasn't enough. She'd accidentally set her hand on the offensive cloth and yanked it more than once while trying to get comfortable on the litter, and it was scratchy. It reminded her too much of the sack that had been thrown over her face when…

No.

She pushed it from her mind. If she let in the grief, the guilt, the anger, she might crumple on the litter and not find the strength to get up. She found a loose thread on the hem of the veil and tugged. Feeling it unravel between her fingers was a welcome distraction.

The agora was packed shoulder to shoulder with Golpathia's citizens. Gonivein twisted her head toward the platform, making an effort to appraise the new statue of Aphrodite. Kelric was keen on her approval, but between the veil and the hundreds of people in between, everything was a blur of shapes and colors.

The litter meandered through the city until it stopped at the temple of Hera and was lowered to the ground. Golpathia's banners hung from the pediments and floated down over the entrance, the deep blue a stark contrast to the white marble behind them. The terrifying five-headed hydra embroidered upon them seemed to slither toward her as the cloth fluttered in the salty breeze. Carved swans and lilies etched in relief along the pediment were vibrant with fresh paint.

Dargos waited for her at the bottom of the polished steps of the porch. Forluna, Gadnor, Tor, *Kubernao* Pallas, Archon Tryphus, several priests, important kyrioi, including Kelric's council members, and guards lined the steps, creating a pathway to the temple entrance. Hedging her in. The smell of burning wood and oil wafted out of the gleaming building from the large open door, and Gonivein hoped the sacrificial animal had already been killed. If she had to see another innocent creature bleed for her, she feared her facade would crumble into a stream of tears.

Dargos stepped forward to take her hand and help her rise from the litter.

She gathered her feet beneath her and stood, grimacing as pain lanced through her hip. Forluna said the pain would lessen, but might never completely go away. A constant reminder of her most egregious failure. The tincture Forluna had given her earlier had helped a little, but it was beginning to wear off.

"You're beautiful," Dargos said, squeezing her hand. She doubted he could truly see her face. The makeup Lokefie, the doula of Aphrodite, had applied that morning was no doubt a splotchy, horrific mess.

She glanced behind her at the city of Golpathia. The thousand citizens before her were faceless silhouettes, but she could *feel* their eyes. Their disdain.

A prickle of heat skittered across her shoulders. She froze, squinting through the linen cloth, searching for some threat, but all she saw were silhouettes of adoring kyrioi, gathered to welcome their new basileia.

This felt wrong.

Drops of sweat ran down her chest despite the cool breeze ruffling her long chiton. Her veil teased glimpses of what lay beyond as the hem waved up and down. She wanted to tear off this confinement. Run. Instead, she turned to face the temple and nodded at her brother.

Dargos smiled back, his eyes shimmering with unshed tears.

The sentimentality riled her. She still hadn't forgiven him for forcing her into this.

No. That wasn't right. She could have refused the marriage. Dargos would have agreed if she had insisted, wouldn't he? Gadnor had said it, too. But Shallinath depended on this marriage. It was the only way to ensure Golpathia's support in reclaiming their lands from Ninenarn's control.

Isn't it?

She'd been over this time and again in her head. Despairing, resigning, bargaining, accepting. No matter how many times she cycled through this torment, she couldn't quell the hope for some vision from Apollo that would reveal a different path for her.

Apollo was silent as ever.

Perhaps she wouldn't have another vision until she was confirmed by the scholars—they had been summoned to Golpathia since she was unfit to travel to the Library with her injury. She had hoped they would arrive before the wedding.

They hadn't.

Gonivein lifted her chin and pushed the intrusive thoughts down. She was done making selfish decisions. Her marriage would save her people. She steeled her resolve and focused her attention on climbing the steps.

Aching, biting her lip, and leaning heavily on Dargos' arm, Gonivein finally made it to the top of the stairs. She paused to catch her breath, and Dargos squeezed her hand.

"Take all the time you need, Gonie," he whispered, and despite her lingering resentment toward him, she was grateful for his presence.

Inside the temple, the statue of Hera waited, poised above the altar to bless her marriage to Kelric. Ironic to seek the favor of a goddess who had plunged their island into famine, but Gonivein had never really taken these rituals seriously, not the way Dargos did. If she asked him, he would probably answer with something cryptic and evasive, like 'Her blessing won't be given if it is not requested.' But she knew this ritual was more for the people of Golpathia than her or the goddess, anyway: their witness to the confirmation of their new basileia.

The walls felt too close in here. Hera's statue loomed too large. The flames of the altar flared behind the priestess and the tall figure standing beside her.

Kelric.

He was a faceless silhouette, like an agent of the Underworld waiting to steal her soul. The prickle along her shoulders became an almost unbearable itch. Sweat rolled unabashedly down her neck and chest. Her hair, loose upon her shoulders, clumped and stuck to her back.

Dargos guided her slowly to stand next to Kelric, squeezed her hand one final time, and then laid it in Kelric's.

Her throat tightened. Her lungs suddenly burned for air as she gazed at the man before her.

Kelric's features were now visible in the firelight. Handsome as ever, his groomed curls soft on his shoulders, piercing gray eyes gazing into hers. A twinge of guilt curled in her gut at the adoration she saw there. Adoration she no longer returned. In truth, she was confused about her feelings for Kelric. She'd fantasized about him for five long years, and she couldn't deny what he'd sacrificed to save her life, but he had revealed a side of himself that she couldn't forgive. The memories of the inlet haunted her when she closed her eyes, every time Kelric approached her, looked at her, touched her. Not only for what he'd done to her, but for what he'd done to Loric.

"Basileus Kelric," the priestess said. "Basileus Dargos offers his sister to you in union. Do you accept this woman, Gonivein of Shallinath, to wed, to stand by your side as you govern these lands and people?"

Kelric's fingers threaded through hers. His jaw clenched, as though he were fighting back his emotions. "I accept."

The woman looked at Gonivein, and it seemed as though she forced her smile. "Do you swear upon the altar of Hera, before the people of Golpathia and Basileus Kelric, that you will perform your duties faithfully as his wife and as basileia?"

Gonivein's tongue was suddenly very thick, her throat dry. She opened her mouth, but nothing came out.

Something flickered in Kelric's gaze. Was he angry that she

might consider refusing him? Afraid of looking like a fool before his entire city?

Gonivein searched his eyes, his face, his posture. There was no hint of pride or anger. He looked… afraid. Terrified she might refuse him, deal a crushing blow to his heart.

Her breath hitched. She could. The gods only knew how many nights she had longed to punish him for abandoning Loric's body to Poseidon's domain, condemning him to wander the fringes of Hades forever. Gadnor had tried to save him, the only noble one of any of them, but it had been too late.

"Yes," she answered, letting her breath go slowly.

A smile broke across Kelric's face as he sighed, his curls bouncing on his shoulders as he glanced eagerly at the priestess for the next part of the ritual.

Hera's servant maintained her calm expression. "And you, Basileus. Do you vow to protect your wife, to maintain a place of safety and shelter for her, and to recognize her offspring as your true heirs?"

Kelric's face sobered a bit with the seriousness of her words. Something akin to reverence—if Kelric were capable of such a thing—sharpened his focus on the old woman. He nodded, the apple of his throat bobbing as he swallowed. "Yes."

"Then," said the priestess, motioning a doulos holding an amphora forward from the shadows. The wine inside sloshed. "Take hold, both of you," she said, and arranged Gonivein and Kelric's hands on the handle.

Their fingers brushed as they held the amphora between them.

Gonivein's hip throbbed, and her knee threatened to buckle at the added weight and awkward twist in her stance. Kelric's other arm reached out to steady the amphora and take the bulk of its weight. Had he felt her hands trembling? Or did she look as thinly held together as she felt?

The priestess' eyes, surrounded by wrinkles of age and wisdom, raked over Gonivein, as though weighing her worthiness.

Gonivein's face burned. Her hands grew clammy and slippery against the clay. Marriages were supposed to be joyful occasions. This woman looked more like she was performing a funeral. Gonivein had known there would be some who questioned this union—Shallinath was at odds with the anax, and this marriage was sure to complicate Golpathia's position—but she hadn't expected such blatant coldness.

Two acolytes stepped forward. One held a brass bowl, the other a dove. The bird cooed, tilting its head in curiosity at the spectacle before it. Gonivein's stomach lurched as the priestess reached for it.

With a practiced hand, the old woman pulled the knife from her belt and drew it across the animal's throat, suspending it over the brass bowl to collect the blood.

Gonivein slammed her eyes shut, tears gathering on her painted lashes. Bile rose up her throat at the sound of the creature's wings, slapping the woman's palms as it died.

The priestess set the dove's corpse onto the coals, then took the bowl and circled the altar, pouring the blood out and chanting prayers.

Gonivein's heart pounded so loudly that she couldn't hear a single word.

An urgent tap of Kelric's fingers on hers snapped her attention back. The priestess was before them again, staring expectantly at her. The bowl had vanished, and her bloodied hands were clasped.

"Pour the libation," she commanded, and Gonivein wondered how many times the woman had repeated herself.

She and Kelric obeyed and stepped forward together. The fire's heat and the stench of burnt feathers was suffocating. Gonivein wondered if her veil would suddenly burst into flames and consume her right here. She half expected it to, under Hera's damning gaze. Perhaps that would be a better fate. *How would Dargos interpret that omen?* She almost smiled.

Kelric tipped the amphora, and its contents sloshed onto the altar. The coals hissed. Steam billowed upwards, adding the scent of grapes and alcohol to the feathers. The orange tongues leapt and licked at the fuel.

The priestess examined the altar as the doulos retrieved the empty amphora, divining the goddess' acceptance of the sacrifice. The assembly seemed to be holding their breath. Finally, the woman nodded to Kelric. "Take your bride, Basileus."

Kelric beamed down at Gonivein. His eyes were bright and shining, yet a hint of caution lingered behind his joy. He stooped and lifted her in his arms.

Gonivein's throat tightened, eyes stinging with relieved tears. Had he known she wouldn't have made it out of the temple on her own? Certainly not down the porch steps.

"I've got you," he whispered, and a pain sharpened in her chest.

'I've got you.' Mist swirled in her mind's eye, and Loric was there on the shores of the Styx, shadows and shades drifting around him, water lapping at his sandals.

She shut her eyes, willing the sobs to stay down. Sunlight reddened her closed lids, accompanied by the deafening cheers of Golpathians. She squinted out at them, emotions roiling within her at the stark contrast between the gleeful people before her and the stony-faced priestess. These people were celebrating their Basileus and his new bride. *Celebrating me.* She didn't deserve their love. How long would it be before they realized it as clearly as the priestess had?

Kelric stepped into his chariot and gingerly lowered her to her feet.

Her hip seared with pain, and her knee buckled. She gasped, clutching at his shoulders to steady herself. Her veil tangled between them and pulled against her face, wrenching her scalp. "Ow."

Kelric's grip around her waist tightened. "You all right?"

She nodded, adjusting her garment. "Yes, just this stupid thing." She didn't want to mention her hip. She didn't want his pity, didn't want his first impression of her as his basileia to be one of weakness.

An amused smile lifted his lips as he leaned closer. "Don't worry.

You won't be wearing any of that for much longer."

A chill rolled down her spine, and it was all she could manage not to push him away and bolt from the chariot, or try to. His flirtatious promise would have melted her knees mere weeks ago, but she wasn't the same silly girl she'd been.

Kelric's smile wavered at her stiffness, hurt flickering in his eyes as he looked away. He grabbed the chariot reins. "Hold on," he murmured.

Guilt twisted in her gut as she put her arms around his shoulders again. At her nod, he tapped the horse into motion toward the villa.

CHAPTER 8

FORLUNA

GUARDS HELD BACK THE EAGER citizens, allowing prominent members of the procession to walk first to the villa. Forluna followed Dargos and Gadnor down the steps and into the street after Kelric's chariot. The cheering crowd thronged behind them, hurrying them faster up the slope.

The street was far too narrow for Forluna's liking. Every brush of a shoulder sent shivers through her, as though at any moment the passive touch might transform into a vice grip and drag her away, swallow her into the belly of the crowd, never to be seen or heard from again.

She rubbed her arms, feeling exposed walking in front, visible. A glance behind her revealed an endless sea of faces craning over the shoulders in front of them. Their focus was directed beyond where Forluna stood, hoping for a glimpse of the bride and groom. Even still, she couldn't shake the feeling of being scrutinized, considered, *remembered.*

But who would remember her as Anassa Iptys' missing companion? Charixes had killed everyone who'd worked in the palace, and only the most prominent kyrioi in Ninenarn had ever come close enough to Iptys to have seen the quiet figure standing in the corner. None of them would have set aside their power and prestige for a mundane existence among Golpathia's citizens.

The leading men of Kelric's polis were all around her. Some were grinning. Some were not. None of them looked her way long enough to do more than dismiss her. In fact, as she stole subtle glances at each of them, she got the distinct impression they were evading her gaze purposely. Shunning her. Adding to her apprehension.

Something else was amiss. *Where are their wives?* Perhaps not all of these men were married, but *some* were, surely. *Are women not allowed to walk in the procession?* The customs couldn't have changed that much during her time in the forest. She joined the crowd in craning over the shoulders surrounding her. She saw no finely dressed women or elaborately styled hair on this side of the guard barrier. *Perhaps they're already at the villa?* Somehow, she found that improbable.

A withering feeling started in her gut and slowly spread through her. She'd experienced tension like this before, in the years and weeks when Charixes' power had begun to steadily eclipse Iptys'. She looked over at Dargos, and his cutting glance told her he sensed it, too. She spotted several alleys through which she could escape. Dark and dusty with neglect, she could easily disappear in any of them, but the crowd was pushing forward too quickly for her to change directions without causing a huge scene. She was stuck.

Why did I agree to this?

Dargos grasped her hand. It was too loud for anything to be heard, so he didn't try to speak. Instead, he gave her an encouraging squeeze. His touch pulled her back from the brink of panic. She closed her eyes and focused on her breathing.

In. Out. Slow.

I asked for this. She and Dargos had both agreed their relationship could no longer be a secret. Dargos was brave enough to take a stand against tyranny, to risk his life to see the heir restored. She wanted to be at his side, no matter how paralyzing her fear might become. *Just breathe.*

But Dargos was only one reason she was parading before everyone in this city. Gadnor was the second. He was stepping out of the shadows, too, battling his own fears of being seen, and she would not abandon him again.

As she tried to calm her fraying nerves, something itched at the back of her skull, scattering her newfound resolve. Her ears instinctively tried to swivel around to catch any strange sounds behind her, but she had tucked them beneath her hair and secured them in place with the celebratory laurel crown. She doubted anything would be discernible, anyway. She twisted around and awkwardly shuffled sideways, squinting down the slope to find anything out of place.

A myriad of faces, headdresses, and cloaked shoulders stretched as far as she could see. Terracotta rooftops and clay houses sprawled before her. Bronze flashed in the sun from the statues of watchful deities from every corner of the city. From her higher elevation, the contrast between the central street and all the rest was striking: buildings shined with fresh paint, and festive drapes rippled in every window. Farther down, she spied something else floating above the sea of bobbing heads: a white banner emblazoned with a red emblem—a sun wreathed in flames. Beside it, a darker banner with a full white moon circled by two rings.

The scholars!

The possibility of being remembered had suddenly become all too real. She faced forward again, her heart pounding as memories surfaced of the months she had sheltered at the Library, hiding the infant Gadnor from Charixes' spies. Anxiety wormed through her.

Stay calm. Even if a scholar did recognize her, they would only recall an unmarried, unlucky mother. Only Brother Neocles, the one who had helped her escape Ninenarn, had known her true identity as Iptys' companion. There was no reason she should feel threatened.

So then, why did she?

She took another deep breath and stared straight ahead, every bump of a shoulder sending a new wave of anxiety through her as they crawled up the street. *Just a little farther.*

The marriage procession finally eased their way through the gates of the Basileus' villa. Fresh grooves from Kelric's chariot wheels sliced through the gravel courtyard and disappeared into the stables. As the dust settled, Forluna saw Kelric and Gonivein standing on the porch hand in hand, observing the throng of people approaching. Gonivein's face was still veiled, but Kelric was beaming.

Kelric motioned for silence, and the commotion ceased. He turned eagerly to Gonivein and lifted her veil. *Oohs* and *ahhs* arose, and the bride and groom stared at one another for a moment before Gonivein dropped her gaze and angled her face away as if to hide. She said something, and Kelric chuckled. Forluna's gaze was drawn to his mouth, and she could just make out his words "you're stunning" before he bent to kiss her and set off an eruption of claps and cheers that rippled through the crowd all the way out the gates and beyond.

Gonivein was officially his wife now, his basileia.

Forluna recalled the many nights when Dargos had passed through the misty veil of the forest and rapped on her door to unburden his frustrations in her arms. Dargos had never liked Kelric, had called him brash, selfish, vile. He'd wanted nothing more than for his little sister to rid herself of Kelric for good. *'Gonivein is too good for him,'* he would say, pacing the grounds in front of her cottage. *'She's obsessed with him, won't listen to reason.'*

Gonivein didn't look obsessed with Kelric now. Her hand hung limp in his, and her unveiled face stretched into an awkward smile that Forluna knew was forced. She'd seen it too many times on Iptys' face. The dutiful smile. The mask that hid the emotions deemed too indecent for the public eye to behold. Too personal for their callous judgment.

Dargos believed Gonivein's indifference of late had to do with the trauma she'd experienced during her journey across the plains. *'She'll remember her love for him again,'* he'd said. Forluna hoped he was right.

With the last wedding ritual complete, the guards motioned the citizens forward to present their gifts. Gonivein and Kelric exchanged quick pleasantries and words of gratitude as the items were laid on the porch steps.

Bronze bowls and weapons gleamed in the noonday sun, scattered among amphorae of every size; sacks of grain; bolts of cloth dyed red, blue, and yellow. There was even a pair of geese honking and flapping their wings against their wicker confinement.

Small talk started among the wedding guests waiting to go inside. Forluna wasn't familiar with these men, but she could easily distinguish the travelers from the city dwellers by the amount of dust on their feet and cloaks. She leaned forward to eavesdrop, doubting she would learn much from such a short exchange, but anything—a tone, a mutter, an affirmation—could allude to their openness to Gadnor taking on an authoritative role.

She couldn't listen long, for a commotion coming up from the entrance to the villa drew everyone's attention. The crowd moved in a wavelike fashion, as though parting for some small party to pass through. The banners of Apollo and Artemis bobbed above the chaos, and she could make out several older men with their youthful acolytes trailing behind.

The anxiety she'd felt before struck her again, and she stepped back. Her eyes darted through the side courtyard and lit upon the path that led upwards to the ancient laurel. *I should hide there.*

Dargos' touch on her elbow made her jump. His brow furrowed in concern as he guided her a few steps away from the chaos. "Are you all right? You look frightened. Did you see something?"

She didn't have time to answer before a sudden noisy clatter rang in her ears, and the pile of gifts avalanched down the steps.

"Gonivein!" Kelric cried, and a collective gasp emanated from the onlookers. The guards thronged, forming a defensive line to keep the curious crowd back.

Forluna scanned the portico where, just a moment ago, Kelric and Gonivein had stood side by side. Now, Gonivein lay in the midst of the scattered gifts, unmoving, with Kelric bent over her. Dargos bolted toward them, Forluna on his heels. Why had she ignored the feeling of foreboding?

Fool! Had someone attacked Gonivein? Had her hip given out? *Should I have given her a stronger potion?* Blackness threatened the edges of Forluna's vision by the time she'd waded through the gawking bystanders and climbed the steps, her chest tight, limbs heavy.

In-out-slow-in-out-slow.

Forluna squeezed between Dargos and Kelric, sweeping her eyes over Gonivein for signs of injury: blood, the hilt of a knife, the shaft of an arrow embedded somewhere. There was nothing. Dargos and Kelric were frantically trying to wake her, calling to her.

Gonivein's lashes fluttered over white eyes, her fingers and hands twitching uncontrollably.

"Gonivein!" Kelric cradled her head between his hands.

"What's wrong with her?" Dargos demanded. "What did you do?"

Kelric's lip curled at the accusation, and Forluna's hand shot out to interrupt them.

"It's a vision," Forluna said.

Almost as soon as the words left her mouth, Gonivein's eyes and fingers stilled. A moan echoed in her throat, and then she was awake. Her brow pinched in confusion, her gaze darting up at the familiar faces. She tried to rise, but Kelric held her down.

"Wait, Gonie, you might be hurt."

Gonivein winced in answer and reached for Dargos' tunic with desperate fingers. Forluna noted that her grip was weak, sluggish, sliding down Dargos' chest without purchase. But her eyes were wild. "Gadnor's in danger."

Forluna shot to her feet, searching the crowd for Gadnor's face.

There he was, peering across the debris field with a concerned expression. "Is she all right?" he asked.

Forluna felt herself nod even as she continued scanning the

courtyard. *'Gadnor's in danger.'* Where was it—the figure sneaking? The misshapen shadow? The glint of a weapon?

There was nothing.

"Danger now?" Dargos asked.

"Coming…"

In the future. The rest of what Gonivein said faded as Forluna's heart beat slowed, too overwhelmed to know what its proper rhythm should be. "We should get her inside. She may have injured herself in the fall." Forluna stepped back to give Kelric more room to acquiesce.

Her attention refocused on eight robed figures standing at the bottom of the steps. Circular emblems hung around their necks on finely braided leather chains: four suns wreathed in flames, and four two-ringed moons. The scholars. At their forefront was a man whose white hair had receded to the top of his head, and whose curly white beard reached just above his sun pendant.

Dizziness washed over her as memories of choking ash and the orange glow of a city in flames bubbled to the surface. The wrinkles of the old man before her seemed to smooth. His white hair darkened, his gnarled fingers and stooped shoulders became straight and nimble. She saw him again, leaping over the rubble and kicking debris, shattering the safety of quiet in his clumsy wake.

Mandus.

Of course it would be him. He was Neocles' brightest acolyte. After helping Neocles smuggle her and Gadnor out of the city, they had become close friends. She'd never thought she would see him again. Her feet propelled her down to him.

"Is she hurt?" Age had deepened Mandus' tone, mellowing out the harsh edge it once held. "I am trained in the healing arts, I can help." His lip curled into a knowing smirk, and Forluna allowed herself to smile back. *Not as well trained as I, dear Mandus.* Neocles had never let him forget it, but it wasn't a fact that had soured their friendship. Rather, they had turned it into a tease between them. Even after all these years, Mandus didn't miss a beat of his humor.

Kelric straightened with Gonivein in his arms. The new bride cried out from the sudden movement, tears spilling down her cheeks. "I'm sorry, Gonie," he whispered. His eyes finally left her tormented face and landed on the scholars staring up at them. His face twisted into a scowl, and the crowd went eerily quiet with anticipation.

Archon Tryphus, standing a few feet away, cleared his throat.

Kelric blinked, his anger dispelled. "She's all right. Just exhausted." He turned to the archon. "Disperse the people back to their homes." Then, to Dargos, he added, "See to the scholars. That's more your expertise, isn't it?" Without waiting for a response from either man, he flashed a wide grin at the gawking citizens and disappeared through the atrium with Gonivein in his arms.

All at once, the courtyard came alive again with gossip.

Forluna reached for Mandus' wrinkled hands. "It's so good to see you," she said. In her heart, the words felt right, but they rang false to her ears. Anxiety hadn't loosened its hold on her yet. Not knowing its cause would drive her to madness before the night was out. She plastered a dutiful smile on her face.

They looked at one another for a long moment, and then Mandus pulled her into an embrace.

"Forluna," he said, squeezing her tightly before pulling. "I thought I'd never see you again." He glanced around. "Where is your child? Is he here? He must be a fine man now."

She caught Gadnor's movement from the corner of her eye, and her smile evaporated. She was torn. Mandus had grown fond of the baby. All the acolytes had. But she couldn't tell him the truth.

"He's..." She lowered her eyes. "He's dead."

Mandus drew in a sharp breath, his stooped shoulders sagging even lower. "Oh, no." He drew her into another embrace. "I'm sorry."

Forluna held onto the old man, the only living soul outside the Forest of Shades who knew a little of what she'd been through. They'd escaped the flames of Ninenarn together. The comfort of that wrenched a sob from her chest.

The mob of people had all but dispersed now, and the guests were filing past her into the villa, where the smells of the evening meal poured out of the open triklinion doors.

Dargos took a step toward her and Mandus. The lines around his dark eyes deepened as they focused. She could almost see his mind swirling erratically. She'd seen that look before, after revealing the heir's identity and her pact with Raleon. A look of curiosity and jealousy.

Guilt curled inside her, and it struck her as strange how two people could be in love without truly knowing much at all about one another. *No more secrets.* She would have to tell Dargos about Mandus now.

She pulled away from the old scholar and brushed her tears hastily from her cheeks. "I must see to Gonivein."

Mandus dipped his head and squeezed her hands. "We will speak again soon."

"Yes," she said, smiling. As she turned and placed her foot on the next step, her gaze lighted on another elderly scholar over Mandus' shoulder. As their eyes met, a flare of recognition—and warning—blossomed within her. The man shuffled his feet, as though trying to ease their ache, but his small movement made him disappear completely behind the other acolytes.

She stumbled up the steps for a higher vantage point and searched the group of scholars. Had she really seen someone? She counted Mandus' companions. *One, two, three, four, five, six...* "Mandus, how many came with you?"

"Including myself? Eight," he answered without hesitation.

I didn't imagine him. But he was gone.

Dargos gave her a puzzled look before she bolted into the villa to find Kelric and Gonivein. Her footsteps echoed loudly in the atrium. All the faces she remembered from the Library swam through her mind, but none of them seemed to fit this man. She didn't recognize anyone else in Mandus' entourage, either, but that wasn't exactly a surprise. A dozen or more people took oaths to become scholars every year.

But he recognized me. She was sure of it. Why hadn't he come forward and reacquainted himself? Why had he run?

Unless he knows me from the palace.

Her feet crunched the gravel of the inner courtyard, and she froze, feeling exposed in the large, empty space. She looked over her shoulder at the crowd waiting outside. She half expected to find the man standing behind her with a dagger in his hand, ready to slit her throat. She sighed, remembering to breathe.

In. Out. Slow.

It's not possible.

But her doubt remained, along with the itch at the back of her skull.

CHAPTER 9

KELRIC

KELRIC GAVE THE BEDROOM DOOR a backward kick, and it closed with a gentle *clink* of the metal latch. Gonivein's ear was pressed against his chest. Could she hear how furiously his heart was beating? He clenched his jaw, wondering if collapsing would be a risk every time Apollo sent her a vision. What if one came while she was on a horse? Or standing beside a cliff? Or mid-stride down a flight of steps?

A chill gripped the spacious room. The fireplace was dark and empty. Kelric tamped down the urge to grumble. It was too early for the douloi to have expected anyone to be in here.

He maneuvered across the room to the large oak bed. He'd ordered the mattress stuffed with fresh straw and lined with sheep's skin. Only the best comfort for his bride. He carefully set Gonivein down, knelt beside her, and smoothed hair out of her face.

Her gaze darted around the room. Her breath shortened. Beads of sweat dislodged from her heaving bosom and ran across her skin. She was afraid. Was it the vision again? Alarmed, he took her hand. It stiffened in his grasp.

It's me. She's terrified of me.

He leaned away, aching to hold her, to slide onto the bed beside her and entangle his arms and legs in hers. Explore her body and soak in her warmth. But it was clear she wanted nothing to do with him.

"The guests…" She pushed herself to the edge of the bed, but he seized her hand.

"They can wait."

She pulled back, and he released her, clasping his hands to his chest. A sickening desperation swelled within him. He had grossly misjudged her feelings about him, apparently. His mind swam with all the clues he'd missed. She hadn't met his gaze in days, hadn't said more than yes or no when he'd spoken to her, practically refused to acknowledge him sitting beside her every night at dinner. What did he think was happening?

That she was tired, hurting, grieving, in shock.

All false, apparently. Or, at least, not the whole truth.

"You need to *rest*, Gonivein." He ran a finger under her chin, directing her eyes to his. *I'm not going to hurt you.* He supposed she had a right to think otherwise. He swallowed down his shame as he remembered his anger in the inlet, his loss of control—of her, of himself, of everything. The result was regrettable. He wondered if she would forgive him if he told her everything he was doing to protect her now, to atone. But now wasn't the time to bring it up.

She stared at him, and he raked his fingers through his hair, breathing a little easier as he saw her body relax slightly.

"Tell me what happened. Why did you faint like that?" he asked, eager to think of something, anything, other than his wife. In his bed. Hating him.

Gonivein swallowed, and he settled back on his heels, giving her more space now that he was sure she wouldn't bolt for the door.

She nibbled her lip—a nervous habit she had broken years ago. Or so he'd thought. "I…"

There was a knock at the door, then it cracked open, brightening the room. Forluna's brown eye peered at them cautiously before she opened the door wider and stepped inside. She made quick strides across the floor and took a seat on the bed beside Gonivein. She reached for her hand, felt her brow, pressed a finger against the pulse in her neck.

"I don't see any injuries." Forluna flattened her palm against Gonivein's hip and gingerly prodded the joint with her thumb. Gonivein winced, and Forluna pulled back. "I don't feel anything out of place. Do you feel all right?"

Gonivein dipped her head. "I'm okay. I was just startled."

Forluna squeezed Gonivein's hand. "You said Gadnor was in danger."

Gonivein's eyes jerked to Forluna's, a swirl of confusion within them. "I did?"

Kelric and Forluna shared a glance.

Great, she doesn't even know what she's saying.

"Can you tell us what you saw?" Forluna asked.

Gonivein withdrew her hand from Forluna's and stared at it, as though her palm might reveal something to her. "I've had this vision before, in Tyldan, the night that..." Her voice trailed off, and her eyes widened as though a ghost stood before her.

Gonivein drew in a shaky breath. "There's a field—beautiful, healthy, green—and a valley. At the bottom is a falcon surrounded by three beasts: a hydra, a stallion, and a lion. They're circling it, waiting to strike, wounding each other when they come close. And then there is a ring of wolves around them, just sitting there, watching everything." Her blue eyes met Kelric's, fear swirling in their depths. "And then the three beasts pounce, crushing the falcon."

"And Gadnor?" Forluna pressed, her body rigid and still. She was barely breathing. Kelric's blood raced a little faster.

Gonivein shook her head. "I don't know why I said his name. He's not in my vision. Just a feeling, I guess."

Kelric waited for Gonivein to look at him, but she didn't. *She was thinking about him.* His jealousy and doubt from yesterday surfaced again, lodging itself like a stone between his ribs. Could they have been up to something in her room, after all? *Was she thinking about him when she was saying her vows to me?*

Was that why she'd hesitated?

"Why didn't you tell us this vision before?" Forluna asked gently.

Gonivein raised her hands to her eyes and rubbed them as she shook her head. "I had forgotten it." She dropped her face in her hands. "What if I missed something important?"

Were visions as vivid as nightmares? He recalled one nightmare he'd experienced as a child. He chased his mother to the Styx, never reaching her, then watched her sail away on Charon's Ferry. She never looked back. It had been so real he could still smell death on the water, feel the mist clinging to his skin. One would think that a vision from a god would be at *least* as memorable as a bad dream sent to torment an innocent child.

Forluna laid her hand gently on Gonivein's knee. "You've been through so much since then. It's understandable that this vision wouldn't be foremost in your mind. What's important is that it's come to you again. It's not too late to understand its meaning."

Kelric's jealousy sharpened into guilt. Forluna was right. Gonivein had been through a lot since she'd fled Tyldan. She was confused, distracted. *That's all.*

Gonivein's trembling voice broke him from his brooding. "How am I supposed to find out its meaning? None of it makes any sense."

"The falcon is symbolic of the one who sits upon the throne," Forluna said. "The beasts—falcon, hydra, lion, stallion—represent the *poleis* which divide Helinthia's lands. The symbolism of the wolves is unfamiliar to me."

Kelric sat straighter. "So, does that mean the falcon is Charixes?"

Gonivein lifted her eyes to the window, focusing on something far away, or perhaps nothing at all. "I don't know. I suppose it must."

Kelric suppressed the urge to laugh. *Why use metaphors when the answer is so obvious?* Did the gods really expect mortals to take visions seriously if they were as silly as this? Perhaps this was the game, to watch humans scramble over ludicrous nonsense for entertainment. He imagined the halls of Olympus booming with laughter at this very moment.

He cleared his throat. "What's confusing? If the three beasts represent Golpathia, Shallinath, and Thellshun, and they crush Charixes, then what else could it mean besides our victory? I don't see anything about this vision that you should lose sleep over."

"I can't explain it, but… I don't feel triumphant watching it. I just felt… sadness." Gonivein stared at her hands again.

"What if the falcon is Gadnor?" Forluna said quietly.

Gonivein bit her lip. "Could it be?"

Kelric dragged his hand through his hair again, snagging a curl and smoothing it out. Frustration was building at his core. This was utter nonsense. "Why would Shallinath and Golpathia attack Gadnor?"

"Why would they attack each other?" Forluna countered, then turned to Gonivein. "You said the beasts wounded each other as they circled the falcon."

Kelric's confidence in his divining abilities faltered. He'd overlooked that detail.

Gonivein nodded dully.

Kelric shrugged. The vision still seemed clear enough to him. His father had once told him, *'People can only see what they look for.'* Gonivein and Forluna weren't looking for a simple explanation, so they were bent on fabricating a complicated one in typical female fashion.

"Well, the scholars are here now. Maybe they can make sense of it," he suggested, feeling a rumble in his stomach.

"No," Forluna blurted, startling him and Gonivein. She looked even more disturbed than before.

"What's the problem?" He could no longer hide the annoyance in his tone. "You're the one who suggested the scholars come here in the first place. Now they can't be trusted?"

"I…" Forluna's mouth clamped shut.

Gonivein met Kelric's eyes, and his heart fluttered at their kindred confusion. Slight, but it was one moment today where they shared a common thought, and that ignited the tiniest spark of hope for reconciliation.

Forluna smoothed the linen of her skirt. "Yes, I did, because Gonivein is not fit for travel and she needs to be confirmed as an oracle. But that doesn't mean we should disclose her prophecies to them. It is their duty to make the will of the gods known to all. They record what the oracles tell them, then relay the information to the anax and everyone else. The scholars are impartial in war. They are loyal to their office and the gods. But we *are* at war, and whatever this vision means, it could reveal things to Charixes that might help him win."

An uneasy feeling squirmed in Kelric's gut. *Great, now I have a city a breath away from revolt and a group of old men to keep an eye on. What next?* He just wanted to enjoy his wedding. Was that too much to ask? His impatience was approaching its boiling point. It didn't help that the smell of roasted meat was wafting through the crack in the door.

Kelric folded his arms across his chest and looked back and forth between Forluna and Gonivein, squinting at their worried expressions. His stomach gurgled and pinched, and he stood, more irritated than ever. He struggled between twin desires to laugh and curse at the gods. Neither action would win back Gonivein's affection, but he was certain this was all some divine prank. It riled him that it was at Gonivein's expense—and his stomach's.

He sighed, reminding himself to keep his voice even and controlled. "Why would Apollo show you such conflicting and confusing information? Why not just say what it means and be done with it?"

Gonivein worried her lip again. Something told him he should stop there, but words continued to fly off his tongue faster than he could figure out how to rein them in.

"All this vision has done is put you in harm's way and interrupted our wedding. You could have cracked your head when you fell. And for what? What useful information has been revealed?"

Gonivein's cheeks flushed, and she quickly looked away.

Guilt stabbed him immediately. *I should have said less.* She probably thought he was calling *her* useless instead of the vision. He blamed his hunger. And Apollo. *Damn him for subjecting the woman I love to this twisted game.*

"Perhaps it's a *warning* not to let our passions divide us," Forluna hissed, her eyes flashing at him.

He couldn't deny she might be onto something, but he returned her glare and offered his hand to Gonivein, softening his voice. "Come, Gonie." He closed his fingers tenderly around hers, relieved when she didn't pull away. "If you're recovered, then let's return to our feast. I know you're hungry, too. Whatever significance Apollo intends…" His mind scrambled for words to rebuild her confidence, but he had nothing but contempt for this whole predicament. He raised her hand to his lips instead and planted a kiss on her knuckles. "We'll figure it out together. *Later.*"

Forluna stood and nodded curtly, meeting Gonivein's eyes. "Don't speak of the vision to anyone, Gonivein. Not yet."

Gonivein nodded and started to rise.

Kelric felt a thrill go through him when she kept her hand in his. She let him help her stand, then leaned on him as they trudged to the door. Her closeness was a balm to his tortured soul.

But she didn't speak, and though her body brushed his as they made their way to the door and across the courtyard to the triklinion, a wall of tension remained wedged between them, made wider now by the meddling of a callous god.

Damn you, Apollo.

CHAPTER 10

DARGOS

DARGOS SURVEYED THE WEDDING GIFTS, scattered in all directions across the porch steps. A gold-tinged substance was splattered on the white marble and snaking through the grooves—olive oil, he presumed. Shards of broken pottery displayed their sharp edges to the sky, and a few bronze bowls had rolled halfway across the courtyard below. A heaviness lingered in the air, like the breath before an arrow flies from the bow toward its mark.

He tucked a loose strand of gray-streaked brown hair behind his ear. So much depended on this day going to plan, but Kelric had committed to nothing, and now Gonivein was hurt. Was her collapse a symptom of the vision—yet another unexpected occurrence—or exhaustion? *Have I pushed her too far?*

"That was your sister, was it not, Basileus Dargos?"

A gravelly voice captured his attention, and embarrassment warmed his face as recognition took hold. "Brother Mandus, I'm sorry I didn't acknowledge you sooner. Yes, that was her."

Mandus waved off his apology. "She's been through much, I see. She is also the bride?"

Dargos frowned, but nodded. What was he getting at?

Mandus' bushy eyebrow rose as he tilted his head. "And also the one we have come to confirm as the Oracle of Apollo?"

Dargos' shoulders slumped as the scholar's chiding tone settled in. He had been so consumed by his plans to fulfill Helinthia's will that he had barely stopped to consider how Gonivein was handling all of this. He'd taken for granted that today would restore some stability for her; marrying Kelric was all she had talked about for the last five years. Until she suffered her traumatic flight across the plains and the injury that was a constant reminder of all she'd lost. *I have pushed her too far.*

"My colleagues are skeptical that an oracle should be chosen after not having one for so long. If she were not the sister of Helinthia's favorite hero, I might agree with them, but your miraculous recovery is still sharp in my memory. In fact, we probably should have seen this coming." Mandus stroked his beard thoughtfully.

Dargos smoothed his thumb over a scar on his hand, a remnant of the plague that had stricken him during his studies at the Library. It was Mandus who had cared for him while his father interceded with Helinthia for a cure.

Mandus dug his fingers into his curly beard to scratch his chin. "If my memory serves, Gonivein has quite a stubborn spirit—never could keep her attention on studies. Forluna will ensure she is restored in no time at all."

Dargos head shot up. "You know Forluna?"

Mandus' other eyebrow rose to the same height as the first. "Do *you* know Forluna?"

Not as well as I thought, apparently. He'd been distracted when Forluna and Mandus were speaking, but assumed their greeting was formal. Now, certain details stood out. Their embrace—twice—and the lingering touch of Mandus' hand on her arm. The simple fact that Forluna had stopped to talk to him at all instead of going straight to Gonivein's side.

Forluna had spent a lot of time at the Library, so it should come as no surprise that the two were acquainted. But Dargos found himself staring at Mandus differently now, all the same. Though there had never been a reason for this to come up in conversation, it didn't stop him from wondering if Forluna had withheld this information from him purposely. She was good at that, keeping secrets. But what would she have to hide about Mandus? He wasn't sure he wanted to know. He had too many things to worry about right now. Dargos had full confidence in Forluna's abilities, too, but he couldn't quell the urge to sprint to Gonivein and see for himself that she was all right, ask her forgiveness for being neglectful, for not considering how overwhelming all of this must be.

"Make yourself useful, girl."

Dargos' attention snapped to a well-dressed man shoving a doula toward the mess of gifts. The girl looked no older than fifteen. She glanced around at the chaos and began collecting each item and setting them upright at the top of the porch, careful not to scratch, dent, or tear anything that remained in one piece. The damaged items she moved to the bottom of the steps, away from tramping feet. The man walked away from her and joined another group of Kelric's guests several paces away. They greeted him with pats on the shoulders and amused grins.

Dargos eyed them. He had yet to be acknowledged by any of Kelric's leading men, and though no one had said it, Dargos knew he was not invited into their circle.

Mandus leaned closer and lowered his voice. "In my experience, wedding feasts are joyous occasions, *even when they're not*, if you catch my meaning."

Dargos did, and it stirred his guilt afresh. Was that how Gonivein truly felt about this wedding? Had her experiences changed her so much without him realizing it?

Mandus' gaze darted from the wedding guests to Dargos. "I observe that *no one* seems particularly happy about this union, except maybe the groom. And there is not much concern about their new basileia, either, unless my eyesight has started to deteriorate. But I still feel rather young for *that*."

Mandus' humor didn't stop the shiver from rolling down Dargos' spine. A heaviness pressed down on him. Like doom waiting to crush them all in one fell swoop.

"Be careful, Dargos," Mandus whispered. "I know every man at this feast, for you were *all* the pupils of Critius, once. Your goal is for peace and prosperity for Helinthia, but many here have less honorable aspirations. Be wary."

By now, the crowd of citizens had fully dispersed and Archon Tryphus was climbing the steps of the porch. He held his arms out to keep his balance as he tiptoed through the debris. "Everyone," he called when he reached clear ground.

The chatter quieted as the everyone focused on the archon.

"The libation will be made soon and the feast will commence. You should all go inside."

The guests began to file into the villa one by one, avoiding Dargos and Mandus as they traipsed through the remaining gifts still littering the porch steps, kicking objects carelessly out of their way.

Shock, and then fury, rippled through Dargos. "Show some respect!" he growled, but his words were lost among the loud laughter and jangling of trinkets. The few men who glanced in his direction just sneered and continued on their way.

The doula, panicking, and perhaps misreading his outburst, began moving faster to clear a path. She got in the way more than the mess she was trying to clean. Several men bumped into her unapologetically. One even stepped on her hand.

Gadnor appeared at her side and swept the objects swiftly out of the way with an unceremonious clatter. A few pieces of pottery dislodged and careened down the steps, shattering on the gravel courtyard at Dargos and Mandus' feet.

The doula looked horrified. She relaxed a little when she recognized Gadnor had done the deed.

Dargos bit his tongue. His rage at the rowdiness of Kelric's guests, and their lack of respect for his property, still pulsed through him too strongly to decide if Gadnor's sweep had made things better or worse. At least the doula was out of harm's way—no doubt Gadnor's intent.

"Poor girl," Mandus muttered beside him. "Having a bad start to her service, isn't she?"

Dargos merely sighed.

"That reminds me," Mandus' continued. "Where is Neocles' doulos, Loric? Is he here? I'd like to see him. He was just a lad when you took him in."

Regret sharpened in Dargos' gut at the mention of Loric, who had been killed after assuming the heir's identity to protect Gonivein from torture. Dargos knew it still weighed heavily on her. Loric had been much more than a doulos to both of them. Speaking of the dead at weddings invited bad luck, but he couldn't bring himself to lie to Mandus, or even make an excuse to avoid explanation. What if Mandus asked Gonivein instead? *Gods forbid.* It would destroy her. "I'm afraid he's dead, Mandus. An honorable death protecting Gonivein." *But no honorable burial.* Dargos kept that thought to himself.

Mandus' eyes closed in a grimace of grief. He sighed. "I'll go inside. My old bones are getting stiff."

Mandus disappeared through the atrium, the other scholars and acolytes close behind. Dargos turned to follow, but found his way blocked by two men. Just behind them, Gadnor straightened with an amphora in his arms and paused, tossing Dargos a worried look.

The men's clothes were finely woven and dyed vibrant colors of reds and blues. Both had polished gold brooches pinning their cloaks over their shoulders. The leather of their sandals looked freshly oiled, and the bronze clasps of their belts had no scuffs or dents. Three-headed hydras were embroidered on their tunics. *One rank below the strategos.* These men would be contenders with Gadnor for the promotion, and Dargos had little doubt they carried far more influence in Golpathia than Kelric's awkward little brother.

Dargos swallowed, his plan becoming more and more complicated with every unfolding moment.

Their suspicious glares killed his hope that they had stopped to offer their heartfelt congratulations and best wishes for his sister.

"Seducing the scholars now, Dargos?" one said, his golden brows pinching with accusation. His tone was even more abrasive than Dargos expected. What exactly was he insinuating?

Dargos straightened his shoulders, unsure how to respond. Starting a fight at a wedding was also bad luck.

The second kyrios merely glared at Dargos, unspeaking, unmoving save for the breeze pushing a loose strand of dark hair over his broad shoulder.

The first continued. "It's obvious to every man here that the gods have cursed you. You have no army, no polis, no people. Talking up the scholars will not curry favor with the gods, and if your plan was to trade a sister for Golpathia's sons, then you have made a grievous error." He stepped nearer, and Dargos resisted the urge to lean away from his breath. To concede any ground was to award them a victory. Both men sneered and stalked up the steps.

The talkative one halted beside Gadnor and stared down at him with a withering look. "Still haven't learned your place, I see." He leaned close to Gadnor's face, and Gadnor stepped back. "What will it take, Gadnor?" He flicked a disgusted look at the doula, and without waiting for an answer, continued up the steps.

Gadnor stared after them, the muscles along his jaw twitching, cheeks flushed red. "That was Alypius. The quiet one was Ephastes."

Dargos knew their names and contributions to Golpathia. Alypius employed and owned the majority of fisherman, and Ephastes owned several sheep farms throughout the polis. It was likely that most, if not all, of the meat they were about to consume was here because of these men.

He suppressed his groan. Of all the obstacles in his way, these two might be the most difficult to overcome. Everything—the rebellion, Gadnor's journey to prominence, the future of Shallinath, the future of *Helinthia*—depended on Golpathia's cooperation.

Kelric would eventually concede to their plan. Of that, he had little doubt; Gonivein was his basileia now. But Kelric was only as powerful as the city he controlled, and the city needed—and wanted—to eat.

Tryphus poked his head through the atrium. "Are you two coming or not?" and he disappeared again.

Dargos sighed and started up, wondering what else would go wrong before Helios finished his journey.

The doula dipped her head to them, then captured Gadnor's gaze. "Thank you for helping me."

Gadnor nodded, his attention horizons away, and the doula hurried through the atrium.

Dargos raised an eyebrow as he considered Gadnor. It wasn't unusual to see the boy flustered, but he seemed more distracted than anything. *I've pushed him too far, too.* He laid a hand on Gadnor's shoulder. "Are you all right?"

Gadnor swallowed and nodded, straightening his shoulders.

Dargos frowned. Gadnor was a terrible liar. "What did Alypius mean by what he said to you?"

"Alypius was one of the men who…" Gadnor swallowed, then cleared his throat, as though the words refused to come out. "He helped my father a lot."

Dargos could guess what that really meant. Raleon's neglect, and sometimes intentional cruelty, toward Gadnor was well-known. Raleon had done it to cow Gadnor out of the spotlight and hide him from the Leirion. Still, Dargos couldn't help but feel the real threat had never been an assassin's blade, and irreparable damage had been done to the son Raleon had sworn to protect. If Alypius had a hand in Raleon's misdeeds, then it was no wonder why Gadnor was upset.

Rage burned into Dargos' knuckles. He wished he could plant them inside Alypius' skull. Instead, he squeezed Gadnor's shoulder encouragingly. "That man owes you his allegiance, and he will give it. Before this war is over, he *will* submit to your command."

Gadnor offered a timid smile, and Dargos smiled back. "Helinthia is on our side. No matter what obstacles we face, we will win. We must. This island cannot withstand this famine much longer." Zeal blossomed in Dargos' chest as he spoke. Gadnor just nodded, wordless. Dargos didn't want to leave until he was sure Gadnor was all right, but he also knew it wouldn't help to press him. Or would it? Dargos opened his mouth to say more, then caught Tryphus glowering at him through the atrium. *Guess that settles that.*

"Come in when you're ready. I'll keep Tryphus distracted," Dargos said, and started into the inner courtyard.

Alypius and Ephastes would be obstacles indeed, but Dargos relished the opportunity to put them in their place. Gadnor was lucky; Helinthia had said it, and despite the day's less than favorable course, Dargos was confident all would go according to plan.

CHAPTER 11

LITHANEVA

BRANITUS KISSED LITHANEVA GOODBYE WITH an enthusiasm that conflicted with the anxiety in his eyes. Charixes didn't seem to notice, thank Hermes. They would be touring the barracks and *palaistra* all day. Poor Branitus.

She stood in the doorway of the *gynaikon*—a location chosen for appearance rather than intention—and watched them leave. The tightness in her shoulders eased, but she couldn't relax completely. Charixes' two guards were practicing their swordplay in the front courtyard. There to keep an eye on her, no doubt.

How could she get a message to Gadnor without drawing suspicion? She'd tossed and turned for hours last night and had come up with nothing. She'd considered sneaking out after dark to meet one of her spies in the city, but her father would have people watching for something like that, waiting to catch her in the act of treachery. She couldn't risk putting herself or her women in danger, not while Charixes was in Thellshun.

Her other option was seeking out Aden, but that would certainly raise eyebrows if they were discovered, for she had no legitimate reason to speak with him—that was Branitus' responsibility. That would spawn an infinite number of rumors, not to mention the headache Branitus would suffer from all levels of his government. She genuinely desired to spare him that.

She tapped the bridge of her nose. *What of the hawk?*

Was it still in the gardens? It had been trained to fly to her. Perhaps it was trained to take a message back.

She strolled out of the guards' view and to the gardens behind the villa. She shielded the sun with her hand and raised her eyes to the branches. *Be here, hawk.* She circled the garden once, then twice. Her heart was beginning to sink, her mind scrambling with other ideas to get her message delivered swiftly when she finally spotted something brown at the top of a tall oak. On one of the branches stretching across the pantheon, the majestic bird peered down at her, looking bored.

Lithaneva grinned, then turned and hurried to her room, trying to maintain an inconspicuous air. She locked the door securely behind her and sprinted to her vanity. She tore a strip of parchment from the journal she'd been gifted at her wedding, dipped her quill in the inkwell, and hovered over the parchment.

Gadnor's message had been simple enough that if intercepted, its meaning couldn't be divined. She should follow that example. Trained hawk or not, it was a beast with a mind of its own, and there were no guarantees the message wouldn't fall off mid-flight and land in the hands of a loyalist. The ships were being built in Hameth. They would attack with the land forces on the spring equinox. How could she convey that?

She examined the tiny paper. Perhaps something poetic would suffice, cryptic enough that if discovered it would be mistaken for an ode or fable, but detailed enough that someone looking for clues would find them.

She brushed the feathery end of the quill back and forth across her chin. Poetry was not her strong suit.

From Hameth's shores, where the Earthshaker dwells
The horns of war will blow.
The lands will quake, the seas will swell

When the tears of Demeter cease to flow.

She stared at her handiwork, debating about crumpling it up and starting over. It was almost too subtle, yet she felt as though any fool would be able to figure it out and somehow link it back to her.

"It'll have to do," she muttered, then hesitated, curiosity itching at her fingertips. She'd forgotten to ask if the heir was safe and well. She had to know that all this trouble wasn't for nothing. Blind faith wouldn't keep her anxiety at bay.

She turned the paper sideways, envisioning how much space the words would require. She sighed and lowered the paper. She would just have to trust that Gadnor or Dargos would disclose that information on their own. Until they did, she would continue on.

Pulling the leather thong from the end of her braid, she wrapped it around the scroll first, then wound the ends and knotted them in the middle. There. Now, if she could fasten it to the beast's leg, there would be no chance it would fall off during its journey.

A shudder rippled through her as she recalled the bird's steely gaze, its sharp beak. Would it let her tie it that securely? She gathered her courage with a deep breath and marched down to the kitchens to tell the douloi to begin preparing the evening meal. It wouldn't do to be seen by *anyone*. That just left two more pesky pairs of eyes.

She approached the atrium, tiptoed through, and peered around the corner. The guards were sitting on the raised edge of the fountain that jutted out from the inner wall, sharpening and polishing their swords. Without the *clang* of their practicing to denote their location, it was possible they could sneak up on her if she took her eyes off them long enough.

"What are you up to, Princess?"

Lithaneva spun, heart launching into her throat. "Larxes!" She swatted him not too lightly.

"Ow," he grumbled, stepping back. "What are you doing?"

"Looking for you," she blurted.

His brows rose. "Why?"

She hooked his elbow and dragged him out of the voice-amplifying tunnel. "I need you to get your lyre and play for those bastards out there."

Larxes eyed the wide opening dubiously. "Why?"

She folded her arms across her chest. "Because I don't want them snooping around."

Larxes swept his long black hair over his shoulder. "Why's that? Got something to hide?"

Lithaneva smiled, her confidence returning. "As a matter of fact, yes." Honesty was never what anyone expected from a spy.

Larxes blinked, curiosity swirling in the green depths of his eyes. "Like what?"

"None of your concern."

"The anax is suspicious of you, you know—your own father." Larxes folded his arms across his chest. "Perhaps it *should* be my concern."

Frustration swelled in her chest. She would have to give him something. "I need to perform… a ritual… in the garden. It requires me to be naked, and I don't want to be seen."

Larxes looked skeptical, but she could tell she was on the cusp of winning him over.

"You have to do it now?"

"Yes, *now*." She thought fast. "Women who don't conceive must perform this ritual every month, otherwise my womb will fall out and I'll bleed… to death." There. If he bothered to investigate, another woman would corroborate her story—at least enough of it to pacify his curiosity. "And if the guards see me," she added, trying desperately to keep the smirk out of her voice, "they'll know *I* haven't been sleeping with Branitus."

Larxes' expression took on a more somber tone. "Fine. How long do I have to play for them?"

"Until I come get you. And if you see *anyone* coming into the villa, you are to stop playing at once to alert me." She stepped closer and twirled one of his dark curls around her finger. "Do this for me, and I'll tell Branitus to get you something nice." She released the curl and it sprang back to his handsome head.

Larxes' face immediately brightened. "A new lyre?"

"Done."

"All right." He grasped her hand and shook it.

Larxes retrieved his lyre, and she retreated to the garden, clutching her precious cargo in her curled fingers.

She waited until she heard the strum of his instrument and the distant sound of his voice rising in song, then smiled up at the tall oak.

The hawk stared down at her. She raised the tiny scroll. "Here. You will return this for me?"

The hawk tilted its head, but stayed put.

She tapped her arm as she'd seen the falconers do.

Nothing.

She whistled and slapped her arm harder until her skin stung and turned red. "Come on, hawk," she cooed, feeling her frustration begin to bubble. "Ferry it," she swore, rubbing her sore arm.

The hawk shifted on the branch, spreading its wings. Her breath hitched. It was going to fly down to her!

But the pompous bird merely flexed its long-taloned toes and settled back on the branch, folding its regal feathers against its belly. She slumped. It was just getting more comfortable.

"You don't have to be afraid of me." She set the scroll down on the ground. "But just in case you are." She stepped back to give it space. "There, see?"

The hawk just stared, then let out a warbling screech that sounded suspiciously like laughter. The beast was lucky she couldn't reach it, or she would snap its neck like she'd seen the douloi do to chickens. She retrieved the scroll and sank onto the edge of a retaining wall, despair threatening to overcome her frustration and determination. Her braid flopped over her shoulder, unraveling in the breeze like all of her hopes.

This was a stupid idea. It was just a hawk. It had performed its duty, and now it was free to do whatever it wanted. It wasn't waiting for her.

Unless...

Its golden eye tilted down at her. *Maybe it's testing me.* It wanted something from her. But what? An idea struck. "You're hungry." She leapt up and dashed into the kitchens where she knew the cook would be carving the meat for the evening meal. She could almost taste victory.

CHAPTER 12

GADNOR

STILL HAVEN'T LEARNED YOUR PLACE... what will it take?'

Alypius' words had Gadnor's feet rooted to the portico steps.

His nursemaid's tear-streaked face as Alypius dragged her away to her new kyrios—some wealthy merchant in Ninenarn, he was told—swam before his eyes, stinging them. He clenched his empty hands. It had happened so long ago, but the loss was still as raw as though it was only yesterday.

I will not be so powerless again.

Alypius, along with most of the prominent men of Golpathia, saw him as timid and weak, a child to be ruled. That wasn't a reputation he could easily change.

But he would. He had to.

"You okay?"

Tor stared up at him from the bottom of the steps. His brown hair tousled in the breeze, and Xios wove in and out between his ankles.

"I don't know."

Tor climbed the steps to stand next to him, leaving Xios glowering up at them. "Kelric still hasn't agreed to Dargos' plan?"

Gadnor's throat was suddenly dry. "No. Did the hawk arrive?"

Tor shook his head, and Gadnor's heart sank. There went his last hope of convincing Kelric to make him strategos today. What if his brother was right and the bird was dead? And the message, discarded by a confused and hungry hunter, left to float away on the wind? Lithaneva would have no idea they had fulfilled their end of the bargain they'd struck. That they'd found the heir.

Gadnor rubbed the long scars on his arm. He couldn't think like that. He couldn't lose hope. The hawk would come, and when it did, it would carry all the convincing Kelric needed to finally give him a chance. It just wouldn't be today.

Tor peered into the atrium at the crowd inside, scanning the unfamiliar faces. His gaze lingered on the scholars, a muscle in his jaw twitching. The oracle confirmation ceremonies would happen soon, and all eyes of the city would be on him. Gadnor smiled a little at their shared aversion to being the center of attention. *Why did the Fates choose us?*

'We are just playthings for the gods.'

He didn't want to believe that, but the more he pondered how mismatched he was for his destiny, the less confident he became that mortal suffering had a purpose beyond divine entertainment.

"Do you think your brother would be offended if we skipped dinner?" A joking grin lifted the corners of Tor's mouth, but Gadnor saw a spark of seriousness in his green eyes.

"Unlikely he would even notice." Gadnor smiled back, and for a moment, he allowed himself to imagine what he and Tor might do instead. Gadnor could show off his favorite places in the city: the mound of hay behind the barracks' stables that he used to jump into from the roof, or the stall in the agora that sold sweet treats made of almonds and dates and honey—had Tor ever tasted sweets? Or the baker's stall near the douloi district with the softest, freshest loaves. Gadnor closed his eyes, remembering the way the dough seemed to melt on his tongue.

"We could go there," Tor whispered.

Gadnor's eyes shot open, heat creeping up his neck.

Tor chuckled and smoothed a forelock out of his eyes. "Wherever you were just now."

Gadnor swallowed, wishing they could. "We will."

Tor nodded in understanding, and they entered the villa shoulder to shoulder. Xios bounded up the steps after them, growling in annoyance at being left behind.

The gossip was in full swing as everyone waited for Kelric and Gonivein to reappear. The priest, Brother Gryphus, and Dargos stood in front of the triklinion entrance, smiling and conversing with the scholars from the Library. An acolyte was beside them, looking bored with the amphora of wine at his feet. The guests were scattered around the altar, which still smoldered from this morning's blessing.

Gadnor had been to enough weddings to know that women were a dominant presence. Men preferred to grumble or discuss politics, but women always brought the conversation back to lighter topics. There was a heaviness with their absence, and he wondered why they weren't here. Warning prickled across his shoulders as he noticed several furtive glances.

"Brother Gryphus." Kelric's voice carried above the chatter, drawing everyone's attention to the approaching newlyweds. Gonivein held tightly to Kelric's arm. Her eyes were still distant, but the color had returned to her cheeks. Kelric stopped beside Gadnor and grinned as he scanned the surrounding faces. "I've kept us from feasting long enough. I know that's why you're all *really* here."

Scattered chuckles rippled around the courtyard, but Kelric's humor faltered. His eyes narrowed, and Gadnor knew he was noticing the absence of wives and marriageable daughters, too. Their gazes met briefly, and dread rushed down Gadnor's spine at the coldness in his brother's stare. He knew that look. Kelric meant to punish him for something.

What did I do?

The wounds on his arm itched suddenly, and Gadnor scratched at them as Kelric raised his hand above the crowd.

"Brother Gryphus, the libation please. I'm starving."

The priest nodded and raised his palms to the sky. The guests crowded around him, giving him their full attention to hurry along the ritual. The acolyte handed over the amphora and Gryphus poured it out before the threshold to the triklinion. "We invite the gods to partake of this celebration. Hestia, bless this hearth with your eternal flame." He turned to Kelric and Gonivein. "Basileus Kelric and Basileia Gonivein have honored Zeus with their hospitality and graciousness. May Hera bless your marriage with many children and much happiness."

Gonivein's cheeks reddened, Kelric's paled, and Dargos began to clap, inciting everyone else to join in.

Kelric and Gonivein went inside first, followed by the priest, the scholars, and the kyrioi, who seemed to have a rank and file of their own understanding.

Gadnor and Tor stepped into the room last, drawing several stares that lingered on Xios. Long tables had been set up for the occasion and were covered in food. Goose, fish, vegetables, dried fruit, bread, cheese, and wine. It was more of a feast than Golpathia had seen all year thanks to the famine, and Gadnor's mouth watered at the sight. Couches that normally rested along the walls had been placed around the tables for the large crowd. Though only half of them were filled. Two lyre players sat in the corner. One, an elderly man Gadnor recognized from the city, strummed his gnarled fingers skillfully across the strings, playing a sweet, lively melody. The second, a younger man—his apprentice, Gadnor assumed—played chords beside him.

Euanthe and the new doula swarmed into the room, replacing empty trays, refilling cups, and keeping the fire blazing in the hearth.

The lead scholar, Mandus, seemed distracted. His gaze flicked around the room as he and his companions conversed with Dargos and Brother Gryphus about their journey. Mandus whispered something to Dargos, then both of them began searching. The seat beside Dargos was empty. *Where's Forluna?*

The doula appeared in front of Gadnor and Tor, a shy smile on her face as she handed them two plates of food.

"Thank you," Gadnor said.

She opened her mouth to say something, then clamped it shut as Euanthe cleared her throat sharply in their direction. The girl sprinted off, grabbing an amphora of wine from the corner of the room and hurrying to fill more empty cups.

Gadnor and Tor found an empty bench along the wall and sat. Tor side-eyed him before taking a bite out of his goose leg. "She's still watching you."

Gadnor refused to look up from his plate for fear everyone would see the inferno in his face. Tor laughed and tossed the rest of his meat to Xios, who tore every scrap of flesh from the bone and gobbled it down in less time than it took Gadnor to eat two bites of bread.

Xios licked his whiskers and stared intently up at Tor, but all that remained on his plate were roasted beets and onions.

Gadnor offered his wing to Xios, but the little cub hissed and spit before scampering into the shadows. He set his wing back down. "He really hates me, huh?"

Tor offered an apologetic look. "Yeah."

Gadnor handed Tor the wing. "He'll eat it if you give it to him, won't he?"

"Yeah." Tor stuffed it into his pocket.

"Girl, come here. Yes, you," Kelric called, motioning at the doula with a small bone before tossing it onto his plate. The *symposium* fell quiet as she hurried over, bowing her head and shifting the amphora to her hip.

"More wine, Basileus?"

Kelric looked her up and down, ignoring the staring guests. Gadnor saw the rage pulsing through the veins in his neck, despite the evenness of his tone. "You're not one of mine. Who are you?"

Her face went red. "Klymene, Basileus. I was brought as a wedding gift for Basileia Gonivein."

Gonivein's head jerked up. "For me? No, I don—" She clamped her lips tight as Kelric covered her hand and squeezed it. She dropped her eyes again, briefly flicking them up once more to glance at Gadnor.

A bitter taste filled Gadnor's mouth, and his appetite vanished.

Kelric scanned the room, amusement twisting his lips. "Who brought you?"

"Kyrios Krastus." Klymene nodded to where the chief magistrate was sitting close to the scholars. He seemed keen on their conversation and raised his cup at Kelric's notice.

"Well, Krastus." Kelric stood and leaned his weight on the table.

Gadnor's stomach churned, the bitterness beginning to scald his throat at the expression on Kelric's face. The same one he'd worn every time he'd bullied Gadnor. Kelric was about to do something regrettable, and Gadnor had an ominous feeling it was going to fall on top of him the same way it always did.

"Thank you for being the only man here to bring female companionship to my wife on her wedding day."

The symposium went still. Even the lyre players ceased their strumming, pressing their palms to the strings to silence the lingering hum.

"Basileus," Alypius said, a devious curl in his lip. "It is our wives and daughters who were slighted, as we understood they were not invited."

Gadnor's brows rose. *That can't be right.*

Kelric's jaw clenched in rage. Gadnor expected him to berate Alypius for such a silly allegation. Instead, Kelric glared at Archon Tryphus.

"Send word to every house that they are to come immediately."

"Forgive us, Basileus, but our women need more than a moment's notice. They must bathe, oil, dress, do something elaborate and ridiculous with their hair." Alypius waved his hand dramatically, inciting a few chuckles from his companions. He laughed with them. "It appears that not even your brother-in-law's woman was invited."

Kelric's eyes darted to Forluna's empty seat, then upward to Dargos in a threatening glare. Dargos' expression remained stoic. Mandus raised an eyebrow beside him.

"No matter, Basileus," Alypius went on, taking a large bite of carrot, chewing as he spoke. "They were assured you meant no offense. After all, everyone is aware that mistakes happen when plans are *rushed*."

Kelric's piercing gaze scanned the faces of his guests, a muscle racing along his jaw. Several men nodded to Alypius. Others observed warily, waiting to see how this drama would unfold.

They're protesting, Gadnor realized. All of them were, some more willingly than others, but all complicit regardless. Alypius' pointed glare, first at Dargos, then Gonivein, conveyed exactly what they were protesting.

But Kelric didn't seem surprised. Was Kelric losing control over his polis?

Why didn't he tell us? Anxiety tingled in Gadnor's limbs, making his scars itch.

"Thank you, Alypius, for making a difficult decision much easier." Kelric downed the last bit of his wine. "Everyone here seems to have forgotten that I need a strategos." He turned his menacing gray eyes on Gadnor.

The blood drained from Gadnor's face. *Oh no.* Kelric was going to deflect all this unwanted attention onto him. He should have seen this coming. He felt light-headed.

Kelric slammed his cup down on the table. Gonivein jumped, pain twisting her face into a grimace. "I had planned to call a Council to decide who among you is best suited to the task. But it's clear that none of you are worth considering."

Gadnor rested his head back against the wall. A glowing endorsement from Kelric probably wouldn't have changed many opinions, but turning him into an insult—a punishment—to his councilmen? How would he ever dig himself out of this? He raised his wine to his lips with a shaking hand and gulped down the bittersweet fluid.

"I trained with all of you, studied with you at the Library. *I* was your strategos. And now…" He held up a finger, pausing as though collecting himself, and then planted it onto the tabletop. "*Gadnor* is."

The weight of every eye fell on Gadnor as though a giant cyclops had just found him for dinner.

It may as well have, for every gaze looked murderous.

Gadnor shut his eyes.

"Basileia Gonivein and I will retire now." Kelric's tone was irritatingly cheerful. "Tryphus!" The archon stood, looking pale and stunned. "See that our guests are escorted safely home."

Kelric helped a bewildered Gonivein to her feet and scooped her into his arms, then strode from the room without a backward glance.

Brother Mandus chuckled as he nibbled a piece of cheese. "Well, well, Alypius, was that what you expected?"

The muttering and grumbling resumed, slowly rising to a querulous timbre.

Alypius stood abruptly, his couch scraping against the tiles and jostling Ephastes sitting at the other end of it. "A duel of swords, Gadnor, and let every man here judge for themselves if there is glory to be had beneath your banner."

Alypius' challenge fell heavily on Gadnor's shoulders, threatening to crush him.

This is my chance. I can salvage this.

Was this how Atlas felt holding up the world?

Gadnor gulped.

CHAPTER 13

DARGOS

DARGOS CINCHED THE BUCKLE OF the breastplate tight over Gadnor's shoulder, hands and fingers quivering with excitement.

Gadnor's eyes stared dead ahead, his jaw clamped, skin pale. The boy was trying to keep his composure, but it was obvious he was nervous.

Kelric had finally committed to their plan, but Dargos had expected him to stay present to keep order among his men, not unleash chaos and disappear. Dargos shook his head. He should have anticipated some dramatic, brash gesture that would leave them vulnerable.

The wedding guests edged the dueling circle in the front courtyard. No one, save Pallas and Tor, appeared friendly.

"Remember to breathe," Dargos reminded the younger man, satisfied when Gadnor's stiff chest suddenly swelled with an audible breath. Dargos began fastening the second shoulder strap, sneaking a glance at the other end of the field where Ephastes was helping Alypius don his armor.

"He's bigger than you," Dargos said, and Gadnor swallowed, the apprehension in his dark eyes unmistakable. "But he's cocky. Use that to your advantage. He's not expecting you to put up a fight."

Gadnor licked his dry lips and nodded, fixating on his opponent as though his life depended on it. Perhaps it did.

A thrill rushed through Dargos. *I will help Gadnor win this.* He pulled the leather straps tight under Gadnor's arms as he continued. "Knowing that, he'll probably try to toy with you at first, bait you into overextending and making mistakes, try to get you riled up and tired. Don't fall for it."

He knelt to double-check the buckles on Gadnor's greaves. "Only strike if you see an opening, but steer clear otherwise." He stood again and clapped his shoulder. "You can do this. He's just like any other enemy standing between you and the throne of Helinthia."

Gadnor mumbled something like, "Let's show him what I'm made of." Though, it might have also been, "That's what I'm afraid of." Dargos couldn't be too sure, and didn't have time to ask before Tor stepped forward, hefting the helmet in his spindly arms with a grunt.

Gadnor settled the helmet over his head, then grasped the sword Pallas offered. Tor held the shield as Gadnor slid his arm into the straps. With a deep intake of breath, he nodded to Dargos and stepped into the circle.

Alypius swiped his sword in an elegant arc and sneered as he entered from the other side.

"Three cuts is the victor," Ephastes announced from the sidelines. "Blood drawn signals the end of a round. The next round begins when both of you are ready, but don't dally or you forfeit." He glared at Gadnor as the last words left his lips.

Gadnor and Alypius nodded their understanding and assumed a fighting stance.

"Begin."

Around the circle, bystanders began to cheer and goad the contestants. Shouting, clapping, chanting, mostly in favor of Alypius, though a few men opted to stay quiet.

Alypius sauntered forward, his advantage over Gadnor in height and muscular girth glaringly obvious with a sword and shield in his hands. Though only a contest, the thought that Gadnor might be in real danger simmered in Dargos' mind, but he pushed it away. *It's three cuts, not to the death.*

He'd witnessed plenty of friendly games that had ended in less than everlasting glory, however. A lost eye or a twisted hand, an uneven gait that impeded the ability to run or climb stairs. Each mangled outcome flashed before him as Alypius' sword came crashing down on Gadnor's shield.

Gadnor kept his balance. Thrust his sword upwards. Alypius deflected the attack with his own shield. Gadnor's blade scraped across the smooth bronze surface. Momentum carried him forward as Alypius twisted around his back and sliced Gadnor's right shoulder with the edge of his weapon.

Blood splattered on the gravel and the crowd erupted in cheers.

Alypius sneered, raising his arms in triumph, eliciting even wilder applause from the spectators. It was more than obvious who the favorite was.

Gadnor can do this. He fought a lion with his bare hands. He could fight a man and win, too. Couldn't he?

If he couldn't, their plans to defeat Charixes—*No!* Dargos shoved the intrusive thoughts down. Helinthia had said Gadnor was lucky, hadn't she? Gadnor would win. *He must!* Dargos caught a worried look from Pallas, and decided it was best not to take his eyes off Gadnor again.

"What's the matter, Gadnor?" Alypius taunted as round two began. Rivulets of blood streamed down Gadnor's sword arm, but he held steady. "You had more fight in you when you were a petulant child."

"Keep your head, Gadnor!" Dargos shouted.

Alypius charged. Gadnor slid his foot back. Braced. Their shields connected. Gadnor stumbled back. Spun away from Alypius' next thrust. Hope surged into Dargos as Gadnor readied himself for the next attack.

Alypius charged again, ramming Gadnor's shield. He leapt, throwing all his weight into it. Then again. Gadnor's knee buckled and hit the dirt. Alypius swept his shield against Gadnor's as though he were brushing an errant twig aside. Gadnor's body twisted as the dented disk was ripped from his arm. Alypius slashed Gadnor's exposed back plate, the tip of his blade searing through the left shoulder.

Alypius pranced around the circle to the rhythm of the cheers, leaving Gadnor panting and bleeding in the dust. Dargos' heart dropped. One more cut would lend Alypius the victory, and Gadnor hadn't inflicted a single one of his own.

"Get up, Gadnor!" Dargos cried, but his voice was lost in the din.

Gadnor finally stood, chest heaving, but his eyes were determined under his helmet.

"I can see why your father never mentioned you," Alypius taunted. "Any father would be ashamed of this sorry display." He waited, as though expecting Gadnor to tear at him, but the boy just stared. Alypius' smirk dissolved. He lunged, swinging at Gadnor's bare shield arm.

Gadnor ducked. Curled under Alypius' thrust. He rolled onto his feet behind Alypius and sliced his calf.

Alypius yelped, stumbling forward. Gasps and shocked whispers rippled through the spectators.

"Yes!" Dargos cried, nearly leaping into the air. Pallas clapped his mighty hands loudly, and scattered applause joined in. Perhaps not all the kyrioi favored Alypius, after all. Gadnor rested his hands on his knees, winded.

Pride swelled in Dargos' chest. Gadnor had used Alypius' own strengths against him, as any champion would.

Alypius glowered at them, and before Gadnor had resumed a fighting stance for the next round, Alypius leapt, smashing the hilt of his sword down into Gadnor's helmet with a vengeful yell.

Dargos' breath hitched as Gadnor collapsed onto the dirt, barely rolling away before Alypius' sword came down on his face. Shock at such an egregious maneuver froze Dargos as Gadnor scrambled onto his hands and knees, shaking his head in disorientation.

Alypius plowed his greaved shin into Gadnor's abdomen, sending him tumbling across the ground. Gadnor lost his grasp on his sword. His helmet flew off and disappeared between the sandaled feet of the spectators, who were leaping wildly and roaring like a bloodthirsty horde.

Up, up, get up! But Dargos couldn't make his tongue work.

A blur of brown burst through the circle and planted itself before Alypius.

Dargos' heart lurched. *Forluna!*

"Stop this!" she screamed, raising her arms.

Alypius grabbed her wrist and jerked her toward him. "Another nursemaid?" He sneered down at her as she fought to pull her hand back.

"Stop," Gadnor rasped, coughing and crawling to his feet. His hands slid across the gravel for his sword, desperation widening his swelling eyes.

Dargos leapt into the center of the circle, plunging his fist into Alypius' gut. Alypius doubled over, releasing Forluna. She stumbled back, and Dargos steadied her with bloodied knuckles.

He was hardly able to blink before Alypius barreled into him, burying a shoulder into his abdomen. Dargos' breath ripped from his lungs. Feet slid out from under him just before the ground slammed into his back, narrowly missing crushing Forluna and Gadnor.

Dargos wrapped his arms around Alypius' head and his legs around his body. Rage coursed through his sinews as he squeezed, leaving his assailant immobile. He wanted this bastard to stop breathing.

The wedding guests shouted obscenities and curses as they cheered and goaded. Alypius raged incoherently against Dargos' chest, pushing up, writhing, throwing his knuckles into Dargos' ribs. Every blow felt like it might have cracked bone, but Dargos held on.

Alypius would taste no victory today. Dargos would make sure of it.

The ringing of swords unsheathing echoed off the courtyard walls. A dozen onlookers pointed their weapons at Dargos' throat. Pallas shouldered through to his side and glowered at the crowd, eliciting several nervous stares and returning more than a few swords to their scabbards.

"Is this how you repay the friendship of Golpathia, Dargos? With an attack on one of our own?" Ephastes barged forward, smirking. "Your treachery has no limits."

"Enough!" An angry voice broke in above the charged crowd. "I said *enough*!"

Dargos raised his eyes to Archon Tryphus, who was shoving through to the spectacle.

Alypius relented on top of him. Dargos waited a moment longer before shoving him away.

Alypius landed in the dirt and scrambled to his feet, panting, scowling, spitting.

Pallas hauled Dargos up and patted the dust off his cloak.

Alypius stalked before them, gnashing his teeth, looking as though he might strike again, but Tryphus stepped between them, hands raised.

"Enough!"

Gadnor shielded Forluna, who was examining the cuts on his shoulders and his eye, which was already swollen shut. Blood dripped from his nose and slid down his back and arms.

"Archon," Ephastes growled, "Dargos viciously attacked Alypius. Arrest him."

"No," Gadnor said, wincing in pain. "Dargos acted in Forluna's defense."

Ephastes raised his hand and snapped his fingers. The wedding guests stepped closer, tightening the circle. "What could your swollen eyes have seen, Gadnor?" he muttered. "I witnessed Alypius acting to remove Forluna from the harm of your sparring, and Dargos unjustly attacked him for it. Isn't that what we all saw?"

Several heads began to nod, others exchanged furtive glances, as if they were beginning to question what they had seen. Or were too afraid to say it.

The archon hesitated, eying the armed men and Dargos warily. He knew the truth, but Dargos wasn't sure if he would take the risk to defend it.

A hawk screamed, flapping its wings as it landed on the porch roof.

Another hawk landed beside it, screeching in rage, and then another. A raven cawed from the inner wall, joined a moment later by a dozen flapping wings of more shimmering black fowl. Scolding cackles rang viciously. Menacing shadows glided over the group, and Dargos' head shot skyward, staring in awe as six vultures hissed from the air, circling.

More birds—gulls, sparrows, and wrens—landed everywhere a perch could be found. A thunderous cacophony of chirping and cackling from branches and ramparts.

The kyrioi huddled, murmuring, their swords redirected toward the birds as though at any moment a swarm of feathers and talons would descend upon them. Dargos' jaw dropped, terror worming through him as he instinctively wrapped his arms around Forluna. What omen was this?

Then…

The birds fell silent, staring with beady eyes at the gathering in the courtyard.

No one spoke for fear it would startle the birds into an offensive dive toward them.

At length, Mandus stepped slowly down the porch steps and waded through the crowd. "This duel has greatly upset the gods," he announced. His words, though spoken in a normal tone, were amplified in the fearful silence. His lip quivered as he turned in a slow circle, examining both men and fowl surrounding him. "You must stop this aggression at once. Return to your homes."

Ephastes motioned for the men to comply and sheathe their weapons. Most of them already had and were slowly backing away toward the gate.

"Archon," Mandus continued, "I witnessed Dargos act in good faith to protect Forluna." He met Dargos' gaze knowingly. "What man here would not do the same if another took hold of his woman? Let the word of a scholar settle this matter. Unless you wish to interrupt the basileus and his bride to have them issue judgment."

Tryphus tore his wide eyes from the glowering birds to study Mandus, seeming to have only just understood what the old man had said. The archon scanned the crowd, waiting for an objection, but all were silent. He nodded. "The matter is settled. There is no offense, either by Alypius or Dargos. The duel is forfeit."

Alypius considered each of them with such malice that a shiver rolled down Dargos' back. The man said nothing as he slowly backed away with the rest of the crowd, but Dargos knew full well that he had no intention of honoring this settlement. Somehow, he would get his revenge.

The courtyard finally emptied, and the birds took flight in a blur of feathers and din of chirps and screams.

Mandus gave Dargos a subtle nod, then considered Gadnor, who was being led into the villa with his arms stretched across Pallas and Tor's shoulders.

Forluna tossed a glance over her shoulder as she followed close behind them. The flash in her dark eyes made his heart grow still. She was angry. Very angry. And he had a sinking feeling it wasn't all directed at Alypius.

"I may have been mistaken, Dargos."

Dargos tilted his head in confusion, and Mandus gave him a crooked smile.

"Perhaps Helinthia has a *new* favorite hero."

CHAPTER 14

GONIVEIN

THE DRAFT AS KELRIC CLOSED the door to their bedroom hit Gonivein like a wave of cold water. She shivered in his arms and pressed closer to his chest for warmth. Her mind was still reeling from everything that had transpired in the triklinion.

The kyrioi weren't happy she was their basileia, that much was clear. Except for Krastus, perhaps. Guilt and turmoil writhed within her. She didn't want to accept his doula as a wedding gift. She didn't want another human beholden to her, but Kelric had made it clear he didn't—and wouldn't—respect her wishes on the matter.

Kelric.

He set her down on her feet beside the bed and went to light a fire in the hearth. How could he throw Gadnor to the wolves like that? Though she hadn't condoned Kelric's behavior, her leaving with him made her complicit in it. She wished she'd said something, but she'd been too stunned, and now it was too late. At least Dargos and Pallas were there. Time for her brother to put action behind his promises to guide Gadnor. And Pallas' mere presence was intimidating. She hoped they would all be in one piece when she saw them again.

Kelric finished with the fire and stood. She quickly averted her gaze to her hands.

She had her own battles to fight now.

The east window facing the sea was cracked open. The gulls chittered above the crashing waves as loudly as though she were right back on that beach, drenched in the ice of an angry sea, sinking into thick sand and clinging to Loric's lifeless body, pleading for him to wake. She'd been helpless before the might of the gods. Her hip ached at the memory.

Loric.

Tears blurred her eyes, smudging out all details of the room around her. In their place she saw him, wandering the shores of the Styx. He turned to her, dark curls brushing over broad shoulders, brown eyes looking right at her. Waiting. *He's waiting for me.*

Kelric's touch on her shoulder made her blink, pushing her tears over the edge. The vision dissolved, and her husband stood before her, powerful, alive.

She recoiled from him, torn, suspended somewhere between life and death, as though she was a wraith herself—her body trapped in the world of the living, while her soul drifted somewhere below in the caverns of despair and darkness.

"Gonivein?" Kelric whispered, dropping his hands, his gray eyes gloomy with hurt. She couldn't bring herself to reassure him. Not when so much resentment boiled beneath her skin.

She glanced at the door, wondering what would happen if she threw it open and ran. Would the revelers outside stop her? How far would she get before she collapsed from pain and exhaustion? Or before she gave up like the coward she was?

The gulls called again, and Loric watched her, drifting among the unsettled spirits. His body was out there, a feast for the fish and vile creatures of the sea. *Because Kelric left him there.*

Other memories of the inlet surfaced then: Kelric's rough hands around her arms, shaking her, fighting her, refusing to believe her warning. Her heart lurched into her throat, cutting off her breath.

Kelric lowered his gaze, as though the trauma of that night were written on her face.

"Gonivein. I'm…" He backed away and sat on the couch under the window, then ran a hand through his hair and looked up at her.

She was struck at how vulnerable he seemed—words failing, his sharp, piercing gray eyes strangely soft, glistening. Something stirred within her. A familiar feeling of longing, of wanting to set him at ease. She waited, too full of emotions to trust her voice.

"I'm sorry for what happened in the inlet. I…" A flicker of something flashed in his expression. Something like…

Shame.

Gonivein swallowed against the lump in her throat, bewildered. Kelric wasn't ashamed of anything. Was he?

"I should have listened to you. To what you were telling me about my father. I'm not sure how different things would be if I'd listened; he would have had to answer for what he did to you. But I'm… I'm profoundly sorry for how I treated you." Kelric's handsome features twisted into a look of devastation that clenched her heart.

What is happening?

"And… I'm sorry about Loric. He protected you and…" Kelric raked another hand through his hair and stared at the ground. "I wronged him severely. And you, too."

She stared, her mouth open, processing his words, his intention. Did he really mean it? She hadn't expected an apology, hadn't wanted one. It was easier to hate him without it. But now?

His validation of her pain cracked something within her.

Her tears came in a rush, sobs scurrying in her chest. Sorrow, anger.

Resignation.

She covered her face with her hands, shaking. Kelric padded across the room to her and circled her with warm arms. Her knees were weak, and he scooped her against his chest and sat on the bed, holding her, not speaking.

She melted into him and cried until her hands and face tingled and her head pounded savagely behind her eyes.

Kelric remained quiet. The steady beating of his heart in her ears created a soothing rhythm that finally calmed her. She pressed her hand against his chest and pushed herself up, his warmth under her palm inviting, familiar. She had lived for his closeness once. There was comfort in knowing she still had that, in spite of everything.

She stared into his eyes and saw a troubled, anguished soul that mirrored her own. They were both responsible for a death through carelessness and stubborn pride. How could she hold this against him when her own hands were stained in blood?

We're not so different.

Could they build on this shared grief?

The sun was low now, purple streaks stretching over the sea. Shadows fell across Kelric's shaven face, but she could still make out his handsome features. The tiny curls falling over his dusky eyes as he struggled for words.

"Alypius had one thing right. This wedding was rushed. If I could have postponed it, I would have. You must believe me." Kelric rubbed a tendril of her hair between his fingers, examining the fine strands in the fading sunlight as if they were threads of gold. "I know this isn't what you want anymore."

A hard lump lodged in her throat.

"*Me*, I mean. After everything that's happened. I failed you. Betrayed you. Hurt you. But I never meant to."

Guilt stirred in her gut at the pain in his eyes, her silence more validating of his sentiments than any words she could say.

He averted his gaze to the floor and continued. "Forcing you to marry me isn't what I would have chosen, but it was the only way to keep you safe. I hoped you would know that, but… I'm not so sure anymore."

She leaned further away from him. "What do you mean?"

He glared at the door, as though he could see through it and find the object of his ire on the other side. "There have been demands that I surrender you and Dargos to Charixes—the citizens are afraid of his retaliation. I've refused to entertain any of it. Our guests' behavior tonight was meant to challenge my authority, perhaps scare me into submission, but I won't let it. The councilmen do not rule Golpathia, *I* do."

He had defied his councilmen to protect her? Defied the anax? Would Charixes send an army to attack them now? Or assassins? *Real* assassins? An unwelcome and familiar warning surfaced.

'Run. Don't stop or you'll be consumed.'

Sweat gathered under her palms, making her hand slick against Kelric's skin. "Do you think Charixes will attack us?"

The alarm in her voice pulled his gaze back to her. "No sooner than he already planned to." He tried to smile, but failed. "I showed them tonight that I will not be controlled, and I will keep showing them until they succumb to *my* demands. Whatever happens, I will keep you safe. I promise, Gonivein. I will never let anything hurt you again."

Her heart softened at the sincerity in his words, and she found herself drawing closer to him. Could she learn to trust him again? Memories of his lips on hers bubbled through the chaos of her emotions. The pleasure of his warm body pressing against hers, his hands smoothing over her skin. Her neck burned, breath shortening as her heart beat furiously in her breast.

She'd convinced herself that her feelings for Kelric had been nothing but a naive girl's infatuation, but underneath the despair that had consumed her were genuine feelings for him. Somehow, he had broken through and reminded her of them. She curled a strand of his hair around her finger, and Kelric seemed as though he might melt beneath her at the small gesture.

Kelric brought her hand to his lips. "I love you, Gonivein. Nothing has changed that. Will ever change that."

Gonivein swallowed. "I… love you, too."

It wasn't a lie.

Kelric brushed his thumb down her tear-streaked cheek. "You're as beautiful as Aph—" He stopped, his face taking on a troubled, almost pained look. "As a goddess."

A familiar warmth from his praise sent a frisson of heat through her.

Kelric leaned closer and grazed his lips against hers.

A thrill raced through her. She ran her fingers through his combed hair and drew him closer, deepening the kiss, tasting the wine on his tongue.

His arm around her shoulders pressed her body close. His other hand roamed over her breast, then slid under the linen fabric hungrily to cup the soft flesh.

Desire surged down her body. She hadn't thought she wanted this, but now all she could think about was Kelric. Beside her. *Inside* her.

Kelric stood and set her gently back on her feet. He rested his forehead against hers. "I want you."

Gonivein lifted her hands to her shoulders and unfastened the broaches of her chiton. Her clothes puddled around her feet with a *swish*. She didn't quite trust her voice, and she hoped this was encouragement enough for him.

Kelric captured her lips in his, pressing his hands to her back and crushing her body to him. He lifted her off the floor and set her down on the bed.

"I've imagined this moment every time I've ever touched you," he said, standing back and looking down at her naked body. Anxiety flickered in his eyes where she expected to see lust. "But, I don't want you to hurt. Your hip…"

Heat burned across her shoulders and up her neck. She'd imagined this moment, too. That he would pull her to him, hungry, and enter her, ravage her as she tangled her hands in his hair, dug her nails into his back, gripped his thighs and pulled him into her even deeper. Then throw him down and ride him until he gave her everything she demanded. She could imagine a similar fantasy dancing through Kelric's mind. Had felt it pulsing at his fingertips the nights he'd crept into her room to be close to her, touch her, tease her, both of them aching for more.

Now she was barely able to stand on her own two feet by herself.

As if mocking her, her hip began to throb, and the gulls screamed louder from the window, drawing her out to sea.

No…

She didn't want to hear the crashing waves. Didn't want to see…

…Loric. Wandering the abyss between Gaia and Hades. Water lapping at his sandals as he stared across the expanse, trying to glimpse the peaceful shore he would never step foot on.

A sob broke from her throat, and Kelric swiftly knelt, caressing her cheek. "Gonivein, it's all right. We'll wait."

"No." Why was she so pathetic? "I don't want to wait."

Kelric dropped his hand, the muscles along his jaw clenching at whatever thoughts were running through his mind. She didn't want to be treated like the broken thing she was. She didn't want to be broken. She *needed* to not be broken.

She reached out and pushed the shoulder of his tunic down over his arm, over his hips. Kelric's shudder under her palm as her hand guided the garment to the floor stirred her desire to new heights. She took in his nakedness, the powerful muscles, broad shoulders, the scar under his ribs where the Leirion's spear had pierced him. She traced the puckered skin with her finger. He was beautiful. She gripped his erection and gazed up at him, unwavering.

"I don't want to wait," she repeated in a whisper, hoping she didn't sound as desperate as she felt.

Kelric drew in a sharp breath, the fire returning to his gray eyes. He leaned down, his proximity encouraging her to ease back against the pillows. He ran his hand up her good leg, sliding his fingers between her thighs, coaxing a moan from her throat. He pressed his lips to where it hummed in her neck.

Gonivein closed her eyes, focusing on the ripples of pleasure stirring all over her body. Kelric's hair tickled her skin as his mouth pecked across her shoulders, down to her breasts, and closed around her nipple. Lightning surged through her, and she dug her fingers into his curls. He pulled lightly on her elbow, and she rolled onto her side.

Kelric nestled behind her, his torso fitting perfectly against the curve of her back. His warm breath caressed her shoulder, hot and husky in her ear. He hesitated, eying the black bruise across her hip warily, as though it were a wall between them he was too afraid to scale.

Gonivein twisted her head, reaching over her shoulder to cup his chin and guide his lips back to hers. A spark as they brushed, and the fire reignited. "Take your wife," she murmured.

Kelric gripped her breast, pinching her nipple as he entered her. She moaned as their bodies melted together. He slid his hand lower, across her navel, between her legs. Pleasure surged through her at his touch, but he was gentler than she expected, than she wanted. She grabbed his thigh, craving more, but he snatched her hand in his and threaded their fingers.

A growl of protest rumbled in her throat, and he pressed deeper into her, filling her. Her body began to move on its own, wanting to find rhythm with his, build the intensity with him, but a sharp pain tore through her hip and down her leg at the effort. She gasped, clenching the furs beneath her. Tears pricked her eyes. The pain and frustration—the guilt—came rushing back.

Kelric seemed not to notice, perhaps mistaking her outburst for pleasure. He buried his face in her neck, his breath growing huskier, hotter.

Suddenly, he pulled away, and a wetness struck her thigh.

Gonivein stared at her violated leg, alarmed, then twisted around to capture her husband's gaze. "Kelric." Her lip curled impishly at his sheepish expression. "We're married. You don't have to do that anymore." She expected her teasing to set him at ease, but his jaw clenched as he rolled away from her and reached for the linen towel draped over the wash basin. A knot formed in her throat as the silence stretched between them, dragging all manner of self-loathing thoughts up from the depths.

"Kelric," she said firmly, cursing at how it sounded more like a squeak. "Tell me what's wrong."

He returned to her side with the towel and gently cleaned her off, then sat on the bed in front of her and sighed.

"I… I thought I could do this… But I can't. Not yet."

His words stung. Was he second guessing everything he said moments ago? *Am I not worth it, after all?* Perhaps this moment of intimacy made him realize nothing he had done—killing his father, jeopardizing his legitimacy with his men, provoking the anax—was worth it. *She* wasn't worth it.

Why would I be? She was battered, broken, sad. Her eyes filled with tears. She felt like screaming, *'If you had listened to me in the cove, you wouldn't have had to do any of this!'* It was on the tip of her tongue, but Kelric spoke first.

"My mother died giving birth. To Gadnor, I thought, but… to another child. Sister, brother? I don't know. They never had a chance in this world. Neither did she."

Gonivein's breath stilled, her rage plunging into her gut and dissolving. She relaxed back against the pillows, relieved she hadn't said those horrible things. She made a note not to immediately assume the worst again. She owed him this second chance. She owed herself too, she realized.

Kelric's hand found hers again and squeezed. "I don't want to lose you, too."

She sat up slowly and caressed his shoulder, wanting to pull him into her arms and kiss him, to guide him back into her and finish their lovemaking properly. Instead, she said, "If I don't give you an heir, I'll be disgraced. You could divorce me. It's my one job as basileia."

"It's not your 'one' job," he argued with a smirk, then stared out the window, where the stars were shining through a black sky. "I would never divorce you or see you disgraced. I won't let that happen. I just… need some time to build my courage for that. And your hip needs to heal. How much unnecessary pain would it cause you to carry and birth a child right now?"

He had a point.

Gonivein tugged him down, and he snuggled beside her and propped himself up on his elbow.

"Can you just let me… love you… like this? Just for a while." He kissed her lips, rubbing her nipple between his thumb and forefinger distractedly. "Please, Gonivein. I can't lose you, not so soon."

"Shh." She pressed a finger to his lips and wove her fingers through his hair. "All right."

Kelric sighed in relief and collapsed onto the pillow. His even breathing soon filled the room, but Gonivein lay awake, a thousand emotions tumbling within her.

CHAPTER 15

GADNOR

PAIN.

THE SENSATION WAS SO strong it was the only thing Gadnor's consciousness could fully comprehend. It throbbed behind his eyes, ached in his ribs, burned in his shoulders.

He didn't know where he was stumbling to—he couldn't see. One eye was swollen shut, the other pinched tight in agony. Steady arms guided his steps forward, turned him, eased him down onto a soft cushion. As adrenaline began to ebb from his veins, reality came rushing into its place. Panic squeezed his lungs.

I lost.

The gods had gifted him one chance to prove himself. To show all of Golpathia what he was capable of.

And that's *exactly* what he'd done.

Blood pounded against his eardrums, drowning out everything but the voice in his head. A self-loathing, gloating hiss, echoing up from the depths of his wounded pride.

Weakling.

Alypius had been so strong and fast, his every blow a struggle to deflect or dodge. Gadnor would be dead if he'd been facing a true enemy. And the entire gathering had known it from the start. Had cheered for it. Shame writhed in his chest at their taunts and jeers. He'd tried to push them out, focus solely on Alypius, but they were so loud. Baying like hounds for his blood. Cheering wildly with every drop that was spilled.

Fool.

How could he have possibly hoped, for one second, that they would accept him? How silly he'd been to think, to *believe*, he could become someone different from the loathsome stain he'd always been. That he could win their praise. Become a leader of men. A hero of the battlefield. Wield the power to make a difference and tear down the injustices that preyed upon the innocent.

Failure.

He prayed to the gods that the fate of Helinthia didn't truly rest in his hands. If it did, then they were all doomed.

A wet cloth dabbed at his eye, and a numbing sensation began to spider across his face, diminishing the misery pulsing inside his skull. Forluna with her potions, so caring, so concerned. He'd never deserved it less.

His cuirass was removed, and he could finally breathe easier, though it still hurt to let his lungs expand as much as they yearned to. Alypius' hard kick replayed in his mind. He didn't think his ribs were broken—the armor had done its job well—but they were surely bruised.

'What will it take?'

Powerless.

He heard a faint sloshing, smelled the sharp, minty scent of Forluna's numbing liquid. The cloth touched his eye again, and he shrank back, raising his hand to gently push hers away. Now he understood why Gonivein preferred pain over potions. Bones and skin would eventually heal, but the emotional anguish, the wound to his pride—that never would. The ache against his skull was a welcome distraction from that intrusive reality.

"I know it hurts, but I need to—"

He pushed her away again. More forcefully this time. "I don't want it."

The words came out harsher than he'd intended, a little high pitched. Like a whine.

Like the petulant child Alypius said he was.

Why did it have to be him? Of all the people who could have challenged him, why did it have to be *Alypius*—the man who had wrenched Cedrila from his arms—*Alypius,* whom Gadnor had vowed to never again be so powerless to stop?

Gadnor lowered his head into his hands, partly to hide his face, partly to guard his eye against further ministrations. He wished Hades would drag him down into oblivion.

"Just leave me be."

"Gadnor, I…"

"Please."

"A man needs time to catch his breath after a defeat."

Pallas.

Defeat.

The word fell as spectacularly as Zeus' lightning bolt striking the earth, validating Gadnor's fears. That was it, then. He had truly squandered his chance to prove he was worth something. He hoped Forluna would listen to Pallas and leave him to his misery.

Worthless.

There was a long stretch of silence before Forluna finally spoke.

"I need to get my bag. You'll need stitches in your shoulders. I'll just fetch it." There was reluctance in her tone.

He tried to reply, tell her not to bother coming back, but a sob threatened to spill out instead. He clamped his jaw tight, angry that his body would even think to heap more embarrassment upon this colossal failure.

He heard feet shuffling, then the click of the door. Finally, he was alone.

He let his tears fall. They burned as they pushed past the swollen flesh. A sob jarred his sore ribs as though it were Alypius' greaved shin colliding with them once again. He wrapped his arms around his torso, trying in vain to secure his bones so his burning lungs could draw in air. The lacerations on his shoulders stretched as he tightened his grip, and he clenched his teeth.

There was no renown he could ever win to reclaim his honor after this humiliation.

'You're lucky,' Helinthia had said.

Bah. What a lying, deceitful goddess she was. Her betrayal stung. Had she built him up, filled him with hope, just to tear him down in humiliation? Had she watched him fail? Were all the signs Dargos claimed to see just an elaborate lie to trick him into believing he wasn't the fool everyone else knew him to be?

'We are just playthings for the gods.'

Gonivein was right.

"Can I help?"

Gadnor froze, heat rushing over him. As if being a pathetic, whimpering child wasn't enough, someone had to be watching him, too. His humiliation was complete. "Who's there?" he croaked out.

"Just me."

Tor.

Just me. As if that made all the difference.

Gadnor forced his eye open to look at Tor, whose worried expression stole the angry rebuke from his throat. Gadnor hung his head. "How long have you been here?"

Tor's feet scuffed on the tiles, and Gadnor imagined the sheepish expression, could feel it in the tension between them.

"I never left."

Gadnor closed his eyes again. His disgrace was complete. What was Tor hoping to see? *He must doubt my ability to protect him after this.* Gadnor had made such a show of strength when they'd first met. Battling a Fury and two grown lions. Defeating Kelric in a duel of words, saving Tor from a life of servitude.

That first impression was nothing but dust in the wind now. Tor didn't belong here. In fact, he needed to get far, far away before he got hurt. Before Gadnor managed to provoke the gods yet again and

Xios met the same fate as the rest of his feline kin. Or worse, before Tor himself paid for Gadnor's failures the way his sister had.

"You shouldn't be here," Gadnor said, bitterness swelling inside of him.

"Where else would I be?"

"With someone who has a brighter future than a worm in the dirt," Gadnor said, his words coming out in a snarl. "With someone who can protect you. And themselves."

Tor blinked at the vehemence, speechless.

Guilt swirled inside Gadnor, but he didn't let it stop him. "Leave."

"Why do you doubt yourself so much?"

Gadnor released a bitter laugh, and pain sharpened in his ribs. He winced. "Were you not watching what everyone else was watching?"

"I watched a man cheat in a fair duel. That's his shame, not yours."

"He did exactly what the enemy will do, and then I and everyone I'm leading will be dead. I'm not fit to be strategos. Kelric was right. I'll never be ready for this."

Tor stepped forward and squatted down in front of him. Gadnor had no choice but to look at him now, unless he wanted to shut his cowardly eye again. He almost did, but he was captured by Tor's fierce gaze.

"As far as I'm concerned, you're the *only* person who can do this."

Gadnor shook his head, slumping further in defeat. Tor couldn't possibly still believe that. "Any one of them would be a better choice, and this proves it."

"Any one of *them* would let a father sell his son and not spare a second thought."

He knew Tor was probably right, but that offered little comfort. "Thoughts are worthless without the power to act on them. I can't even defend myself, nevermind someone else."

"You're not doing this alone."

Gadnor couldn't stop himself from glaring. "I will be, after today. No one is going to stand beside me. Even the gods laughed at me."

Tor's brow furrowed in confusion. "What are you talking about?"

The cackling, chirping, and screeching rang in Gadnor's ears. "You saw the birds, didn't you? Flocking like flies on a rotten corpse to feast on my disgrace."

Tor shook his head, a small smile tugging at his lips. "The birds weren't there because of the gods. *I* summoned them to stop the duel, to stop Alypius from killing you."

It was Gadnor's turn to be speechless. He didn't know if he should feel gratitude or even more shame.

"I told you." Tor smiled in earnest now. "You're not alone."

Dargos had expressed the same sentiment. Yet sooner or later, everyone who cared about him either rejected him or was taken from him.

"You can't save me every time I'm in over my head."

Tor sighed in exasperation. "Why are you being so stubborn? Just because you're chosen by the gods doesn't mean you have to be perfect. And one defeat doesn't mean you just give up."

The conviction in Tor's voice sapped what remaining energy Gadnor had left to argue. He sensed there was something beyond the current situation fueling Tor's words, but what, he had no idea, and he didn't have the mental stability to investigate it.

Forluna took that moment to reappear, bag in hand. She stood in the open doorway, cognizant that she had interrupted something. Gadnor was glad she had. He wasn't ready to forgive himself. Not yet. And he was afraid that if he stayed alone with Tor any longer, he might be forced to plaster a dutiful smile on his face and lie about it.

Tor stared down at him. There was clearly more he wanted to say, but Forluna's presence seemed to have stymied the flow of words begging to be let out. Finally, he turned and slogged out of the room.

Gadnor watched him go, his heart aching more than before. He remembered a time when he shared Tor's optimism—even this morning he'd still had hope.

But it had been beaten out of him for the last time.

CHAPTER 16

LITHANEVA

THE STRIP OF MEAT LAY crusted with dirt in the garden. So many flies buzzed around it now that they almost drowned out the sweet notes of Larxes' lyre drifting across the villa grounds. The hawk showed no interest in the offering and remained perched on the limb stretched over the pantheon.

Lithaneva wasn't sure how long she'd sat there, waiting, hoping, muttering prayers to all the gods. Except Hera, of course. When her eyelids grew heavy and her chin began sinking toward her chest, she knew she'd waited long enough. This plan wouldn't work.

She eyed the temple underneath the hawk's perch. The marble statue of Helinthia stared from inside, just as hopeful that Lithaneva would find a solution for this. *I could ask her for help.* Except any help Helinthia might offer would constitute interfering in the decisions of mortals. Helinthia might lose her island forever if she were caught breaking that rule. The memory of the goddess' nervousness that morning entered Lithaneva's mind. It risked too much.

Lithaneva had to figure this out on her own. She leaned forward on her elbows and rested her head in her hands, rubbing her temples with her thumbs as she stared at a line of ants making their way to and from the piece of meat. It was possible Helinthia wouldn't be able to help her anyway. Animals were Artemis' domain.

Lithaneva sat up straight. *Artemis could command it.* She hadn't worshiped at Artemis' altar since she was a girl. Since she'd seen Helinthia for the first time. Did the divine huntress even know who she was anymore?

How can I get her attention? Her mind spun, then her eyes wandered down to her boots. She wiggled her toes in the soft rabbit fur, an idea forming in her mind. She stood and hurried back into the villa. The smells of cooking had grown strong while she'd been wasting precious time. Branitus and Charixes would be back soon to eat. "Charon's rotting ferry," she muttered, going room to room, searching for something that might catch the goddess' eye. An offering, a sacrifice, a pledge of devotion, anything.

As she passed one of the sitting rooms, her eyes lighted on a fur-lined couch shoved against the adjacent wall and buried under a basket of what looked like laundry or old bed sheets. She stopped mid-stride and stood on the threshold, scrutinizing the room, trying to remember if she had ever set foot in here before. She approached the couch, removed the basket, and ran her fingers across the coarse fur. What a majestic wolf it had once been. She could tell by the sheer size of it—it would more than cover her entire height if she were to stretch herself out on it.

It was perfect.

Without another moment's hesitation, she pulled the wolf skin from the couch. Underneath was a linen cushion stuffed with old straw. Little dusty tufts had crept through the threads, and at the sudden movement of exposing it, featherlight specks flew into the air. Lithaneva stepped back, coughing and clutching the wolf skin tightly to her chest.

Artemis valued every animal's life. She showed leniency to hunters when their intent was food, especially when that food was to feed their children. But this? This majestic creature was killed for nothing but sport and turned into a soft seat. It was as undignified an end as a creature could possibly have, especially a creature as magnificent as this. And then to be stashed in this room, unadmired, unused, left to rot and suffer the insult of dust and hidden away underneath discarded scraps of cloth?

If Artemis was to accept a sacrifice in exchange for a favor, it would be this, Lithaneva was sure. *It has to work.*

She slung the wolfskin over her shoulder and hurried to the store room. Along the way, she paused outside the kitchens to make sure she still heard the cook busy inside. Larxes was still playing the lyre, though he was only plucking now. He'd been playing for a long time. She could only imagine how sore his fingers were. No doubt plucking was the best he could manage at this point, but it was enough to ensure her safety. She would have to make sure Branitus picked out a *nice* lyre for him when this was over. The nicest one Thellshun had to offer.

She grabbed two *amphoriskoi* of oil and wine and tucked them under her arm, then set off. The hawk eyed her as she crossed the garden grounds, and she met its gaze with confidence. *This will work.* She stepped inside the pantheon and laid the pelt down reverently before Artemis' altar, then busied herself making a fire, piling sticks, pouring oil to make the flames leap. She sprinkled wine, and the fire licked higher.

She glanced behind her to make sure she wasn't being watched, then whispered, "Goddess Artemis, mistress of animals, protectress of the woodland and the innocent creatures who refuge there, I beseech you." She paused and stooped down to grab the wolf skin in her arms. She raised it high, reaching toward Artemis' marble face. "I return this graceful creature to your care. A creature taken from your refuge unjustly and abused in death in a most undignified manner…"

Was that enough?

"… in the hope that you will command your hawk to bear me a message to…" She paused, listening for footsteps or voices—any indication of someone who might overhear, but she heard nothing.

"… a message to Gadnor in Golpathia."

She paused, but couldn't think of anything else, so she draped the wolfskin onto the altar. Thick, viscous smoke wafted from underneath, tongues of blue and green licking at the soft furs. It finally caught, burning bright and hot. Lithaneva waited until all traces of the animal were gone, then stepped back, bowed to the goddess one final time, and turned to leave the temple.

She looked up into the tree at the hawk's perch. It was empty.

Her heart fluttered in panic. She whirled around, scanning the tree branches. Had it gone? Had it not been waiting for her, after all? The wind ruffled the leaves as if laughing at her. An angry curse formed on her lips, but it melted into despair before she could get the words out of her throat. *How am I going to tell Gadnor?*

Aden would know of a trustworthy soldier who could carry the message, but it would take days to cover the distance between Thellshun and Golpathia. So much could go wrong along the way, and she doubted an errand could be invented to escape Leirion suspicion.

She turned back to look inside at the altar, now smoldering and spent. She wasn't sorry she had sacrificed the wolf pelt—the creature deserved to be at peace and removed from such a dishonorable state—but she dearly wished all this effort had resulted in more than mere sentiment.

She turned to stomp back into the villa, then froze.

There, waiting on the stone bench where she had sat for so long, was the hawk. It tilted its golden head at her. Daring her, as before.

Her heart fluttered wildly in her breast. For a moment, she was too shocked to recall why this sight filled her with such elation. She untied the scroll from her belt. Giddiness welled inside her, but she forced it down. Bursting into a childish fit of glee would surely scare the bird away, if not compel it to launch at her face with outstretched talons.

Lithaneva eased forward and knelt. The bird was elevated this time, so it was less awkward to reach underneath the smooth belly.

Blood pounded in her ears. The hawk's head swiveled to eye her hand, displaying its sharp, hooked beak.

She gulped, remembering to breathe as she tied the scroll around its scaly leg. She dearly hoped the message wouldn't fall off. Or get wet; what if it decided to go fishing on the way? The writing would smear, be illegible.

No. Focus! It will work.

Lithaneva straightened slowly and stepped back, eying her handiwork. It wasn't too tight to cause discomfort, she thought, but there was no chance it would slide off the bird's leg, either. Or so she hoped.

Without ceremony, the hawk launched into the air, tucking its legs, and her message, against its brown-flecked belly. Joy tightened in her chest as it soared over the temple and the villa wall, higher and higher, until it was just a speck soaring toward the horizon. Toward Gadnor and the rebellion. Closer to her victory.

Grinning, she turned on her heel to go back inside. Poor Larxes' fingers were probably bleeding by now.

She didn't get a chance to take a step before terror froze her in place. There, in the doorway, stood her father, watching her with an emotionless expression.

Silence rang in her ears. When had Larxes stopped playing? Panic skittered up her back as the more important question hammered into her. *How long has he been watching me?*

A figure emerged behind her father: tall, broad-shouldered, bushy eyebrows raised.

Branitus.

Charixes glanced at the sky, squinting.

Lithaneva's heart pounded. Had he been there long enough to see her with the hawk?

If he had, he wouldn't say so. He'd rather watch her squirm.

Charixes lowered his gaze to hers, and Lithaneva forced herself to approach in a confident stride.

There was only one thing to do. *Make him doubt everything.*

"You're back, Father," she chirped, clasping her hands in front of her to hide their shaking.

"I've seen enough." About Thellshun's soldiers, or about her? Charixes' expression gave nothing away.

She silently seethed. The challenge with trying to overthrow her father was that she had learned all her tricks of persuasion and tactics for subversion from him.

I perfected them. Yet she found herself second-guessing that truth. But wasn't that exactly what he wanted? To make her doubt herself, panic, become sloppy, make mistakes?

"To your satisfaction, I trust?" she probed, pushing the anxieties aside.

Charixes hesitated, his eyes flicking again to the sky before narrowing on her. "Hmph." He turned and shouldered past Branitus.

Branitus raised an eyebrow at her and gestured with an upturned palm as if to say, *'What was that about?'*

Lithaneva reached him and leaned close, barely managing to keep her rage confined to a whisper. "How dare you sneak up on me. I'm your *wife.*"

Branitus' face turned red. "You *saw* me come up; I didn't sneak. Your father was only a few steps ahead. How could I have known he wouldn't announce himself? What were you two staring at, anyway?"

Lithaneva merely scowled and stormed past him, willing her anxiety to calm within her. If Branitus' accounting of time could be believed, then the hawk should have already been airborne when Charixes arrived. All he could have seen was her fixation on it. And, perhaps, her inexplicable joy at it flying away. That would certainly raise questions, and none with ready answers.

She had to be extra careful now. *That was too close.*

CHAPTER 17

FORLUNA

ORLUNA STOOD BACK AND EXAMINED her handiwork. The lacerations to Gadnor's shoulders were stitched and covered in salve and bandages. His eye, swollen shut and black as night, glistened with ointment. His ribs were bruised, and she could tell they pained him when he breathed too deeply, but they would heal soon enough. It was the blow to Gadnor's pride she couldn't remedy. He hadn't spoken a word since she'd returned, hadn't even flinched as she'd poked her needle into his flesh and sewed his skin back together. Only stared at a chip in the tiled floor.

For herself, she'd been too angry to even try to say anything to him. Nothing would have come out soothing, and the idea he might think her rage was directed at him mortified her. She despised duels. She'd never understood their purpose. They rarely resulted in the everlasting renown the contestants hoped for, but irreparable damage was plentiful enough. And *this* duel…

She bristled, recalling the sound of Alpyius' greaves connecting with Gadnor's body, flinging him through the air.

This duel should never have been. There was no doubt in her mind that Alypius had intended to kill, or at least maim, Gadnor.

She hated herself for not being there to put an end to it before it began, but she'd allowed her fear to drive her back into hiding, leaving Gadnor vulnerable. Again.

With only the laurel tree for company, she'd sought refuge on the plateau, hoping to catch a glimpse of the eighth scholar, place him in her memory, or at least determine if he was really a threat. Instead, she'd seen the men of Golpathia filing out onto the front courtyard, armor and weapons assembled, and heard a din of jeering and taunting. Gadnor's blond hair was difficult to miss at the center of their bloodthirsty circle. She'd immediately recalled Gonivein's vision, but even scrambling as fast as she could, she couldn't reach him in time to prevent this.

She rinsed the blood from her hands with a pitcher on the vanity, then wiped her instruments clean and returned them to her bag.

"I've done everything I can, for now," she said, trying to keep her tone as neutral as possible.

"Thank you." Gadnor didn't look up.

Her heart wrenched to see him like this. What vile things was he thinking about himself? The fact that Alypius had cheated wouldn't offer comfort, she knew, so she didn't bother saying it. At this point, anything positive she said about Gadnor's performance would probably sound patronizing. She bit her lip.

"Are you all right?" Gadnor's eye scrutinized the bruises around her arm—perfect purple circles where Alypius' fingers had jabbed into her.

"Yes." She placed an amphoriskos of pain serum into his palm. "Get some rest." She squeezed his hand and turned to go.

"Forluna?"

She stopped. "Yes?"

"How did you come to know my mother?" Troubles she ached to remove churned within Gadnor's brown eye like a storm of Poseidon. He had Iptys' eyes.

She swallowed. The box into which she'd shoved all her grief slid open. Why was it her lot in life to watch them suffer, to want to help, but be so utterly helpless?

She sat beside him on the couch. "Helinthia commanded me to go to the palace and mentor your mother. To become her family, because she had none left." The words felt hollow, but she was too conflicted to put emotion into them. So much pain had come from that command, and yet Gadnor was here, alive, with her.

"Did you want to do it?"

Forluna stiffened, remembering the way the forest smelled when Helinthia had given the command. Rich, like just after a fresh rain. The animals called out for her, and the laurel blossoms wept their petals along her path as she walked through the veil out into the world of men. Every step was heavier than the last, fear overtaking her from what other nymphs had said about the gods condemning them to a life of mortal service.

'You think you won't love them. You plan not to. Inferior, weak beings. But then you do. And then they die. And us? We're cursed to live with our pain for eternity.'

Forluna couldn't find her voice to tell Gadnor how she had screamed. Argued. Bargained with the goddess to choose someone else. All in vain. Her silence seemed to say enough, or perhaps his immortal blood made him more perceptive.

"Do you regret it?" he asked then.

She didn't hesitate. "No, but I thought I would. I loved Iptys. She was so much more than a pupil, she was…" Forluna stopped as her voice cracked.

"Does it get any easier?"

She wanted to say yes. Precious moments of joy at the palace flashed into her mind, but that happiness had been fleeting. Iptys' death had broken her. But giving up Gadnor? That had shattered her completely. Finding him again had restored her hope and pride, but also brought bitterness. *I should have been there for him.*

Despair clenched in her stomach as she studied his swollen eye, the scar running across his cheek. How would this end in anything other than more heartbreak?

They will crush him.

She couldn't decide who the imminent 'they' were. Perhaps Charixes, the Leirion, the gods, Kelric's councilmen, or someone—or some*thing*—else. The odds were stacked against him more than ever.

"No," she finally said.

Gadnor lowered his eyes and nodded, as though she had resolved some conflict for him. "Thank you."

She put her hand on his shoulder, wishing she could somehow convey how much she loved him, how proud she was of him. She wanted to say it, but the words lumped together in her throat. He reached up and squeezed her hand, telling her he knew.

Tears pricked her eyes.

"Good night, Forluna," he whispered.

Her stomach knotted painfully as she left, pulling the door closed. She drew in a deep breath, hands trembling as much from her nerves as the bite of the breeze tickling her skin. She stuffed them under her arms, hugging herself, and scrutinized the shadows.

The eerie feeling of being watched was omnipresent, despite the fact that she hadn't glimpsed the mysterious face again.

The moon was still ascending toward its zenith, bright, nearly full. Stars glittered, and a few torches flickered in the city below. She saw no movement, save for an owl perched on the roof on the other side of the courtyard. It swiveled its head toward her, the soft feathers around its thick neck ruffling in the silvery moonlight. Were these the eyes of Athena, weighing her worth, or just a wary owl drawn to what moved in the darkness?

She met its eyes. *A guardian.* Summoned by Tor, perhaps? A small smile pulled at her lips as she turned away and walked along the balcony to the stairs. She froze, gripping the banister to keep herself upright as her eyes lighted on a dark figure waiting at the bottom.

She debated sprinting back to Gadnor's room, barring the door. They would both be safe.

The shadow moved toward her, and her legs tensed to spring.

"Forluna?"

"Dargos!" Her apprehension melted into anger as she stomped down the stairs. He held out his hand, but she shouldered past him and continued under the peristyle to their room at the front of the square villa.

He trailed behind her, quiet, tension building between them.

As soon as the door closed, she rounded on him.

"How could you let him be beaten like that? Why didn't you stop that bastard?"

Dargos wore a stoic expression. The mask he put on to hide his emotions. It made it easier to sling her fury at him, but she hated it because she never quite knew when she had successfully gotten her point across.

Tonight, though…

Tonight, she didn't care.

"You promised me you would protect him!" All her repressed rage and fear suddenly boiled to the surface. The face in the crowd, the eyes at her back, the doom hovering above her, Gonivein's cryptic prophecy, the danger Gadnor had narrowly escaped—all of it surged upwards with vehemence and exploded into her fists.

She pounded them against Dargos' chest. His eyes widened, body stiffened, but he didn't move, didn't speak. It enraged her even more. Did he have no defense? No excuse for his negligence? His disregard for all she had done, risked, endured, *lost* to keep Gadnor safe?

"For *what*?" She beat his chest again and again. Exhaustion finally caught up to her, and she slumped, sobs catching in her throat.

Dargos' arms went around her, holding her up, as though he sensed she might collapse on the floor right there and refuse to move.

"You promised," she muttered against him, feeling the heat of his chest, hot from her aggression. She thought he understood how important Gadnor was to her. *I trusted you.*

She would have taken her secret of the heir's identity to her grave if she'd known Dargos would turn on her like this.

He lowered her onto a chair and walked to the other side of the room. She heard him pour a cup of water, and a moment later he held it down to her. She took it, considered throwing it at him, but she didn't have the energy anymore, and her throat was parched. So she drank it all and handed the cup back, refusing to look at him.

He took it, and she noticed the cuts on his knuckles where they'd scraped the lip of Alypius' cuirass when he'd saved her. He sat on the edge of the bed facing her, rubbing his hands, gathering his thoughts. The tension in the air was almost enough to chase her back outside, find somewhere else to sleep. But the knowledge that someone, or some*thing* was lurking out there sapped her will.

"You're right," Dargos said finally.

She looked at him, surprised he was already conceding. Was he being honest, or just trying to put an end to the argument as quickly as possible?

His face was sincere. "I'm sorry, Forluna. I misjudged what was happening. I thought…"

"You thought Helinthia would come through for him."

The color blooming in his cheeks was all the confirmation she needed.

Her ire reignited. "You trust her too much. She will not interfere. Don't you understand? Not to save *him* or anyone else."

"But she did come through, the birds—"

"The birds were *Tor's* doing, not Helinthia's!"

Dargos gaped at her.

She dropped her face in her hands and took a deep breath, then combed the loose strands of her hair behind her long ears as she looked up again, crossing her arms over her chest. "You think Helinthia's favor means something, but it doesn't."

"How can you say that?" Dargos' tone finally donned an edge of its own. "I'm living proof it matters."

"She abandoned Iptys to die!" She clamped her mouth shut. *I said too much.*

Dargos studied her, curiosity burning in his brown eyes. She'd never spoken of this to him before. Why should she? She'd had no intention of helping him on his foolish quest to placate Helinthia. Except now, she *was* helping him, and Gadnor had already made her open that box of hidden grief. Perhaps it was time to let it all out. *No more secrets.*

His mouth opened, eyes fixating intently on hers, and she knew he was searching for the right words to say. He needn't try to be so articulate.

"You want to know the real reason for this famine? The real reason Hera is angry?"

His mouth closed. He was barely breathing.

"The oracle of Hera came to the palace. She knew a famine was coming and how to stop it. Do you want to know what she said?"

Dargos' head dipped ever so slightly, his eyes still locked on hers.

"She said the only way to prevent the famine was to renounce Helinthia and prove we were not made of the same offensive stock as our goddess. Do you want to know why the scholars never recorded this prophecy?"

Blood pumped hard in her veins, thrumming in her head. Grief gathered in her chest as the memories burst forth. She had kept this secret for so long. Part of her screamed to hold her tongue. What if Helinthia suddenly materialized from the shadows and snapped her neck, like she had Eraia's?

But at Dargos' nod, she pressed on. *She* had never promised Helinthia anything, save that she would be companion to Iptys. And now Iptys was gone.

"Helinthia *murdered* the oracle. Right at our feet. Because she craved power more than she cared for her own people. And then? The goddess you revere so much swore to protect Iptys if she kept her secret. When Charixes came, Helinthia was nowhere to be seen."

Dargos' eyes glistened, but he still didn't speak.

"I will *never* trust Helinthia. Gadnor isn't safe." Her eyes blurred with tears, and she half expected to feel immortal hands sliding around her neck. Her arms prickled with gooseflesh, but she refused to give in to her fear and look for the vengeful goddess over her shoulder. If Helinthia wanted to kill her, Forluna would let her. At least Dargos would know the truth, would no longer be blinded with devotion for her. Helinthia didn't deserve his reverence.

Dargos stood slowly and walked, dazed, to the head of the bed. He slipped off his clothes one article at a time and draped them over the couch, avoiding her gaze. He didn't say a word.

I should have told him all of this the moment he stepped foot in my forest. But she knew he wouldn't have believed her then. If not for the tears sliding down his cheeks and disappearing into his beard, she might think he didn't believe her now.

Now he shared her grief, or at least understood it. She hoped.

Guilt gnawed at her. Restoring Helinthia's glory had been the focus of his entire life, and she had destroyed it all in a few heated breaths. She wasn't sorry the truth was finally free, but she regretted how carelessly and recklessly she had thrown it at him.

Dargos had never truly been the object of her anger, not really. Her rage was for Helinthia. Helinthia, who'd forced her to love a mortal and then ripped her away. Helinthia, who beguiled everyone she loved with the same fruitless promise. *'Do this, and you will have my favor.'*

Helinthia's favor rewarded nothing but death and grief.

Dargos slid under the covers and rolled onto his side, away from her.

'Perhaps it's a warning *not to let our passions divide us.'* Her own words haunted her as Gonivein's vision of beasts lashing at one another flashed into her mind. She had let her passions drive a wedge between her and her lover. She felt ashamed.

Dargos was one of the only two reasons she still cared to live.

She stood, undressed, and crawled under the cover beside him. Her eyes traced the faint lines on his back—scars from a plague's painful boils. Helinthia had healed him. Forluna worried her lip, sensing how deeply she'd hurt him.

How could she begrudge him his devotion? She hadn't been fair. She pressed against his back and slid her arm around him, threading her fingers through the fine hairs on his chest. She half expected him to ignore her, perhaps shove her away. But after a moment, his hand curled around hers, entwining their fingers. He didn't let her go.

CHAPTER 18

KELRIC

D AWN'S ROSY FINGERS REACHED THROUGH a crack in the window, teasing Kelric's eyes open. A chill burned across his naked shoulders, and he burrowed under the furs to wrap himself around the warm body curled next to him. Gulls called from outside, a perfect serenade to usher in a perfect morning. A morning where Gonivein was asleep beside him. For the first time, he didn't have to sneak away.

The sliver of sunlight illuminated her face. A tiny snore rumbled in her throat on every exhale, and he sighed in contentment. He'd been having a dream just now. His waking mind remembered none of it, but his body did. He grinned wickedly and smoothed his hand around the curve of her rump, sliding his erection between her thighs.

She roused slightly as he kissed her ear.

"Mmm," she said, angling her cheek toward him. Her eyes remained closed, but her lips curled into a sleepy smile.

From somewhere behind him, a cricket began to chirp. It didn't bother him at first—his senses dismissed it as easily as they dismissed the quarrelsome gulls outside. Exploring her warm skin with his hands and laying seductive kisses along every inch of her jaw took up all his attention. But the insect was insistent. No sooner had he coaxed a moan of pleasure from her sensuous lips than the high-pitched whine began to drill into his skull.

He looked over his shoulder, scanning the dark corners and window ledges. With his sexual advances delayed by his search, her body began to relax again under his hand. She was falling back to sleep. *Ferry this damned creature.* She had almost been ready for him.

He slid across the mattress and set his feet on the cold tiles. The noise was coming from the corner. He stood, and the chirping immediately stopped. Perhaps it had jumped away. He waited a moment longer before sitting back on the bed, eager to finish what he'd started.

As soon as the blankets were over him, the chirping started up again.

Kelric threw off the covers.

The cricket quieted, but Kelric would not be fooled this time. He crouched on hands and knees, squinting under the couch and between vanity table legs, pushing aside piles of clothes and sandals. He thought he heard skittering once, but saw nothing. He stood, anger keeping him warm. Maybe his rummaging had really scared it off this time.

Kelric turned his attention back to Gonivein. He admired the curve of her body under the warm furs, the soft rise and fall of her chest as she breathed. Then something else caught his attention. Something lying just on the other side of her pillow.

He walked around the bed for a better look. His stomach twisted and knotted at the thing lying so innocently beside his wife. A small linen handkerchief, dyed black, embroidered with a vibrant white flower.

A lily.

He snatched it up, rubbing his thumbs over the stitches, unbelieving. His eyes darted around the room. How long had this been there? Could they have missed it in the dark? Or had it been placed there after they'd gone to sleep? Had someone been in their room in their most vulnerable state?

No. That's impossible. He would have heard someone enter. Surely…

But he wasn't sure. And somewhere, deep in his gut, he knew the truth. A Leirion had crept into their room while they slept and left this for him to find. A demonstration of power and stealth, a warning that not even the bedroom of the basileus was beyond reach.

He touched the pillow where the kerchief had lain, so near to Gonivein's face he could feel her breath on his trembling fingers. How could they get this close? They could have killed her, and he wouldn't have been able to do a thing to stop them.

He sank onto the edge of the bed, heart pounding. His burning desire leached from him, replaced by a cold chill. He looked over at his wife. Her face, a portrait of grace and beauty in slumber, was blissfully unaware a Leirion had threatened her yet again.

An inferno of rage blazed in his chest. The Leirion wanted something from him. Wanted to toy with him, scare him into submission, or make him anxious, careless. Anything to make it easier for Charixes to get his way. Kelric thought of the wedding guests. Was one of them the culprit? Or was it someone else?

Alypius and Ephastes had made a point to make their displeasure with his leadership public. Were they so confident of their influence that they would threaten him like this? They had to know he would suspect them and order their arrest. Or was that what the Leirion, whoever he was, wanted Kelric to do?

Kelric rubbed his temples. His head ached with all the information bouncing around inside.

There was a scuff outside the door.

He stilled, heart slamming against his chest. He stood as the door handle began to slowly lift. *Fool!* He hadn't bothered to bar the door last night. He'd been so wrapped up in his emotions and their lovemaking that he hadn't even thought about it. Perhaps the Leirion was back to finish the job.

He reached for his razor lying on the vanity and crept over behind the door just as it inched open. He wouldn't give the intruder a second chance to kill them.

A figure slunk into the room, shadowed by the alcove of the threshold. Kelric grabbed their elbow and jerked them into a chokehold. Pieces of kindling and logs dropped from their hands, scattering across the tiles.

Gonivein bolted up in the bed, gasping and staring wide-eyed at them. "Kelric!" Shock and pain tinged her voice.

Kelric hooked his arm under the intruder's jaw and lifted it higher, stretching it to expose a slender neck. He pressed the razor against it.

The slight build, hardly more than a twig, the whimper from their lips, the lack of defensive retaliation from Kelric's assault…

The doula!

He uncurled his arm from her neck and shoved her away.

She cried in surprise and twisted around to face him. She tripped on one of the logs and fell hard on her rump, a strangled yelp flying from her lips.

"Kelric!" Gonivein's tone was noticeably sharper this time, but he didn't take his attention from the doula, whose eyes lit on him in terror. Her face, at first pale, suddenly flushed red, and he remembered he was naked.

He had half a mind to slap her eyes away from him, but she lowered her face and covered it with her hands, her voice cracking with sobs. "I'm sorry, Kyrios. I'm sorry… Please don't kill me."

"What are you doing in here?" Kelric slammed the razor down on the vanity with a loud *crack.* Some of the pent-up tension he'd hoped to release by opening the Leirion's veins dispersed, but not enough to dispel his rage completely.

"Kelric!" Gonivein repeated, and he finally looked at her. Fire blazed behind her icy eyes, an evident rage of her own that he quickly realized was not for the same reason as his.

Why was she angry at *him?*

He furrowed his brow, confused, waiting for an explanation.

Gonivein didn't give him one. She stood on shaking legs, grimacing in pain as she settled her weight on her hips.

Kelric squashed his instinct to help her stand. Until he knew why she was angry with him, he had no intention of touching her.

She grabbed her robe from the floor and drew it over her shoulders. Then took his robe in hand. She shoved it against his chest as she hobbled past, not even looking at him.

"Stand up, Klymene," she said, offering her hand to the girl.

Kelric jerked his arms into the robe, suppressing the urge to rend the garment in two at the absurdity of the situation. Gonivein was in no position to be helping a perfectly able-bodied doula stand—she'd likely be pulled down to the floor.

The girl seemed to have sense enough to understand the danger to her kyria's kindness and stood quickly on her own, bowing her head and twiddling her hands. "I'm so sorry, Basileia. I was just coming in to stoke your fire." She gestured stupidly to the mess of wood around them.

To make matters worse, the cricket began its irritating chirping again.

"I thought… I thought you would still be sleeping and… it would be cold, so…" Klymene swiped the tears from her cheeks. "I thought you would like it to be warm when you woke up."

Kelric jerked the sash of his robe tight. *Stupid girl. She should know better than to barge in unannounced.*

"My previous kyrios, he… he always wanted it that way."

Gonivein's eyes sharpened on Kelric like daggers. He refused to meet her gaze, even as a tendril of guilt scratched at him. Maybe the doula didn't know better. And she couldn't have anticipated that Kelric was expecting a threat to emerge.

"It's all right, Klymene." Gonivein rubbed the girl's shoulders soothingly. "*You're* all right."

Kelric's frustration boiled over. He didn't have time for tears and hurt feelings. It was a lesson worth learning never to barge in on them again. And if she hadn't learned, then next time he wouldn't hesitate to cut her throat and be done with the nuisance. He folded his arms across his chest, drawing the doula's gaze. It was time for her to leave.

The doula flinched, and Gonivein moved to stand between them, as though the girl was the victim in all of this. It was Kelric whose privacy had been violated—Gonivein, too. How could she not see that? *Women and their stupid sensitivities.*

He opened his mouth to enlighten them both on what really mattered—the Leirion—then thought better of it. Gonivein had looked so serene as she slumbered. Would she be able to sleep at all if she knew what lurked in the shadows? She had enough things to keep her awake already.

Kelric curled his fingers tight, the handkerchief disappearing inside of them. "Is this the first time you've come in here?"

Klymene nodded, avoiding his eyes. "Yes, Kyrios."

"Did you see anyone else come in?"

She shook her head furiously.

He scowled. *Useless girl.*

Gonivein narrowed her eyes at him. Any more questions, and she would make him tell her about the handkerchief.

He turned away from her, eager to escape her suspicion. He disrobed, no longer caring if the doula saw him naked or not, and grabbed his clothes from the floor. Keeping the Leirion cloth balled in his fist, he used his thumb and forefinger to pull his tunic over his head, tie his belt, and cinch his sandals.

Despite his simmering resentment for Gonivein's anger toward him—which he still didn't understand—he couldn't resist planting a kiss on her cheek as he passed. She barely looked at him. No doubt she would hurl all of her frustrations at him later. He resolved to keep his distance as long as possible. Maybe she would forget about it and spare them both a needless argument.

Klymene was cleaning up the wood and stacking the pieces neatly beside the fireplace now. Kelric ignored her as he stepped through the mess, kicking stray pieces carelessly out of his way. It was time he had another chat with his archon.

CHAPTER 19

LITHANEVA

LITHANEVA STOOD, HANDS CLASPED ON the porch steps beside her husband, waiting for her father to emerge from the villa. He was taking his time, as usual. He loved making people wait, especially her. She sighed impatiently, and Branitus gave her arm an encouraging squeeze.

"Only a little longer, Lithie. Then we can breathe."

She held onto those words like a lifeline.

Finally, Charixes appeared through the atrium, crunching gravel beneath his polished sandals. Branitus stiffened beside her, and she felt her own nerves fray again as her father stopped beside them. With a dismissive nod to Branitus, he turned the heat of his gaze solely upon her.

Since yesterday, she had maintained the charade of annoyed housewife to perfection, shutting down her mind every time it tried to pine after Helinthia or worry about what traps Charixes might be scheming up for her. Now, as she raised her blue eyes under the bright morning sun, she almost couldn't contain her glee at the cloud of anger and disdain, thicker than she'd ever seen, contorting her father's expression.

Only one thing could evoke such a reaction. A puzzle he couldn't solve.

He has no idea what I was doing in the gardens, and he can't stand it.

Triumph ached to stretch a smile across her face, but she managed to suppress it and bow her head respectfully. Anger made him more dangerous and volatile. She dared not push him.

He leaned forward, his hot breath on her neck sending a startled chill down her spine. "The next time I see you, it better be to show me how you have solidified your place as Basileia of Thellshun."

Defiance whirled in her belly like a storm, but she managed to keep the scowl off her face and bow even deeper.

Charixes flashed Branitus a warning look, and her husband dipped his head low.

"Anax."

"I've gifted you my most precious possession, Branitus. Make sure she fulfills her potential."

Lithaneva clenched her jaw. He would come to regret how much he underestimated her 'potential'.

"Expect a visit from the Chancellor before the next full moon," Charixes announced before turning away and stalking down the porch steps.

A stable boy held the reins of Charixes' horse. The stallion's bronze coat gleamed in the afternoon sun, his black mane tangle-free and fluttering delicately in the soft breeze. The boy knelt and held the reins aloft, not daring to lift his eyes above Charixes' sandals when they stopped in front of him.

Charixes lifted the leather straps from the small, upturned palms and pulled himself onto his horse's back, swinging his muscular leg over the saddle with the grace and ease of a man in his prime.

Keeping her lip from curling in disgust might be the most difficult challenge she'd had all week. The least her father could do was age poorly.

The two men Charixes had arrived with were already mounted and waiting. They dipped their heads to Branitus and Lithaneva in farewell as Charixes heeled his steed into motion. Without a backward glance, they trotted off across the courtyard, kicking up dust, gravel, and bits of straw in their wake.

Lithaneva and Branitus waited like statues on the porch steps as Charixes passed through the gate and disappeared into the Kyrioi Quarter. They waited still longer until they saw him traverse the lower levels of the city. Citizens thronged like ants around him, cheering and groveling as he pressed through clusters of them. Finally, Anax Charixes disappeared around a temple dedicated to Hephaestus.

He was out of their lives at last.

Lithaneva only wished it was permanent.

"Gah!" Branitus heaved.

Lithaneva jumped, gazing wide-eyed at him as he doubled over at the waist and caught himself with his hands on his knees. He sucked in a greedy gulp of air, as though he'd just finished a lengthy sprint.

He made several more loud, obnoxious noises—growls, curses, and what sounded like gurgling—before whipping himself up straight again and shaking himself like a wet dog. Amusement twisted her mouth as he turned to her, wild-eyed. His hair, perfectly groomed a moment ago, was now tousled from his exertions.

"I *hate* your father," he hissed, leaning close to her face in mock anger before turning on his heel and striding back through the atrium.

Lithaneva couldn't contain her laughter. Tension from the last three days rumbled out of her in a fit of giggles, leaving her breathless, knees weak.

Her father was gone.

And she was still in one piece, physically, emotionally, metaphorically, and every other way imaginable. Charixes had still not broken her, despite all his best efforts.

"Now you understand," she gasped, wiping tears from her face.

"Yes!" Branitus threw up his hands. "How did you survive to

adulthood with your sanity intact?"

"A bold assertion." She smirked, and he grinned back.

They reached the inner courtyard side by side before he stopped suddenly and grasped her elbow, turning her to face him. His humor dissolved into seriousness, and she stilled, wary of whatever was going to come out of his mouth.

"Did you mean what you said, Lithie?"

Lithaneva narrowed her eyes, her head spinning with everything she had said over the last two days. "Said when?"

"When you said Thellshun was your home now, and you wouldn't see it fall into ruin?" His voice was low but soft, kind eyes searching hers for truth.

The city and its inhabitants swam through her mind. Their joy at her arrival on her wedding day, their devotion and love for their polis, their willingness to do anything to ensure Thellshun's glory and survival. Even commit treason—like Archon Aden. Here was a people who wouldn't be bullied or made to lose sight of their identity. A smile curved her lips. There was much to love and fight for in Thellshun. "Yes."

Branitus gave her arm a gentle squeeze. "There's no infatuation between us, Lithie, but I am fond of you. I'm glad you are here. Away from him."

Lithaneva swallowed the lump in her throat, too stunned to speak. That might be the nicest thing Branitus had ever said to her, perhaps the nicest thing *anyone*—besides Helinthia—had ever said to her.

Branitus dropped his hand from her elbow, looking embarrassed. "Aden will arrive soon for his evening report. I'd like you to attend."

Aden was just the person she needed to see. Now that Charixes was no longer around, it was safe to convey their next move.

"Of course. For what reason?" she asked innocently, tucking a stray tendril of hair behind her ear.

"You remembered the census—you remember all the details I don't. I hate your father, and I'm not enthused with what he wants me to do, but I must acquiesce to his demands." He sighed, kicking a loose pebble across the path. It smacked into a broad-leafed plant lining the tiled pathway and disappeared between the stems. "I'd like your help softening the blow to our people. I trust you."

Lithaneva nodded, trying not to appear overly excited. "Of course."

Branitus smiled, suddenly appearing distracted. "Good. Well… until then."

From the corner of her eye, she spotted Larxes' large green eyes peering out from the crack in the door to his bedroom. Resentment stirred in her gut, but she had to admit that Larxes deserved special attention for yesterday. She still hadn't had an opportunity to thank him for playing the lyre for so long. And Branitus had played his part well these last few days.

She pretended not to see him waiting. "I'm going down to the agora. My loom is bare."

Branitus didn't seem to hear her as he turned with a nod and disappeared into his bedroom.

Lithaneva retrieved her coin purse. Now that she knew what her father was up to, she needed to find out every detail. How many ships was he building? Who was building them? Where were they getting the wood and bronze from? What weapons of war would they carry? How many men were guarding the shipyard?

Obtaining this information required a more delicate hand.

The crowds in the city were denser than normal, on account of her father traipsing through the streets. Everyone had poured out to glimpse the anax go by, hoping to put a face to the rumors of the man who'd single-handedly usurped the throne. Now that their curiosity was satisfied, they were eager to gossip.

Familiar stories met Lithaneva's ears as she walked brusquely down the cobbled streets. She refrained from rolling her eyes at the variations of how Charixes became 'the hand of divine justice'. Allegedly, a witness to the murder of Oracle Eraia had come forward, asserting that Iptys was the murderess. Even before Helinthia confirmed that was a lie, Lithaneva hadn't believed it.

Charixes had managed to fool the kyrioi in Ninenarn, however, and the rest of the island was too far removed to risk the repercussions of questioning such allegations.

Lithaneva picked her way through the crowded agora, delighted that most people ceased their chatter when she neared. They exchanged quick pleasantries to hurry on their way or skirted closer to stalls to feign interest in the wares displayed. Were they afraid of offending her?

How adorable.

She reached her destination stall and made a show of examining the spools of thread before her. Wool, flax, and linens were arranged in a rainbow of vibrant colors that would make even the goddess Iris pause to admire them. The woman behind the counter stood, sweeping her gray-streaked hair out of her face as she bowed in greeting. "Basileia, welcome!"

"Hello, Melitha."

Melitha tipped one of the baskets toward Lithaneva. "Fancy a closer inspection of the golds?"

Gold. A color of calm. Inquisition.

"Basileia, you grace us!" The merchant in the next stall blurted out just as Lithaneva opened her mouth to respond. "Fancy something sweet and tasty?"

"She's mine, Telechus, mind yourself," Melitha snapped back.

"Everyone loves sweets," Telechus retorted, grabbing a handful of dates from the basket on his counter and thrusting them toward Lithaneva.

Lithaneva tried to keep the amusement from her tone. "Perhaps tomorrow… Telechus, was it?" She turned away from his crestfallen expression and plucked a spool of red wool from a basket. "I'm looking for something close to this."

Red. The color of blood and violence. The color of a mission.

"Ah." Melitha swept her hand over the other spools in the basket. "These were dyed and spun by Thellshun's maidens of Aphrodite. Beautiful scarlet shades, don't you think?"

Lithaneva petted the soft thread, spun fine enough to weave a chiton for an anassa. Perhaps there was something to be woven there for another day, but Thellshun's threads would not supply her the materials she needed this time.

Three men passed behind them, discussing architectural refurbishments to the *bouleuterion*. They paused an arm's length away from Lithaneva, right in front of the sweets seller. The merchant leaned toward them with an eager grin. "Welcome, Kyrioi!"

One of the three half-heartedly examined the dried dates as he tried to listen to what his companions were saying. The merchant shifted anxiously from foot to foot, deciding how he could gain their full attention without appearing insolent.

Lithaneva eyed the exchange warily, wondering if she should wait until they moved on to continue her acquisition.

"Oak may be cheap, but we need limestone if we want to avoid this discussion in ten years." The man examining the dates turned away from the stall to engage with his companions again.

Men paid so little attention to the activities of females. Lithaneva doubted they would consider anything amiss if they overheard her exchange. She decided she was more annoyed at the raucous they were causing than concerned. She straightened her shoulders and nodded confidently. "It's beautiful, but do you have any imports from the capital?"

Melitha blinked, a pained look swirling in her eyes at the mention of Ninenarn. Melitha's uncle and brother had been palace guards before Charixes executed all those loyal to Iptys. When the Leirion had begun searching for their families, she'd hidden herself at the temple of Aphrodite. There, her position allowed her to gain the trust of young Ninenarn brides. That's where Lithaneva found her, before helping her escape to Thellshun. Now, Melitha's enterprise connected her to nearly every household in Thellshun. Lithaneva was never without a wealth of information.

But this was the first time Lithaneva had ever asked Melitha to return to Ninenarn. Would she do it?

Melitha returned the spool to its basket, arranging the threads attractively for display. "I do not have anything from Ninenarn at the moment." She threaded her fingers and tapped her thumbs together in thought. "But I am due for imports. Do you have something particular in mind?"

Lithaneva sighed with relief.

"I have fresh apples, Kyrios!" The merchant beside them practically shouted, claiming the trio's attention, and everyone else's, in the square. Lithaneva seethed as faces turned toward them.

"Picked yesterday," the eager man continued, oblivious to everything but the potential sale.

The kyrios, clearly annoyed, threw a few *drachmae* onto the counter and snatched three apples from the offered basket. Then promptly left with his two companions.

Most of the crowd resumed their shopping as the trio walked away. Only a few stares lingered on her, but she pretended not to notice. Discomfort with attention was unbecoming of a basileia, and odd behavior for a princess, besides. She straightened her shoulders. "Where were we?"

"Any particular qualities you're hoping for?" Melitha twisted a green flax thread around her finger.

"I'm weaving a new cloak for Branitus to wear with his armor." She held Melitha's gaze, ensuring the gravity of her words were understood.

This is war, Melitha.

Melitha nodded, slowly winding the flax back onto the spool. "That will be lovely."

"Not just any cloak, something *exquisite* and *regal*. There can be no doubt he is a great leader of men."

And there could be no doubt that only the most privileged of Ninenarn would have the information Lithaneva sought.

Melitha tucked the spool alongside the others with a downcast, resigned gaze. "I understand." She rested her hands on the worn wooden counter and examined the grains thoughtfully. Lithaneva waited, wondering if the older woman would decline. To gather information about war from the highest-ranking individuals in Ninenarn risked everything Melitha had built for herself here.

Finally, Melitha nodded. "The basileus will be pleased with such a fine garment. I will do my best to obtain everything you need."

Lithaneva released her breath, relief pulling at the corners of her lips. "I need it by the next full moon. *Whatever* you can get your hands on."

The spring equinox was only three full moons away. The rebels would need every day possible to prepare a defense. The timeframe was impossible no matter how it was divided.

Fresh surprise flashed across Melitha's face, but she quickly composed herself and bowed. "Of course, Basileia."

Lithaneva pressed her coin purse into her spy's palm with an appreciative squeeze. "An advance."

"Thank you." The woman's eyes widened as her hand dipped under the weight of the purse. There were enough drachmae inside to bribe a god.

It could take just that to complete the mission.

Satisfied, Lithaneva turned and made her way back to the villa.

CHAPTER 20

GONIVEIN

GONIVEIN SAT ON THE EDGE of the bed, braiding her hair as she watched Klymene. The doula, red-faced and eyes puffy with her efforts to keep her tears in, had finished stacking the scattered logs by the fireplace and was now sweeping up the stray chips strewn across the floor.

Saying something would probably set the girl at ease, but Gonivein didn't trust herself to speak yet. Her emotions—her rage—still roiled inside her. She didn't want to frighten the girl further. Kelric had done enough of that.

She yanked the strands of her braid, wishing she could displace the violent image from her mind. The way Kelric's arm had whipped around her neck, stretching it for the blade, as if she were a goose in his grasp rather than an innocent girl. Why was aggression always Kelric's first instinct?

Klymene finally finished with the wood and stood before her with clasped hands. "That's all of it. Can I help you dress, Kyria? Perhaps draw a bath?"

Gonivein finished tying her braid and released a slow breath, collecting her thoughts. She was surprised Klymene wasn't trying to get away. That would certainly make this much easier. "Do you have family somewhere in the city?"

A flicker of panic pinched the girl's brow. Her mouth moved, but no words came out, as though a lump had been stuffed down her throat.

Gonivein tilted her head. *Was that such a strange question?* Loric hadn't acted like this when she'd asked him where he had come from.

Loric...

Guilt immediately replaced her curiosity. Perhaps the girl had lost her family and the question grieved her. "I'm sorry, Klymene, you don't owe me that explanation. It's just that I hoped you would have somewhere to go."

What remained of the embarrassed flush drained from the girl's cheeks, leaving her pale. She looked a heartbeat away from fainting.

Can I say nothing right? Gonivein almost retracted her words, conjured some menial task for the girl to do, but she stopped herself. *No. I won't apologize for this.* "It's not that you aren't welcome here, it's just that I don't want anyone subservient to me. You should be somewhere you want to be."

Klymene's color slowly returned, her own brow furrowing in confusion. "But I'm... I..." She trailed off and stared.

"We're going down to the Magistrate today, and I'm going to free you. You can—"

"No!" Klymene blurted.

Gonivein leaned back as though slapped, her next words jumbling in her throat.

Klymene's hand flew to her mouth. She knelt, clasping Gonivein's knees. "Forgive me, Kyria, I didn't mean to shout, nor deny such a gracious gift. I just... I just... I..." Her breaths were coming too fast and short.

Gonivein laid her hands over the girl's. *What have I done?* "Calm down, Klymene, I promise I'll listen. Catch your breath, then tell me what is the matter."

Klymene nodded, pausing to collect herself. Finally, she raised her eyes to Gonivein's, and they were filled with tears. "Please don't free me, Kyria. I have nowhere to go."

"Well…" *Think!* "I'm sure there are many families in the city who would gladly pay you for your help," Gonivein offered her. "I will help you find someone—"

"It's not that, Kyria, it's Kyrios Krastus. He's the chief magistrate. He'll punish me if you bring me before him. He'll think you're trying to be rid of me for some offence."

"I'll assure him that's not true." Gonivein braced to rise, but Klymene's grip tightened on her knees.

"Then he'll think you are trying to offend *him* by publicly rejecting his gift. No one would dare go against him and hire me. He's too powerful. He'll hurt me, or cause trouble for the basileus. Please, Kyria, just let me stay. Please…" Klymene buried her face in Gonivein's lap, her shoulders shaking with sobs.

Gonivein's mind raced in bewilderment. How could one man instill such a fear in Klymene that she would feel safer here, after narrowly escaping having her throat cut open? *Could I have imagined Kelric's aggression to be worse than what it really was?* Gonivein rubbed her eyelids, allowing the offensive images of Kelric back in, but they didn't offer any clarity.

"What about the temples? You could dedicate yourself to Aphrodite, or Artemis, or Hera, anyone. Krastus wouldn't dare harm you in the presence of the gods. Nor could he find offense in such a noble sacrifice."

Klymene's hands slid into her lap as she slumped back onto her heels, defeated. She wore such a resigned expression that Gonivein's heart twisted. "I would like to have a family one day, Kyria. The temples…"

"Require chastity," Gonivein finished, sighing. She stared at the girl's bowed head and thought of Loric again. Her heart ached. She didn't want another person determining their footsteps according to her words, suffering for her. *Dying* for her. Klymene didn't understand the risk in staying by her side.

Warmth rushed under Gonivein's skin, pushing out beads of sweat that she wiped away with the back of her hand. Every fiber of her rejected the thought of Klymene staying here. There had to be another way. If life in the city wasn't feasible, then Gonivein would help her find a family in a village that would employ her, away from Krastus' influence.

A village like Tyldan?

Embers and ash from the dead scattered into her mind, and she bowed her head in defeat. Forcing the girl to leave the protection of the city, waiting to be consumed by the fires of war or be carried away as spoil, was no offer of freedom.

A gull screamed from the cliffs outside the window, and she closed her eyes, allowing herself to give in to her torment. Klymene's bowed head dissolved into a cloudy abyss. Loric's face turned from the misty shore to look at her, his dark eyes piercing hers across the veil. Her heart raced in her breast as she gazed back at him.

What is freedom?

'Choice,' he seemed to say. Choice she had never given him.

"Kyria?" There was a subtle shake on her knee and the image of Loric blurred with unshed tears. She blinked, wiping away her grief as it plummeted down her face, and smothered the sob in her throat with a deep inhale. "You may stay, on one condition—two conditions."

Klymene's brown eyes widened with hope as she squeezed Gonivein's knees. "Anything."

"When you are ready for your family, say the words, and I will free you. And you must stay out of Kelric's way. He…" *Would sooner kick you aside than alter his course.* "He has a lot on his mind. He doesn't always have time to think about how his actions might be a little…" *Brutal. Callous.* "… excessive."

Klymene's smile widened as she leapt to her feet. "Of course, Kyria, thank you!"

Somehow, the girl's gratitude only heightened Gonivein's

remorse. Was this truly the right thing? She directed her to help Euanthe in the kitchens. She hoped, since Kelric adored the cook, that Klymene would have a chance of avoiding his ire if she could get in the old woman's good graces. It was a fleeting hope, but the best Gonivein could manage at the moment. She prayed Aphrodite would ensnare a husband for her soon and take her away from here.

Gonivein made her way to the triklinion for breakfast. As soon as she stepped foot inside, tension gathered around her like a cloud. She'd expected some awkwardness the morning after her wedding night, a sly smile or two in her direction, or maybe excitement for Gadnor becoming strategos—especially from Dargos. But there was none of that. Everyone's shoulders were slumped forward in defeat. Then she saw Gadnor. She gasped. "What happened to you?"

Gadnor turned his head. One brown eye, whites shot red with busted blood vessels, opened to her. The other was swollen shut, the battered skin shades of black and purple. He attempted a smile, but there was only sadness in it.

Her eyes instinctively searched for Kelric. He sat in his usual place at the table, eyes glaring into his plate of cold, untouched food. Her muscles tensed at the rage she detected from his rigid posture. He was a breath away from doing something brash.

She looked at Dargos and Forluna. They were sitting at opposite ends of the table today.

Gonivein crossed the room on wooden legs and cautiously took her seat beside Kelric. He didn't even acknowledge her. She looked around the table expectantly, her eyes landing on her brother. For once, he was reluctant to speak, but finally he began to explain everything. Alypius and Ephastes, the argument at the table, the duel, the birds.

Kelric stood, pushing the couch back and jostling Gonivein. She flinched at the harsh scrape of wood against the tile. The whole room seemed to hold its breath, then release it when he stomped out. Gonivein hoped he was on his way to put Alypius and Ephastes in their place. How could such violence have happened at their wedding? Under Dargos' scrutiny, no less? She shot her brother an accusing stare, but he had refocused his attention on his food and didn't see it. Why hadn't he tried to stop the duel?

The scholars began to trickle into the triklinion, taking seats on the couches around the tables in the room, throwing curious glances at Gonevein and her group.

Mandus stopped beside Gadnor and smiled down at him. "Glad to see your injuries were not beyond Forluna's capable hands."

Gadnor raised his head, but didn't meet the old man's gaze as he nodded. Gonivein's heart tightened in her chest at the familiar scene. Gadnor, bullied and bruised. She had hoped those days were behind him, now that he was destined for greatness. How cruel the Fates were to continue subjecting him to such abuse.

Mandus turned to her. His compassionate gaze deepened her shame, as though he could peer into her mind and see her resentful thoughts.

She looked down at her hands, feeling his gaze linger on her.

"The winter solstice is three days away, Basileia. There are preparations to be made for the confirmation ceremony, preliminary sacrifices and offerings to be given. I request your company today to instruct you on how to honor Apollo."

Apollo. His very name scalded her. She kept her eyes on her knuckles as she nodded. If she raised them to Mandus, he would see the irreverence burning there.

"Where is the young Oracle of Artemis? Tor, is it? I must speak with him, as well."

Gadnor cleared his throat. "He is on the plateau further up the mountain."

Mandus stroked his long gray beard. "I see. I will spend today with you then, Basileia."

"Are all of you here, Mandus?" Forluna asked, eying the scholars breaking their fast around the tables in the room. "I only count seven."

Gonivein impulsively counted them, too. Why did Forluna find this worthy of note?

"I sent one to the agora just as Dawn awoke. I thought it best to get ahead of the crowd."

Forluna nodded. "Of course. May I come with you?"

Gonivein's brows rose. Forluna usually avoided the agora. Dargos shifted from the other side of their table, and Gonivein could tell he was bursting with curiosity. *At least I'm not the only one surprised.*

Mandus' smile widened, the lines around his eyes crinkling in genuine delight. "Of course, dear Forluna."

Forluna bit into a slice of bread, and Gonivein let her curiosity die in the rhythmic chewing noises around her. It wasn't even midday yet, and she was already exhausted. She hoped Mandus' instructions wouldn't be as intense as his lectures from her youth at the Library.

CHAPTER 21

FORLUNA

SAND GRITTED BETWEEN FORLUNA'S TOES as she walked at the back of the group bound for the agora. Gonivein's litter, resting on the shoulders of four armed guards, bobbed above the heads of the acolytes. Four more guards flanked the basileia, keeping a watchful gaze on the surroundings of the Kyrioi Quarter.

Gonivein looked regal, riding so high above everyone else, eyes attentive, unassuming, kind. *Like Iptys.* Gonivein even resembled the anassa a little. Iptys' blond hair had been a deeper gold than Gonivein's, her face rounder, but their quiet, anxious natures were the same—their naivete, perhaps. Both saddled with enormous responsibility in service to gods and men at a young age.

Both under threat by the same man and his wicked spies.

For all their similarities, Forluna prayed Gonivein would not share Iptys' fate.

Mandus trundled beside Gonivein, one gnarled hand grasping the edge of the litter to help him keep his stride even. His cheerful voice carried high on the breeze as he detailed the finer points of the confirmation ceremony. Gonivein smiled at the right times to follow his words, but she seemed distracted.

Forluna was, too. Somewhere ahead of them was the mysterious eighth scholar. She couldn't shake the feeling of familiarity—of danger—that had gripped her when she captured his gaze at the wedding. She had to remember him. She would not be able to relax until she did.

The bustle of the agora grew louder as they exited the Kyrioi Quarter. Children laughed, people talked and called to one another, hurrying to and fro. Forluna despised agoras. There were too many people, too many emotions, too much going on at once. Chaotic. Like a city in the throes of an uprising.

She shivered, ears straining beneath her hair in response to the offending noises. There was something even more tense about the city today, like everyone was holding their breath. Forluna examined her surroundings, but couldn't put her finger on why.

Forluna was so distracted she almost slammed into the back of the acolyte in front of her. A glance to her right revealed the tall columns of Apollo's temple beside them.

The litter-bearers lowered Gonivein to the ground. One of them helped her stand and held her arm as she secured her crutch.

"Thank you," Gonivein said. "How long will we be here?"

"There is much work to do," Mandus answered.

Gonivein frowned.

"That probably means you'll be here forever," Forluna interpreted with a smirk.

Mandus shot her a glare, but his eyes crinkled with humor. "Not *forever*, but that depends on how well the basileia pays attention the first time I go over the instructions." He arched a bushy brow at Gonivein. "Perhaps I should ask *you* how long we will be here."

It was clear there was a prior history between Mandus and Gonivein as teacher and student. She wondered what stories Mandus had of the youthful, willful Gonivein at the Library Critius.

Forluna had expected a quick retort, but Gonivein seemed to give it thought as she nibbled her lip.

The basileia untied her purse from her belt and shook eight

drachmae into her upturned palm. She held them out to the guard who had helped her stand. "Get yourself some food. We'll be here a while."

The guard shared a nervous glance with his companions, then cleared his throat. "We've been ordered to stay with you at all times."

Gonivein's brow furrowed, and Forluna shared a kindred look of surprise with Mandus. Eight guards was excessive for a short trip to the agora, but in light of everything that had happened yesterday, she understood the extra precautions. Yet something in the guard's tone made Forluna wonder if Kelric knew more than the rest of them.

Gonivein rattled the coins at him and reassured him with a dazzling smile. "This is the temple of Apollo. I'll be perfectly safe here."

"I'm sorry, Basileia. My orders came directly from the basileus."

Gonivein's shoulders slumped as her eyes passed over each guard, then their surroundings. She was clearly frustrated at having her authority stripped away as though she were a child—the always unanticipated consequence of marriage.

Pity stirred within Forluna as desperation deepened in Gonivein's face.

"Then, can just one of you go and bring something back for the rest? It would set me at ease if I knew you were at least comfortable while you waited for me. I know you're hungry, I heard your stomachs gurgling all the way here."

The guard opened his mouth, no doubt to protest again, but Mandus cleared his throat, interrupting him.

"It is your duty to make things as easy as possible for the basileia as well as to protect her, is it not?"

The guard's face reddened, and Forluna smiled.

Mandus raised his hand toward the sun. "She has already devoted considerable time thinking about your well-being at the expense of her own. She should be sitting down, resting her hip. Will you argue with her until she collapses, or will you grant your basileia this small compromise so we can get on with Apollo's work?"

The guard bowed his head and accepted Gonivein's coins. "You are most generous, Basileia."

Gonivein smiled, then hobbled up the temple steps with Mandus and disappeared inside.

The guard handed the coins to one of his companions, who set off in the direction of the food stalls. The scholars, having received prior instructions from Mandus, scattered in different directions.

Forluna followed them into the belly of the bustle, skin crawling as the chaos closed around her. She would almost rather enter a cavern full of spiders than go farther into this sweaty, jostling fray. Either would ensnare her in a tangled web for some monster at the end of it, she was sure.

The acolytes' long gray robes weren't difficult to spot through the crowd, and she saw each of them again and again as she wandered. *Where is he?* How could she have seen the other acolytes multiple times over, and the one she sought not even once?

Her frustration built until at last she froze in the middle of the street. An aged acolyte stood before a candle merchant two stalls away. His gray robe was like all the others, but there was something about his posture, the tilt of his chin as he conversed.

Forluna ducked her head and moved closer to a bead stall next to her. She nodded with a forced smile as the merchant launched into a spiel about the superior quality of her oyster shell beads. Forluna plucked a strand of iridescent slivered beads and held them up to the midday sun, pretending to examine them while peering beyond at the scholar.

She tried to imagine the man without his curly beard and fewer streaks of gray in his dark hair. Had he, in his youth, found a clean-shaven face fashionable? She could tell he used to be very muscular—a soldier or guard, perhaps. He stooped to lift his basket of newly-purchased goods. Something in the slope of his body, the bend in his knee…

A shadow of her past itched at her skull. A man hunched on the ground, something—no, *someone*—underneath him. Had he hurt them? Killed them? Her mind strained at the memory.

The scholar straightened and turned in her direction.

All her thoughts fled. She twisted on her heel and flung the strand of beads back into the basket as she skirted around the stall to hide.

"Mind how you treat my wares!" the woman snapped, drawing eyes from all around.

The air left Forluna's lungs in a rush, and she found herself gasping to pull it back as she darted into the safety of the crowd.

Was he following her? Surely he'd seen her.

She hadn't been completely sure what her plan was in tracking down the eighth scholar, but she'd thought to approach him, speak to him, learn who he was and where he'd come from. Put her irrational fears to rest. Yet something about the brief flash she'd pulled from the recesses of her mind screamed caution. A primal instinct at the core of her being urged her not to let herself be alone with him.

She ducked behind a cart full of amphorae and cautiously peered back around. He was gone again. She scanned frantically, to no avail.

In. Out. Slow. In-out-slow. Inoutslow—inousl—

Darkness pressed at the edges of her vision, her heart thundering. Any moment now, she expected him to leap out and surprise her, plunge a knife into her, bound and gag and drag her away.

A shadow glided overhead, drawing her gaze skyward. A large bird circled above the city, riding an updraft. *A hawk.* That was important for some reason.

In-out-slow. In. Out. Slow.

The majestic creature rose higher and higher, then broke toward the villa. Toward Tor.

The hawk! Lithaneva had finally sent word.

Forluna stood cautiously, gripping the side panel of the cart for support as the blood tingled back into her legs. She examined her surroundings, but there was no sign of the scholar. Only the crawling sensation of being watched. He was there. She could feel his eyes.

Not alone.

Forluna tensed to sprint, but an iron grip cinched around her elbow. Panic exploded in her chest as she spun, fist balled, ready to fight for her life. A scream built in her throat, but confusion kept her from releasing it.

A woman stood before her. Scars gouged her face, and bolts of silver hair cascaded over her shoulders. There was something wild in her eyes, but kind. The look of a woman who had experienced more at the behest of others than by her own intentions. "He will never stop hunting you."

Forluna's breath came in sharp, inadequate gasps. How did this woman know she was being hunted? She scanned the market, trying to pull free. Was this woman part of a ruse to trap her here until her enemies could overpower her?

"Perhaps it's time you hunted *him*."

Forluna's gaze sharpened on the woman. A silver medallion around her throat glinted in the sun.

A gorgon's head glowered up from the round disc.

"Who are you?" she managed.

The woman released her elbow, a triumphant smirk twisting her scarred lips. "A woman who wins her battles."

A shiver shot down Forluna's spine. She opened her mouth to ask more, but a flash of gray in the crowd caught her eye.

Forluna spun and ran.

CHAPTER 22

GONIVEIN

GONIVEIN'S HEAD ACHED ALMOST AS much as her hip. The information Mandus poured into her swirled and blended together in her mind. Histories and deeds of oracles who had come before her, duties, rituals, expectations, festivals. Given what little information she'd retained so far, she was destined to ruin a long-standing legacy.

Gonivein found her attention drawn to the acolytes of Apollo as Mandus droned on. They moved with quiet grace around the temple, cleaning, arranging offerings, greeting visitors. The arrogant priest she and Loric had spoken to had emerged from his lavish lair only once to accept offerings from a wealthy woman and her son. He'd eyed Gonivein contemptuously upon spotting her with Brother Mandus. Learning she was Apollo's oracle had won her no favors with his ilk. Not that she wanted it.

Mandus had warned that she needed to find common ground with Apollo's priests and priestesses to perform her oracle duties successfully. She anticipated that would be her first failure.

A strong scent of sweat tickled Gonivein's nose. She turned to the temple entrance. A skinny old woman stood there, looking around with wide, reverent eyes. Her chiton was little more than a dirty rag clinging to her bony frame. Long white hair lay over her shoulder in a messy braid. The veil shrouding her head was faded and frayed at the edges. With trembling fingers, she clutched at a linen wrap draped across her body. It looked designed to carry something, like a baby, or perhaps clothes or food, but it was empty.

Gonivein's heart twisted. She stepped forward to offer a welcome, but before she could get close enough to say anything, the haughty priest emerged from the back room with a wrinkled nose.

"This is a sacred space, Kyria, not the public baths," he huffed, waving his hand at her as though she were a fly. "They're farther down. Turn left by the forum and keep going. You can't miss them."

This vile little man! Rage surged down Gonivein's arms. She clenched her fists, tensing to charge over to him as fast as her broken hip would allow.

Mandus wrapped gentle fingers around her elbow. "Wait. I think she'll surprise you."

The woman stiffened her spine. "You're the high priest?"

He clasped his hands in front of him. "I am."

"I am here for someone closer to the gods than you."

Gonivein would have laughed if not for the dangerous flare in the priest's eyes.

The woman craned her neck around the thick columns, searching. "I've been told there's a new Oracle of Apollo. Where is she?"

"The *oracle*," the priest hissed, tossing a glare at Gonivein. He was set on denying her authority as long as he could.

Mandus released her arm, and Gonivein hobbled forward. "I'm the oracle. How can I help?"

The woman smoothed her hands down the skirt of her dress. "I'm from the refugee camps." Tears glistened in the woman's proud eyes as they flickered to the hovering priest.

Sensing the woman didn't wish to disclose more in front of him, Gonivein took the woman's arm and led her outside. Her guards closed around her, but Gonivein waved them back.

"What is your name?"

"Agni."

"How can I help, Agni?"

"Forgive me, Basileia. I've misled you." Agni lowered her eyes and bowed her head. "It's not to Apollo that I request your intercession. It's to Basileus Kelric."

Unease knotted in Gonivein's stomach. "What do you want with my husband?"

"Dozens of us arrive every day from the *khora*. We've been herded into the lower ring of the city like sheep. There's no place for all of us. We're hungry. The children shiver at night." Agni clutched the linen wrap in a bony grip as her voice cracked. "We've made appeals to the archon, but our pleas go unanswered. A few priestesses and a handful of kind-hearted kyrioi have come to us, but our numbers overwhelm their charity. I beg you to ask the basileus for help. We need food, blankets, medicine, shelter. We came here to escape a violent death from Charixes, but many of us are wondering if that would be preferable to this."

Horror tightened Gonivein's throat. She considered finding Kelric right now and bringing this to his attention. *He must help them.*

But how could he not already know? She thought of his foul temper that morning. Could this have had a hand in it? Regardless, trying to say anything to him before they had resolved their own issues would likely end in disaster. But maybe…

A smile spread across her face. *I could help this woman.* It would ease Kelric's burdens. Maybe give her life meaning. She'd promised Loric she would do something that mattered. She owed him this.

Gonivein gently squeezed Agni's arm. "Show me the camp."

"Basileia…" The guard stepped forward with a stern look. "Our orders are to—"

"Ensure I'm protected while I receive my training from Mandus?" Gonivein eyed the old scholar watching them from the doorway. "I believe the scholar has much to teach me in the lower city today."

Mandus grinned. "Indeed. An oracle is duty-bound to those who worship the god she serves." He winked at Agni.

The guard merely sighed and bowed his head. Gonivein was relieved there wouldn't be an argument this time.

"Lead the way, Agni," Gonivein said, then hobbled to her litter.

The guards lifted Gonivein and followed the old woman.

Mandus grasped the rail of her seat to keep pace. "Well done, Gonivein," he murmured. "I may have an easier task preparing you for your duties than I thought."

Warmth flooded Gonivein at his praise—the first time she'd ever received it.

Citizens stepped aside as they made their way toward the outer wall. The statue of Aphrodite gleamed from her pedestal in the agora's center—a vision of serenity and loveliness. The craftsmanship was exquisite, but Gonivein could see no resemblance to herself in the beautiful features. There was a time when she might have, but that was before she understood the rot in her soul. She stared at her hands.

Outside the agora, a towering bronze statue of Poseidon presided over the crossroads. The main road continued on a few more paces to the gates of the city, where guards checked travelers with their carts and wares and made a note of their business. Branching to the left and running parallel along the outer wall was the path to the lower city. Agni led the way.

Pristine walls and swept streets faded into derelict, dirty conditions. Debris and animal droppings littered the road. Bones of fish and empty shells of oysters long since eaten were pounded into the cracks of the cobblestones from years of hooves and wagon wheels. Terracotta roofs were chipped, walls were stained by years of dirt, shutters creaked or hung crookedly from windows, retaining walls crumbled.

An overwhelming stench of sweat and urine was the first sign they were close to their destination. Poorly constructed lean-tos stood at haphazard angles all around the lower plaza and against the outer wall of the city. Dirty faces and bone-thin bodies peered out from them, looking scared and hungry. Still more thronged her guards, pressing toward her couch with palms upturned, anxious to receive a scrap or handful of something to extend their miserable existence.

The wails of children met her ears as she glided through the camp. Horror tightened her lungs the deeper they went. There were dozens of people here, with nowhere to go and no way to know if they would ever see their families again. Gonivein's chest ached at the frailty and fear surrounding her. Flashes of her escape across the plains only weeks ago surfaced, stealing her breath. How much more terrifying would it have been if she were a child?

Agni led them to the center of a crowded plaza and stopped.

A few Golpathian guards stood watch nearby, the glittering points of their spears enough to keep the throng orderly. She spied clusters of acolytes from the temples of Hephaestus and Artemis distributing alms. Their banners floated over the sea of squalor further down the slope. Gonivein was annoyed that Apollo's banner was nowhere to be seen. She would remedy that. Several citizens from higher in the city had come to help, too, distinguished by their clean—albeit modest—clothes.

Gonivein motioned for her guards to lower the litter and stood shakily. "What can I do, Agni?"

Agni spread her hands wide, gesturing to the crowd. Her lips moved helplessly, but no words came out.

No words were needed. Gonivein could see the problems plainly enough. Nearly everyone here was under ten summers or over fifty, or else had a baby at their breast or a toddler on their hip. They had left their homes to seek safety from Charixes' tyranny.

Safety that her presence in Golpathia jeopardized.

'There have been demands that I surrender you and Dargos to Charixes—the citizens are afraid of his retaliation.' Kelric's words held new meaning as Gonivein stared at the downtrodden faces. Her role in their misfortune weighed heavily. Would these people have

felt the need to flee their homes if Kelric had agreed to his councilmen's demands? She held tightly to her crutch, her hip aching more than usual. Her eyes stung.

I will make this right.

Her gaze fell on the dried-up fountain near Agni. It was large, almost as long as a full-grown man, nearly two feet deep, and edged by a wall as wide as her hand. It would do nicely for the plan forming in her mind.

She turned to her guard and removed her purse from her belt. The coins inside jangled as she held it up. "I need you to return to the agora and acquire some things."

CHAPTER 23

KELRIC

KELRIC RAISED HIS KNUCKLES AND knocked on the wooden door. It opened a moment later and Archon Tryphus' ten-year-old son appeared. His eyes widened before he dipped his head in a bow.

"Basileus, it is an honor. Please come in." The boy stepped aside to allow Kelric entry.

Kelric moved past him into an elegant atrium. His feet scuffed against a mosaic of waves spiralling outward from the center of the floor. An alcove carved into the wall beside the door housed statuettes of the Olympians Zeus, Hera, and Helinthia. Hooks on the opposite wall held the family's cloaks. Beside those, Tryphus' military shield and spear were displayed.

"I'll get Father for you, Kyrios," the boy said, hurrying away.

Kelric watched him go. He had the same confident gait of his father, the same quiet, contemplative expression in his brows. He was still clearly a youth, but the muscles in his arms were already filling out. Archon Tryphus must train with him frequently.

An unfamiliar longing stirred in Kelric's belly. What would it feel like to have a son? Especially one as respectful and obedient as Tryphus'.

He shook the thought away as his archon appeared in the entryway.

"Basileus! I was just about to ride for Theskyra. What can I do for you?" There was an urgency to Tryphus' tone.

Kelric's lip curled in satisfaction that he was inconveniencing Tryphus with this visit. He had planned to be brief, but the temptation to drag it out longer enticed him. He pulled the kerchief from his pocket, the image of the white lily reigniting his rage. "Explain why I found this on my wife's pillow this morning."

Tryphus' eyes widened. He stepped forward, glancing over his shoulder as though fearing his son or wife would see. "Come with me, Basileus." He turned quickly and walked deeper into the house.

Kelric followed him to the villa's inner courtyard. Sunlight shined brightly through the open roof. Smells of mint, basil, and thyme wafted from the plants around the cistern at the center. Tryphus opened the first door on the left and ushered Kelric inside.

Tryphus' andron was cramped, with one window and three couches surrounding a small table. "Sit," he said, opening the shutters and peering outside before grabbing an amphora from the corner and pouring two cups with water. He set them on the table and scooted one toward Kelric. "May I see it?"

Kelric relinquished the cloth and accepted the cup, draining the contents in three gulps. He hadn't realized how thirsty being angry made him. He wanted to strangle Tryphus. His archon was supposed to ensure the protection of the Basileus' villa, his household, the city, and the villages across the khora. Tryphus had failed miserably. Kelric had half a mind to order his execution, but he sensed Tryphus had more to offer alive than as carrion for Hades' birds. He had served Raleon for over a decade. That knowledge would be hard to replace.

"This was on the basileia's pillow?"

"Yes, and I was lying beside her all night. How did they get into my room? Onto the grounds at all? You have men stationed on the perimeter. Explain to me how this happened without your knowledge. Unless you want to confess that you knew."

Harsh furrows appeared in Tryphus' brow. "Of course I didn't know. I had the guard doubled after what happened with Alypius. No one would have gotten through last night without my knowledge."

"Then one of your guards must have let him in," Kelric accused.

Tryphus' eyes narrowed. "Or perhaps it's one of your household."

Kelric scoffed, feeling that jab a little too close to home. Had Tryphus known his father was a Leirion? Was Tryphus one himself? "Just who are you accusing? Euanthe? My *wife*?"

Tryphus merely shook his head, wisely discontinuing that line of questioning, and handed the kerchief back to Kelric. "Whoever he is, if he didn't slit your throat, then he wants something from you."

"I don't care what *he* wants. *I* want him found and brought to me. I don't like being toyed with."

Tryphus sighed, tapping his finger against his cup. "I've been informed that even the Leirion do not know the identities of everyone in their ranks."

Kelric sensed Tryphus knew much more, but wasn't sure how to get it out of him.

"This Leirion may be the one behind the vandalism of your statue."

Kelric's fists clenched, fury boiling in his veins. "I will flay him alive."

Tryphus' finger traced the rim of his cup. "The Leirion draw power from fear. They fan it like flames in the direction they want to force change. Whoever this man is, be assured he has considerable power and influence."

Kelric resisted the urge to slam his cup down. Dargos had warned him that, as a new leader, people would try to manipulate him. It was one piece of counsel he actually appreciated from his brother-in-law. He and Dargos had more differences than the colors of a sunset, but Dargos had been a basileus for far longer, and this warning was one Kelric had kept close.

"That," Tryphus pointed at the kerchief lying across Kelric's knee, "was a warning. Until we find the one responsible, I advise caution."

As much as Kelric hated it, Tryphus was right. He couldn't help but rebel against the idea, anyway. Ceding any ground to this threat would be a sign of weakness.

"It's one of the council members, I know it." Kelric recalled the sneering faces of Alypius and Ephastes, the cowed expressions of the other men at the feast, and Gadnor's battered face this morning. Though, Kelric wasn't as upset about that as he probably should be. He had a feeling his little brother had brought that upon himself. He had his heart set on becoming a hero, and Kelric had warned him he wasn't ready. Gadnor's stupidity, and all the consequences that followed, were his own fault.

Still, Alypius' audacity to resort to violence at his wedding! It was too bold.

"That seems plausible, given their positions of authority. But if it's true, then there is more than one Leirion. I personally escorted all of your guests from the villa grounds. One of them could not have left this in your room."

The idea that there was more than one Leirion wreaking havoc sent a chill through Kelric. How dare they ruin his wedding. Threaten his wife. Challenge his authority!

He slammed his cup down on the table. The amphora wobbled. "I will not hand my wife to Charixes to appease cowards hiding in the shadows." He didn't care how much influence these Leirion had—they would never convince him to give her up. He would not lose her.

Memories of his father leaning over Gonivein, pressing the pillow over her face as she kicked and struggled beneath him, invaded his thoughts. His stomach soured. He swallowed, tasting bile. *I murdered him for her.*

He would murder every Leirion who tried to take her from him.

Tryphus swirled the water in his cup, seeming to contemplate his next words carefully. "It's probable it's Dargos he wants, not Gonivein."

"I will not break my alliance," Kelric stated flatly. "Gonivein would never speak to me again, and Dargos would nullify our marriage immediately."

"You must consider what is best for your people." Tryphus' voice was even, but Kelric could sense the archon's frustration building. "Thanks to your wedding, Charixes has justification to march to our gates—it would be too easy for this Leirion to prey on the fears of your people and incite violence in your streets. There are already people pouring in from across the polis. Did you read the report from Tetra? Golpathia will not survive a war on two fronts."

Heat crept up Kelric's neck. He'd forgotten about the report. Had forgotten why he cared about reports in the first place. On his rides across the polis, Tryphus gathered crucial information Kelric needed to prepare for war: the number of fighting-age men, how many of them were trained for combat, harvest bounty, disease, births, deaths, and any major complaints the kubernao wished to address with the basileus. Kelric scowled, shaking his head. How could he be expected to care about the concerns of outlying villages when his city—his capital—was in disarray? His *wife* threatened in their bed?

"What do they want me to do? Hand the woman I love to Charixes and beg for his mercy?" Kelric's imagination ran wild with horrible things Charixes might do. Let his army have their way with her. Parade her in chains through jeering, hateful crowds. Have her publicly tortured. Make her a doula in his house. In his bed.

Kelric would never subject her to any of those possibilities.

"I would rather see this whole city razed to the ground than bow to the whims of a faceless fool."

Tryphus' eyes flashed. "You can't be a spoiled brat anymore, Kelric. You are the basileus. Your duty is to your people, not your pric—"

Kelric sprang from his couch faster than the older man could blink. He grabbed the archon's tunic and jerked him close, bumping the small table between them. The amphora fell over, and the quiet *glugging* of its contents pouring onto the floor filled the silence. Neither moved to pick it up.

Kelric debated making this bothersome fool swallow his own teeth. He hadn't provided any useful information to this predicament, no guarantees of protection, not even an apology. He recalled Tryphus' soft stance toward the mob who'd thrown shit on Gonivein's likeness, his advocacy of their protests. Perhaps his archon was enabling this Leirion, or secretly supporting him. Maybe Tryphus *was* the Leirion.

"I think you should focus your attention on finding the man threatening your basileia's life and spend a little less time questioning my loyalties." Kelric shoved him away. "I could have you executed for your negligence. Don't tempt me."

Tryphus smoothed his tunic, then stooped to pick up the amphora and set it back on the table. His face was pinched in anger, but at least he showed the proper restraint. "I'll double the guards and put my men on full alert throughout the city."

"I want all talk of unrest, any inkling of displeasure for me, my wife, or Dargos investigated fully."

Tryphus shoved the cork back into the spout with an audible *squeak* that made Kelric wince. "As you wish."

Kelric moved toward the door. "Pick someone else to go to Theskyra. I want you here until the culprit, or cul*prits,* have been found and executed. The Leirion will not gain a foothold here. They will not undermine my authority over my own city, over my wife! I alone will decide what's best for Golpathia."

Tryphus bowed his head. "Yes, Basileus."

CHAPTER 24

GADNOR

THE ACHING IN GADNOR'S RIBS roused him. Pain tightened his lungs, making it hard to breathe. He wasn't happy about his agony, but he was glad it had freed him from his nightmare. Only fragments of the horrors remained as awareness of his waking surroundings took hold: a pair of outstretched arms that he couldn't reach, no matter how hard he ran or fought.

As he struggled to sit up on his bed, that also slipped away, and only a deep, hollow anguish remained.

His shoulders felt tight. He touched them, feeling a dried, crusty substance over the gashes in his flesh. When he pulled his hand back, the smell of turmeric and marigold lingered on his fingertips. Forluna's medicines.

Sunlight squeezing through the cracks in the shutters told him it was afternoon. He'd probably slept through the midday meal. He was glad no one had come to get him. Breakfast had been brutal with everyone staring at him, judging him, probably laughing at him when he wasn't looking. Not that he wasn't used to that by now. But Kelric's fury had been the worst of it. Gadnor had never seen him so angry. He'd half expected to earn another set of bruises—not that he wouldn't have deserved them. Kelric hadn't wanted to make him strategos, after all, and Gadnor had failed as miserably as predicted. Kelric had probably stormed out to promote someone else, instead.

At Forluna's encouragement, Gadnor had gone to rest after breakfast, welcoming the opportunity to escape into the shadows again. He stood, legs shaky, and opened the window. He filled his lungs with the salty sea air, and was surprised when he felt a little better. The day he'd been dreading for weeks was finally behind him. Undesirable outcome or not, it was done.

When he turned back around, the brightness flooding the room seemed to have banished some of his hopelessness. He splashed water on his face from the bowl on the vanity, fingertips brushing lightly over the scar that ran across the bridge of his nose and left cheek. He dragged his fingers through his hair to pull the tangles free.

A knock at the door froze him in place. Probably Forluna coming to check his wounds.

A mess of tousled brown curls framed the face that greeted him, and a lump lodged in Gadnor's throat.

Tor's fist was clenched, and Gadnor steeled himself for a blow. He deserved it from Tor even more than from Kelric. Gadnor recalled his spiteful and dismissive words yesterday, and regret roiled within him. *I told him to leave.*

Just where, exactly, would Tor have gone if he'd listened? Gadnor was relieved he hadn't.

Tor opened his palm to reveal a tiny scroll tied with a leather string.

Gadnor stared, surprised and confused.

"The hawk came," Tor said, holding his hand out.

Gadnor took the tiny object, his mind trying to register too many things at once. Tor was here, and he wasn't angry—at least, he didn't seem to be. The hawk had returned. There was a message. *From the princess?*

"Aren't you going to open it?" Tor asked.

Gadnor's neck and cheeks warmed. Somehow, that thought

hadn't occurred to him yet. He retreated inside his room, holding the door open for Tor to follow.

He sank onto the bed, twisting the scroll between his fingers, scared to read the words inside now that he'd made such a colossal failure of his mission. *She still doesn't know I'm the one she agreed to marry.* What would she have thought of his performance yesterday if she'd witnessed it?

He felt sick.

Failure or not, there was no backing out of his destiny. He sighed and picked at the knot, expecting it to come free easily, but it didn't. Time slowed to a crawl as he struggled to loosen it, Tor's amused eyes watching him.

"I had to cut it off the hawk's leg," Tor offered, but it didn't quell Gadnor's embarrassment.

His face was on fire by the time he finally pulled the first knot free. Lithaneva must have really been concerned it would be lost. Finally, the leather thong released its grip, and he unraveled the tiny strip of paper.

From Hameth's shores, where the Earthshaker dwells
The horns of war will blow.
The lands will quake, the seas will swell
When the tears of Demeter cease to flow.

Tor sank onto the bed next to him and peered over his shoulder at the words, one eyebrow raised. "She sent an ode?"

Gadnor read it again. Coupled with the intricacy of the knots, he sensed the phrasing was one more precautionary layer. He should be more careful with his own messages, too. But what did her words mean?

"Hameth is an ancient city in the far north," Gadnor mused. "It was destroyed by an earthquake a couple centuries ago and abandoned."

"Perhaps it's not abandoned anymore," Tor offered. "The lands will quake, the seas will swell. Some kind of warning?"

"When the tears of Demeter cease to flow." Gadnor tapped the pad of his finger against the corner of the paper. "The end of winter is the spring equinox."

"So something is coming from Hameth on the spring equinox?"

Gadnor shrugged. "That could be one interpretation."

"What could be coming?"

Gadnor shook his head, his mind spinning. "I don't know, but I think she sent us this to find out. It has to be important. We should tell Kelric."

Tor nodded, but neither of them moved.

"I'm sorry about yesterday," Gadnor said, the lump in his throat making his words warble. "Nothing that happened was your fault, but that's how I treated you. I shouldn't have told you to leave." He drew in a deep breath and then let it out, resigned. "I'm the one to blame for this mess, and somehow I've got to figure out how to fix it." *Before the spring equinox.*

His only interaction with Lithaneva had been very brief at her wedding, but she hadn't struck him as the poetic type. If she'd been compelled to send them a warning in verse, then there must be a lot at stake if the wrong person found out about it. Whatever it was, she probably expected the hero of Helinthia to win renown thwarting it. That last thought filled him with dread. "If I can."

Tor reached down to the floor. When he righted himself a moment later, he cradled something in the cup of his hand. Beady eyes peered between Tor's fingers. Tiny whiskers wiggled at him.

A mouse?

Gadnor raised his eyebrows, then winced at the pain lancing through his swollen eye at the small movement.

Tor rubbed his thumb across the mouse's round back. "My father saw every creature that crossed our path as food or a resource for skins. He was always afraid we would starve or freeze. Even when we had enough, he wanted more. When he found out I could speak to animals, he wanted me to use my powers against them so he could kill them easily. But I didn't want to. I didn't want to betray them like that."

Gadnor's heart ached at the pain in Tor's words, the tremble in his hands.

The mouse combed its face and ears with tiny pink hands, then rubbed its head against Tor's thumb. Tor watched it as he continued, a tremor in his voice. "Sometimes…" He cleared his throat. "Sometimes he would beat me until I did what he wanted. Cana… not even she could stop him."

Gadnor remained still, trapped between the urge to say something comforting and the fear that Tor would stop talking if he did.

"The goddess gave me the power to speak to animals. She entrusted their safety to me." A muscle raced along Tor's smooth, angular jaw as he fought his emotions. "I failed a lot before I finally found the courage to do the right thing."

Gadnor could finally breathe normally. "How did you find it?"

Tor leaned back down to the floor and released the mouse, who scurried off and disappeared into the dark corner. "I surrounded myself with lions."

A shudder went through Gadnor as he remembered the lion's jaws closing around his arm, ripping the flesh from the bone. His scars itched, and he rubbed at them harder. He tore his gaze away, regret sharp in his chest. "I'm sorry about what happened to them, and for my part in it."

"It wasn't your fault," Tor answered quietly.

"I was the reason the Fury was there."

Tor sighed, rubbing his palms. "That's not why I told you the story."

Gadnor's cheeks burned.

Tor's voice softened. "I'm not trying to tear you down."

Gadnor swallowed against the lump in his throat. Dargos, Forluna, and Gonivein had expressed the same sentiment, but he was more confused than comforted by it. He hadn't done anything to earn their affection. Not yet, anyway.

"I thought that only I could protect Artemis' animals," Tor continued. "I thought because she chose me, I had to be strong enough to do it by myself. But that was a lie I convinced myself was true, because it was easier to fail alone than to believe I was worthy of help."

Gadnor stared at him, feeling more than a little targeted by the similar experience.

"I know you don't believe it yet, but you're worthy of help, too."

Before he could respond, Tor stood and disappeared out the door. Gadnor's heart beat wildly in his breast, and for the first time in a long time, he didn't feel quite so alone.

CHAPTER 25

DARGOS

ARGOS SAT ON THE PORTICO steps, staring across the courtyard and through the open gates of the villa grounds. He'd thought to go to the agora, buy something worthy of an offering, and take it to the temple of Helinthia. He craved the connection to his goddess and the familiarity the ritual provided.

When he'd set out to Branitus' wedding three weeks ago, he'd been so sure of the future, of his role in the world and the goddess' favor guiding him. The shocking brutality of Tyldan's destruction was the first time he'd questioned that reality. Somehow, after learning the heir's identity and finding two new oracles, he'd allowed himself to overlook the goddess' absence at Tyldan. He'd seen it not as a warning to desist, but as justification to press on in his quest to overthrow the anax. Perhaps some divine working his mortal mind couldn't fathom had pulled Helinthia away from his innocent citizens.

Now, he couldn't decide if it was fear of running into Forluna in the agora that kept him grounded to the marble steps, or something else. What if he gave his offering to Helinthia's priestess and didn't feel the goddess' blessing? Or worse, what if he realized he'd never felt it? What if it had all been in his head?

"Dargos!"

Gadnor's voice behind him jolted him from his thoughts.

"What?" Dargos' tone was a little sharper than he'd intended, but Gadnor didn't seem to notice as he hurried up.

"The hawk arrived. Look." Gadnor waved a tiny scroll in his face.

Dargos unraveled it. A new revelation streamed into his mind as the words on the tiny paper danced before his unfocused eyes. What did Lithaneva's involvement in this rebellion mean if Helinthia was to blame for all of this? Did the princess suspect her goddess could not be trusted? Worse, did she *know*? Was this alliance—this rebellion—not as righteous as he'd believed? Would overthrowing Charixes even stop the famine?

He thought again of the victims he'd buried in his village of Tyldan, wondering if their deaths were all for nothing.

"Dargos?"

Dargos looked up.

"I thought we should ask Gonivein what her interpretation might be. Since she's Apollo's oracle, maybe she could get a feeling about what it means."

Dargos read the paper and handed it back to Gadnor, nodding. Helinthia aside, one thing was clear: Charixes was planning something sinister in the region of Hameth. He stood. "I'll find Gonivein. You find Kelric."

Gadnor nodded, and Dargos bounded down the steps toward the agora.

What could Charixes be doing in Hameth? Nothing was there but the ruins of a civilization destroyed by Poseidon's wrath centuries ago. Much like the Forest of Shades to the west, spirits were believed to hide in the mist that crept over the forest floor. Superstition and strange howls had kept most people from seeking to re-inhabit it.

Dargos furrowed his brow. Perhaps Charixes wanted the timber. Or the game. Was the famine finally clawing at the borders of Ninenarn, forcing Charixes to seek higher hunting grounds?

Whatever the anax was doing, Lithaneva meant for them to know of it. Prepare for it. Maybe try to stop it. Gadnor was right to seek out Gonivein's guidance. Who better to unravel a mystery of the future than the oracle of the prophecy god?

When he arrived at the temple of Apollo, the litter and Gonivein's guards were nowhere to be seen.

The high priest sniffed at Dargos. "They went off with some filthy wretch."

Dargos' brow furrowed. He'd thought Gonivein was exaggerating when she'd mentioned the priest of Apollo had a rotten temperament. "Where?"

"How should I know?" The priest turned to go.

Dargos grabbed the man's elbow, a sudden spark of impatience seizing him. "What do you hope to gain from interfering with a god's business?"

The priest's eyes widened in a brief flash of fear. He yanked his arm away and straightened his tunic. "Until she's confirmed, she is but a *woman*. Check the refugee camps in the lower city. I'm sure you'll be right at home."

Dargos stared in shock as the priest stormed off. Blood rushed in his ears at the vehemence, the disrespect, the unwarranted hostility. He had half a mind to call after the man, but turned away. An altercation wasn't worth his time. *Apollo will put him in his place soon enough.*

For Gonivein's sake, he hoped that was true.

Dargos started down the steps and turned onto the main street. Several citizens stopped along the roadside to stare. He pretended not to notice. He wasn't near enough to understand everything they were murmuring, but the venom in their tone carried clearly in the few words he overheard. No doubt they blamed him for the refugees he was going to see.

He was halfway through the agora when a figure moving through the crowd drew his eye. He only caught a glimpse before it disappeared again. Something in the purposeful stride, the wave of brown hair…

Forluna.

He froze, unease gripping him. Part of him wanted to keep walking. Following her might force the conversation he wasn't ready to have. Yet something about the way she'd dashed off spoke of urgency. A cord of fear rippled into him, as though some tether bound his soul to hers. A shiver rolled down his spine.

Dargos pushed through the crowd. "Forluna!" He wove between shoppers, unapologetically bumping into several people. Curses and scowls followed in his wake, but he didn't slow down. His eyes searched frantically for her, for danger, for a Leirion. They had never stopped hunting her. It was why she had denied a life with him for five years. Had her fears come true? Was someone, even now, pushing their way through the crowd to get to her?

Dargos clutched his dagger, pushing and searching, panic zinging through his limbs as though Zeus himself had struck him with a bolt of lightning. "Forluna!"

He pushed one more body out of his way and stopped.

She stood at the end of an aisle of stalls, staring up the tall cliff face blocking her way. Merchants flanked her on either side. There was no through traffic here. "Forluna."

She spun, her brown eyes glazed in terror. Her chest heaved, glistening with sweat. Strands of hair floated around her face, wrenched from the careful braid she'd woven this morning.

At the sight of her so distressed, Dargos' heart plunged into his gut. His resentment over their quarrel scattered from his mind.

"Dargos," she choked out. Her eyes never lingered on him. They scanned the crowd instead.

He reached her and took her hands in his. They were trembling. "What's happened?" He gathered her against his chest with one hand and turned around to search the crowd for… what? "Who is chasing you?"

He would gut them.

"I…" Her voice sounded so strained and frail. "I saw…"

When she didn't finish, he pulled away slightly to look at her face. Her fear ripped his heart.

"Saw what?"

Her brown eyes met his. Conflict swirled within their depths.

He squeezed her shoulder, shaking it gently. "*What?*"

Forluna blinked and gazed into the crowd a final time. Then she laid her palm against his chest, pushing herself upright. The place where her body had pressed against his felt ice cold. He wanted to crush her to him again, let her warmth seep back in, melt beneath his skin. He never wanted to let her go.

"I saw the hawk. I was trying to get back to the villa, but I…" Her eyes froze on something behind him.

Dargos whipped around again, but saw nothing.

"I just got turned around in the crowd." Her voice was calmer now, her breathing even.

He studied her. He knew she was withholding something. He was too familiar with her half-truth mannerisms not to recognize them, but she wouldn't tell him anything until she was ready.

She continued to stare around him, over him, through him, anywhere but *at* him. The tension from the previous night crept between them. Now wasn't the time to resolve it, but he wanted her by his side.

"I'm on my way to find Gonivein."

Forluna nodded in understanding.

"Will you come with me, or wait back at the villa?"

"I'll come with you," she said, looping an arm through his.

He squeezed her elbow to his body, securing her place beside him. They walked in silence to the refugee camp.

A pit opened in Dargos' stomach at the squalor stretching before them. Every possible inch of space had been claimed by a weary woman, elderly person, or child. The stench of too many bodies was stifling.

Forluna gasped softly beside him, her hand on his arm tightening.

To the left, an entourage of priestesses stood in a circle of eager refugees. "Gather, good people," said one. She wore a gray, shapeless chiton, but the finely embroidered sash around her shoulders suggested she was the high priestess. Women and children thronged eagerly around her and her attendants. "Gather and receive Helinthia's blessings."

The children squirmed, and some of the littlest ones cried. But for the most part, everyone tried to remain orderly as blankets, clothes, and bags of food were distributed into their upturned palms.

One of the younger acolytes noticed Dargos and Forluna and approached.

"Are you here to help?"

Dargos couldn't get his tongue to move for a moment. His conscience would disown him if he said no, yet that was the truth. He was here for Gonivein.

"We're here to assess and see what supplies are needed," Forluna answered.

Dargos should have known she would have already set her mind to this. He squeezed her hand appreciatively. "Is the Oracle of Apollo here?"

The girl pointed down the street, where a wisp of smoke was rising above the crowd. "A makeshift kitchen has been assembled in the center of the plaza. The oracle is there. Will you be so kind as to take some items to her?" She hurried over to where a cart was hitched to a sleepy-looking donkey. Several crates were arranged inside. She dragged one to the ledge and poised to lift it.

Dargos quickly intervened, releasing Forluna's arm to grab the crate and pull it to his chest. It was heavy! "Of course."

The girl smiled, tucking a strand of hair behind her ear. "Thank you, Kyrios."

Dargos nodded dumbly and started off in the direction she'd indicated. Forluna fell into step beside him. A tiny wisp of a smile played on her lips. She kept whatever thought had just popped into her head to herself, but Dargos felt some of the tension between them slip away.

The wails of children met his ears as they picked their way through the camp. Horror constricted his chest the deeper they went.

'She craved power more than she cared for her own people.'

Dargos had awoken this morning intending to renew his faith in his goddess with an offering, hoping her blessing would breathe life back into his inner fire. That goal seemed a frivolity in the face of this desolation—desolation *his* actions had wrought upon Golpathia's citizens. How much worse were his own people faring back in Shallinath? Were they suffering under Charixes' occupation? Were they even alive?

The smell of roasting meat and spices rose above the stench of refuse, and he knew they were getting close to their destination. He stopped to readjust his grip on the crate and catch his breath.

Ahead was the plaza with a dried-up fountain at its center. Instead of clean water, the pit roared with a hearty fire. On one side, a swine roasted on a spit. On the other, a large cauldron full of bubbling lentils was suspended on a long metal rod. Along the tiled edge of the fountain were dozens of tiny bread loaves, baking from the heat of the coals. It was the most efficient setup Dargos could have hoped to see in a place like this.

Gonivein sat on a stool nearby. She pulled blobs of dough from a large wooden bowl in her lap, rolled them into buns, and placed them on the edge of the fire pit to bake. An elderly woman sat beside her, critiquing her technique as she mended a tunic with a bone needle.

"Gonivein?"

His little sister jumped at his voice, a ball of dough tumbling from her hands and plopping down amongst the coals. "Styx," she cursed, quickly snatching the dough back and bouncing it between her palms to cool.

The woman *tsked*, but her lip curled into an amused smile.

"Sorry," Dargos said. "Where do you want me to put this?"

"Just set it there." Gonivein jerked her head to the side as she rounded out the slightly blackened dough ball and plopped it into an empty spot on the edge of the fountain.

A boy no older than six summers hurried up to them. His ragged tunic was streaked with soot and dirt, but his hands were clean. Gonivein smiled down at him and pointed across the flames to the other side of the fountain. "Those over there should be done, I can see they're browned. Take one to your mother, too, and tell her the soup is almost ready."

The child nodded and skipped off.

"Did you organize all of this?" Dargos asked, gawking stupidly around the plaza. One woman stirred the lentils with a long wooden spoon. Rows of more women sat around in a circle, weaving baskets, mending clothes, grinding wheat. Children played together, far enough away from the fire that they wouldn't be at risk of being burned or disrupting the cooking with their antics.

Gonivein's eyes cast downward, red tingeing her cheeks. "I should have done much more before now."

"No one wanted to step up before the oracle came," said the older woman. "Too afraid to draw unwanted attention." Her yellowed eyes peered up at a group of finely dressed men standing at the border between the camp and the middle city. They watched the gathering with sour expressions.

Forluna immediately turned her back to the group and began weaving through the rows of women, gravitating to the sick or injured.

That cord of fear rippled through Dargos again. "Who are they?"

The woman pursed her lips, returning her attention to the garment she was mending.

Gonivein answered instead as she grabbed more dough to knead, avoiding looking at the men. "I'm not sure, but I think they work for some of the more prominent kyrioi, maybe a council member. Agni informs me they have been less than kind to the people here. Even badgering others who have come to help." She nodded to various groups of people scattered around the plaza. "I plan to have words with Kelric about it."

Dargos' chest swelled with pride and admiration for his little sister. How changed she was from the girl he'd left behind in Shallinath. Her crutch leaning against the fountain beside her and her thin, bony hands pinching and prodding the tiny balls of dough were jarring reminders of her cruel transition into womanhood. A transformation marked by pain and loss, rather than the joy and hope he'd always wanted for her. His heart wrenched.

Dargos doubted his brother-in-law would do anything about the vulturous men. With the Council actively challenging his authority, Kelric would be loath to risk escalation on behalf of poor women and children. But if anyone could convince Kelric, it would be Gonivein.

The girl stirring the lentils set her spoon down and pulled an amphoriskos from the crate. She popped its cork and sniffed it, then grinned. "Salted oil!" She stepped closer to the roasting swine and drizzled some of the savory liquid across its back. Droplets ran down the hot flesh, sizzling and releasing a mouth-watering aroma.

Dozens of eyes lifted to stare at the food, tongues licking cracked lips.

"Has anyone come from Shallinath?" Dargos asked now.

Gonivein shook her head, biting her lip as she pinched another dough ball into shape.

Dargos' heart sank. The rest of his queries died on his lips as the desolation seeped back in. His admiration for Gonivein wasn't enough to fill the void in his soul where his purpose and conviction had once been. Before yesterday, he might have been able to see a sign from Helinthia in the work being done here. Now, all he saw was the goddess' absence, her indifference.

Dargos recalled every sign he'd seen, or thought he'd seen, which had guided his decisions to this moment. Had they all been figments of his imagination? A wishful hope that his life held meaning—that he had been spared from a deadly plague for a higher purpose?

If what Forluna said was true…

Helinthia was never there at all.

He felt light-headed as the weight of that realization settled on him.

"Why have you come here, Dargos?" Gonivein asked now, pulling him back from his dark thoughts.

"The hawk arrived."

Her brow furrowed.

"We need your oracle eyes."

Gonivein glanced around at the camp, hesitant.

Agni touched her arm and smiled gently. "You've done more than we could have hoped, Basileia. We'll be all right, at least until tomorrow."

Gonivein nodded, but didn't look convinced. "I will return soon."

The girl stirring the lentils took the bowl of dough from Gonivein, and Dargos stepped forward to take his sister's hand.

She smiled gratefully, leaning on him as she stood and secured her crutch.

"This is incredible, Gonie," Dargos murmured.

Her head ducked.

Dargos frowned. The little sister he knew would have giggled in delight at such praise, perhaps returned with some snarky remark such as "about time you noticed," or "did you expect less?" How stingy he'd been with words of encouragement and reward, always finding a reason to chastise her instead. There had been so much to praise her for that he'd never acknowledged. He had taken the simple joys of family for granted. Was his opportunity to hear her laughter behind them? His throat closed up at the thought.

She climbed onto her couch, and her guards lifted her onto their shoulders.

Forluna's fingers threaded through his. They still trembled, and he sensed it was just as much to do with whatever had happened in the agora as it was her heartache for these people. Instantly, he squeezed her hand, wanting to reassure her. She pressed closer to his side.

Her unexpected tenderness pushed the tears he'd been trying to

hold back over his eyelids and down his cheeks.
I've been such a fool.

CHAPTER 26

GONIVEIN

GONIVEIN'S HIP THROBBED AS SHE settled back against the cushion on her litter. Mandus had tried to convince her to rest—that seemed ages ago. He'd invited her to accompany him back to the villa, but she had waved him off, intent on staying for as long as it took to make the camp better than she'd found it. Despite Agni's assurance, she wasn't sure she'd accomplished her goal. But she didn't have a choice now. Her oracle eyes were needed elsewhere.

The couch swayed and bobbed beneath her, allowing the exhaustion she'd been denying to wash over her body. There was no rest for her mind, however. It galloped with ideas on how she could help these people. Perhaps provide them more permanent accommodations. Her thoughts kept wandering to her wedding gifts. The answer lay in that exorbitant pile—she was sure of it. She eyed the vulturous men as she passed them. They remained at the fringes of the camp and still scowled at the innocent, ailing women and children, doing nothing to help. Well, if these arrogant, rich men felt themselves above kindness, she would turn their gifts into aid. The thought twisted her lips into a smile.

Her confirmation ceremony would delay her plans, but once that was over and she was officially the Oracle of Apollo, she could direct that pompous priest to help, too.

The confirmation. A twinge of panic fluttered in her chest. Mandus' careful instructions from this morning were a blank spot in her memory. Her focus on Agni and establishing a reliable means for food had consumed all her attention. What if she messed up the ceremony? Did something wrong? Offended Apollo? As the guards carried her through the streets, she latched onto the thought that all she needed to do was walk straight to the altar and do exactly what she was told—most of it would be explained during the ritual for the benefit of the crowd, anyway. All would be well if she could just pay attention.

When they arrived at the villa, Klymene was waiting at the top of the porch stairs, twisting her fingers nervously. She bowed, glancing between Gonivein and Dargos, as though unsure who she should address first.

Dargos held up a hand. "Where are we expected, Klymene?"

As Gonivein rose from her litter and positioned her crutch under her armpit, she eyed the girl. The doula's shaky gestures were worrying. Had Kelric done something else to her? Gonivein sighed in dismay at how easily that thought sprang to mind, but Kelric was more capable of harm than self-restraint.

"Basileia, Basileus." Klymene said, curtsying to each. "Everyone is assembled in Basileus Kelric's andron. He said to tell you to meet them there when you arrived." Klymene's eyes darted to the path that led through the side courtyard to Kelric's andron. "We should hurry. They're waiting."

Dargos offered Gonivein his arm, and she looped her free hand through it. Forluna followed closely behind. The nymph hadn't offered Gonivein a draught in several days. It seemed she had finally accepted that Gonivein didn't want the dulling tincture. Today, Gonivein would have welcomed the offer, but she didn't have the heart to say so.

They followed Klymene to the andron and knocked on the door.

"Thank you for escorting us," Gonivein said. "You may go. If Euanthe has nothing for you to do—"

"I hoped I could wait here for you, Basileia." Klymene's cheeks turned bright red as she fiddled with her hands. "Please."

Dargos raised an eyebrow.

Before Gonivein could think of what to say, the door opened. She managed a feeble nod as Dargos ushered her inside. Kelric, Gadnor, and Tor were already seated on the couches. This room had always been larger than most androns, but it felt cramped with this many people stuffed inside. Not even the open windows helped dispel the stagnant air.

"What's this about?" she asked, as she and Forluna sat side by side.

Kelric's jaw was clenched in fury. He didn't even look at her. Hurt pinched in her chest, but she swallowed it down.

"The hawk arrived carrying this note," Gadnor said, placing a tiny strip of paper into her open palm. "We wondered if it might mean something to you, as the Oracle of Apollo?"

Kelric folded his arms across his chest and rolled his eyes. Gadnor offered her an apologetic grimace, and she sensed he and Tor had exchanged aggressive words with her husband before her arrival. She had a sinking feeling that her assessment of the tiny paper would not support Kelric's opinion, whatever it was, and she dreaded his deepening displeasure. She took a deep breath, preparing herself.

As an oracle, she could not let fear of reprisal dissuade her from sharing the god's truths. She remembered that much from Mandus' lectures. And yet, conflict churned within her all the same. Husbands were the supplier of truths that wives weren't allowed to contradict. Would Kelric be understanding of her position? She glanced at him again. This time, his piercing gray eyes stared back, annoyed and impatient. *Doubtful.* There would be no discussing the camps tonight. Or anything, for that matter.

She took a deep breath and read the cryptic message to herself.

The words brought flashes of color behind her eyes. Adrenaline raced through her veins. Thunder roared in her ears.

"There are bodies in the water." The room blurred. Waves of red splashed onto the shore and receded, leaving behind men splayed and mangled on the sandy beach. "The walls are bathed in blood." The paintings of hydra and dolphins on either side of Golpathia's gates were cloven by sprays of gore. "The ground has turned to mud. Starving animals gorge on the dead."

Dargos' hand tightened on hers, and she opened her eyes, not even realizing she had closed them. The gaping mouths of everyone in the room startled her after such vivid images. Even Kelric's expression was one of alarm. She wasn't sure if that was better or worse.

"Thank you, Gonivein." Dargos' gaze remained steady on hers. He squeezed her hand and took the paper, then turned his attention to Kelric. "You need to assemble the Council. If Charixes is planning an assault on Golpathia, then you must prepare your citizens for war."

Fear constricted Gonivein's chest. Memories of buildings in flames and screaming mothers assaulted her. Pallas' wife, Yulie, bruised and bloodied, her dead son lying a few paces away. Gonivein's fingers instinctively grazed her neck, where the Ninenarn soldier's hands had tried to crush her throat. Loric, a dark shadow, hurled a spear through the air, flames flashing on the bronze tip before it plunged into their pursuer's chest. This danger was coming for Golpathia. Agni and the hundreds of others had been right to flee the villages.

"The Council will question how we learned of this." Kelric glared at the paper between Dargos' fingers.

"You can't tell them," Forluna said suddenly.

Kelric raised a brow at the forcefulness—or was it desperation?—of her tone. "I agree. But they may be less inclined to cooperate with urgency unless I give them something."

"I should go to Hameth," Gadnor said quietly. "See for myself what this threat is, and either stop it or bring proof back that will convince the Council to act."

Forluna met Gonivein's gaze, fear swirling in her eyes. She seemed to be waiting for Gonivein to say something to support Gadnor's idea. Gonivein considered her vision of the falcon surrounded by the other beasts, then the ode on the paper. Neither made her feel strongly for or against Gadnor's proposal.

"I'll call a meeting," Kelric said finally. "Golpathia is on a path of conflict with the anax. There's no escaping that, and everyone knows it. Perhaps suspicion of a threat will draw enough support for a small expeditionary force under the guise of cautionary exploration."

"Call it after the confirmation ceremony," Dargos suggested. "Seeing proof that your marriage has brought the voice of a god into their midst might make them more agreeable to your authority."

Kelric seemed to wrestle with something before he finally nodded. Gonivein waited for him to look at her, hoping for a clue that she hadn't angered him. But he avoided her gaze as he followed everyone out of the room. His cloak brushed against her shoulder as he passed, leaving her feeling cold, hollow, as though she were little more than a piece of furniture. She was eager to escape the confines of this tiny room and clear her head.

Klymene stood outside, waiting for Gonivein to emerge. She seemed excited to help Euanthe with the evening meal, which was already producing savory smells from the kitchen. Gonivein's stomach churned at the thought of eating. She was hardly able to drag herself to her bed before her strength gave out. She collapsed onto the wool mattress and pulled the furs around her.

She wanted to move past this animosity between her and Kelric. His aggression toward Klymene couldn't go unanswered, of course—the poor girl hadn't known she would startle him, and she couldn't safely stay here if Kelric did not promise to be more patient. But this festering tension helped no one, not Klymene, not Gonivein, and not the camps and the dozens of scared women and children confined there.

Gonivein pulled the blanket tighter, wondering how the conversation would go. Would he listen, or turn defensive? How quickly would it devolve into an argument? Did she even have the strength to argue with him?

She clenched her pillow tight, resisting the urge to scream into it. She shouldn't be having these doubts. She should feel comfortable approaching her husband.

But she didn't. The very thought sapped her of energy.

Gonivein focused on her breathing the way Forluna had taught her. *In. Out. Slow.*

I promised I wouldn't think the worst of him.

Perhaps he'd had a reason for grabbing Klymene in such a violent way. *But what could his reason be?* Gonivein had been the last person he had spoken to before he'd done it. The last thing he'd done—*they'd* done…

Heat burned her cheeks, hair rising on her skin as her thoughts wandered away, delving into their passion. Kelric's body pressed against her, around her, *in* her.

It had felt good. And yet, she'd been left wanting more.

But I should *want more.*

Then why did it seem like something was missing? Why had he become so angry? And what was making him cling to that rage?

What am I doing wrong? She stared up at the wooden beams in the ceiling, drained and defeated.

Waves crashed, gulls screamed, and she let the sobs out, succumbing to the ache.

Crash.

Scream.

Crash.

Scream.

The light faded from the room. Soon after, she heard the door creak open, then close again after a pause. Someone had come to alert her that dinner was ready—the smells of roasted meat and herbs were strong, but she didn't want to go. The thought of experiencing another meal, forcing herself to be the gracious hostess with so many thoughts jumbling in her head…

When no one said anything, she raised her head from the pillow just a little to glimpse the door, then sank back down, groaning at the throb behind her swollen eyes. Whoever it was had gone—blessedly deciding to leave her be.

A cricket chirped from somewhere near the window.

Chirr-up. Chirr-up.

The soothing song drowned out the waves. Masked the gulls. Soothed her mind.

The next thing she knew, Kelric's arm slid under her pillow, his body nestling against her back.

Now was her opportunity to speak. To ask. To learn what was wrong and fix it.

"I love you," Kelric whispered, smoothing the hair from her neck and kissing her skin.

Her heart raced, her tongue tied, and confusion tightened on her brow. Had she imagined the distance between them? The abrasiveness, his avoiding gaze? The doula's distress had been real enough. "Kelric, I need to talk to you."

His arm stiffened beneath her head. A moment later, his lips closed around the lobe of her ear, sending a jolt of pleasure through her. "I know, I know. I'll be nice to the girl, I promise."

The strength she'd conjured to advocate for Klymene withered in her breast. Kelric had agreed and she hadn't even spoken. Yet somehow, it didn't quite feel resolved. How could she press this conversation without sliding back into that unbearable tension?

Chirr-up. Chirr-up. Chirr-up.

A half-growl, half-sigh rumbled in Kelric's throat, and he pulled away. "Ferry that cricket!"

Her breath hitched in her throat, and before he could roll completely away and onto his feet, she grabbed his arm. "No, leave it, please!"

Kelric turned back to her with an incredulous expression, piercing gray eyes wide, mouth ajar. "What? Why? It's annoying."

A smile curled her lips upward. "Please let it be, it… helps me sleep."

Kelric glanced into the darkness, looking for the insect, unconvinced it should live. "You can't be serious."

"I am." Gonivein tightened her grip on his arm. "Please. The waves remind me…" Her voice cracked, and she clamped her mouth shut, too late to hide her pain.

Kelric jerked his head back to her, his gaze softening with understanding. And guilt.

She rolled away from him. Ashamed at the onslaught of tears blurring his face from her vision. She was so tired of weeping. Tired of grief controlling her body, her thoughts. Tired of not being sure of anything.

His arms went around her again, his chest warm against her back. Strong, secure, soothing. As though he were a completely different person. Disrupting this sudden tenderness filled her with dread.

Perhaps it was better to let the matter drop for tonight. He had worked through his emotions. Her own anger had been tempered, too—albeit by exhaustion. Perhaps both of them needed to rest and start fresh tomorrow.

The cricket sang, and she closed her eyes, welcoming oblivion.

CHAPTER 27

LITHANEVA

LITHANEVA HID HERSELF AWAY IN the gynaikon when she returned from the agora, but left the door cracked open. She didn't want to be disturbed, but she wanted to be the first to know when Aden arrived for his report.

He was early, as though anticipating she would want to see him after her father's visit. He paused in the center of the courtyard where he would be most visible.

The doula, Torine, led him in. "I'll find the basileus, Archon," she said.

Lithaneva opened her door wider and stepped through. "That won't be necessary, Torine. I will escort Archon Aden. You may return to the kitchens."

Torine bowed her head and disappeared through the triklinion.

"Welcome, Archon." Lithaneva smiled at Aden and swept her eyes over him. Dust covered his sandals and calves, his golden hair was messy and windblown from his ride across the polis, and the faint scent of sweat and horse lingered. A leather bag was slung over his shoulder, his fingers worrying the flap.

"Princess," he said, bowing his head.

"You're early."

Aden tossed her an impish grin. "I thought it pertinent I should be."

"You thought correct." She ushered him into motion with a sweep of her hand.

She had met Aden at the Library in their youth, where they had studied together under the scholars' tutelage. Their competitive drives to be the best and brightest students had initially set them at odds, but had eventually warmed into an ardent friendship. The only thing that eclipsed Aden's devotion to her was his devotion to Thellshun. So long as her plans benefited his homeland, she never had to doubt his loyalty.

Lithaneva wondered what his report would say today. From the worry creasing his brow, it would likely contain some hard truths to swallow. Charixes' demands would add to his headache, which she was genuinely sorry for, but it couldn't be helped.

"Branitus has asked me to attend your report this evening. He was not expecting you this early, however, so we'll wait." *And figure out the real plan.*

Aden's lips twitched, itching to speak, but he waited until they were safely in the andron with the door closed. "Asked you to attend my report? Such a strange expectation for a wife." He chuckled. "I should have known it wouldn't take you long to begin your usurpation. You're more like your father than you think." He flashed her a sly grin as he took his usual seat on the couch, his back to the door.

His acknowledgment bolstered her confidence for the scheme playing out in her mind. She sat on the opposite couch and leaned forward to examine a bowl of almonds on the center table.

"Charixes is building ships to attack Golpathia."

Aden's eyes widened.

"I've already sent word to the rebels—"

Aden tilted his head.

"—goddess stuff," she explained, plucking up a nut with a flourish of her hand. His curiosity seemed satisfied with this, and she continued. "Charixes demanded we assemble one thousand fighting men to accompany his land forces to the polis gates. He wants to trap them in, force them to surrender."

Aden shook his head slowly. She could almost see the information sorting behind his furrowed brow. All traces of his earlier humor were gone. "Good strategy for him, except we don't have one thousand men to spare."

"He insisted, and Branitus is determined to comply. Even if it means training douloi in warfare and leaving no one behind to plant our crops, but I won't leave Thellshun so vulnerable." She straightened her shoulders, resolve surging through her and tingling in her fingertips. "I will not see Thellshun brought to harm because of my father's arrogance."

Aden rubbed his stubbly chin, his eyes troubled but determined, attentive. "What do you suggest?"

"We lie."

"Lie?"

"Lie."

Aden blinked. "One thousand men is a difficult thing to lie about."

"I know my father's strategos, Marham." Lithaneva popped another almond in her mouth. She savored the crunch between her teeth as she pictured the man's vile face and entitled air. "He's lazy, and would never bother to count every single soldier that marches from Thellshun. All we need to do is ensure that our commanders report whatever number we tell them to."

Her stomach swooped as she imagined her plan enacted on the plains of Golpathia. The intimidation of Strategos Marham and his captains would be strong. Stronger still if they suspected they'd been duped. If even one of the Thellshun commanders cracked, the plan would fail, and Charixes' retribution would be brutal on them all. But especially her. *He's too smart not to know I wouldn't be behind it.*

"To safeguard against his suspicion, should it arise, tell every kubernao you visit, even the ones we can trust, that pockets of plague have sprung up across the polis. Don't say where." She rolled an olive between her thumb and forefinger. "Should Marham question the numbers, there will be multiple alibis and a plethora of rumors to explain their absence."

Aden nodded slowly, his mind calculating the risks and costs. She knew he was thinking of everyone he would need to involve, weighing their trustworthiness and loyalty. "Some of our captains and commanders will do it. Some won't and would have no qualms with ratting out their comrades if they thought it would buy them favor with the anax. It's very risky."

Lithaneva grabbed several more almonds from the bowl. "This plan ensures the survival of Thellshun. My father believes Golpathia will fall within two weeks. It will not—it can't. Thellshun will starve without our crops."

Aden nodded. "How many men are we sending then?"

Lithaneva shrugged. "Five hundred."

"Half the number requested? That will be too obvious."

"Six hundred then, and tell the ones loyal to us to bring another horse if they have it and an extra tent to house their belongings. When Marham gazes out from a high point, he'll be none the wiser. And if he does start asking questions, every single man will offer the plague as the culprit." She took a sip of wine, studying the lines of doubt creasing Aden's forehead from over the rim. "Don't underestimate the power of misinformation, Aden. My father would not be the anax without it."

Aden pinched the bridge of his nose, obviously worried. "The numbers Charixes demands would ensure his victory, but this, *this* will guarantee our defeat."

"Yes."

Aden plucked an almond from the bowl and rubbed it between his fingers. Her stomach swooped once again at his hesitancy. The plan would not work without his cooperation. *Hear him out. You trust him, or you wouldn't be speaking to him now.*

"Tell me your concerns."

"Are we to just sacrifice six hundred men? Whether by sword or surrender, they will be lost to us."

She reached over to touch his arm. "Ensure they surrender. I will secure guarantees from the Golpathians that they will be protected. Their loss will only be temporary, and we will still have our crops."

He lowered his eyes, the almond still suspended between his thumb and forefinger. "Are you *sure* we can trust the Golpathians?"

She gave his arm a confident squeeze. "I'm sure."

Aden nodded and drew in a deep, resigned breath. "Then I will do what I can to see your plan come to fruition. I will get six hundred men. As for the battlefield…" He put the almond between his teeth, crushed it in one chew, and swallowed. "If Ninenarn marches alongside them, even our most loyal men may not have a choice but to fight."

"Then make sure they know who they should be fighting."

A flicker of something flashed in the depths of Aden's cerulean eyes. He leaned back, studying her face, then nodded once again.

They waited in silence then, chewing almonds and listening to the cuckoos outside.

Finally, they heard a scuff outside the door just before it swung open.

Branitus sauntered in. "Ah! Good, you're both here." He made straight for a wine amphora on the sideboard counter and poured three cups full. He handed them out and took his seat beside Lithaneva.

"First, your report," Branitus said. "What of Relium?"

"The harvest was poor—barely three carts of olives, and not even that much of figs and grapes." Aden's tone was grim. "It seems the famine that has ravaged Shallinath for so long has finally poisoned our orchards. The farmers have begun planting barley, but they are insistent that only half the fields can be maintained. I promised the kubernao I would request a lower tribute of their exports. If we take the current requirement, they will starve."

The spark of joy faded from Branitus' eyes, and his shoulders slumped forward a little. "What of the city's needs? We depend on those exports for our survival."

Aden's look became troubled. "Perhaps we should begin rationing our food stores."

Branitus glanced at Lithaneva. "If we provide Charixes the numbers he seeks, will he be lenient in sending along some of Ninenarn's harvest?"

It was a good proposal. Ninenarn was well-positioned to withstand the famine and would be a powerful ally in that regard. Lithaneva couldn't help but notice how carefully Aden was watching them. *Is he trying to decide if our plan is worth the risk?* If Marham found out they'd inflated their numbers, there would be no compassion for Thellshun's starving widows.

She had told Aden of Helinthia's will, that restoring Apollo's line on the throne was the only way to end the famine. Aden had believed her and promised to do everything within his power to make her anassa. But what if the famine became unmanageable before they overthrew Charixes? They might need his favor to survive.

It was a risk. *Will he take it?*

She met Branitus' eyes steadily. "That is not an unreasonable request to make of my father. Unlike what he expects from us."

Branitus nodded. "Lower the tribute from Relium, then."

"The anax has made a request?" Aden asked, giving Lithaneva a subtle nod.

She crunched another almond as her doubts melted away.

CHAPTER 28

GADNOR

S TARS STILL TWINKLED ON THE western horizon when
Gadnor stepped out of his apartment. A cool breeze blew,
carrying a sharp scent of salt and sand. Tor waited for him at
the bottom of the stairs, leaning against one of the pillars supporting
the peristyle. His sandaled foot glided back and forth over a loose
pebble. He seemed nervous—or was it excitement? Gadnor couldn't
really tell in the half light.

Xios bristled from his perch on the retaining wall at the center of
the courtyard as Gadnor quietly descended.

"Ready?" Tor asked.

He hasn't changed his mind, then. Not that Gadnor thought he
would. Tor wasn't the type to agree to something if he didn't intend
to follow through. After the meeting in Kelric's andron yesterday,
Tor had expressed his intention to accompany him to Hameth. So,
now they were going to train.

Gadnor led the way through the atrium and across the courtyard
toward the stables. The smell of hay, sweat, and manure permeated
the space when they stepped inside. The horses leaned over their
stalls to greet the newcomers, whickering softly.

"Through there is the training yard." Gadnor pointed to the door

215

at the other end of the long corridor.

Leontes and Inan, Dargos and Forluna's steeds, were stabled side by side, one white, one black. Their long beards tickled Gadnor's knuckles as he scratched under their chins. Damsel, Kelric's mare, was across the aisle, beside their father's stallion. Three other horses lived there as well, a black war mount who had carried Gonivein and Loric away from Tyldan, an old brown workhorse, and Kubernao Pallas' gelding, who was here only because Pallas' cousin didn't have a place for him at his residence in the lower city.

Gadnor petted each as he made his way down the aisle toward the smaller room at the back.

Kelric's chariot rested in the corner, and a disorderly heap of armor lay beside it in the dirt. Gadnor's dented helmet rested on top. Alypius' sword had cracked the plating, leaving a jagged edge just over the vizor. Gadnor's eye throbbed. The swelling had finally gone down enough to open it. He was lucky a bruise was the extent of the injury.

"All of these look too big for me." Tor eyed the suits displayed along the walls. Tor had a small frame, partially due to a meager diet and a less strenuous exercise regimen than most boys, but also because he wasn't done growing. His upper lip had only just started showing signs of maturity.

"Those are my father's and Kelric's," Gadnor said, then pointed to the opposite corner, where the hook for his damaged armor hung empty. A second hook held the smaller suit of armor he had outgrown the previous year. He pulled the cuirass down and held it up to Tor. It might be a little snug, but it would do for training. He grabbed the other items and shouldered open a door that led to the training grounds.

A brilliant dawn greeted him, and he breathed in the crisp morning air. They were on the other side of the villa's inner wall, on a secluded plateau that offered a breathtaking view of the sea. Gulls were beginning to wake and spring from their nests in the cliffs below. Gadnor deposited the armor on the ground, then returned to the armory to retrieve two practice swords, two bows, a quiver of arrows, and a spear. He propped everything against the armory wall.

A practice dummy wearing dented bronze plates stood on one side of the small, dusty plain. Its wooden limbs were splintered and worn down from frequent strikes. Three targets, vaguely shaped like cattle, had been placed at the far end of the court. Straw spilled from holes in their leather hides where arrows had punctured them.

Gadnor had never enjoyed training for battle. He'd done it because his father had made him do it, because he was told it was important, and because Kelric belittled him for being terrible at it. Growing up, he'd thought if he practiced hard enough, long enough, his brother would leave him alone, and then he could pour his energy into activities that enhanced the nurturing of things rather than their destruction. Now, it seemed, his father and brother had been right all along.

Xios busied himself nosing in some brush that had escaped the stamping of sparring feet. Gadnor began fitting the armor around Tor, wrapping the cuirass around his chest and securing the leather straps under his arms.

Tor squirmed behind the leather and bronze plate, trying to shift it.

"Is it too tight?" Gadnor was already moving toward the ties to loosen them, but Tor twisted away from his reach.

"No." Tor cleared his throat. "It's just heavy." He pointed at the remaining pieces on the ground. "Those too?"

Gadnor nodded.

"All right, then."

At Tor's wave, Gadnor began fastening the greaves around his calves, then the braces around his forearms. The ensemble was complete when Gadnor placed the helmet over Tor's dark curls.

Gadnor stepped back and examined the soldier before him. The eyes peering out of the helmet looked anxious and uncomfortable, hot beneath the rising sun despite the chill lingering in the air. Beads of sweat were already running down his neck.

Xios growled and hissed, crouching as if readying to pounce on this new threat. A cricket leapt beside him, stealing his attention.

Tor laughed and traced the nose guard with a timid finger. He grabbed the crest of the helmet on his head and wiggled it, moved his neck side to side to test his range of motion. After a moment, he pulled the helmet off. Strands of hair were already plastered to his scalp, and a sheen of sweat glistened on his bare forehead.

"How can you wear this and see anything?"

Gadnor shrugged. "Not easily." Especially when the sun warmed the bronze. His head would burn and salt sting his eyes. He kept that to himself. "In formation, what's in front of you is what's most important."

Tor set the headgear down and picked up a wooden sword. He stepped toward the dummy and swung the blunted blade at its body. Raising an imaginary shield in his left hand, he lunged and thrust the sword forward, sliding between the plates under its wooden arm.

Gadnor's brows rose in surprise at Tor's form. "Have you practiced with the sword before?"

Tor turned back around, hanging his head. "Cana and I would sometimes play with sticks and pretend we were Hector and Achilles. Father would encourage us, teach us a few things he learned as a soldier. Cana was always better than me, though." He smiled at the memory, but his joy quickly faded. "This is my first time in armor."

Tor clawed at the cuirass, trying unsuccessfully to shift or loosen it. He stooped, shoulders sagging under the weight. "You have to carry all of this while someone is trying to kill you?"

Gadnor bit his lip and moved to unlace Tor's cuirass. "Yes. And a shield too." The armor dropped onto the ground with a soft clang.

Tor removed the greaves and bracers and stacked them. "I don't understand how anyone survives a battle wearing that."

His tone bore a discouraged edge, and they'd only just started training. Gadnor felt stupid for putting him in armor first—he hated wearing it, too. *I should have shown him a defensive strike, or how to hold a spear properly.* Something to raise Tor's confidence instead of tear it down.

Building a body that could move fluidly in armor took years of dedication, and even then, practice didn't always bring skill. *Like me.* But revealing those truths would do neither of them any favors.

"We can get the movements down first, and worry about armor later," Gadnor said lightly, hoping to dispel the doubt lingering between them.

Tor didn't seem convinced, so Gadnor reached for one of the bows. "Archers usually wear lighter garments, even in battle." He thrust the curved stave toward Tor.

Tor eyed the weapon warily, but took it, testing the grip. "It's heavier than a hunting bow."

Gadnor picked up the second bow. "War bows are reinforced with bronze, the strings double-braided. Designed to pierce armor." He strummed the bow string. The soft *thrum* was soothing as it vibrated through his arm, almost like it had its own pulse.

A vague memory floated up from the recesses of his mind. Small hands, *his* hands, holding a smaller weapon. His father crouched behind him. *'Don't lock your elbow.'* His large hand covered Gadnor's, helping to pull the string back and steady the fletching against Gadnor's cheek. He hit the target on the first attempt, and his father's proud chuckle rumbled in his ear.

Tor knocked an arrow and slid the fletching between his fingers. Gripping the string, he pulled, aiming at the bull at the end of the plateau. He closed one eye, grimacing at the strain, then released. The bolt sailed through the air and pierced the dirt just under the bull.

"That's pretty good," Gadnor praised.

Tor shrugged, but a smile danced on his lips. "Your turn."

Gadnor took a deep breath and readied his arrow, pulled the string back and rested it against his cheek. The tense of every muscle in his upper body thrilled through him as he trained the bronze tip on the target. There was a slight breeze. Gadnor shifted his aim.

Released the bolt. It sailed, whistling, and embedded into the eye of the bull.

Tor's eyebrows rose. "Clearly you need no practice with the bow. Why not lean into this instead of the sword?"

Gadnor plucked another arrow from the quiver and twirled it between his fingers. "Kelric says archery is the weapon of those too weak to throw a spear and too clumsy to wield a sword. He says only cowards refuse to look their opponent in the eye before they kill them."

Tor looked at the weapon in Gadnor's hands. "Do you believe that?"

Gadnor stared at his arrow. "I don't know." Archers were a key strategic asset in any battle. Their efforts could slow an enemy advance, giving footmen more time to prepare, recover, or retreat. An arrow could save a life, especially if one's aim was sharp. "I respect archers a great deal, but I've never really felt proud of my skill with a bow."

Tor tilted his head. "Because you believe archers are cowardly and weak, or because Kelric has made you believe that about yourself?"

A lump formed in Gadnor's throat. He didn't have an answer for that. At least, not one he felt brave enough to voice. It wouldn't matter if he did. It wasn't just Kelric who scorned archers, it was everyone who wasn't one. No matter how good he might be—he could be as great as Apollo—it wouldn't earn him the respect of the Council or position him to win the renown needed to marry the princess. Not in the eyes of mortals, anyway.

Tor grabbed the spear leaning against the wall and examined it, blessedly deciding to let the matter drop. "And why is this so special?" He widened his stance and held the weapon at his hip, giving it an awkward thrust toward the dummy that was neither straight nor sturdy.

Gadnor chuckled. "You won't survive long wielding it like that. Here." He held out his hand, and Tor relinquished the spear. Gadnor positioned himself shoulder to shoulder beside him. "In a battle, you would be in a formation with comrades on either side of you. Your shield would be here, like this." Gadnor demonstrated with his arm, and Tor replicated the movement.

"Widen your feet—bend your knees a little. Perfect. Now your spear will rest on top of your shield—like this. When you advance, you can thrust it cleanly through the enemy and draw it back."

Gadnor picked up a wooden shield and slid it onto Tor's left arm, then handed him the spear again. "You try."

Tor widened his feet and hefted the shield up, resting the shaft of the spear over the bronze lip as Gadnor had shone him. He thrust the lance forward and drew it back.

"That's almost right." Gadnor stepped close. "Grip the spear here." He took Tor's hand and slid it back several inches along the spear's shaft. "Open your shoulder here—just like that. It feels a little awkward, but holding it this way will let you thrust it farther with less effort. Now keep your arm close to your body. Not that close…" Gadnor tugged lightly on Tor's elbow, moving it into the correct position.

Tor tensed in his grip, and Gadnor immediately dropped his hand, wondering what was wrong. He stepped back, concern sharpening his gaze on Tor's reddened face. He opened his mouth to inquire, but closed it again as Tor's focus remained fixed straight ahead, as though the only thing bothering him was the imaginary foe in front of him.

Did I imagine it?

"How does that feel?" he asked stupidly, latching on to his first intelligible thought.

Tor just nodded, the muscles along his jaw twitching, waiting for the next instruction.

"Remember to breathe." He wished he knew how to ease whatever anxieties were swarming through Tor's mind.

Tor drew in an audible breath.

Gadnor cleared his throat, refocusing his thoughts. "When you thrust the spear, twist your whole body, don't just move your arm. Like this." Gadnor replicated Tor's stance and demonstrated the movement.

Tor completed the movement with the grace of an experienced foot soldier. If a foe had been standing in front of him, they would be severely wounded, if not fatally so.

"That was excellent," Gadnor said, grinning.

Noises from the other side of the wall reached his ears. Scholars called to one another. Feet crunched on gravel. He glanced at the sky, surprised to see how far the sun had risen. "We should get something to eat before Gonivein's confirmation."

Tor nodded, looking relieved as he set down the spear and gathered Xios into his arms.

Gadnor frowned, wondering what he'd said or done that had upset his friend. He was about to ask, but Tor gave him a lopsided grin that made him question everything he'd seen.

"Come on." Tor nudged Gadnor's shoulder with his elbow. "Maybe Euanthe made some of those honey cakes."

CHAPTER 29

DARGOS

THE DARK CIRCLES UNDER GONIVEIN'S eyes captured Dargos' notice in the chill of the morning. Her gaunt appearance—eyes sunken and hollow, collar bones protruding at the base of her throat—made her seem more wraith than human. Guilt and sorrow pierced his chest, and he extended a steadying hand to her as she neared.

A light fog had descended from the mountain behind the villa. As she slowly descended the steps, her booted feet disappeared beneath the otherworldly swirls. She looked closer to taking a step toward the gloomy caverns of Hades than the bright temple of Apollo.

She took his hand, but didn't smile.

How blind I've been.

It was hard to believe the giggling, joyful, vibrant girl he'd grown up with was the same person standing before him. She made to step past him to climb onto the litter that would bear her through the city, but he pulled her to his chest and wrapped his arms tightly around her. He needed to feel her heart beating against his. How lucky he was that she had survived. That of everything he had lost—his lands, his people, his faith—his little sister wasn't among them.

"Dargos?" she said, more an expression of her surprise than the

223

beginning of a question.

Emotions and thoughts tumbled through him as he held the bitter fruit of his quest for Helinthia's favor in his arms. Gonivein was all that was left, barely recognizable after all she had suffered. Here was all the reward he had to show for his devotion to the goddess.

He and Forluna had avoided conversation with each other, despite the closeness they'd shared in the agora yesterday. Her revelations, coupled with Gonivein's visions, painted a harrowing future. Their rebellion had progressed too far to turn back now. The refugees were proof of that. Had his faith in Helinthia truly been misplaced? Would she really abandon them when they needed her most? Or—he couldn't scrub the harsher question from his mind—even if she did come through for them, would there be anything left to save?

He pulled away from Gonivein and looked down into her icy blue eyes. There was too much he wanted to say, so he kept silent and helped her get situated on the litter.

My sister, the Oracle of Apollo. How that would have filled him with pride once.

She kept her gaze on him, a spark of curiosity flickering within and bringing a little life back into her features. He smiled and squeezed her hand, then motioned to Kelric's guards to lift her and begin their descent to the temple of Apollo. Whatever doubts he now had about the gods, the scholars remained an imposing force that he didn't dare keep waiting.

Kelric, Gadnor, and Forluna fell into step beside him as he trailed behind Gonivein. Forluna pressed close. Her flattened ears beneath her hair and her rigid shoulders alerted him to her heightened anxiety. He threaded his fingers through hers and squeezed, relieved when she squeezed back and didn't pull away. Something frightened her, and no matter what unresolved tension lingered between them, he would always protect her, soothe her.

They met the scholarly procession at the gates, where the acolytes of Apollo arranged boughs of laurel and bay on Gonivein's couch. All eight scholars were assembled in a line, two abreast, with

Mandus at their head. All carried something in their arms: amphorae, wicker baskets, bundles of twigs and sticks, wooden boxes, and more laurel branches. One also carried a lyre, and when the litter had been blessed with Apollo's sacred symbols, the acolyte strummed her fingers across the strings. The scholars raised their voices in a hymn to Apollo and began to march slowly and methodically down the city street.

Just as with the wedding, citizens were gathered along the sides of the path, waving colorful linens as they passed by. Some lifted their voices in song. Dargos would have joined them, but he couldn't find it in him to sing.

It felt wrong to show such lack of enthusiasm for this sacred ritual, but he didn't have the energy to care. A fact he recognized was out of character for him. He was losing himself, and he didn't know how to stop it before he unraveled.

Priests, priestesses, and kyrioi crowded the steps when they arrived at the temple of Apollo. The council members had brought their wives with them this time. Dargos also noted an unusual number of guards standing along the route and watching from the high places. He cut a glance at Kelric, surprised that his hot-headed brother-in-law was exhibiting caution rather than arrogance for once, but it worried him. Was Kelric concerned there might be violence at an oracle confirmation ceremony? Kelric looked straight ahead, giving no indication that anything was amiss.

The litter lowered to the ground before the temple. One of the guards helped Gonivein stand. She and Mandus led the procession up the stairs and through the grand entrance.

The music's timbre amplified off the walls of the vestibule and rose to such an electrifying height in the antechamber that it shook Dargos to his very bones. The words of the hymn danced in his mind as he gazed at the golden statue of Apollo looming above the assembly. Just when the urge to sing had finally overcome his state of melancholy, the song ended.

Dargos was breathless, almost disoriented by the sudden silence.

Somewhere during his trance, Gonivein and Mandus had reached the altar, where the high priest of Apollo waited.

The priest didn't smile as he gazed upon Gonivein. She straightened her shoulders and lifted her chin, undeterred by his coldness. Dargos smiled a little. Not all of her fire had been extinguished. *Good.*

The priest turned to Mandus. "Brother Mandus, you have brought forth one alleged to be Apollo's chosen oracle. Come forward, venerable scholar, and make your sacrifice."

Dargos' eyes swept over the row of scholars. His brow furrowed. Had they forgotten the sacrificial animal? Surely Mandus wouldn't have made such a mistake.

At Mandus' bow, the priest stepped back into the shadows, and the old scholar turned to face Gonivein and the assembly. "Gonivein of Shallinath, Basileia of Golpathia, Apollo has laid claim to your voice, and by your voice, all shall know you are his vessel. By your blood, he will know your devotion."

Kelric snapped his head to Dargos. "What does that mean?"

Fear twisted inside Dargos as he met his brother-in-law's eyes, trying to appear confident and calm despite feeling nothing of the kind. What, indeed? Forluna's hand tightened around his, grounding him, reassuring him. He returned the pressure, grateful that she was still here with him.

Brother Mandus extended a shaky hand. An acolyte brandished a polished bronze knife with a hilt shaped like a swan and laid it in his gnarled palm.

Kelric bristled, and Dargos shuffled closer to him in case he needed to interfere with some brash reaction. However alarming this ritual seemed, all the oracles Dargos had ever known were alive and well after their confirmations. Gonivein was in no imminent danger. He doubted Kelric realized this.

"You have been called, Basileia Gonivein. Will you heed the god's voice?"

Gonivein's eyes flicked to the knife, then to Mandus' face. She nodded. "I accept."

"Then may your blood bear witness that Phoebus Apollo, far-shooter, light-bringer, has bestowed his gifts upon you. Your hand, my child."

Gonivein swallowed and gave Mandus her upturned palm.

A kind smile parted his curly white beard. He guided her gently toward a bronze bowl perched on top of a tripod before the altar.

Kelric legs tensed to lunge forward, but he stayed put as Mandus drew the blade along her palm. Gonivein's eyes closed, and rather than the grimace Dargos anticipated, her features seemed to relax, as though the pain was a comfort to her. Tears stung his eyes. He suddenly felt sick as her blood streamed into the bowl. Too much blood, but Mandus squeezed, coaxing even more droplets from her.

Mandus laid the knife on the edge of the altar with the blade resting on the coals, then motioned for the scholar carrying the bundle of sticks to come forward and arrange them to be burned. Next came the acolyte with the wooden box. Mandus reached inside, grabbed a fistful of fine powder, and sprinkled it over the wood. The sweet scent of incense filled the room as the grains sifted down to the embers, and wisps of smoke curled upwards to caress the bronze face of Apollo's statue. Next, Mandus turned and raised the bowl of Gonivein's blood high before the god and the assembly.

"By your blood shall all peoples of this isle know that Apollo has chosen you to utter the threads of the Fates." He poured the crimson fluid onto the sticks. Immediately, he traded the empty bowl for the amphora of wine and drizzled it across the offering. The flames leapt, consuming sticks, blood, and incense. A sweet, metallic tang filled Dargos' nostrils and he couldn't help but grimace.

Mandus stepped back into the shadows and bowed his head, leaving Gonivein alone before the blaze.

Gonivein's calm demeanor as she stood alone at the foot of the giant statue of Apollo eased the racing of Dargos' heart. The moments passed. Everyone waited in silence for… something.

Then, he saw it. The flames licked higher and higher, elongating into the shape of a man. It moved in ways unnatural for any fire, separating from the altar.

A gasp rippled through the assembly. Kelric's hand flew to his hip to seize a sword that wasn't there, then curled into a frustrated fist.

The flame stepped in front of Gonivein, who hadn't moved an inch. A serene expression settled on her face, as though it wasn't a giant flame moving toward her at all. An orange tongue licked out, but she remained still.

Adrenaline pumped into Dargos' limbs. *Why isn't she moving back?* He didn't understand her desire for pain, but it had been unmistakable in her eyes as the blade tore into her flesh. Was her paralysis in the face of this inferno some desire for self-destruction? He looked to Mandus, but there was no sign of fear from the old man's face or stance. He wore an expression of awe and reverence.

What is happening?

"Gonivein!" Kelric's voice cut across the chamber as he stepped forward. Gadnor grasped his shoulder, pulling him back.

"Wait, Kelric, it's Apollo."

Shock thrummed in Dargos' chest. He looked to Forluna to contradict the claim, but she didn't.

Kelric wrenched his shoulder free of Gadnor's hold. "Are you mad? It's a burning flame." He turned an accusatory glare on Mandus. "What kind of ritual is this?" His words echoed harshly. Several people turned to stare, but most of them were too enamored with the divinity to pay a mortal any heed.

"It is a flame to you, but it *is* Apollo, Kelric," Forluna said.

They can see him. By their immortal blood.

The priests, priestesses, and scholars bowed, shielding their eyes from the fire entity. The rest of the onlookers followed suit. Only Kelric remained standing, glowering. Dargos elbowed him in the ribs and glared. Kelric refused to submit, his eyes riveted to the otherworldly scene before him.

Dargos had never been in the presence of a god. Despite all his devotion to Helinthia, he had never laid eyes on her. Perhaps Forluna had been right in her declaration that the goddess didn't deserve his love. Then again, maybe it didn't matter if she was right. Helinthia wasn't the only deity who had promised her favor. Apollo had chosen Gonivein, and the gods did not choose their oracles thoughtlessly. Oracles were favored, prized, even loved.

Apollo is with us.

Dargos' heart hammered wildly in his chest, reinvigorated by the joyous revelations spinning through his mind. He side-eyed Tor bowing respectfully beside Gadnor. His confirmation as Artemis' oracle would occur when the moon reached its zenith mere hours from now.

Artemis is with us, too.

Dargos didn't understand why Helinthia had not protected Anassa Iptys as she'd promised. Perhaps they would never know. But two other powerful gods favored their cause, and he could not lose sight of their mission now. Neither could he continue to turn a blind eye to the suffering of those he loved. What was it all for if he lost them?

Once again, he had wasted too much time on idleness, on regret, on uncertainty. He had to find Pallas after the confirmation. Plan a way to assemble his scattered forces under Golpathia's banner. Reclaim Shallinath and end Charixes for good.

"He's going to burn her alive," Kelric hissed.

Dargos raised his eyes to his sister, and his stomach twisted as the flame stepped forward and engulfed her. Every instinct screamed to launch himself forward and whisk her out of reach of danger, but her face was calm. Her clothes did not burn, Neither did her hair or skin. Dargos had no words to explain the phenomena before him besides *power.*

"He's not burning her, Kelric," Gadnor assured him, tightening his grip on his brother's arm. There was something off about his tone, something… afraid?

No. *Embarrassed.*

The fear in Kelric's eyes transformed into rage. He whirled on Gadnor and grabbed his tunic with both hands, wrenching his brother's face close.

"What is he *doing* to her, then?"

Gadnor swallowed, his cheeks red, eyes shifting between his brother, the god, and Gonivein.

Dargos had a sinking feeling he knew exactly what Apollo was doing. And Kelric did, too.

CHAPTER 30

GONIVEIN

GONIVEIN DREADED SEEING THE GOD again. Apollo embodied a man newly graduated from boyhood, with broad shoulders and chiseled muscles beneath glowing bronze skin. Gold hair cascaded around his beardless face, and mischief sparked in his cerulean eyes. He was the most beautiful being she had ever seen. She recalled her adoration the first time he'd appeared to her—the all-consuming urge to fall at his feet and serve him. She remembered the last time, despair and contempt writhing inside of her like an insatiable fiend. She'd screamed at him. Berated him.

The last time she'd seen him, Loric had lain dead in her arms.

A gasp rippled through the crowd as Apollo stepped down from the altar, stealing the flames from the coals with him. Heat burned her cheeks under his watchful eyes, but the room turned cool with the absence of the fire, teasing her arms with gooseflesh.

From the shadows, that vile little priest of Apollo stared slack-jawed in disbelief before prostrating himself on the floor behind the god. Satisfaction bloomed within her.

"You may stop running now, Gonivein," Apollo whispered, extending a hand to brush her cheek.

Could she? She doubted it. She struggled for something to say as she gazed upon him. The hair rose on her arms and beads of sweat formed on her chest as Kelric's voice rose from the fringes of the crowd. His tone was urgent and demanding. Something was wrong.

Apollo cupped her face between his hands, keeping her from turning to find her husband. Her breath hitched as the god stepped closer, brushing his body against hers, spreading warmth through her that had nothing to do with fire. For a moment, she thought he was going to kiss her.

Kissed by a god. Her heart thumped wildly in her breast, and she couldn't tell if the idea intrigued or disgusted her.

Kelric is watching. A shiver rolled down her spine. She dreaded how a fit of jealousy might manifest in his heightened state of anxiety. How that would jeopardize the tenuous peace between them.

"Can they see you?"

He shook his head. "They are too afraid."

'Fear blinds the eyes of men.' He had told her that once.

"Can they hear you?"

"A god speaks to his oracle, not the rabble. They hear the roaring blaze of my glory."

Relief flooded her. She hoped his disguise as a disembodied flame was enough to avoid Kelric's jealous ire.

"I sent you a vision," Apollo said.

Images overpowered her. A green hillside stretched before her, bursting with blades of green and white flowers. Lilies. It was a scene of tranquility, except for the loud screech that cut through the valley—a frightful, jolting sound. Gonivein stood on a peak, high above the ground.

The first time this vision had come to her in Tyldan, she had sprawled in the grass on the hilltop like a carefree child, still full of hope and joy, blissfully unaware of the bloodshed about to occur. The second time, at her wedding, she had stood on a high ledge looking out, searching, anticipating the violence. She shut her eyes.

I don't want to see it again. No more death. No more blood. But the vision wormed its way through her. There was no choice but to obey. She opened her eyes, breathing in the scent of the clear air, and moved toward the edge of the cliff to peer at the valley.

The wounded falcon fluttered on the grass, circled by a hydra, a lion, and a white stallion. All were of similar stature—too large to be anything but mythical. They roared in rage and anger, thirsty for blood and violence. Their focus was on the bird, but they lashed out at one another when they closed ranks, inflicting deep wounds that stained the grass crimson. Around them were hundreds of wolves, timid and leaderless, eying the battle in their midst with fear and uncertainty—as though they wanted to help the falcon, but couldn't.

"Why do you show me this again and again?"

Apollo's voice was gravelly, sharp. "Because you're not *seeing* it, Gonivein."

Her breath hitched at the note of desperation in his tone. *What did I miss?* She scanned the scene again, focusing with intent this time, analyzing every detail. The three beasts continued to circle the falcon, but then... *The ground!*

Brambles sprouted from the earth, twining around the wolves. They pulled and tugged to get free, but to no avail. The vegetation spread, swallowing the wolves and crowding the mythical beasts closer together. The creatures eyed the vines warily as they encroached. Anxiety and aggression in the shrinking space grew and boiled, until at last they all pounced on the falcon. The bird screamed in agony.

Her heart lurched into her throat. She'd known what was coming, but it still surprised her. The vision faded and she was back in the temple, face to face with Apollo again. He was even closer now. His warm breath brushed her lips, a hint of something sweet reaching her nostrils. It made her mouth water.

"Do you see?" he asked.

She searched his eyes, trying to recall the details. "The vines."

He nodded slowly, waiting for more.

"They were taking over everything."

"Do you *see*?" His fingers grew rigid around her head.

A burst of panic flared in her chest. "I… I don't… I don't know. What am I supposed to see?"

His jaw clenched, a small muscle spasming in his cheek.

She grew breathless at the disappointment swirling in his bright eyes, fearful that he might lose his patience and crush her skull between his palms like a bug.

"I'm not allowed to say. You are the one chosen for this. *Think.* What do you see? What do you *not* see?"

Despair filled her eyes with tears. "I don't know what you want from me," she croaked out, shame flooding through her. "Why did you pick me for this?"

Apollo's eyes softened, but he didn't answer her. Instead, he grasped her bleeding hand and ran his thumb along the sacrificial cut. Immediately the skin sealed, leaving only a red smear of dried blood. Not even a scar remained.

Her eyes widened in shock.

"When you have need of me, sprinkle your blood on my altar, and I will come. I cannot tell you what your vision means, but I will show it to you as many times as it takes for you to *see*."

Kelric's voice broke through again, sharper, determined, furious, and something tugged within her. She needed to set her husband at ease, to assure him she was safe, that she was his, and only his.

'I can't lose you too.'

"There's one more thing." Apollo took a strand of her straight blond hair and rubbed it between his fingers. "As my oracle, you may request a gift of me."

"A gift?"

"A rule Helinthia imposed to allow gods to interact with her mortals." At her confusion, he shrugged. "I told you, she's young. Far too eager to exert her power, even when completely unnecessary."

Granting a single gift in exchange for a lifetime of servitude seemed like the *least* a god could do for their oracle, but Gonivein dared not say that.

A gift from a god...

A thought bloomed within her mind. What if she could remove one more burden from Kelric's shoulders? Enable them to escape in each other's arms with total abandon? Such uninhibited intimacy could draw them closer. Bridge the tension between them.

"You can manipulate a body," she said.

Apollo lifted a brow in curiosity, and she raised her newly healed palm in answer.

He smiled.

"If I am to perform this duty for you, then I can't afford distractions. I..." She swallowed, her resolve beginning to falter. All her vulnerabilities sprang into her mind. Her broken hip, her grief, her inability to sleep. She wondered if Apollo could remove these for her, but she brushed the selfish desires aside. She had found a purpose for her life, and she couldn't do it with a child latched to her breast. Or worse, die in childbirth as Kelric feared. What good could she accomplish then?

Apollo's shoulders straightened, and he appeared taller as he stared down at her, his expression blank. Somehow, he was closer than before, his body pressing against hers. Fire roared inside her, warning her. She trembled, knees growing weak, beads of sweat bursting from her skin.

"I want to choose when I have a child," she blurted, and Apollo's mouth pinched into a thin line before opening. "Please!" She grasped the folds of his tunic before he could say no, partly in desperation, partly to keep herself from crumpling to the floor. Her knees shook uncontrollably.

Apollo's eyes narrowed down at her, considering. Then he slid an arm around her body, supporting her. His other hand slid down her belly.

"You do not fear me."

She didn't know if that was an observation, a command, or an accusation. A numbness crawled under her skin behind his palm and spread through her middle. Before she could decide the meaning of his words, his mouth captured hers. Her lips parted in surprise, and his tongue plunged between them. The sweet scent on his breath tasted of honey and figs.

Then he was gone. Her weight settled back into her own feet, and her knees buckled. She sank to the floor, gasping for breath, shivering.

Everything was so cold. Blackness clouded the edges of her vision, and her blood hammered in her ears, drowning out the gasps and shrieks from the assembly around her.

Kelric's face appeared before her, twisted into an expression that made her shrink from him. Pain surged from her hip and she released a cry, shaking. She avoided his gaze, wishing she could melt into the floor to escape it. Her hand strayed to her belly. A dull ache began to spread there, sharpening with every inhale. Apollo had done what she'd asked. She knew it.

The old scholar, Mandus, appeared at her other side, gentle, kind—a refuge. "Basileia, are you hurt?"

Dargos came into view behind him, concern deepening the lines around his eyes.

"It's… s-so cold," she managed, her teeth chattering.

Kelric unfastened his cloak and draped it around her shoulders. "Are we done here, Mandus?"

The scholar nodded, giving Gonivein's shoulder a gentle squeeze before he stood and addressed the assembly, stretching his arms to the sloped ceiling tiles.

"Phoebus Apollo, far-shooter and light bringer, has graced our presence and embraced Gonivein, Basileia of Golpathia, in the flames of his power. By her blood, we have borne witness that she is blessed with his gifts and has custody of his voice in all of Helinthia." He motioned to the other scholars, who immediately took up the hymn to Apollo, then nodded to Kelric.

Kelric lifted Gonivein in his arms. Despite the warmth of his cloak around her and his body against her, she still shivered. He didn't look at her, and she sensed something wild and aggressive churning within him.

CHAPTER 31

FORLUNA

RESENTMENT BURNED THROUGH FORLUNA AS she stomped across the plateau to the laurel. It was so easy for a god or goddess to appear whenever or wherever they wished, engulfed in a blaze of glory. Why—*why*—had Helinthia not protected Iptys as she'd promised? Was Charixes' sword opening her veins not enough blood?

Her eyes stung as she sank to her knees between the roots. She scraped the tears away with her palms and examined the delicate leaves of her herbs: basil, chamomile, and coriander. She'd planted them here shortly after she'd arrived in Golpathia. Several of the children at the camps had rashes—most likely caused by poor hygiene from being cooped up in a tight area with limited access to fresh water. The shoots were tender beneath her fingers, but they would do. She would make a salve mixed with a bit of olive oil and honey. She would not abandon the innocent.

She pulled the small knife from her boot and cut the stalks cleanly. Then tied the bundles with string and placed them in the sack beside her. She touched her hand to the bark of the ancient tree. "Thank you," she whispered.

Life hummed beneath her palm in answer. The tree appeared dead to everyone but her, with brittle, gray limbs and scaly bark. But she'd awakened it, called to it by name, and it had answered. Slowly, daily, life began to pulse once more through the pulpy passageways beneath the bark sheath. The earth under her feet vibrated with a healthy thrum from reinvigorated roots. Like a weary old friend refreshed after good company and rest. How long had this laurel been alone up here? It was massive, so Forluna knew it had been centuries. Why had it chosen to be here, of all places? Why not the Forest of the Shades with its kin?

Forluna wondered, but hadn't probed. Every nymph carried some secret into its afterlife. Every nymph had earned that right ten times over. When her own time came, she would hold her mysteries close, too, if for no other reason than to spite the gods who had used her without care for the toll they extracted.

She settled into an open space between the roots and leaned back against the tree trunk, gazing at the city sprawling before her. The streets were dotted with pockets of festivities for the winter solstice. It was a beautiful view. She should get a move on with making her medicines, but found her limbs suddenly weak. She hadn't allowed herself to think about the scarred woman in the market. Between the refugee camps and the confirmation ceremony this morning, not to mention the strain between her and Dargos, she'd kept herself busy. Purposely, she admitted, because she didn't want to succumb to the whirlwind of anxiety threatening to scatter her focus.

There was just one more confirmation ceremony remaining. It would be over tonight, and then the scholars would return to the Library. She needed to decide what to do about the eighth scholar before he disappeared forever. Or returned to the shadows to lurk.

'He'll never stop hunting you.'

Forluna dismissed the idea that the woman knew her exact circumstances. The old scars disfiguring her wizened features told of a past filled with suffering—at the hands of men, Forluna was sure. The woman had undoubtedly seen an opportunity to impart her wisdom on another soul desperate to escape a life of abuse and fear.

A fate driving scores of women and their children behind Golpathia's walls to avoid.

Charixes would burn every village, just as he had Tyldan, slaughter the men and the elderly, and take the women and children as spoils to abuse and exploit. Horror swelled in her gut at the thought of any of those terrified, innocent faces from the camps subjected to such cruelty.

Charixes was a monster. Regardless of how she felt about Helinthia's involvement in the creation of this mad world, Dargos was right to risk so much to end Charixes' tyranny.

'There are bodies in the water. The walls are red. The ground is muddied with blood. Starving animals gorge on the dead.'

Gonivein's trembling words sent a shiver down Forluna's spine. That was the future Charixes offered. Her hands tightened around the linen sack full of herbs, instinctively trying to reach for something to ground herself.

Forluna thought of the falcon trampled under the hooves of the stallion and ripped apart by the claws of the hydra and lion. She hoped Kelric's assumption that Charixes was the falcon was correct, but worry had creased Gonivein's forehead when she'd described the horrific vision. Forluna couldn't shake the hollow feeling in her gut. *What if the falcon is Gadnor?*

She drew a deep breath. Could Dargos and Kelric stop Charixes before Gadnor succumbed to this dreadful fate?

'Perhaps it's time you hunted him.*'*

The old crone might be onto something. But how could she hunt Charixes? She doubted he would allow anyone close to him, least of all *her*. He would recognize her immediately, and then it would be over. She thought of the gorgon's medallion the woman wore, the symbol of Athena. Was she a priestess of the powerful goddess of war and wisdom, or just a loyal worshipper?

Athena knew how to win battles.

But she was a god. Fickle and feckless as Helinthia. And yet…

Had she aided that woman? Was that why her wrinkled skin had no fresh cuts or bruises? Why her eyes gleamed so deadly and sharp?

'A woman who wins her battles.'

Forluna wished she had such confidence, that her first instinct wasn't to flee or hide, but to stand and fight.

She wished she wasn't so afraid.

CHAPTER 32

GONIVEIN

GONIVEIN JOLTED AWAKE AT THE sound of the door banging open. Kelric's arms tightened around her, grounding her as he stepped across the threshold of their bedroom.

Kelric nudged the door closed behind them with his foot, and she glanced up at him, trying to determine his mood. She couldn't tell. He avoided her gaze.

Did he carry me all the way back here? She wished she wasn't trapped in his arms. She tried to remember leaving the temple, but failed. *I must have fallen asleep.*

Kelric set her down on the bed. "You're awake." His emotionless tone unsettled her.

Her heartbeat sped up.

"Is something wrong?" Her words came out more like a croak. She cleared her throat, eying the water pitcher beside the window with longing. Her eyes trailed Kelric as he went over to it, but instead of pouring water into the cups, he reached for the amphora of wine resting on the floor beneath the table. He filled a cup to the brim with the ruby liquid and took a lengthy swill.

Her mouth watered. "May I have some water, please?"

Kelric gulped another mouthful of wine, pondered the cup in his hands, then looked over at her as though he hadn't heard her request. "What did he do to you?"

Her breath hitched at the accusing tone. His piercing gray eyes bore into her, and her earlier relief that Kelric couldn't see Apollo's true form disintegrated. She should have known his jealousy would be roused no matter what. Heat crawled up her neck and bloomed in her cheeks. She moved her tongue against her teeth, tasting honey and figs, recalling the warmth of Apollo's mouth against hers. His body. The chill of his absence. She shivered, averting her gaze from Kelric's face.

"He gave me the vision again. Told me that I wasn't *seei*—"

"I don't care about the vision," Kelric snapped.

She jumped. The inlet flashed in her mind. Kelric's face crumpling in rage as he lunged for her, fingers biting into her arm. Fear swelled in her gut like a wave about to crash.

She stared at him from across the room, holding her breath, wishing the floor would open up and swallow her.

Kelric set the wine cup down and stepped toward her.

Instinctively, she leaned back, digging her fingers into the fur blanket.

"The flames engulfed you. I saw them. But it wasn't just fire, was it? It was *him*. Apollo."

Blood pounded in her head now, beads of sweat matting her hair and clinging it to her neck. "Yes."

His eyes narrowed, raking her body up and down. "What did he do?"

She suddenly felt vile under his gaze, and defiance sparked within her. "What difference does it make, Kelric? He is a *god*."

"You belong to *me*." He towered over her now, brows furrowed. "He touched you, didn't he? Did he kiss you? Did you even try to push him off?"

Gonivein's gaze fell to her lap. She hadn't tried. The idea hadn't even crossed her mind. Perhaps Kelric was right to be upset. But the defiant voice persisted. *Apollo didn't ask my permission to kiss me.* And it was over so fast she barely even registered what was happening. *Could* she have stopped him?

"I take your silence to be no." Hurt and anger dripped from his tone. "I was foolish to think you really wanted a future here."

She looked up at him, confused. "What?"

"I thought I was what you wanted, but if you'd rather have a god, then I won't stop you." He returned to the wine and poured himself another cup.

Her heart slammed against her chest, panic seizing her with a sudden chill. "What are you saying?"

Kelric took another swig of his drink.

Her hand strayed to her belly. What had led Kelric to such a drastic conclusion? "I didn't choose to be Apollo's oracle. I don't *want* him. I didn't even want to *see* him, but I had to for the ceremony. What choice did I have?"

She hadn't chosen to be Kelric's bride, either, not willingly, but she kept that thought to herself. She was more than willing now. Didn't that matter?

"I want *you*, Kelric."

He turned back to her, his eyes searching, disbelieving, hoping.

She swallowed, feeling the need to explain herself, to convince him of her devotion. "But I did ask him for something. I didn't want the concern about children between us so… I asked him to make it so I could choose when to conceive. He… had to touch me to grant my request."

Kelric nearly choked on his wine. His knuckles tightened around the cup, eyes widening in shock and… *revulsion*?

Her hands shook as desperation sprouted within her. "We can decide when it's the right time to have a child. When I heal, when this war is over, when Gadnor takes the throne and the island is at peace again. You can love me without fear of losing me now."

He set the cup down on the table and rubbed his temples with his fingers, his shoulders more rigid than ever. The silence stretched, humming with tension like an aching limb. Her hip began to throb.

"So," he began slowly. "You told Apollo you wanted to choose when to conceive a child, then you let him kiss you."

A pit widened in her stomach. "I didn't *let* him kiss me—"

"So you asked him to?"

"No."

"You just said you did!"

"I didn't know what he would do." How had she misjudged this so horribly? *Why can't I do anything right?*

Kelric shook his head. "He's a *god*, Gonivein. Why wouldn't you want him?"

"Where is this coming from?" Her own anger was building now. "I want you to be passionate with me without fear of a child. That's all." She grabbed her chiton to steady her shaking hands.

Kelric began to pace. "We were already passionate without fear of a child. Just admit that you want him. That you don't want *me*."

"I *want* you!" Her thoughts scattered, sticking her words in her throat as he stormed back and forth across the bedroom floor. Each scuff of his sandals against the smooth stone raised her anxiety higher, disorienting her. How could she get through to him? Finally, she managed, "I just wanted to help."

"You thought betraying me in front of the entire city would help?"

She grabbed her head. Heart broken. She couldn't remember being so confused in her life. She'd been sure he'd be relieved at her news. "That's not—"

Kelric whirled to face her. His fingers splayed like talons in his frustration, as though he wanted to grab her and rip her apart. "What do I have to do to be good enough for you?" His voice broke, and he ran his hand through his hair, snagging a curl and dragging a snarl from between his lips.

She was so stunned. This was ludicrous, but she had hurt him, and that was the last thing she'd wanted to do. "I'm sorry."

He stopped pacing and rubbed his temples with his fingers, trying to calm himself. Finally, he looked over at her again. "I don't want you to speak to him again." The contempt she saw in his eyes made tears sting her eyes.

Her defiance reared. She shook her head. "I'm his oracle. I *have* to speak to him."

His eyes flashed. "Then tell him to find someone else to be his harlot."

Something inside of her snapped. She stood, needing to get away from him, get out of this room. The walls were closer than ever before, the air thick and hot with anger—from both of them.

"I won't do it." The words were out of her mouth before she could check them.

His chest heaved with anger. "Ferry it, Gonivein, you will!" He slammed his palm down on the table with a loud *thwack*. The wine pitcher wobbled, and one of the cups fell over and rolled off, landing with a loud *clang* on the stone floor.

She jumped, heart beating fast. Her words twisted in her throat, but she forced them out, flustered and desperate. "Do you know what happens to women who refuse the gods?" She recalled stories of mortal women who had—Cassandra, Daphne, Medusa. She used to find Kelric's irreverence for the gods funny. What a stupid girl she used to be. "I won't risk his wrath for something that doesn't change anything."

"It changes *everything*."

"This is madness!" Her frustration boiled over now, her jaw set. She'd had enough of this. Her heart was broken, closed. She needed space, time to think.

"It is madness for me to always wonder if Apollo has had his hands on you. You will, tomorrow morning. Sacrifice a dozen goats to placate him. I don't care." He flicked his hand at her, as though she were a doula with new instructions for some menial errand. As though this settled everything.

Gonivein lifted her chin, willing it not to tremble, willing the tears to stop flowing down her burning cheeks. How had her brilliant idea gone so awry? She'd wanted to prove herself to him, but what he demanded she do now was a new level of insanity. Better to offend a husband than a god. "No."

Something moved from the corner of her eye. A small thing, black, crawling along the windowsill.

Chirr-up. Chirr-up. Chirr—

Kelric spun toward the window. His hand already sailing out.

Gonivein screamed at the sharp *crack!* The strength of her defiance rushed out of her body. The inlet swam before her, Kelric's rage, his unreasonableness, his violence.

Kelric whirled back to her, and in her mind's eye she saw him lunge at her, face twisting with malice as he jerked her toward him, fingers digging into her arm, the explosion of pain as her hip wrenched from its socket.

Her hip throbbed with the memory, and her knees buckled. She wobbled for balance as Kelric advanced. Terror sharpened like a knife in her chest. She fell in a heap and put up her arms, curling herself against the bedside and squeezing her eyes shut. What would break this time? Her ribs? Her back? Her neck?

But the blows didn't come.

She peeled her arm away from her face to look at him.

Kelric stared down at her, his mouth open, a look of horror swirling in his silver eyes. His lips twitched as though they wanted to form words, but he spun on his heel and left the room instead. The door slammed behind him.

The shutter over the window dangled at a strange angle. Snapped from the force of Kelric's hit. Shimmering cricket guts were smeared across the grains. The crushed body had fallen on the floor, but one crooked leg remained caught in the stickiness. Twitching.

Sobs choked her. Despair, memories, her failure again to do something that mattered, tightened around her like chains, paralyzing her, pulling her down. Down. Down. The gulls screamed from outside, louder now that the window was broken.

Louder now that there was no cricket to mask her grief with a song.

Even an insect had paid for its loyalty to her with its life.

Mists and shadows swam before her eyes. She let the images come this time. She wanted—no, *needed*—to see him again.

Loric took his eyes from the river before him to settle on her, his black hair tousled, his cloak floating down his back and around his calves. His eyes sparked as they met hers, as though death didn't lay between them at all. She could almost smell the river at his feet, the petrichor of the surrounding bank, the wet of the enveloping mist on her skin.

The ache in her chest swelled and sharpened. She could hardly breathe. And then…

Loric stepped toward her.

Her breath hitched. In all her nightmares and visions, he had never done that before.

He took another step, then another. She was afraid to blink away the tears lest he suddenly vanish into the abyss. His deep brown eyes were so close, she could almost reach out and touch his face.

"Gonivein?"

A voice pulled her back to the bedroom, and Loric dissolved before her. She'd lost him all over again.

She grabbed her hair and pulled as hard as she could. A strangled cry ripped from her throat. Pain exploded across her scalp. She pulled harder, relishing the feel of something other than the torment that haunted her soul.

Firm, gentle hands slid around her wrists. "Please stop."

She opened her eyes, and through her messy strands, she recognized Gadnor's face.

He let her wrists go and swept her hair back, tucking it behind her ear. Tears glistened on his cheeks as he smoothed away the ones streaming down hers with his thumbs. He didn't ask her if she was all right. He didn't have to.

She sagged forward, and he knelt on the ground before her, catching her against his chest and holding her tightly as she cried.

CHAPTER 33

GADNOR

ANGER SIMMERED IN GADNOR'S VEINS, burned in his gut. It was all he could do to sit still while Gonivein calmed herself. He wanted to charge after Kelric and give him a piece of his mind, maybe a bite of his knuckles. Things he hadn't believed himself capable of before Artemis came to him in the Forest of the Shades. Her words had unlocked something deep within him. Something he'd shoved away and tried to forget.

That he could make a difference.

Hiding in the shadows wasn't his only option. Wasn't an option at *all*. Not anymore. He'd believed for the longest time that his best efforts to help those he loved were doomed to fail. That he wasn't strong enough, smart enough, quick enough. That it was better if he kept his mouth shut and stayed out of everyone's way. Alypius had almost convinced him of that again, but Tor reminded him how wrong that was.

Doing nothing hurt the ones he loved far more than trying to help, even if he failed. And he refused to do nothing now.

Gonivein finally quieted and pulled away from him. Her face was drawn and gaunt from famine and poor appetite, her bloodshot eyes pushed even further into her face now by red, swollen lids. She wiped her nose on her chiton and stared at her hands in her lap. "I'm sorry, Gadnor. I just… need to lie down."

"I'm going to speak to him," he said, rising.

Gonivein grabbed his arms with more strength than seemed possible for her fragile frame, pulling him back to the floor. "No." Her eyes widened with fear.

"Your devotion to your people and to this alliance isn't contingent on Kelric's abuse. You don't deserve that."

She lowered her gaze. "It's not completely his fault."

"Yes, it is." Gadnor's tone was sharp, but gentle. "Kelric is patient enough when it comes to getting something he wants. He's more than capable of keeping his anger in check after he has it, too."

Her shoulders slumped. "You can see the gods, can't you?" Her voice was barely above a whisper.

Gadnor swallowed, already sensing where this conversation was going.

"You saw Apollo," she answered for him. "Saw what he did. And Kelric is no fool."

"Apollo should not have kissed you." He squeezed her hand, drawing her downward gaze back to his. "That's actually why I came." He curled his other palm helplessly in his lap, ashamed that Apollo's blood flowed through him. It seemed not even gods were above the vilest behaviors of mortals. "Kelric should be your protector. You're not to blame for a *god's* actions." He smoothed away the fresh tears that rolled down her cheeks.

Gonivein pulled away and adjusted her weight evenly across her seat, her face pinching in pain as her hip shifted. "It wasn't all Apollo, Gadnor. I asked for something, and he granted it."

He recognized the guilt in the pout of her lip. Felt the same emotion boiling at his core from his own years of Kelric's bullying. How did Kelric convince others so easily that they were to blame for his rage? As though he, a grown man and now leader of the free peoples of Helinthia, bore no responsibility for maintaining his composure?

Feelings of helplessness, confusion, and conflict solidified in Gadnor's gut. He loved his brother, but hated how he hurt everyone around him without remorse. Gadnor had no idea how to reconcile these opposing sentiments.

"Please don't confront him," Gonivein whispered, drawing his attention. "What happened must stay between Kelric and me, or he'll think I betrayed him even more. *I* have to fix this, and *you* have to let me." Her blue eyes searched his, and a faint smile twisted her lips. "You were right. I am not powerless, so don't start treating me like I am."

He swallowed against the lump in his throat. She'd used his own words against him, and he knew he had lost.

"Apollo gave me the vision again." Her brows knitted together. "I saw the falcon surrounded by the other beasts, just as before. But this time, I noticed vines crowding around them, engulfing the wolves. And the beasts..." she massaged her temple with her fingers. "I don't think they attacked the falcon on their own. It seems like maybe... maybe they were provoked."

Gadnor tried to picture the image in his head. Just as before, he had no idea what future this foretold. "Perhaps the scholars could provide an interpretation?"

Gonivein shook her head. "Mandus told me the scholars are obligated to record the vision and share it with anyone who seeks the prophecies of the oracles, including the anax. I don't know what I'm supposed to learn from this vision, but whatever it is, it can't reach Charixes."

Gadnor's arm itched. He rubbed his scar absently, conscious of the fragile skin despite the irritation that begged to be scratched away. "What good are visions of the future if we can't learn their meaning?"

Gonivein bit her lip, and he realized how callous his words had sounded. "I'm sorry, I don't mean it like that," he said quickly. "I just... Maybe telling the scholars isn't the worst that could happen. Brother Mandus seems to know Forluna and Dargos. Perhaps we can trust him."

She shook her head again. "I don't want to risk it, not until I've thought it through more. Apollo seemed insistent that I would figure it out on my own. I just need a little more time." Her eyes darted between him and the door.

She was ready for him to leave.

He nodded and stood. Forluna and Dargos might have an opinion on this new development as well. Nothing need be decided right now.

"Can I help you up?"

Gonivein seemed to consider it a moment, then shook her head. "No, I'm fine here."

Gadnor frowned. The stone floor was hard and uncomfortable. His own aching legs testified to that fact, but he wouldn't wound her pride by coddling her. "Please come to me if you ever need help. I'm not afraid of my brother anymore."

Gonivein swallowed and nodded, squeezing his hands with what he was sure was a forced, albeit convincing, smile. "I will. I promise."

With a final nod, he turned and left, closing the door softly behind him. He sat on the lip of the fountain in the center of the courtyard to catch his breath and let the needles ease from his legs. Anger raced through him. At Kelric. At himself.

He should have tried harder to convince her to call off the marriage, or postpone a little longer. *I could have made Kelric promise to honor the alliance without a marriage. Why didn't I try?* He dropped his head in his hands and massaged his temples. *Why didn't I think of that?*

Somewhere deep within him, he doubted Gonivein would have agreed to such a proposition. Even deeper simmered doubts that Kelric would have agreed. The embarrassment of such a publicly anticipated ceremony being postponed would have been too much of a blow to Kelric's pride to brush aside.

Smells of the evening meal began to waft out of the triklinion.

The douloi began bustling to and from the kitchens and the storerooms to prepare the meal. Every now and again, he heard Euanthe scold Klymene for doing something incorrectly, dawdling, or retrieving the wrong item. The girl popped out of the kitchen and skirted along the edge of the peristyle, muttering something that sounded like "screechy old bat" before disappearing into another storeroom. Although, it could just as well have been "I'll get that."

Humor twitched his lips despite his roiling emotions. He would never reveal which one he thought it was.

CHAPTER 34

KELRIC

KELRIC STEPPED INSIDE HIS ANDRON and slammed the door. His blood boiled, head spun in confusion and hurt. Gonivein had *betrayed* him.

The room was dark, the dampness strong. He kicked the leg of a couch as he made his way to the window and threw it open. A breeze rushed through the room, ruffling parchment and quills haphazardly piled on the small desk against the wall.

He stared across the room, eyes unfocused. Tiny dust motes filtered through the beams of light shining in from outside. He wished his father were here, rambling about some problem happening in the city. *He* would know how to handle the mess Kelric found himself in. How to quell this rage. How to think through the pain and find the root of the problem. Find a solution he could stomach. He could teach him how to argue with his wife, make her understand.

He couldn't recall his parents ever raising their voices at one another—his father must have nipped those tendencies quick. He remembered laughter and love, playfulness, strong arms, and a constant, warm, full feeling inside of him whenever he was with them.

Kelric reached for memories of his mother's face, but try as he might, he could only see a blur surrounded by dark hair.

A sudden ache in his chest sucked the breath from his lungs, and he slumped onto the crooked couch. Grief at the loss of her image, which he'd held so close to his heart all these years, trembled through his limbs. There was nothing but an empty, gaping hole. She was gone. Completely. And the only person who could have helped him reclaim those memories was gone, too.

Because I killed him.

He was alone. Alone with a wife who despised him and a polis on the brink of an uprising against his leadership. Alone in the crumbling ashes of the future—a future he had dreamed would be filled with the joy he'd lost in his childhood. And somewhere in the midst of it all, a Leirion lurked in the shadows, toying with him, turning his kyrioi against him, shattering whatever safety and comfort there was to be had in the last stronghold standing against Charixes' tyranny.

He fished inside his pocket and pulled out the handkerchief. He crushed it in his hand, the hurt of Gonivein's betrayal writhing through him, tangling with his grief and remorse for what he'd done to save her.

They had come to an agreement on their wedding night, hadn't they? Found new hope for their love and their future, despite all the horrible things they'd endured. Somehow, she had convinced him that it hadn't all been for nothing. That she wanted him. That she *loved* him.

She lied.

She'd made him feel safe laying his soul in her hands. Why did she want to be near Apollo again? What had that *god* ever done to prove his love to her?

Kelric sat at his father's desk and dropped his head in his hand, rubbing the ache growing behind his temples. *She said she wanted to help me. To make it so I could love her without fear.* Was that really her aim? Or was it revenge that fueled this betrayal?

Retribution for letting a doulos' body float away? For not leaving her to die in the inlet?

And after everything he'd done to assure her he would never hurt her again, she had cowered before him—as though all his efforts meant nothing, as though his promises to her meant nothing.

Haven't I atoned enough?

Grief, guilt, and hatred swelled inside of him, twisting and coiling. He clenched his fists, snagging a few curls and yanking his scalp. He had made mistakes, but he had made them for *her*, for his city, for everyone he loved, for a future where they could be happy. *Why can't she see that?*

A five-headed hydra embroidered on silk threads hung on one wall. A glorious and fierce tapestry that signified the might of Golpathia—the benevolent leader feared by his enemies, adored by his kyrioi, revered by his councilmen and kubernai, loved by his wife. His father had made it look so effortless, dining and entertaining guests every other day, always with an attentive ear and quick solutions that fostered loyalty among all levels of the polis. His presence had demanded respect from everyone.

I killed him. For her.

He opened his eyes and stared at his cluttered desk. His attention landed on a scroll—the unopened report from Tetra. He broke the seal and unraveled it, desperate to direct his attention anywhere but the sickening churn in his gut.

Fields seeded: 3 wheat. 1 barley.

Kelric frowned. Tetra had twelve fields to sow. What had happened to the rest?

Olive oil: 3 amphorae.

Figs: 1 cart.

A knot formed in Kelric's throat. There were three groves each of olive and fig trees in Tetra. The village was located closer to the mountain, where melting snows created more fertile soil than any other place in Golpathia. He'd expected far more than three amphorae of oil and one cart of figs. He read on.

Goats: Births, 20. Deaths, 18. Total, 80.

The list of livestock went on. Kelric skimmed, skipping notes about sacrifices and observed rituals. He didn't care about those silly provisions—if he could *take* sacrifices from the gods, he would.

Men: 33, Battle trained: 24

Douloi: 15, Doulai: 5

Women: 5

Kelric blinked. *Five women?* He squinted, noting Tryphus' additional scrawl beside the census.

35 women, 38 children, and 10 elders were sent to Golpathia on the last new moon as a precaution against attack. The men have established a night watch. Talk of abandoning the village, orchards, and seeded fields to follow their women to Golpathia is frequent. Assurances of Tetra's protection against Charixes is paramount to maintaining stability.

So, that was what Tryphus had been so concerned about. Kelric lowered the scroll, a hollow feeling spreading in his gut. Was it too late to give assurances to Tetra, or had the village already been abandoned? How many more villages were on the verge of desertion? Of burdening the city with their dead weight?

"What assurances do they want?" He growled. He had none to give. His anger rekindled. He should be focused on planning a defense against Charixes—planning a *war*—not chasing after Gonivein like a lovesick puppy, trying to prove himself to her. Why was everything falling apart?

In a rage, he swung his arms across the desk, sweeping everything—scrolls, quills, trinkets, bowls—onto the hard tiles. Pottery shattered, bronze jangled loudly, parchment fluttered. He released a bellow of rage and kicked the desk. Wood splintered as the leg cracked in two.

An empty amphora rolled across the tiles. A moment later, a mouse leapt out of its wide mouth and scurried off into a dark corner. A bronze platter spun like a top, creating a warbling racket against the stone floor. At last it stilled, and the silence brought a finality to his outburst that left him exhausted and drained from the inside out.

"My, my."

Kelric spun toward the voice, drawing the dagger at his belt. "Who's there?"

A shadow elongated from the wall just under the tapestry and stepped closer to the shaft of light shining through the window.

"I have come on behalf of one we both held in highest regard." The man's voice was gravelly and deeper than any voice he'd heard before.

A disguise.

Kelric tightened his grip on the dagger. "I doubt such a person exists."

"Your father."

Rage sparked at his fingertips. "If that's true, then show me your face." He couldn't see it so much as *feel* the man smile.

"I can't do that."

"Why not?"

"I think you know."

Kelric did. This was the Leirion.

The figure tilted his head. "Kill me, if you must, Basileus—if you *can*—but know that another shall take my place. You will never be rid of us."

Kelric squeezed the hilt of his blade, wanting to rise to this challenge. If he knew it was a bluff, he would, but the Leirion had all but admitted there was another. He needed to find out who before he eliminated this one. "What do you want?"

"I want to help you."

Kelric scoffed. "You're nothing but a doulos to Charixes' tyrannical ravings."

The man spread his hands out, palms up. "I answer the anax's summons, yes, but I am Golpathian, and my allegiance is to Golpathia. A delicate balance, but a necessary one. Your father recognized this, too."

Kelric didn't like the control this man had over the conversation.

"You threatened my wife."

The man's head tilted beneath his fur hood. "*Threat* is a strong word. I wouldn't call it that."

"Then what would you call it?" Kelric ached to feel his enemy's warm blood slicking down the hilt of his knife and coating his fingers.

"A simple greeting. To let you know we are here."

"Here to slit my throat if I don't do what you want, you mean." Kelric evaluated the cluttered room. The brass platter within range of his foot was in perfect alignment for a well-aimed kick to the intruder's stomach. It could stun the man long enough to get the upper hand.

The Leirion shrugged. "Killing you would... complicate matters."

"Killing *you* would complicate nothing. Say what you came for, or I'll make sure your death is painful rather than quick."

The man chuckled. "I've come to extend you an offer to join our ranks, as your father did before you."

"What makes you think I would ever agree to that?"

"Because the Leirion are necessary to Golpathia's survival."

"The Leirion are cowards and murderers."

"The Leirion are businessmen, merchants, and soldiers. We are the cornerstones of this city, and our allegiance to Charixes has ensured Golpathia's prosperity."

"Golpathia is prosperous because of the food the sea and earth provide, not Charixes' good nature." *He's lying.* But the man's confidence rattled Kelric.

"Yet your markets are filled with more than just fish and wheat: goats, geese, wine, fruits." The man's eyes flicked to the report from Tetra, crumpled on the floor. "The harvests are dwindling, Basileus. Think. The fruits of our labor cannot begin to account for our abundance. The dead palms and olives in your own courtyards are a testament to this fact."

Kelric's eyes narrowed. The extravagance and variety of food at his wedding flashed into his mind. Tetra was the best of his villages, and it was doing poorly. Alypius and Ephastes seemed to be doing exceptionally well, despite the drought. Could Charixes be supplying their farms? Kelric hated how much sense that made.

Tryphus. His archon had to have known about this. Perhaps Kelric had been wrong to dismiss the possibility he was a Leirion. Was it the villages' instabilities fueling his caution? *Or is it his loyalty?* Tryphus was well placed to fan the villages' fears and encourage them to bloat the city with all their helpless and useless population, pressure Kelric into submission to end the chaos.

Yet something still wasn't quite right.

"Why would Charixes feed a potential threat? Our friendship with Dargos has never been a secret. He had to know we would eventually take his side."

The Leirion rested his hand over his chest, his calm riling Kelric. "Charixes wants *peace*. It is Dargos pushing for bloodshed. Would you have us suffer as Shallinath suffers for his insolence?" The man's smooth tone donned a sharp edge. "Bare markets, absent merchants, starvation driving innocent children down to Hades in faster numbers than Demeter's grief?"

Kelric's heart began to drum in his ears, and he lowered the knife. *This Leirion doesn't know my father's loyalty to Charixes was to protect Gadnor.* But Kelric knew how cunning his father had been. He would have used the situation to every advantage for himself and Golpathia.

Perhaps Kelric should consider doing the same.

If a large part of Golpathia's economy relied on Charixes, then waging a war could cripple Golpathia. How many people involved in the supply chain were Leirion? Enough to start a revolt? Kelric's disgruntled councilmen and their disdain for Dargos' presence made much more sense now. He seethed. *Those bastards knew all of this, too.* This wasn't just personal politics. Golpathia's security was at stake.

Kelric was even more out of his depth than he had dreamed.

"Should you agree, you must hand over Dargos as proof of your commitment to our oath. His sacrifice will ensure our city continues to thrive and will solidify your power as basileus."

Kelric raked a hand through his hair. Joining the Leirion was one solution, but it was a betrayal to everything he held dear. How many times had the Leirion tried to kill him? They would murder Gadnor if they ever found out who he was, and they *would* find out eventually. And Gonivein would never forgive him if he betrayed Dargos. *I will not follow my father in this.*

But he needed to play along. Learn as much as possible. Every Leirion had to be dealt with. Removed. Replaced with someone loyal. "Let's say I do what you ask. What then? What happens when the famine doesn't end? When even Charixes has no more goods to smuggle into our agora? How do the Leirion plan to counter that?"

The man seemed to grow taller, and Kelric sensed a scowl beneath the dark hood. He smirked in satisfaction that he'd riled the man.

"Do you know why this famine is happening?" the Leirion asked.

"Charixes usurped the throne from Helinthia's anassa, and the goddess punished us with a famine." Kelric plucked every word directly from one of Dargos' speeches. "When Charixes is dead, she will send rain."

"A falsehood spun by Dargos to stir up the populace," the man snarled. "This famine began because Iptys murdered the Oracle of Hera. This famine is *Hera's* vengeance, not Helinthia's. It is *Hera's* favor we must seek."

Kelric scoffed. This allegation had been never been entertained by his father or Dargos, and for an obvious reason. "Iptys is dead. Why would Hera still punish us?"

"Because Iptys didn't act alone." The man brandished a finger at Kelric. "Her companion was an accomplice. She escaped. The Leirion have searched for her ever since."

Unease skittered across his shoulders. *'Iptys' companion...' Forluna? Murder?* If it was true, how had they not recognized her right under their noses? Kelric side-eyed the man, forcing a smirk. "The most elite spies on the island, and you can't find one woman?"

"Too few people ever noticed her presence—why would they, when the anassa was their object? Fewer still could identify her after all this time. This famine may never end until she dies as nature intended. But in the meantime, Golpathian citizens need not be manipulated to their deaths by Dargos' lies. Heed my words. Charixes rose to power at Hera's behest, to deliver justice."

Kelric's heart hammered in his ears. Had Forluna lied to them? Was that the real reason the nymph had hidden herself away in the Forest of the Shades, why that Leirion had tried to kill her? She had claimed they were after the child, after Gadnor. What if that was just a story to cover up her crimes? To hide her role in this famine?

A chill ran down his spine. *The Fury in the Ordan*—the one who had turned the lions against Tor's command. It was Forluna who had said Gadnor was its target, to remove the last threat to Hera's victory over Helinthia. *What if she lied then, too?* What if the real target was Forluna all along?

His head spun.

"I see you have much to consider."

Kelric's attention snapped back to the Leirion. His adrenaline spiked. He'd been so stunned, so distracted, the man could have easily killed him.

"I will leave you to think it over. When I come to you again, you will tell me your decision."

Kelric gaped at the man, speechless, dazed.

The intruder brazenly turned his back to him and climbed out of the window, disappearing before Kelric could reconsider plunging his dagger into him.

He's lying. This can't be true.

But what if it was?

CHAPTER 35

GONIVEIN

GONIVEIN PUSHED HERSELF UP FROM the floor, wincing as pain lanced across her hip and surged into her lower back.

She had to get up. She couldn't stay here waiting… waiting for what? For Loric's ghost to come back to her? For the cricket to spring back to life and sing? For Kelric to storm back in and crush a little more of her fractured soul?

She glanced at the broken window. The cricket's mangled black leg had stopped twitching. Its guts had hardened, encasing it onto the wood like some trophy a hunter put on display. Tears slipped over her eyes.

Kelric.

She bit her lip, recalling his tenderness on their wedding night, the way he had melted through her reservations and rekindled her devotion to him. How easily she had forgiven him.

She felt stupid.

She rubbed her swollen eyes, guilt coiling inside her like a viper dripping venom.

'He's more than capable of keeping his anger in check.' Gadnor's words replayed over and over in her mind. They were logical, but

somehow, she couldn't believe she was completely blameless. She was never blameless.

But the cricket had been.

Loric had been.

Eltnor and Yulie and all the people of Tyldan had been.

The women and children suffering in the camps were, too.

She covered her face with her hands.

I'm to blame for all of it.

She dearly hoped Gadnor would do as he promised and say nothing. He had been the target of Kelric's ire long enough, and to become that again on *her* account made her stomach churn. She wished Gadnor hadn't come at all. She loved him for wanting to help, but she hated worrying for him now.

Gadnor had broken free; it had to stay that way. She couldn't let him see her hurting anymore. No one could, or they would put themselves in Kelric's way. She recalled the concern etched into Dargos' face this morning and nibbled her cracked lips. She would have to be extra careful around him.

Though Dargos had relinquished his role as her protector, she knew he would never stand by and see her abused. Especially by Kelric. And Kelric…

How would his retaliation manifest if Dargos interfered?

Dargos was a fugitive of the anax, a walking target for everyone outside the villa walls. It would be too easy for Kelric to exact revenge. She wanted to believe he wouldn't, but Dargos had always said Kelric was brash and reckless, prone to letting his anger control him.

Deep down, caution whispered. *'Build a wall around yourself. Don't let anything in. Don't let anyone see.'*

I won't be the reason anyone else gets hurt.

She struggled to rise, using the bed frame as a crutch. Her muscles shook in protest. Pins and needles surged through her as the blood rushed back into starving limbs.

Her feet now under her, Gonivein drew in a long steady breath, held it, then slowly let it out. She couldn't wallow in this room anymore—people would start to wonder where she was, to worry, come looking for her. Then they would see the broken window. Ask questions.

Besides, Apollo had shown her something of import in the vision. *The vines.* She would see its meaning revealed to her. Perhaps it could save Helinthia. Save Dargos and Gadnor and Forluna, and all the innocent people inside these walls.

Forluna. If anyone had any idea what the vines could mean, it would be her.

Gonivein hobbled over to where her crutch rested against the wall beside her vanity and tucked it under her armpit. The hard wood dug into her raw skin as she leaned her weight into the rough cradle. She gritted her teeth against the burn. The ache of her hip lessened considerably, however—an uneasy compromise she made for speed.

She reached for the door handle and pulled it open a sliver. Voices floated through from the courtyard. Blood raced in her veins as panic surged. Her throat closed, restricting precious air to her lungs.

Breathe.

She peered through the small crack to find Klymene drawing a bucket up from the well as Euanthe explained the special herb concoction she always added to the wash water to make the linens smell fresh and 'help Basileus Kelric sleep'. How long had Euanthe been doing this for him? Her stomach pinched. *Since he lost his mother?*

Gonivein drew steady breaths and released them, just as Forluna had taught her. Slowly, her racing heartbeat calmed again, lungs expanding and contracting in a steady rhythm.

Euanthe and Klymene disappeared into the washroom, and Gonivein hobbled over to Forluna and Dargos' door and knocked. There was no answer. She rapped her knuckles against the solid wood, harder this time. Still nothing. Had they stayed in the agora after the confirmation? There were festivities today for the winter solstice, but she doubted Forluna would stay for them. Had she gone to the camps? Her supply bag hadn't been with her during the confirmation. The nymph would have come back for it.

That only left one place she might be.

Gonivein's eyes turned toward the slope that rose behind the villa. Her eyes followed the winding path, lined by sharp-edged tombs, to the plateau, where the laurel once flourished over the glorified dead. Forluna was also growing a garden there, full of herbs for her tinctures.

Gonivein could just make out the leafless branches of the tree reaching toward the sky like claws—all that was visible from this far below. Yes. Forluna would be there. She knew it.

She could enlist a guard or Klymene to fetch her, but that would involve more people than she wanted. *The fewer involved, the better.*

She straightened her shoulders and started forward, slipping past the washroom, where soothing scents of camphor, vanilla, and lavender wafted through the back archway. She followed the gravel path to the back row of apartments. She hoped she didn't run into Kelric coming from his andron. To her relief, his door was closed.

Beside the left-most apartment, the path up the mountain began. She stared at the place where she and Loric had once hidden from a Ninenarn captain, then looked away. She drew in a deep breath and began to climb.

Every step shot pain deep into her pelvis, jarring her spine and surging down her leg. She gritted her teeth and jammed her crutch into the earth in front of her, hoisting herself forward and up with her arms and pushing as much as possible with her good leg. But she was forced to use her broken one, too, and before she got to the plateau, tears streamed freely down her face. After the first ten steps, she had decided to stop looking at her destination. It never seemed to get any closer, no matter how many agonizing steps she climbed.

"Gonivein!"

Forluna's voice had never sounded sweeter.

Gonivein nearly collapsed where she stood. She had reached the plateau.

Forluna leapt over the gnarled, curled roots of the ancient laurel and rushed toward her. She slung Gonivein's arm over her shoulders and grasped her around the waist.

Forluna was surprisingly strong. Pain eased from Gonivein's hip as she allowed Forluna to help her to the tree. "What Furies possessed you to climb all the way up here?"

Gonivein eased down between the roots and leaned back against the giant trunk. Her body trembled with too much agony to respond.

Forluna held a water skin to her lips. Gonivein drank greedily, staring up at the boughs, shocked to find tiny buds on the ends of its branches. She swallowed her last gulp and looked at the nymph with wide eyes.

"I thought this tree was dead."

Forluna nodded wistfully. "It was suffering."

"How did you bring it back without rain?"

Forluna stroked the gnarled trunk soothingly, as though it were sentient, like a baby or a grieving friend. "Sometimes a thing just needs to know it is not alone to thrive again."

"A tree?"

Forluna smiled. "This 'tree' is much more than it seems. Most laurels are." She spoke with such respect and adoration. Love, even. Gonivein wished she could feel such a deep connection with something.

Rather, she wished everything she connected with wouldn't die before their bond could thrive.

Forluna cocked her head. "Mind telling me why you braved such agony to come up here? Is it about the camps? You could have sent someone for me."

Gonivein shook her head. "I didn't want to involve anyone else."

Forluna's ears perked forward. Up here in this secluded place, the nymph had felt secure enough to pull her hair back, letting her long, cat-like ears breathe.

"What has happened?" Forluna's eyes grew serious as her hands instinctively wandered to Gonivein's broken hip, checking to see if any damage had occurred.

"It's the vision," Gonivein said.

"What about the vision?" Forluna's brow pinched in trepidation.

Unease crept through Gonivein in a rush of heat. She was already sweating from her exertion up the mountain, but the fear in Forluna's face sparked an unyielding flame of anxiety that made her skin weep all the more profusely. Her clothes and hair stuck uncomfortably to her body.

She knows this vision is the key, too.

"I saw vines encroaching on the beasts as they circled the falcon, springing up and trapping them where they stood." The images swirled into focus in her mind's eye. "They grew and grew until all the wolves suffocated beneath them. And the beasts… I always thought they wanted to kill the falcon, but now…" The beasts had pressed closer together, agitated as their freedom diminished beneath the encroaching vines. "Now I think the vines *made* them do it."

The color leached from Forluna's face.

"Do you know what it could mean?"

"Were there lilies on these vines?" Forluna's voice was barely above a whisper.

Gonivein closed her eyes, willing herself back to that raised dais. Her stomach roiled inside her as she forced herself to focus on the details, to *see*. The falcon stood at the center of the circling beasts. Around them were hundreds of wolves, calm, watching, waiting.

Vines sprouted from the earth, green tendrils snaking upward, wrapping around the legs of the wolves, who yelped in terror and squirmed to break free.

Gonivein wanted to flee, knowing their deaths were imminent.

A little longer. The vines grew and thickened, smothering the wolves and encroaching on the beasts, whipping them into a bloodthirsty frenzy. And there, at the tips of the green shoots, tiny white buds formed and burst into white trumpets with five delicate petals.

"Yes," she said.

Forluna drew in a sharp breath. *"Leirion."*

Hearing their name froze Gonivein's blood, sapping her warmth. "It could be anyone." She had trusted Tendior, one oath sworn to protect Shallinath, and he had killed Loric in front of her. She had *loved* Raleon—he was to become her father. And he had nearly killed her.

"Yes." Forluna's face turned slack, eyes distant.

Gonivein waited, knowing the nymph was formulating a plan.

Finally, Forluna put her hand on Gonivein's shoulder. "I will tell Dargos of this after Tor's confirmation tonight. You should rest."

Gonivein nodded. Chills crawled along her neck as she considered which was worse, the nightmares that haunted her dreams when she slept, or this new waking terror she found herself living?

CHAPTER 36

LITHANEVA

HELIOS DRAGGED THE LAST RAYS of the sun below the horizon, and Lithaneva pushed herself away from the tiny, now indiscriminate, letters on the scroll before her. She sank back on the couch and rubbed her aching neck.

Branitus released a sigh and looked gratefully at the sprinkling of stars shining through the window. "Same time tomorrow, then, Aden."

Aden nodded and began rolling up the parchments they had spent most of the afternoon and evening poring over. Maps, harvest and census records, military lists. Aden had cleverly inserted an inkblot on the first letter of every commander he believed to be trustworthy. Branitus hadn't given them a moment's peace the entire day. As inconvenient as his presence was, Lithaneva had to give him credit. Branitus had maintained attention on the task at hand and considered every village, their inhabitants, and their harvest projections carefully.

The picked-over carcass of a roasted goose sat on a table nearby. A plate of crumbs was all that remained of the bread loaf, and the amphora of wine was almost empty.

Aden stuffed the documents into his leather bag and bid them goodnight.

Branitus rubbed his eyes. When he pulled his hand away, Lithaneva noticed new lines at the corners and between his bushy eyebrows.

Her very first impression of him at their wedding had been that of a blubbering fool who enjoyed the luxuries of life and delegating important tasks to others far too much. Seeing him now, she knew that was untrue, and something within her softened a little more for him. Branitus enjoyed fine things, but he cared for his polis, and Charixes' demands worried him deeply.

If only I could share my plans with him. But anxiety made men wild and unpredictable, and the possibility that Branitus could react the opposite of how she hoped was too great a risk. It would endanger Aden, too. Better to keep her husband in the dark. At least for now.

She stood, aching for a release from the stress and tediousness of the last few hours. She wanted Helinthia. To share all she had learned with the goddess and coax a smile from those delicious lips, feel the warmth of Helinthia's approval rushing through her body.

"I'm going to the garden," she said. Branitus nodded as he reached for the amphora and splashed what remained into his empty wine cup.

"Good night, Lithie."

The villa household was accustomed to her spending long hours in the temple. She'd explained to Branitus when she first arrived that being there soothed her. Of course, she'd neglected to mention that a particular statue within the temple was responsible for most of the soothing. He hadn't questioned it. Devotion to the gods wasn't out of the ordinary, after all. But she wouldn't put it past Charixes to have bribed one of the douloi or villa guards to keep a closer eye on her activities.

She laid her hand on the door handle, considering. She wasn't afraid of being caught in Helinthia's company. Mortal eyes couldn't see Helinthia unless the goddess wanted them to, but they might find her behavior questionable, all the same.

She turned back around. "I think I'll give the guards and douloi the night off. Perhaps bequeath a few drachmae to go into the city and revel a bit. I think they've earned it after suffering through a week of my father's tyranny."

Branitus shifted his jaw thoughtfully, then nodded. "Fine." A tense silence stretched between them.

The way Branitus looked at her stirred her anxiety. There was something dark behind those eyes, a scheme she knew she would loathe. She wanted to escape this room, but if she didn't address whatever it was in his mind head on, it might grow beyond her ability to squash it. She sighed. "Out with it, Branitus."

He shifted uneasily. "What are we going to do about the other thing your father wants?"

"Other thing?" Her mind spun, then her stomach flopped. *Oh no.* "A child?"

She wished the ground would open up and swallow her right here, right now. *Remain calm, logical.* It was obvious Branitus wasn't fond of the idea. *He's just scared of Charixes. I can get out of this.*

"Simple." She shrugged as though the idea didn't make her want to lose the contents of her dinner. "We lie."

Branitus quirked a brow. "Lie?"

"Women sometimes have difficulty conceiving. I could have difficulty."

Branitus rubbed his neck, unconvinced. "Wouldn't a… physician need to be involved?"

"Not until we've been married much longer. It's only been a month. My father is just trying to scare you. Don't let him."

Before he could say anything else, she pulled the door open and stepped over the threshold, eager to be out of his presence. She didn't think Branitus would try to follow her, but just in case…

She stopped herself mid-stride and turned around again, swiveling on her toes. "Perhaps you should go to the market too, get Larxes something nice. Maybe a new lyre."

Branitus paused his wine midway to his mouth. Suspicion narrowed his eyes, as though she might suddenly transform into a viper before him and strike him for his infidelity. "Oh?"

She laughed at his expression. "I enjoy music, you know. His lyre sounds a bit... hollow? Besides, he makes you happy, and that matters to me." Not a total lie, she was glad to realize.

Branitus remained quiet, studying her, but his eyes lit up with a skeptical hope as her words lingered between them.

"Perhaps one with pearl or gold inlays. Can you imagine his handsome grin to hold such a fine instrument?" She shrugged and stepped out into the night, satisfied she had effectively planted the seed in Branitus' mind to get him far away from her this evening.

She sought out the douloi and guards—finding them all finishing their meal in the kitchen—and informed them they were free to go into the city. She smiled when she caught Branitus slipping away after them. Most of the market in the agora was closed this time of night, but Branitus wouldn't let that stop him from finding the doorstep of the most skilled lyre craftsman in Thellshun and making demands. No doubt the taverns would be welcoming to him, as well. There should be plenty of time to accomplish all she wanted to without being seen.

She grabbed an amphora of wine from the storeroom, an alabaster box of incense from her bedroom vanity, and her knife, before hurrying to the gardens.

The full moon filtered through the leaves, illuminating her path through the bushes. Even if it had been pitch-dark, she would know the way into her goddess' arms from anywhere. She stepped into the marble temple and made quick work of stacking kindling and setting a blaze on the altar. She sprinkled a pinch of incense on the glowing embers, and a sweet floral scent wafted upwards.

Helinthia's statue stared at her from the other side of the flames. Curls of smoke caressed her painted marble features, and Lithaneva licked her dry lips. Helinthia was so close!

She closed her eyes, willing herself not to fidget with impatience, and tilted her head, listening for footfalls or snapping twigs. She couldn't afford another incident like what had happened on her wedding night when they'd discovered Gadnor skulking in the leaves. He was lucky Helinthia hadn't killed him or turned him into something that couldn't spill their secrets, but the goddess must have known he would be an important ally.

'~G,' the note had said. Strange it had been Gadnor who sent the message. He'd seemed so timid and inexperienced at her wedding. Wouldn't Kelric or Dargos have been a better choice to interact with a princess?

She furrowed her brow. Why *hadn't* Helinthia killed him? Lithaneva wished she could ask the goddess, but whatever rules Hera had established for this divine conflict, Helinthia wouldn't break them to satisfy frivolous curiosity.

A soft breeze blew outside the temple, rustling through the trees and sending a shower of yellowing leaves to scatter across the tiled floor. The cuckoo called from the villa eaves, but she detected no unusual noises. No mortals creeping in the bushes.

She raised her blade to her palm, cold and sharp. Her skin prickled with gooseflesh in the nighttime chill, but underneath, her veins burned to feel the warmth of her true love against her body. Revel in the light of her smile when she told her the good news of their plan. Taste the victory as their tongues intertwined.

She sliced her palm and squeezed the droplets onto the glowing embers of the altar. The coals hissed and sizzled, and Lithaneva stooped to grab the jar of wine at her feet. She added a splash to her offering. The flames leapt briefly, consuming the fuel.

Lithaneva cut a glance at the other stone deities circling her in the small temple. In her early days as Helinthia's oracle, she'd worried one of them might answer her summons instead, but Helinthia assured her that the blood sacrifice of the oracle ritual could only be answered by the deity who'd chosen them. So far, that had proven true.

The features of Helinthia's statue softened, and the carved drapes of her gown melted into buttery soft fabrics that swayed as she stepped down from the stone plinth. Raven curls bounced upon her shoulders, floating across her maroon eyes.

Lithaneva rubbed her thumb over her fingertips, slick with blood.

Helinthia's gold sandals scuffed against the marble tiles as she maneuvered around the altar. Her expression was regal and unreadable. "Why have you called me, Lithaneva?"

The goddess' tone wasn't very welcoming.

Lithaneva swallowed. "Is this a bad time?" She fought the urge to bite her lip, hoping the answer was no.

Helinthia's gaze drifted over Lithaneva's shoulder to peer through the doorway into the night. Lithaneva followed her gaze, suddenly afraid she hadn't checked the shadows well enough and someone was out there, watching them.

Helinthia turned back to her, relaxing her shoulders.

"What's wrong, my goddess?" Lithaneva clasped her hands to keep from reaching forward and cradling Helinthia's face, caressing the smooth skin. Her fingertips burned with desire. "Are you angry with me?"

Helinthia's expression softened. "No, Lithie. Never."

Lithaneva released the breath she'd been holding. "Good, because I thought for a mom—"

Helinthia swept forward and gathered Lithaneva into her arms, crushing her lips and smothering the rest of her words with her soft, sweet tongue. Surprise and pleasure surged through Lithaneva at the sudden passion. She slid her non-bloody hand around Helinthia's waist, pressing her palm against the muscles beneath her shoulder blades, drawing their hips together. Heat burned where their bodies touched, intensifying with every ragged breath that escaped between kisses.

The goddess pulled away, licking her lips, and rested her forehead against Lithaneva's. Breathing deeply. "I worried for you."

Lithaneva rubbed her fingers along the trench of Helinthia's spine. "Why?"

"Because your father is a bastard, and I know how hateful he is. How *hurtful* he is."

"He'll never break me so long as I know you are waiting for me." Lithaneva stole another kiss. "I have good news." Her eyes wandered to Helinthia's perfect heart-shaped mouth, eager for it to curve into a smile. "Charixes divulged his grand plans to me and Branitus." Lithaneva stroked the goddess' bare arm. "I am so close to giving you victory."

Helinthia leaned back to look at her fully. "Did you call me here to scheme? You know I trust you to do what needs to be done without my constant oversight. It's why I chose you."

There was no mistaking the chastising in her tone, but Lithaneva was still too breathless from their passionate reunion to let the false assumption sour her mood. She swirled her finger around a strand of Helinthia's hair. "*I* thought you chose me because I satisfy your sexual desires."

Helinthia smiled, eyes sparkling. "I can have more than one reason for doing a thing, can't I?"

Lithaneva's heart fluttered in triumph. "Aden and I have already done all the scheming necessary to foil his plans." This time, she did cradle Helinthia's cheek in her palm. "I just wanted to see you. Wanted to taste you. And yes, my father's presence was agony."

"Mmm." Helinthia slid her arms around Lithaneva and drew her body close again. Her fingers tangled in Lithaneva's long, dark hair as the kiss deepened. She tugged, pulling her head back and exposing her neck to her lips. The goddess' kisses trailed along her jaw to her earlobe.

Lithaneva sucked in a breath as a thrill surged down her body. She grasped the folds of Helinthia's chiton and pulled it upwards, knuckles brushing over smooth, muscular thighs to her hip bones. She planted her palms over the protrusions, swirling her thumbs over Helinthia's soft navel with just enough pressure to tease.

Helinthia moaned in her ear.

Lithaneva needed her. Now. "Down," she commanded.

Helinthia's eyes flashed, and pleasure knotted in Lithaneva's belly as the goddess obeyed. She stretched out on the floor, grasping Lithaneva's forearms and pulling her down with her. Both of them trembled in anticipation.

Lithaneva pushed the fabric of Helinthia's skirt up around her waist, then slid her hand down to the tender flesh between her thighs. A soft sigh escaped Helinthia's beautiful throat as Lithaneva stole one more kiss, then moved lower. Down Helinthia's neck, across her shoulders, chest, stopping briefly to swirl her tongue around one perfect pink nipple, savoring the taste of the goddess' honey skin, breathing in her sweet lilac scent.

Something fluttered near the door, and both of them froze.

Helinthia sat up, practically shoving Lithaneva off.

Lithaneva rolled onto her rump and stared at the entrance. She expected to find a person standing there. All she saw was a cuckoo, perched sideways at the top of one of the columns. Its claws dug into the ridges of the capital as it angled its head curiously at them.

Lithaneva sighed in relief and tensed to take Helinthia in her arms again, but stopped short as she took in the goddess.

Helinthia was completely still, fearful eyes locked on the bird as though the tiny creature was Medusa herself. She clutched at her garments with white knuckles, trying to cover her exposed flesh.

"What's wrong?" Lithaneva whispered, shivers snaking down her back and arms. She'd never seen Helinthia so afraid.

Helinthia turned tear-filled eyes to hers. "I've stayed too long, my love."

Lithaneva gaped in confusion, gaze darting between the goddess scrambling to her feet and the cuckoo with its black, beady eyes. She leapt up and reached for Helinthia, wanting to soothe her, understand this sudden fear.

Helinthia quickly spun away, avoiding her embrace. "I'll come again when I can."

Then she was gone, dissolving back into a statue behind the curtain of thin vapors still rising from the dying coals of the altar.

Lithaneva glared at the tiny intruder, furious that victory had been snatched from her arms.

She wanted to murder this bird.

'Caught you. Caught you,' it warbled at her.

She ripped her boot from her foot and hurled it as hard as she could, but the fowl took flight, and the soft fur slapped against the empty column and ricocheted out into the night.

CHAPTER 37

KELRIC

KELRIC HID IN THE SHADOWS of the side courtyard, watching the procession for Tor's confirmation gathering. A stirring in his gut told him to join them, make himself seen for his people. The citizens would be anxious at the confirmation of yet another oracle, and the absence of their basileus would likely provide fuel for the Leirion and his fickle kyrioi.

But he was still too angry. About Gonivein, Apollo, Charixes' spies. About the fear of war squeezing the life from his polis. He had no more control over any of it than he did the seas. His grip on power was feeble, and Gonivein belonged to Apollo more than she did him—the two things he'd counted on to ground him through any storm. Both had slipped through his fingers like dust. He didn't have the heart for a facade.

Not until he found a way to reclaim everything he had lost. He would *not* be made a cuckold.

He scanned everyone present, but didn't see Gonivein. Panic jolted his heart into a thundering beat. He left, adrenaline pumping through his veins. What if something had happened to her? The masked man might have acted on his threat… Perhaps the Leirion wouldn't kill her, but they might do other things in their attempt to punish Kelric, bend him. Break him.

He skidded to a stop outside his bedroom door and grabbed the handle. Locked. He knocked. His knuckles rapped against the wood in rhythm to the blood pounding in his ears. "Gonivein? Are you in there? Open the door."

Footsteps approached from inside, soft and uneven, like legs cumbered by a limp. His breath rushed out of him in relief. He nearly collapsed against the doorframe.

She was safe.

His mind meandered back to the way she had cowered before him as though he was something to be feared rather than loved. Shame coiled inside him. Her refusal to extricate herself from Apollo's service had burned him, but his temper had cooled. Perhaps he shouldn't fault her for fearing the god's wrath—she was Dargos' sister, after all. But it still cut him deeply. The oak between them seemed to stretch the length of the world. A hollowness spread in his chest.

"Gonivein." He jiggled the handle once more. "Let me in." He sighed. "Please."

Another moment of hesitation passed before the bolt slid back and the door creaked open.

A sliver of moonlight fell on Gonivein's face, and his frustration sharpened at her haggard appearance. Her eyes were sunken, lids swollen like she had been crying. Her hair was frazzled and fuzzy where strands had come loose from her braid. Darkness cradled her cheeks, and he couldn't tell if her face was dirty or shadowed by the protruding bones of her skull.

Gonivein resembled a crone more than a maiden. Weary and weak. Or a corpse.

She lowered her gaze, as though she could feel his eyes judging her, and began to hobble back to the bed, every step stiff more agonized than he remembered.

"You didn't undress." He examined her chiton, creased with wrinkles on her frail frame.

She didn't answer.

"It's freezing." His eyes darted to the dark hearth. "Did that doula run off? Why is nothing done?" That stupid girl deserved a scolding for letting this room drop to such a frigid temperature. Had she no thought for her basileia, alone and helpless, inside?

Gonivein slowed her steps for just a moment, as though she might answer, but she resumed her uneven gait to the bed and crawled back under the covers.

Her indifference to his concern riled him, but he forced himself to stay calm. He hadn't seen her since this afternoon. He knew she hadn't eaten, nor was it likely she'd had one of Forluna's pain potions. Gonivein must be miserable.

Irritation overshadowed his empathy. He bolted the door and made his way to the fireplace, brooding. She chose to decline dinner. Chose to remain isolated, mourning an *insect*. Chose to lie here in the cold. To ignore how she had hurt him. It was her choice to be miserable.

Yet I'm the one she blames.

He lit a fire in the hearth and stared at the flames awhile. He waited quietly, hoping Gonivein would say something. He wondered if it would be best if he spoke first. Set the tone. He rubbed his chest, trying to quell the dull ache of longing inside.

Finally, he stood and crossed the room to the bed. The broken window caught his eye. The sound of the waves breaking against the cliffs buzzed through the crooked gap.

He didn't care what his people thought of him. Only Gonivein mattered tonight. He undressed, slid under the covers, and stared at the back of her head, annoyed by the loud silence. He propped himself up on his elbow and peered down at her face.

Gonivein's eyes were closed, the fire's warm glow dancing across her soft features. A strand of messy hair fluttered in rhythm with her even breathing.

Of course, she would be asleep, safe and ignorant of the threats lurking outside their door and infesting his city like a den of roaches.

Threats he was protecting her from. Protecting *everyone* from. Threats he had to find some way to eradicate. Threats that wouldn't let *him* sleep.

Gonivein twitched beside him, first her eyelids, then her head and body. Short, jerky movements. A moan vibrated from her lips.

A nightmare. They'd tormented her sleep for years. All thanks to Apollo.

Apollo. Kelric could still see the flames consuming her—Apollo putting his hands on her. And she'd let him. *Invited* him. In exchange for what?

For nothing I couldn't give her, nothing I hadn't promised *her.* Kelric wished he could stab Apollo through with his sword and scream, *'She's mine!'*

Gonivein flailed wildly, her muffled screams and cries sending shivers through him.

He shook her shoulder. "Gonivein, wake up." Harder this time, squeezing her bony arm. "*Gonivein.*"

Her eyes shot open, and her chest heaved as she gasped, eyes blinking furiously to reorient herself to the waking world.

"You were having a nightmare."

She pulled her shoulder away from his hand.

No gratitude for waking her, not even a glance in his direction, as though he were not even there. He glimpsed the cricket leg still glued to the windowpane and shoved down the guilt that threatened to emerge.

Kelric clenched his empty hand. "You're still angry?" He'd expected her to be, but the validation of it frustrated him all the same. "I've given you space, let you brood all day in peace. It's Apollo you should be angry at. He's the one sending you these nightmares. I'm the one who pulls you back from them."

Gonivein's lips trembled, but she didn't look at him.

He sat up, raking his fingers angrily through his hair, trying to calm his emotions before he lost control of them again. There was just too much to worry about. Why couldn't Gonivein try to not be one of them? Why couldn't she support him? Trust him? *Love* him?

Her silence deepened the wound of her betrayal.

"What do you want me to do?" He was unable to quiet the sharp edge in his words, and he hated the desperation ringing in them. "Be happy Apollo kissed you, that he bestowed this *gift* upon you?"

Gonivein stiffened. "I'd like you to go." Her voice was barely above a whisper.

Shock plunged into his gut, and for a moment he wasn't sure he'd heard her right. He swallowed the hurt down, but she didn't retract her words, didn't even look at him.

"Go?" he repeated, unable to think of a better response. "Go where? This is my room."

Gonivein sat up slowly. Hope sprang that she would turn to him, acknowledge him, say something. Even yelling at him was better than this abrasive calm. But to his surprise, she stood, legs shaky, and began hobbling to the door.

"What are you doing?" He had a sinking suspicion he knew, and he was already out of the bed and crossing the room after her.

"If you won't leave, then I will." She reached for the handle the same moment he pressed his full weight against the door.

She stepped back, clenching her thin knuckles into a tight ball. Tears gathered in her eyes. "Let me go."

Kelric bit back the fury gathering on his tongue. First she betrayed him, then she ignored him, now she was abandoning him? Without even trying to discuss anything?

He should tell her of the threats, the cracks in the wall of his power. If he did, she might forgive his anger. At least *listen* to him. But the knowledge that she couldn't simply trust him and accept that he was doing what was best irked him.

"You're not going out there."

Panic flickered across her face. For a moment, he thought he had won, but she lifted her chin in defiance.

"I'm the Basileia of Golpathia. It's my duty to join the procession—"

"They've already left." A lie.

"Then I will catch up to them."

He clenched his jaw. His impatience was approaching the bounds of his control, and he wasn't sure how many more words he could muster before forcibly removing her from the door.

"There aren't enough guards to bear you." There were. Tryphus had tripled the guards after their discussion this afternoon, but she didn't need to know that.

"I'll walk alone."

"It's too dangerous." The words were out of his mouth before he could stop them.

Her head tilted, her expression unreadable, sharp. A shiver snaked down his spine.

"What danger, Kelric? What's out there? Is this not the safest place in Helinthia?" Her tone was mocking.

This was his opportunity to tell the truth. Would she set aside their quarrel if he did? He studied her blue eyes, wanting to tell her everything, about the Leirion, their demands, their threats, their influence in every layer of the city. He wanted to let her in.

Memories of her torture sprang to his mind—horrors she'd endured at the Leirion's hands, his own father's hands. Not all her nightmares were Apollo's doing. If she knew how close her tormentors walked beside them, would she cling to him for protection? Or would she recede even further?

A voice whispered from the darker depths of his soul—a voice that was far more truthful than he wanted to admit. What if he couldn't eradicate the Leirion before they got to her? What if playing their game was the only way to take his power back? If he told her the truth, she would insist she be involved. He wouldn't be able to hide his complicity in their atrocities, and she would never forgive him. Even if it was all to save her.

Is that why Father kept his allegiance to them a secret from me? Had he feared Kelric's scorn? Thinking on it now, Kelric realized he hadn't forgiven his father yet. Perhaps his father had been right to hide this from the ones he loved.

But I can't lose her.

She could put a sword through his heart and he would still crave her touch.

"This is the safest place in Helinthia," he lied, sharpening his gaze and praying to all the gods that she wouldn't argue with him. So, he did the only thing he knew to do. Deflect.

"You had no intention of joining the procession before I came in." His words were more of a snarl than he'd intended, and she stepped back from him. "Whose bed are you wanting to fling yourself into? Apollo's? Gadnor's?"

She took another step back. Her eyes flashing.

Kelric had won now. But he didn't want to have this argument ever again. He wanted to make her squirm. "I saw him leaving your room the day before our wedding. Is there something you want to tell me?"

She stared at him, her beautiful lips parted in shock. Beads of sweat glistened on her neck and chest. A few broke free and rolled down her skin, disappearing into the linen chiton covering her breasts.

His knees trembled as he took in the astonishment on her face. He half hoped she would throw herself on him and try to reassure him that his accusation wasn't true. Proclaim her undying devotion and love for him. Stillness settled deeper between them. His hope withered. He'd only heightened her hatred of him. He was one breath away from taking it all back, pulling her into his arms, and begging forgiveness. The thought of losing her, whether to Charixes' spies or by her rejection, was more than he could bear.

"You know me better than that."

He did.

She climbed back under the covers and tucked the blanket around her as tight as she could, like a shield to keep him out. He sagged down to the floor. He ached to hold her, but she might try to sneak away if he left his vigil.

Kelric retrieved his cloak from the couch and wrapped it around his shoulders, then curled into a ball with his back pressed against the door, and tried to sleep.

CHAPTER 38

GADNOR

THE FULL MOON SHONE DOWN on the courtyard of the Golpathian villa, outlining the forming procession of scholars and acolytes as they carefully arranged every item for Tor's confirmation ceremony. Villa guardsmen were stationed around them, holding torches aloft.

Gadnor sat beside Tor on the porch steps, watching the silent and speedy efficiency of the scholars. He wondered if he could ever be half so successful in organizing a military expedition—the topic of tomorrow's Council.

Unlikely, he thought, but he pushed his doubt away as quickly as it had come and focused on Tor. Tonight was about him. Gadnor wanted to put off thinking about tomorrow for as long as possible.

Xios trembled in Tor's arms. Ears down and eyes wide, the cub clung to Tor's shoulder in terror. His tiny, sharp claws were outstretched and snagged in the fabric of the boy's cloak, tail tucked under his belly. Pity stabbed Gadnor. How frightening all these strangers must be for him.

Tor wore the same somber, calm expression as always, his fingertips methodically massaging Xios' neck.

"Are you nervous?" Gadnor asked.

Tor shrugged. "I've seen Artemis before."

That wasn't an answer, but Gadnor smiled as he recalled his own interactions with the goddess. She was tall and beautiful, and had an air of sovereignty about her that demanded respect and reverence. But she was also kind and compassionate. Wise. Good at understanding and helping others understand themselves.

"Will Alypius attend the meeting tomorrow?" Tor asked.

Gadnor stiffened at the name, then nodded, palms turning clammy. After what had happened during the duel, Gadnor half expected a revolt tomorrow. It would be his first official appearance as strategos. The first time exercising the authority his title granted.

Stop thinking about that, he scolded himself. "Tomorrow will take care of itself."

Tor glanced sideways at him and raised an eyebrow, as if to say, *'Who do you think you're fooling?'* but said nothing. Gadnor was happy to let the subject drop.

Mandus beckoned to Tor from the front of the assembled procession. Tor stood, cradling the cub close as he took his place beside Mandus at the front of the line.

Gadnor rose, dusting off his tunic as he glanced around the courtyard. Forluna and Dargos retreated to the back of the procession, but Gonivein and Kelric were nowhere to be found.

Gadnor hoped the two weren't arguing again, or worse. He joined Forluna and Dargos. "Has anyone seen Gonivein?"

Forluna nodded. "I spoke with her earlier."

Gadnor breathed a sigh of relief. Forluna's insight was usually good, her judgment even better. Perhaps she had remedied the situation.

The procession lurched into motion and passed through the villa gate, over the bridge, and down into the city. Despite the late hour, citizens had congregated once again along the route to watch them pass.

The journey to the temple of Artemis was much like the one to the temple of Apollo, except it was the full moon that guided their feet, not the blazing midday sun. The scholars and acolytes sang a hymn the whole way. The notes were beautiful, but were almost shrill in the reverent quiet.

They passed through the western gate and marched to the base of the plateau where Artemis' temple stood, purposely situated en route to the Ordan Forest so hunters could make sacrifices to the Mistress of Animals.

Stone steps led up the slope to a marble archway connected to the free-standing colonnade that circled the entire grove. The arch was undecorated, archaic, ominous as it towered high above their heads against a backdrop of bright stars. A temple from a more ancient, untamed time in Helinthia's history.

The priestesses of Artemis were gathered in rows on either side of the steps, and as the procession began their ascent, the priestesses joined their voices to the hymns. As Gadnor passed through the arch and stepped into the grove, the notes reverberated off the stone columns surrounding them. Despite the open roof, it was every bit as cacophonous as Apollo's temple had been, and Gadnor couldn't help but wince.

The altar crackled with a hearty flame at the center of the circle. The orange glow reflected off the smooth columns and sprayed sparks to the stars, driving out the darkness. From this elevation, one could see the lower city stretched out on one side, and the outer ring of houses in the Kyrioi Quarter ascending the peak on the other. Beyond the altar, visible through another stone archway, sprawled the Golpathian plains. The scraggly outline of the Ordan Forest cut a jagged line across the starry horizon.

More priestesses lined the perimeter of the circular temple, standing shoulder to shoulder. Their white garments glowed in the moonlight, making them appear more like a second ring of columns than people. Mysterious and otherworldly. Gadnor followed the scholars' lead in spreading out to form an inner, third ring around the sacred grove.

The head priestess of Artemis waited beside the altar. Mandus stopped before her and bowed. The hymn crescendoed for a few more beats and then stopped. As the last human notes reverberated off the stone, the crickets took up the melody.

"Brother Mandus," the priestess said, and Mandus righted himself. "You bring us one with whom the Huntress has found favor. Come forward, venerable scholar, and make your sacrifice."

The priestess stepped back, and Mandus turned to face Tor.

"Tor of Golpathia, Artemis has laid claim to your blood, and by your blood, she will know your devotion. By your communion with beasts, all shall know you are her vessel. Will you heed the call of the goddess?"

Tor cleared his throat. "Yes."

Mandus extended his shaky hand to him. "Then may your blood bear witness that Artemis, Mistress of Animals, Huntress, protectress of youth and innocence, has bestowed her gifts upon you. Your hand, my boy."

Tor stooped to place Xios on the ground and gave Mandus his upturned palm. The cub flicked his tail and stared up at the old scholar with glowing amber eyes, his fur bristling with suspicion.

Mandus drew the ceremonial blade at his hip and a low growl emanated from Xios' throat.

Mandus grinned down at the cub. "Don't worry, little one," he crooned in his deep shaky voice, "I will leave him plenty." He motioned with his bearded chin to an acolyte, who stepped forward and held a brass bowl underneath their hands. Mandus cut Tor's palm with a quick slash.

Tor flinched, and Xios hissed and crouched, but a quick downward glance from Tor stopped him from doing more.

Blood dripped into the brass bowl. As with Gonivein's sacrifice, Mandus waited until the blood slowed before squeezing for a little more. He released Tor's hand, then cleaned his blade with a cloth and sheathed it. He took the bowl from the acolyte and held it up to the altar.

"By your blood shall all peoples of this isle know that Artemis has chosen you, Tor, to bridge the divide between the animal realm and the human." Mandus poured the blood onto the fire. A metallic tang rose into the air on a puff of steam. Another acolyte stepped forward with the box of incense, then a third with the amphora of wine. Mandus took each in turn and made his offering to the flames.

An eerie silence filled the void as everyone waited for another miraculous occurrence. Would the blaze elongate and consume Tor? Moments passed, and the altar's fire remained low and confined to the coals.

Gadnor leaned closer to Forluna. "What happens now?"

"Just wait," she said.

An owl hooted, and then the faint swish of rustling grass arose from somewhere in the darkness of the plains beyond the colonnade. Gadnor craned over the priestesses' heads to get a better look.

Through the arch leading to the Ordan, the silver silhouette of a tall woman materialized. Her chiton swished around her knees above tightly laced leather boots. A short deerskin cloak was fastened at her throat, and her hair was bound into three long braids draped over one shoulder. Vibrant blue-fletched arrows shimmered from a quiver strapped to her back, tucked beside a silver bow that reflected the moon beams like a mirror. Her faithful white hound, Peithie, trotted at her heels.

Excitement bloomed within Gadnor, and a wide grin spread across his face as his brown eyes met her purple ones. She returned his smile.

A gasp rippled through the onlookers. Several stepped backward, on the verge of breaking ranks and fleeing back to the safety of the city walls. Their companions admonished them in sharp, hissing tones to stand their ground as Artemis sauntered into the heart of the grove.

Apollo had been perceived as a flame by everyone except himself, Forluna, and Gonivein. Gadnor wondered how Artemis appeared. He couldn't resist whispering into Dargos' ear. "What do you see?"

Dargos' throat bobbed as he swallowed. "A panther," he whispered back. "Please tell me that's Artemis and not the last thing I'll ever see."

"It's Artemis." Gadnor was unable to hide a smile. He'd never seen Dargos so petrified. "Do you see the hound?"

"What hound?"

"Shhh!" one of the priestesses admonished behind them.

Dargos straightened as though he'd been slapped.

Gadnor coughed to mask the bubble of mirth in his throat, his cheeks burning.

Mandus bowed low and moved aside as Artemis approached.

The Huntress stopped before Tor and extended her open palms. Tor laid his hands on them, and Artemis' fingers closed gently. Her lips moved, but Gadnor couldn't hear her words—nor Tor's when he answered. It seemed as though the sounds of the night—crickets, the rustling wind, the crackling fire—had amplified, drowning out the conversation between the deity and her oracle.

It's a trick. Now he understood why he couldn't recall anything Lithaneva and Helinthia had spoken in Thellshun. He'd thought his fear was to blame, but he simply hadn't heard them. Now that he considered it, Apollo and Gonivein's discussion had been muted, as well.

Artemis knelt down to Xios and scratched the cub's ears. Xios brushed his sides against the goddess' legs in affection and flopped onto his back, pawing playfully at the graceful hand. Peithie nosed the cub, wagging his tail, tongue lolling.

Artemis petted Xios a moment longer before straightening to examine the crowd of worshippers. Tor spoke again, and Artemis' expression grew serious, thoughtful.

At once, both Artemis and Tor looked at Gadnor, and a chill rolled down his spine. Even Peithie turned to him, perking up his ears and stilling his tail.

Why are they staring at me? His curiosity burned, but he found himself equally terrified to find out what they were discussing. Their fixation reminded him too much of the moment Helinthia and Lithaneva had caught him spying. It unsettled him, and he sensed something looming over his future that, if not for the arbiters being Artemis and Tor, he would certainly fear.

Goddess and oracle focused their attention on one another again. Then Artemis nodded to him, turned, and stalked back across the grove and through the arch. Her silver bow flashed as she disappeared under the moonlight, Peithie trotting by her side.

CHAPTER 39

FORLUNA

THE POLIS BUZZED WITH GOSSIP AS Forluna walked to the villa. Citizens lingered in the streets, debating what *two* new oracle confirmations meant after so many years of silence from Olympus. Murmurs about the birds surrounding the guests at the wedding fed the tension further. And whispers of their basileus' absence were laced with disdain for his competing priorities between his people and new bride. Forluna's ears twitched beneath her hair as they strained to make sense of the many voices.

Forluna understood their fears. Deities rarely concerned themselves with mortal affairs in times of prosperity. With the lingering drought, talk of war, and refugees, sudden attention from Olympus was a sure signal that conditions would deteriorate.

A lump formed in her throat.

Fear made people vulnerable to manipulation. Drove them to do desperate things to reclaim some semblance of certainty and security.

Fear had once cost her everything.

Forluna's skin prickled with gooseflesh. After Gonivein found her beneath the laurel, Forluna had enlisted Pallas' protection to return to the camps with her medicines, under the guise that he could assist with fortifying the derelict structures that sheltered the people. Pallas was happy to comply, and she'd seen no sign of the eighth scholar today.

Now, the man was right in front of her. She eyed his back warily as he walked ahead, seemingly oblivious to her scrutiny. She had considered remaining hidden at the laurel to avoid this proximity, but she would feel safer if she could watch where he was at all times. Besides, Dargos and more than a dozen guards were there. This man wouldn't dare try anything.

She wished that was enough to set her at ease. But in reality, the eighth scholar might be the least of her worries since learning the new details of Gonivein's vision. The Leirion were here. Everywhere. Lurking. Skulking. Waiting for their opportunity to destroy everything and everyone she loved. Again. She knew it was true from the way her skin crawled on her body.

She eyed the shadowy figures along the path. Instinctively, she drew closer to Dargos and took his hand, relieved when he squeezed back. Her revelations hung between them like a thick curtain. She was ready to tear the barrier down, and she sensed Dargos was ready as well.

There was no more time to waste on petty feelings. Gonivein's vision couldn't wait a moment longer. Dargos' mind was on whatever attack Charixes planned on the spring equinox, but it was the threat *inside* the walls that was important. The threat Dargos didn't know about. The threat that could not be stopped unless Charixes was dead.

The owl perched once again on the roof. Its head swiveled toward them as they walked through the gate and crossed the courtyard to the porch steps. Gravel crunched under their feet, the scent of smoke promising the warmth of hearty fires. She watched the scholars disperse and return to their apartments. The eighth scholar did not even glance her way as he stepped inside his room and closed the door. She kept second-guessing her recognition of him.

She worried a jagged fingernail. It seemed more likely the danger she had sensed was from the Leirion. This poor man, because he had turned away so quickly when she'd first seen him, had fallen victim to her paranoia.

As they parted ways with Gadnor and Tor, Dargos gave the oracle a heavy clap on the shoulder and flashed him an excited grin. She was glad to see Dargos' mood had significantly improved. It was almost enough to lift her own spirits. Almost.

A fire crackled merrily in their apartment, emanating a warm, orange hue. Forluna eyed the darkened corners warily. Relieved to find them empty.

Dargos closed the door and turned around, unmoving.

She met his gaze, and they stared at one another. Saying everything with their eyes that both of them wished they could speak aloud.

I'm sorry.

I understand.

I forgive.

"Forluna," Dargos whispered, finally breaking the silence. The tenderness in his tone made her arms ache to hold him, made her body crave his touch, but she stayed put. Conviction swirled in the depths of his dark eyes, and she owed him this opportunity to set it free.

"You were right about… everything. Helinthia, my devotion to her, how blind I've been to the truth. I believed we lived in a world where the gods are in control, and our future has to be bright because destiny demands we survive this. But I'm no longer sure that world even exists, or ever did. I've been blind to the cost of my faith—the toll it has taken on everyone I love. Everything I thought I understood, I realize now that I don't."

Dargos stepped forward and took her hand, sorrow deepening the lines on his face. His acknowledgment of their doom was bittersweet. She had opened his eyes and crushed his soul.

"But I have to believe that world still *can* exist." He stepped closer, connecting his body to hers. Tongues of fire from the hearth danced in his eyes.

Her breath hitched. Could there be something bright left to shine on this dark existence?

Convince me, her heart begged. *Give me hope.*

His hands cradled her face, palms warm and rough against her cheeks. His fingers traced her long ears, sending shivers down to her toes. "I have to believe the gods chose Gonivein and Tor for a reason, that they are helping Gadnor succeed in every way they can. What you said about Helinthia… I *have* been blind, and I have made too many mistakes because of it. Too many people I love have suffered. I just can't bring myself to believe this is what Helinthia wanted to happen, that she is working against us.

"But whether she is or isn't, my determination to see this war through hasn't changed. Though all the gods rise against me, I will keep fighting to save this island. Because if I don't, then very soon there won't be anything left to save. There won't be anyone left to *love*."

He rested his forehead on hers, their noses touching. His lips were so close now. She ached to taste them.

"There are many gods, Forluna, and their desires do not always align. This is the lot we bear as mortals, to be caught in their storm. Tossed in the winds of their fury. Not because we are the object of their malice, but because we are the *weapons* they wield against one another. It isn't fair. And no matter which god claims victory, mortals will always lose.

"I'm under no illusions about what Helinthia's favor grants me. Death is coming, riding a war horse of bronze and fire, and I'll be damned if I'm the only man standing to meet it. I can't be. Gadnor has chosen his side, as have I." His voice was husky. "We cannot cower. We cannot hide anymore."

Forluna pressed her palms against his chest. The heat of his heart pounding against her skin chased the chills from her arms. Her ears perked toward his voice, hanging on his words. There was doom in them. But also courage, honor, and justice.

'We cannot hide anymore.' Something focused in her mind, a missing piece finally locking into place.

"No one should suffer as you have—to lose what you have lost, to sacrifice everything and be rewarded with betrayal by the goddess who swore to protect you."

Tears slipped down her cheeks.

"But you are *alive*. You are *here*, with *me*. And I will fight for this life until the Shades of Hades drag me down to the shores of the Styx. Not because the gods demand it, but because I will not bury your corpse in a shallow grave and cover it with rubble to keep the dogs from your bones. Nor Gonivein. I lost my city, I failed Pallas. I will *not* lose you to my mistakes, too."

She searched for words, but nothing worthy enough to convey her feelings formed. This man who would not be broken or moved was hers. Willingly and completely. Words failed to convey her relief to hear it from his lips, see it in his eyes. Only her body could voice the depth of her feelings for him. And that voice was loud, screaming through her veins, echoing in her belly. She lifted her chin and closed the slight distance between their lips, capturing his mouth with hers.

Dargos sighed and kissed her back, finding her tongue with his.

She dug her fingers in his hair. His hands circled her rump and lifted her, crushing her to his chest as he moved to the bed.

He set her back on her feet. Her body slid down his torso, igniting the fire between them. Their arms tangled, fingers fumbling with the broaches on their shoulders. Their clothes fell into a puddle around their feet.

She crawled backward onto the bed. He followed her, planting kisses on her thighs, stomach, breasts, shoulders. Sensation rippled beneath her skin. He pressed her body into the wool mattress, gliding between her legs. She wrapped them around his back as he entered her. Pleasure surged through her as their bodies found a sensual rhythm, building with every hot breath they shared, breaking down the walls they had built. Welcoming the intimacy they had denied one another for too long.

Gasping. Sweating. Spent. They lay in each other's arms, a tangled mass of limbs.

Dargos pressed his face against the side of her head and kissed her ear. "I love you, Forluna."

"I love you too, Dargos."

She wished she didn't have to ruin this moment. She wished they could lie like this forever, at peace with their fears, of one mind with their destinies, their emotions, their devotion to one another. But she couldn't. Dargos was fading into slumber, and he had to know the truth before he was overcome.

"Dargos?"

"Mmm?"

"I learned something today."

Dargos' lashes fluttered against her long ear as he opened his eyes. His heartbeat against her shoulder increased at the seriousness of her tone.

"Gonivein had the vision again, at the ceremony. Apollo revealed something new."

"The same vision as before?" He propped himself up on his elbow to look at her fully.

She nodded, her eyes following a bead of sweat that ran down the channel of his sternum. Like Kelric, Dargos had interpreted Gonivein's vision positively for the rebellion. The three beasts working together to stamp out Charixes. "She said vines were springing from the earth, pinning and choking the wolves, creeping toward the beasts. She said the *vines* provoked the beasts to attack the falcon."

Dargos' brow furrowed.

"Vines blooming with white lilies."

"Leirion."

"I don't think the Falcon in her vision is Charixes. I think it's Gadnor." Panic at the thought of Gadnor crushed, shredded, and torn asunder by the beasts fluttered in her chest.

Dargos rubbed her bare shoulder. "I believe Lithaneva to be loyal to this rebellion. At least for now. Something may change. But I *know* that Kelric and I would never betray Gadnor. This vision must mean something else."

Panic crept into her tone. "But what if the lion and hydra aren't you and Kelric? What if it's whoever takes your place when the Leirion dispose of you?" A new thought struck her suddenly. "The meeting tomorrow. You will all be there, every leader in one place, unsuspecting of danger. What if they strike you all down?"

Dargos raked his hand through his hair. "If Charixes' assassins are here, I'd wager at least one of them is a member of the Council, and I have a good idea exactly who it is."

"Alypius?"

Dargos nodded. "Possibly Ephastes, too. Once they learn we have information about Charixes' plans, they'll want to know how we came by it. They wouldn't risk killing us before then."

"I fear it is not just a few men we have to worry about," Forluna said. "Gonivein described many vines, as though they are woven into the fabric of this city—the whole island. I never would have dreamed Charixes' cult could grow so vast."

Dargos pinched a strand of her hair between his fingers.

She recalled the night of Iptys' murder, the blood, the screams, the acrid, inescapable stench of smoke and burnt flesh that clung to her skin no matter how many baths she took in the weeks that followed. Her stomach churned, horror and dread seizing her lungs and constricting her air flow.

In. Out. Slow.

Dargos stroked her shoulder again and planted a gentle kiss on her forehead, reminding her he was there to draw strength from.

She nuzzled closer to him, letting him be her fortress against the Shades that haunted her. "It wasn't just Charixes' armies marching on the palace that night. His decisive victory was won by forces *inside* the palace. Guards, sworn to Iptys, spilled the blood of their brethren without a second thought. I saw the bodies littering the halls as I fled. Before Charixes even set foot inside. He will do it again. He will strike from inside these walls as well as without. It is how he *knows* he can win. His spies are here to see it done."

Forluna was sure of it. "Every time I think Gadnor might be safe, I'm reminded of the danger that hunts him, that will *always* hunt him."

Dargos kissed her head again. "Apollo gave my sister this vision to help us, to tell us this future is coming so we can stop it. And we *will*. We *must*. This city is the last stronghold against Charixes. He will try to break us, but we know his plans. We know our doom, but he doesn't know his. That is our advantage."

Though she had doubts about the eighth scholar now, Forluna knew she should tell Dargos about him. About the ominous presence that stalked her steps. Only under the boughs of the laurel tree did she not feel its venom so close on her heels. But she kept those words in her throat. She could already see Dargos' mind spinning with thoughts of tomorrow—how to combat whatever Alypius and Ephastes might say during the meeting to thwart their plans and sow division among them. Telling him she might know this man from her past would only distract him. He had to keep a clear head.

Dargos rolled from the bed and stood, his naked body glistening in the dying embers of the fire. He threw two more logs in the hearth and stoked the coals before checking the window lock. He strode to the door, jiggled the bolt, then dragged a couch in front of it. He returned to the bed with his dagger in hand. Laid it beside the pillow and slid under the covers once again, wrapping her securely in his arms.

As his breathing grew even beside her, her mind spun with threats and strategies to thwart the Leirion. She would leave whatever Charixes was doing in Hameth to Dargos and Kelric.

But the Leirion...

They had hunted her. Tormented her. Taken everything from her. Now they threatened to choke out everything she loved once again. If they were truly as prevalent as Gonivein's vision revealed, it would be impossible to track them all down and remove them one by one. No. She was aware of only one way to be rid of such an invasive vine.

Rip it out from the roots.

I will kill Charixes.

CHAPTER 40

LITHANEVA

LITHANEVA PUSHED HER PLATE AWAY, the braised duck and vegetables cold and untouched. She tried to convince herself to eat, but she couldn't. The roasted wings reminded her too much of the cuckoo that had ruined her night. She still had no idea why such a tiny creature had scared Helinthia. Lithaneva had tossed and turned for hours, wrestling with possibilities.

She knew people could experience heightened fears of things barely noticed by others. One of the kyriai she'd studied with at the Library was afraid of bees. Every time she saw one, she ran to the nearest sheltered place with a door she could slam and latch. Could Helinthia have such a fear of cuckoos?

A goddess? Scared enough to flee from a night of celebratory, ravenous love-making with me?

"What is troubling you, Lithie?" Branitus' voice drew her gaze up from her plate.

"Nothing," she lied. "I'm just not feeling very hungry."

Her stomach burbled loudly, and Branitus and Larxcs shared a look, jaws pausing their chewing.

She dug her nails into her palms. How dare her own body betray her like that.

"Does this have something to do with…?" Larxes trailed off, and she met his squinting hazel eyes with a daring brow. "You know… the, um, thing you did? In the garden?"

Lithaneva's cheeks burned as panic fluttered into her throat. *Did he see us?* Then she remembered the lie she'd told him about the conception ritual, and relaxed. *That* thing in the garden. She almost laughed. "Yes, in fact."

"What thing?" Branitus demanded, looking between them with an offended expression, as though they had intentionally excluded him from some juicy secret.

"A woman's cleansing ritual."

A knowing expression lit Branitus' features. "Ah yes, my kyrioi have mentioned similar such practices their wives perform. Can I… fetch a doula or something? I hear that helps."

Lithaneva's smile was genuine at their concern. "No, but I'm tired. I think I'll go lie down for a while."

"Oh," Larxes pouted. "I wanted to play something for you on my new lyre."

Branitus beamed as a hungry look passed between the two men.

Branitus followed my suggestion, then. She wished she could nurture her resentment that Branitus and Larxes could share their love openly and without restraint, but she didn't have the energy to stamp out the gentle sigh of happiness she had for them. Happiness that *she* had played a role in cultivating. That lifted her spirits more than she would have thought possible.

"Perhaps this evening, Larxes." She stood and nodded at them before heading to her room.

Though her body ached with exhaustion, her mind wouldn't rest, replaying Helinthia's strange exit over and over as she walked. Every step closer to her room made her heart and body ache more for her lover.

I earned that moment of bliss. And Helinthia knew it. All that work securing the information, forcing smiles and displaying a loyal facade to her father, organizing a clever counter to his monstrous plan, winning over the hawk's trust. What could have been so significant as to overshadow all of that? *To drive her from me in such haste without a backward glance?*

Helinthia better have a good reason for this stunt, and not just some divine game to make her jealous, make her crave her even more—was such a thing even possible? Never had Lithaneva been more ready to please and be pleasured.

She shoved her bedroom door open and slammed it shut behind her. She drew in a deep breath, nostrils flaring as her rage continued to build inside her chest. She felt its spark enter her throat. She strode to the bed and grabbed the pillow, the one Helinthia's head had rested on just days ago—it still smelled like her—and gave it the full brunt of a vengeful scream.

That felt good. But it would feel even better if—

Lithaneva slammed the pillow against her bed, once, twice. On the third strike, the seam ripped. A cloud of feathers burst around her, assaulting her mouth and eyes and ears like a nest of hornets.

She waved her hands furiously and retreated, spitting and holding her breath to keep from sucking a fluff of down into her lungs. She bumped into a low piece of furniture. It snagged her behind the knee, and she wobbled for balance. She fell backward. One half of her bottom slammed onto a hard edge, pitching her into the floor. She barely caught herself in time to stop her head from smashing into the hard tiles.

Feathers showered down around her. Humiliated, her rump smarting and her rage even more roused, she glanced backward at the object that had assaulted her—a couch—and kicked it as hard as she could. It screeched across the floor, but didn't break. Instead, pain jolted into her heel and up to her knee.

"Furies take me!" she howled, grabbing her foot and cradling it.

Someone laughed from a dark corner of her room.

Lithaneva's head shot up. "Goddess?"

For a moment, her hope that this had all been some horrible prank tempered her rage. Oh, she would make Helinthia pay for that laugh.

She would pout, she would guilt, and Helinthia would beg for forgiveness for teasing her to such an extreme. But then she would pull back, let the goddess soothe her, coddle her. Make it up to her with passion and pleasure.

Two can play games. And she had no intention of losing *this* time.

But it wasn't Helinthia who stepped into the light.

Lithaneva's breath hitched. She scrambled to her feet, adrenaline racing through her. "Who are you?" But even as she said the words, she knew *exactly* who it was.

And it was the last being she ever wanted to see.

The figure stepped forward, the swish of her chiton breathing a soft olive-blossom scent into the room. A thin, elegant veil floated over honey-colored curls. A golden crown, perfectly smooth and gleaming like the sun, circled her head. She wore a cloak with exquisitely embroidered birds in gold threads, and tiny tassels all along its hem. Sunlight shined through the window on her noble visage. The shape of her nose and brows cast intimidating shadows over half her face, as though she were a being of both light and darkness.

Just as Lithaneva knew her to be.

Lithaneva pressed her face to the floor. "My goddess, Hera." Her heart pounded so hard against her chest she could barely hear her own words. Her heavy breath pushed tiny feathers across the floor until the tile beneath her face was bare.

"Who are you?" Hera said. The very ground trembled in terror at the timbre of her words—Lithaneva felt it under her palms.

"I am your humble servant, Princess Lithaneva," she choked out. At first, she thought Hera was doing something to her—changing her, strangling her—but then she realized it was her own body, succumbing to the swelling panic in her lungs and throat.

Why was Hera here? Helinthia's sworn enemy. Her bitter rival. The true power behind Charixes' ambition, his hatred, his malice, his arrogance.

Where are you, Helinthia?

Hera laughed again. "*My* humble servant? I think not."

She knows. Had Helinthia suspected Hera had found them? Is that why she fled? *Did she abandon me to face Hera's wrath alone?*

She couldn't accept that. Helinthia would never—

"Tell me who you *really* are."

Lithaneva closed her eyes and drew in a deep breath. She raised her torso, sinking her bottom back onto her heels. She lifted her eyes to Hera's. *Voice, be steady.*

If these were the last words she ever spoke, then she would say them with all the passion and conviction of her soul. She would die proud of her birth, proud of her obligation. "My name is Princess Lithaneva, daughter of Anax Charixes, Oracle of Helinthia."

"Oracle," Hera repeated. Her emotionless tone was unnerving. It would almost be preferable if the goddess flew into a rage. At least the suspense would be over. "I don't recall witnessing Helinthia claim you. The people of this island certainly do not. *How* do you know you are Helinthia's oracle?"

Lithaneva gulped, willing her heart not to beat itself out of her chest. "I asked for the honor, and Helinthia granted it."

"Get up."

Lithaneva scrambled to her feet, pins and needles shooting along her legs as blood rushed back. She kept her head bowed, clasping her hands tightly to keep them from shaking.

"Tell me, how long have you been lying to the entire island?"

"I haven't lied—"

"Omitting truths is a lie, and you have omitted your existence as their oracle. Lie again to *me* and see what power I will wield over you." Hera's presence seemed to expand forward, despite the fact that she hadn't moved an inch closer. "*How long* have you deprived them of their goddess' voice?"

Lithaneva shuddered, clutching her hands so tight her white knuckles seemed to glow in the darkness. "Three years." Tears stung her eyes.

Coward! How easily and quickly she gave up her truths. Truths she had safeguarded against her father for those same three years, now to spill them without even attempting to slide out of it.

She wished there were a sword nearby she could fling herself upon and end this interrogation before she said something Hera could use against Helinthia. Her eyes flicked to her vanity. Somewhere beneath the dark mass of clutter was a dagger—one which had spilled her blood for Helinthia's love countless times. Could she reach it before Hera stopped her?

"Three years." Hera clucked her tongue.

Doom seemed imminent, but rather than utter despair, Lithaneva was emboldened. Perhaps she could steer the conversation. "How did you find me?"

"I have my eyes and ears all over the island. In the shadows, in the skies. *Under the eaves.*"

The cuckoos. So Helinthia *had* known. *And she left me here.* The betrayal sank deep into Lithaneva's core, but her heart protested. *She's coming for me. She'll be here. I know it.*

As though to prove Hera's point, the irritating creature began to warble outside. Hera smiled. "Beautiful creatures, aren't they? Loyal creatures." Hera tilted her head, a hint of admiration softening the deep furrow in her brow. "She hid you well, but not well enough."

"What will you do to me?"

"No less than what she did to *my* oracle."

Lithaneva's heart lurched at the veiled threat, even as curiosity wormed through her.

Hera smirked and sat elegantly on the crooked couch. She stretched out her legs, her beautiful toes peeking through golden sandals, and propped her elbow on the windowsill. "Oh, she didn't tell you?"

Lithaneva swallowed. "Oracle Eraia?"

"Yes. Eraia." Hera's tone was wistful.

"She collapsed. Some said it was exertion, others blamed Anassa Iptys—that is what my father did, how he rallied the people behind him to usurp the throne."

"Both wrong," Hera snapped. "*Helinthia* killed her. And now, I will kill you."

Lithaneva felt her knees begin to shake for more reasons than one. *That's not true!* But there was no lie in Hera's golden eyes, only conviction—and something else. Pain. Loss. Regret. Lithaneva's stomach swirled as the betrayal seeped in further. She was glad she hadn't eaten this morning.

"Why would Helinthia kill her?"

Hera gazed coldly at Lithaneva for a long moment, as though considering whether or not to indulge her. The goddess' gaze softened again. "I sent Eraia to give the people a choice: worship me and prevent a famine, or worship Helinthia and suffer it. Helinthia was afraid they would abandon her, and in her jealousy—her rage— she took *my* favorite." Hera's eyes shone with unshed tears.

She must have seen Lithaneva's confusion, because she scoffed. "Omission, lies. Tell me their sting isn't the same."

Lithaneva's breath hitched. Her lungs burned as she struggled for breath. The garden couldn't be the last time she saw Helinthia. *It can't.*

Yet she knew it would be. She honestly didn't know if Hera was speaking the truth—Helinthia had never told her this—but it didn't have to be true. Hera *believed* it was true. That was enough for a goddess' vengeance.

Hera petted a silk tassel on her cloak. "Before I kill you, humor me. What did she promise in exchange for your service?"

Despair washed over Lithaneva as tears slid down her face. Every kiss, every embrace, every tender moment she had shared with Helinthia flashed through her mind. Her arms ached for her lover, fingers tingled with longing to cup her goddess' face.

"Her heart." Her voice was barely audible.

Hera stopped petting the tassel. She narrowed her eyes and swept them up and down Lithaneva, judging her. Weighing her worthiness of such a bold claim, or perhaps truth.

She will surely kill me now. It would be the ultimate revenge.

The silence stretched so long between them that Lithaneva had to pinch herself to make sure this wasn't all just a dream gone horribly awry. Finally, Hera stood, towering over her.

"I want Helinthia to understand just how much power she really has, and what destruction can be wrought from it. She is young and foolish. No combination is more destructive and harmful than power and arrogance."

Hera's fingers slid around Lithaneva's neck.

This was it. Her doom.

"I am vengeful, but I am just. Words have consequences, lies most of all. Helinthia will know what it is like to lose one she loves."

Hera's fingers tightened around her throat. Lithaneva tried to fight back, tried to beg for mercy, but she was paralyzed, rooted to the floor, arms limp at her sides.

"I *curse* you, Lithaneva, daughter of Charixes. Your tongue, your lying, deceitful tongue, *despises* you and rises against you. May you reap the truth of the lies you sow."

Lithaneva dropped into a heap as Hera released her. She grasped her throat, shocked, confused, relieved it wasn't crushed, and looked up.

Hera was gone.

CHAPTER 41

DARGOS

DARGOS RAISED HIS HAND TO knock on Kelric's door, but it opened before he could, revealing a startled Kelric on the other side.

"Ferry it, Dargos." Kelric emerged from the dark room with bleary eyes and a scowl. "What do you want?" He closed the door and pushed past Dargos—not in the least interested in a response.

Before Dargos could speak, Kelric was already across the courtyard.

"Klymene!" Kelric shouted—more like a barking hound than a human call. His eyes darted around, peering into storerooms. "Klymene!"

The girl burst out of the kitchen door, looking flustered and breathless. "I'm here, Basileus," she stammered, staring at the ground and twisting her fingers into a knot.

Pity stabbed Dargos as he watched the scene unfold. Kelric towered over her, looking menacing in his bedraggled state, his piercing gray eyes elongated by dark circles, but no less intense.

"Go to the basileia, and do not leave her side until I say so."

Dargos straightened at the mention of his little sister. The urgency in Kelric's tone suggested something was very wrong. He recalled her gaunt face and frail frame from the day before, her exertions at the camps before that. Had she exhausted herself? Was that why she hadn't attended Tor's procession?

The doula bit her lip. "The basileia has told me she does not—"

"You do as *I* say," Kelric snapped.

Klymene flinched, her lip trembling. "Yes, Basileus."

Kelric glared down at her, and she bowed again and sprinted away.

"What's wrong with Gonivein?"

Kelric's attention snapped to Dargos as though he had only just noticed him standing there. "I don't owe you an explanation." He started to move away.

Anxiety ignited into anger at Kelric's evasion, and Dargos grabbed his shoulder. His little sister was no longer his responsibility, but he would be ferried before he stood by and watched her suffer. Kelric may have earned a shred of respect for saving her, but that shred was a breath away from snapping in two.

"*What* is going on, Kelric?"

Kelric shoved his arm away, squaring his shoulders for a fight. "My *wife* has a broken hip and is being stubborn. Let me take care of her in peace, Dargos, or get out of my city."

Adrenaline raced through Dargos' limbs at the vehemence. He would have never thought it possible for Kelric to become even more insufferable, but he should have known his taking on the mantle of basileus would have accomplished exactly that. Dargos had foolishly hoped it would force him to be more level-headed, and in some respects, it had. The doubled guards around the city were evidence of that. Yet Dargos couldn't help but wonder if that decision had been spurred on by something far more rash. The details of Gonivein's vision and Forluna's interpretation of the vines wormed through him. Did Kelric know more than he had shared?

Clenching his jaw, Dargos reminded himself to choose his words carefully. Golpathia was Kelric's domain, and so was Gonivein. He couldn't do any good for his little sister if Kelric forced him to leave.

"Is she all right, besides the hip?" He willed his voice to lose its sharp edge.

"She's fine," Kelric growled. "She'd be better if Apollo didn't exist."

The hair raised on Dargos' arms. He half expected the god to appear and loose a bolt into Kelric's chest for his arrogance.

"We need to talk about the Council." Best to change the subject before the god did materialize.

"What about it?" Kelric ducked through the kitchen doorway.

Dargos followed on his heels into the warm room, where Euanthe had already set out a basket of dried fish and fruit on the wooden table just inside the door. Dargos crossed his arms over his chest as Kelric stuffed his pockets with dried raisins and several strips of fish.

Across the room, the cook stirred a large kettle of lentils for the midday meal over a merry fire. A brass pan sat on the hearthstones, warming loaves of flat bread. Savory smells of garlic and herbs permeated the air.

Euanthe beamed when she saw Kelric. She set the ladle down and hurried over, reaching into the pocket of her *himation*. "I saved this for you." She placed a ripe apple in Kelric's hand.

Kelric grinned. "Thank you, Euanthe. You've always made my day better."

"Took me a little while to find one. The markets are a bit scarce, but your smile was worth the trouble." She squeezed his arm before hurrying back over to her kettle, not noticing the way Kelric's smile faltered at her words.

Dargos frowned, snatching two strips of dried fish and following Kelric into the sunlight.

Kelric took a bite of the apple and looked expectantly at Dargos. "Well?" he said, crunching loudly.

"The vision." Dargos was annoyed, but not wholly surprised Kelric hadn't taken the threat as seriously as Forluna had.

Kelric swallowed. "What vision?"

The look on Kelric's face quickened Dargos' pulse. "Gonivein told you, didn't she?"

Kelric wore the expression of a little boy caught shirking his chores. He shrugged.

Dargos' anger flared, fingers curling tightly around the dried fish in his hands. Why must Kelric be so dismissive of anything to do with the gods? He wanted to take Kelric by the shoulders and shake him until his apple-crunching teeth rattled in his skull.

"The vines," he hissed. "It's probable that one of your councilmen is a Leirion, maybe more than one." *Why is he being so daft?* Was it possible Gonivein *hadn't* told Kelric of this yesterday? He was about to ask, but Kelric waved his hand as though that clue had jarred his memory.

"I know."

So, Kelric *was* keeping things from them.

"They may try to rid themselves of us at the meeting today. Create chaos and division so they can exert control over Golpathia."

Kelric took another bite of the apple. The way his eyes were narrowed unsettled Dargos.

"What do you already know about this?"

Kelric scowled. "I'm not convinced these visions are anything more than Apollo's twisted idea of entertainment. But I've already ordered extra guards present at the bouleuterion, if it makes you feel better."

"To be honest, I'm not sure it does. How can we be sure your guards are not with the Leirion?"

Kelric opened his mouth, no doubt with a sharp retort, but closed it without speaking. How could Kelric refute that? His own father had been a Leirion right under their noses.

"What choice do we have?" Kelric eyed Gadnor as he emerged from his bedroom. The swelling had gone down over his eye, though the white around his pupil remained bloodshot. The black-and-purple bruise was beginning to fade to yellow, and the skin beneath the stitches on his shoulders was a healthy pink.

Gadnor nodded to them and drew up a bucket from the well in the center of the courtyard. As he rinsed the sleep from his face, Dargos relayed the new insight of Gonivein's vision and Forluna's concerns about the Council.

Whatever trace of confidence Gadnor might have had was scrubbed from his face by the time they were on their way down to the bouleuterion to meet with Kelric's most influential kyrioi. The boy looked as nervous as ever. Dargos drew closer to him. "You're the strategos. Sit proudly beside Kelric. Your duel was forfeited because of Alypius' treachery, not lost because of any lack of skill on your part. Remember that."

Gadnor nodded. If he hadn't straightened his shoulders just a little, Dargos would have thought his words had made no difference.

Dargos stepped between the columned entrance of the bouleuterion and waited for his eyes to adjust to the dimness. The rectangular structure was lined with rows of tiered seating, enough for fifty people to discuss public affairs. Today, it was completely empty.

We're early. They'll come.

Unless they planned to stage another protest and ignore their basileus' summons. Dargos moved to the altar in the center of the room to build a fire, hoping busy hands would quiet the anxiety thumping in his mind. Gadnor retrieved the wine from the corner. Kelric folded his arms and stood perfectly still, glaring at the altar as though it were an adversary. Dargos ignored them as he struck the flint and caught the tinder.

He was so absorbed in his task, he hardly noticed when the assembly members began to arrive, murmuring greetings to Kelric. None of them formally acknowledged Gadnor or Dargos. A few glanced at them as they entered, but quickly looked away as if afraid they might turn to stone if they stared too long. Alypius and Ephastes were the last to arrive and sat closest to the exit. At their appearance, the tension thickened, and the already cramped space became almost suffocating.

With the fire crackling heartily and the seats filled, Dargos signaled for Gadnor to hand Kelric the wine.

Kelric stared at it, confused.

Dargos looked pointedly at the altar, hoping he didn't have to tell his brother-in-law what his duties were. The assembly watched like hawks.

Kelric finally took the amphora and splashed it on the coals. "Gods' blessings," he grumbled. The flames leapt. He took his seat at the back of the room on the center bench. Gadnor sat on his right side, and Dargos his left.

Dargos folded his arms across his chest, touching his fingers to the hilt of his dagger fastened at his waist. He eyed these prominent kyrioi warily. Any one of them, or all of them, could be a Leirion. He especially didn't like Alypius and Ephastes sitting by the door. It felt threatening, as though they intended to prevent his escape.

As though they anticipated he might have reason to try to.

"Thank you for coming on such short notice," Kelric said. "This matter cannot wait."

Expectation hung in the air, and Dargos experienced the strange sensation that everyone knew something he didn't. He shared a glance with Gadnor, who also seemed uneasy. At least Dargos wasn't the only one.

Kelric shifted on the seat beside him. "We have received word that Charixes is planning an assault on Golpathia."

Anxious murmurs arose from all around the circle. Kelric raised his hand to quiet them.

"We expect an attack by the spring equinox."

Voices erupted in the chamber. Kelric waited for the shock to subside before raising his hand again. "We should be prepared well in advance."

Dargos studied each face carefully. Most of the men seemed genuinely surprised and outraged by the news.

"How did you come by this information?" Ephastes asked.

Dargos met Kelric's gaze, praying to Hermes that he wouldn't fumble his words and give Lithaneva away.

"I have my sources." Kelric smirked. "And they are reliable."

"If Charixes is planning an attack, it's because you're harboring a traitor." Alypius pointed at Dargos. "We should turn Dargos over to him now, before his armies are at our gates and there is no more hope of negotiating a peace."

Dargos had expected this, but anxiety skittered across his shoulders all the same as the councilmen began to speak in favor of the idea. A few said nothing, eying each other from their scattered places around the circle. Dargos recognized some of them as the ones who had not cheered for Alypius during his duel with Gadnor. Hope sparked within him that they might object, but it fizzled out as the moments drew on.

Kelric raised his hand once again. "Golpathia has been threatened. Is it your suggestion, Alypius, that we cower under these threats like whipped dogs?"

Alypius glowered from across the room, shooting menacing stares at his quiet companions. Some pretended not to see, some averted their eyes to the floor.

What power does he have over all of them? Dargos was reminded that Alypius and Ephastes were responsible for most of the food brought into Golpathia. Was that the only reason no one wanted to cross them? In a famine, perhaps that was enough. Still, Dargos found it more likely he was the leader of the lurking threat. He wished he had proof.

"Better to cower like a dog than be skewered like a fish," Ephastes muttered. "Which is exactly what will happen if we allow Dargos to remain here."

"Before our basileus' wedding, I might have agreed with this action," Krastus said. "But the appearance of those birds still unsettles me. The scholar said the gods were angry with Alypius' aggression, and that is not an opinion we should dismiss out of hand. If we turn Dargos over to Charixes, we may anger the gods more."

So, the kyrioi had interpreted Tor's summoning the same way.

Good. Dargos had no intention of correcting them.

"They could have just as easily been angered that we haven't finished Dargos off," Alypius countered.

The men began to bicker. Echoes of their anger rebounded in the domed space to an ear-splitting degree. Suggestions for every possible scenario merged into one indistinguishable roar that made Dargos want to flee the walled space. He stayed put, gritting his teeth.

When would Kelric order silence? His brother-in-law seemed uncharacteristically subdued, despite the chaos.

Gadnor met Dargos' gaze, a kindred curiosity passing between them.

Finally, Ephastes rose, drawing all attention to him. Blessedly, the noise subsided. "Charixes occupies the city of Shallinath. No one has had word of their welfare in weeks. He decimated Tyldan for their defiance, leaving only a trail of blood, tears, and ash as proof they ever existed at all. Every day, our own villages empty their rabble behind our walls to avoid the same fate."

A few heads began to bob, and a cold chill swept over Dargos.

"Our markets strain to provide enough food to those who live here as it is. If we do not wish to be overrun by useless women and children, never mind Charixes' army, then we should negotiate Dargos' surrender in exchange for peace and expel this hoard back to their homes. Birds be damned."

Dargos' heart thumped wildly as Alypius thrust his fist into the air in support. At least a dozen others followed suit. Even the quieter ones wore contemplative expressions. The Council seemed on the verge of a unanimous decision.

"My army is pledged to defend Golpathia against this assault." Dargos knew the census records of every village in Shallinath by heart, knew the number of able-bodied warriors in each. And his doulos, Crusates, after having warned Dargos not to return to Shallinath, would have alerted at least three villages to prepare for war by now. If Dargos could get to them, they could be ready to march to Golpathia's defense by the spring equinox.

Dargos looked to Kelric, waiting for confirmation that would put an end to the Council's dangerous and misguided ideas.

Kelric remained tight-lipped.

A prickle of warning skittered across Dargos' shoulders. This wasn't like Kelric. Dargos would have never thought Kelric would stand for such a brazen challenge to his authority. *What is holding him back?*

Realization struck him like a harsh blow.

He's considering their demands. Dargos' heartbeat thrummed in his ears as the walls closed in. The flames crackling in the center of the room burned what little air remained for his straining lungs.

This can't be true. This can't be happening. Kelric wouldn't betray him like this—they were brothers now. Gonivein was his wife!

He stared at Kelric, waiting for that piercing stare to meet his eyes. But it didn't.

White-hot rage kindled in Dargos' gut. He should have seen this coming. Kelric had always loathed Dargos for making him wait to marry Gonivein, for reminding her of his faults and encouraging her to break off their engagement at every opportunity. *Fool!* Why had he let himself believe this animosity was behind them?

I've been wrong about so many things.

Dargos wondered now if Kelric had planned this revenge all along. Was that why he'd been acting so strangely earlier? Why he had refused to let him see Gonivein? *Does she know?*

Dargos dragged his hand through his hair to keep himself from throwing his knuckles down Kelric's throat. As his fingers slid through the tangled strands, the very last of his hope slipped away. His city, his dignity, his pride, his position—they were all memories of a not-so-distant past he had once lived, led, fought for.

Now they were ghosts.

CHAPTER 42

GONIVEIN

VINES ENTANGLED THE HELPLESS WOLVES in the valley below. Gonivein could not tear her eyes away. The beasts' jaws snapped as they circled the helpless falcon, claws and paws swiping angrily. The stallion's hooves pounded, shaking the earth. Even high on this ridge, she felt the reverberations through her feet. Her stomach swooped. A gust of wind would be all it took for her to career over the edge. She crouched low to the ground, clutching blades of green grass to keep from plummeting to her doom.

She'd fallen from a ledge like this once before. No—she'd been thrown.

She licked her lips, tasting salt. The deafening roar of crashing waves drowned the screams of the dying falcon. She clenched the grass tighter, digging her nails into the dirt. But it was no longer the earth she clung to. It was a body. Loric's body. A sob caught in her throat. She prayed for the sea to drag them both away this time.

Then Kelric was there, his fingers clamping around her elbow, trying to pry Loric from her arms.

"No!" She tightened her grip around Loric's shoulders. "He's not dead!"

Loric's eyes opened.

Her breath hitched.

"Gonivein," he whispered through pale blue lips. He raised his hand, gently brushing her shoulder. "Wake up."

Gonivein startled awake. A face swam before her, black hair and dark eyes. *Loric!* The name was on her tongue, aching to be set free, but as she blinked the last of the nightmare away, it was Klymene whose features came into focus.

"Basileia." Worry creased the girl's features. "Are you all right? You were screaming."

Gonivein licked her lips, tasting salt. When she moved, she noticed the moisture clinging to her linen gown, the chill in the air tightening her skin with gooseflesh. She sank back into the wet pillow, drawing in a deep breath. She tilted her head to peer across the room at the door. "Where's Kelric?"

"He's gone to the bouleuterion." Klymene dug in a trunk and pulled out a clean yellow chiton.

Gonivein sat up slowly, rubbing her shoulder where Loric had grazed her with his fingers. *'Wake up.'*

She held her aching head. Cryptic nightmares had plagued her for over a decade, and Loric had been there with a gentle hand to wake her from them night after night.

'I'm the one who pulls you back from them.' Kelric's words made her seethe with rage.

'No!' she wanted to scream at him. *'It was Loric who pulled me back.'*

Loric still pulled her back.

She eyed Klymene warily. The girl held a broach in one hand and sifted through the trunk with the other. She pulled out a red veil and examined it, then put it back and continued searching for the second broach. Before she'd found it, she'd pulled out a blue veil and laid it beside the chiton, and tucked a comb under her arm. She stood, letting the lid slam shut. She grinned at Gonivein. "There, I think I've found everything we need."

"Is Euanthe treating you well?" Gonivein asked, rubbing the sleepiness from her eyes.

The girl's smile dimmed somewhat, but she nodded. "Yes."

Gonivein furrowed her brow. "Did she dismiss you for the day?"

"B... Basileus Kelric commanded me to help you today." Klymene bit her lip, the color draining from her face.

Commanded. Gonivein despised that word. She doubted Kelric's temper had been soothed by a night's sleep on the cold floor. Guilt scratched in her stomach—not because she had angered Kelric, but because Klymene had borne the brunt of it this morning. Her own anger thrummed through her veins, temporarily masking her exhaustion. She'd been sleepless most of the night, waking every time a wave crashed louder than the rest. She eyed the window pane, still hanging crookedly on its hinge. The cricket was gone, the wood cleaned and polished with oil.

"I suppose I have you to thank for the window?"

Klymene chewed her lip, nodding.

"Thank you."

The girl visibly relaxed, and Gonivein motioned her over. "I do need your help today, actually."

"Really?" Excitement buzzed in Klymene's voice, tugging a smile across Gonivein's face.

"I need to sort my wedding gifts. I'm going to sell them to raise funds for the refugees."

"That's very kind of you," Klymene said, helping Gonivein change out of yesterday's dirty clothes and step into the yellow chiton.

Gonivein didn't answer. Not so long ago, she would have agreed with Klymene and been pleased with herself for giving up her expensive things for someone else's benefit. But in truth, her view of kindness had shifted. Ensuring her citizens were fed and sheltered wasn't a kindness, it was her obligation as their basileia and as the Oracle of Apollo. Anything less would be a failure of duty.

Klymene combed and braided her hair, then placed the veil

delicately over the plaits. The long blue cloth draped down her back and over her shoulders like a cloak.

In the kitchen, Gonivein had little appetite, but she ate because Euanthe was eying her from across the room as she kneaded a large portion of dough into smaller loaves. Gonivein didn't want the old woman to think her meals weren't tasty. The scholars trickled into the room, helping themselves to the food spread on the sideboard table and talking animatedly about their journey back to Critius the next morning. They seemed in good spirits, delighted and excited to share the news of two new oracles with the rest of Helinthia.

Mandus stopped beside Euanthe to thank her for preparing so many loaves for their journey, to which she beamed and winked flirtatiously. Only one scholar did not have anyone to talk to. He stood near the door, waiting for his companions with clasped hands and glancing outside occasionally. He seemed anxious. Perhaps he disliked the noise as much as Gonivein did. When he noticed her looking at him, he smiled kindly.

Gonivein shoved the rest of her dried figs into her mouth and stood, eager to begin sorting through her gifts. Klymene bolted to her side. Gonivein eyed her. Euanthe had a considerable amount of work to do between preparing provisions for the scholars and meals for the villa, and Gonivein had won no special treatment from Kelric last night. Was he hoping to use the girl to spy on her? Report back to him all of her comings and goings? Her interactions? His accusation that she'd intended to throw herself into another's bed burned through her. She wished she'd slapped him, but she'd been far too stunned to react appropriately.

"What, exactly, was my husband's reason for making you my shadow today?"

Klymene's face turned bright red. "H-he didn't say, Basileia, but he was adamant."

Gonivein's anger for Kelric rekindled. She wanted to probe the girl further, find out exactly what happened, but she didn't want to risk Klymene misinterpreting her emotions. The poor girl had gone through enough.

Gonivein sighed and turned away, unsure if she wanted to destroy something, or crumple to the gravel and sob. She turned to the storeroom door which led to the pile of gifts and flung it open. It banged against the wall. The sharp cracking sound it made was satisfying. She wanted to do it again, but didn't wish to cause a scene. The last thing she wanted was to draw Mandus' attention. She couldn't suffer through his droning voice offering ancient wisdom on gods and marriage, or whatever other nonsense he might conjure up.

Inside the storeroom, crates, baskets, boxes, amphorae, bronze trinkets, bolts of cloth, and at least a hundred other knickknacks littered the space, piled almost to the ceiling. For a moment, Gonivein let herself imagine charging into the pile and shattering every breakable thing. She took a calming breath, then let the thought go. As satisfying as that violent fit would be, her people needed these items intact.

"You look terrible, dear."

Gonivein jumped, her senses sinking back into her. Euanthe stood beside her with clasped hands, studying her with a concerned expression.

"What?"

"Are you sleeping well?"

Euanthe was *definitely* not the one to confide in.

Gonivein forced a smile. "I'm fine, Euanthe, thank you for asking. Just getting ready to sort through these gifts." She took a step forward, hoping the woman would leave, but Euanthe took her gently by the elbow.

"Sit a moment, Basileia. Please?"

Something in the old woman's eyes convinced her to agree, though her instincts warned her to stay guarded. Everyone in this villa answered to Kelric, and Euanthe *adored* him. Gonivein didn't want to give away anything he could twist and use against her.

She followed Euanthe to the retaining wall surrounding the dried up fountain and sat. Klymene busied herself sorting the gifts in the storeroom, separating out everything bronze and expensive looking to one side.

Euanthe took Gonivein's hand and petted it affectionately. Despite having always seen this woman working something with her hands, her touch was soft and silky. The scent of yeast and flour soothed Gonivein, encouraging her to breathe deeper. Guarded intentions or not, she felt herself relax.

"I was a new bride myself once," Euanthe began. "It's hard, giving yourself to another. I don't just mean physically, either. You are not one person anymore, you are two, and that is a difficult thing to figure out how to manage. Especially, when you both have such different burdens to bear."

Warmth rushed beneath Gonivein's skin. She maintained her gaze on Klymene, suddenly afraid she would burst into tears.

"You and Kelric have been through many changes in a short time. He has you to look after, but he also has the entire polis. Trust me when I say that he finds it difficult to divide his attention between the two."

Gonivein resisted the urge to pull her hand away. She didn't want to feel guilty for her fury or her reluctance to forgive Kelric. She sensed no remorse from him.

"I know Kelric can be quick to anger, but it wasn't always that way. He was such a cheerful boy, devoted to his mother. And she was gracious and patient with him—with everyone. The two were inseparable. Kelric would ask me to make her little honey cakes. He never asked for any for himself. Only for his mother. Of course, I always made one for him, too."

Gonivein looked at the woman then. There were tears in Euanthe's eyes.

"Kelric was devastated by her loss. We all were, but for him, it seemed he'd lost everything that held meaning. I thought I would never see true joy in him again. And then he met you."

Euanthe captured her gaze, smiling as she squeezed her hand.

Gonivein squeezed back. Sadness in the woman's tone tugged at her heart, softened her rage. She sensed an unhealed grief for Kelric's mother there, but even more for the little boy who had been changed forever. Gonivein's eyes stung, and she had a sudden urge to find Kelric and hold him.

"There's been anger in him ever since. But if there's one thing that has never changed, it is how fiercely he protects the ones he loves. He always will."

Klymene had wandered closer and was listening to the story. She dipped her head. "You care very deeply for him."

Euanthe smiled. "There's no one who can replace his mother, but I tried as much as my station allowed. I'd like to think I've brought him some comfort over the years. I've seen a glimpse of that joyful boy once or twice. But it's you, dear Gonivein, who can truly make him whole again. And he would let you, if you choose it."

Gonivein swallowed the knot in her throat. She couldn't think of a response, so she simply nodded.

Euanthe stood and clasped her hands in front of her. "Well, I need to check on the loaves." Then she was gone.

Gonivein stared after her, moved to compassion for Kelric despite the wounds he'd inflicted on her soul. Could his happiness really be as simple as Euanthe seemed to suggest?

And would that result in her own happiness if it was?

CHAPTER 43

GADNOR

ANXIETY WORMED THROUGH GADNOR'S CHEST as the noise in the bouleuterion rose to a deafening height. Alypius and Ephastes seemed ready to spring at Dargos and rip him limb from limb. Kelric showed no signs of intervening if they did. Dargos' face flushed red as rage pulsed through his body. A fight seemed inevitable. He looked to Kelric, wondering why his brother remained silent through it all.

Krastus, the chief magistrate, waved his hand, shouting to refocus everyone's attention on him. Finally, the chamber calmed enough for the older man to speak clearly.

"Your concerns are valid, Alypius. Dargos' presence complicates matters now that he is a fugitive. However…" Krastus extended one hand, pressing his fingertips together. "Even if we hand Dargos over, we have no reason to trust that Charixes will abort this planned attack. The anax has proven he needs no provocation to invade—Shallinath received no warning."

Dargos visibly relaxed. Several heads nodded, faces turning thoughtful.

"You think Charixes had no provocation?" Alypius scoffed. "Dargos has made his thirst for blood no secret. Was Charixes to allow such an affront to his authority go unchecked?"

Kelric shifted in his chair, and Gadnor noticed a curious look pass between him and Archon Tryphus. Still, Kelric remained silent.

"How do we know this 'information about an attack' wasn't contrived by Dargos to force us into *his* war?" Alypius narrowed his eyes on Dargos. "He's squandered his means to wage it himself, so he's set his sights on our men—our sons and brothers—to do his dirty work."

Dargos leaned forward as if to launch himself across the room, but Kelric raised his hand, stopping him. Gadnor could tell it was taking nearly all of Dargos' willpower to obey.

Calls of '*where did you come by this information,*' and '*who is your source*' echoed. Kelric waited for the din to die before opening his mouth. He seemed to have gotten his bearings now, and Gadnor allowed a little more confidence back into his lungs with grateful breaths.

"I will not expose my source to scrutiny from the likes of you, Alypius. Trust that they have no connection to Dargos. Or is it *my* loyalty you're questioning?"

Alypius glowered from his seat.

Not bold enough to challenge Kelric directly, then. Good.

Kelric smirked. Gadnor had never been happier to see that visage of pride and confidence return to his brother's face. "I'm sure many of you can appreciate a man who wishes to remain anonymous."

Tryphus shifted uneasily, and Kelric's eyes swept the room as though searching for something. Confusion pinched Gadnor's brows together. He studied his brother, hoping for a hint, but Kelric gave nothing away as he settled back onto his stone seat. He waved to Dargos to speak.

"Charixes is the aggressor here." Traces of anger remained in Dargos' sharp tone. "He usurped the throne from Anassa Iptys, and he took Shallinath from me with *no* provocation, no terms, no warning. Now he moves to do the same to you."

"Golpathia has no quarrel with Charixes." Alypius pointed an accusing finger at Dargos again. "You made a gadfly of yourself in disputing his legitimacy. From where I'm sitting, you brought your misfortunes upon yourself. Don't drag us into your fate."

Alypius' triumphant smirk in the nervous silence that followed made the hair bristle along Gadnor's arms.

Dargos was rigid with rage. Kelric's expression was once again unreadable, and Golpathia's leaders and councilmen seemed ready to agree with Alypius.

Gadnor clenched his fists. He wouldn't be silent and watch someone he loved succumb to a fate not of their choosing again. He stood, locking his knees to stop their trembling.

Ephastes' mouth curled into an amused smirk. "And what do you have to say, *Strategos*?"

Warmth flooded Gadnor's neck and face. His arm itched, and he dug his nails deeper into his palms to keep them from tearing into his scars.

Hermes, give me words…

He cleared his throat, collecting his thoughts. "War with Charixes became inevitable the day our father negotiated a marriage between my brother and Dargos' sister." He nodded down to Dargos. "Father knew the risks. He accepted them, and all of us celebrated the announcement—including you, Kyrios Ephastes."

Ephastes' eyes darkened, his smile waning.

No one dared move, but agreement flickered across several faces. Gadnor swallowed. "He allied with Dargos because he disputed Charixes' legitimacy every bit as much as Dargos does, and because the armies of Shallinath and Golpathia together make a formidable foe that can defeat the anax and restore prosperity to our island."

The faces before him suddenly blurred as his mind caught up with his emotional impulsivity.

He was speaking. In public. To a room full of angry, powerful men who despised him. His words might very well decide the fate of the rebellion and Golpathia's sovereignty as a self-governed polis of Helinthia.

What am I doing?

His heart thrummed in his ears. He lifted his gaze to the mosaic waves etched into the wall just above the men's heads. To his relief, his sight focused, and he followed the blue spirals around the room as he spoke. He hoped no one realized he wasn't looking at them.

"Dargos is our ally." His blood raced through his veins so fast his limbs were beginning to tingle. "If we abandon him now, we will leave ourselves isolated and exposed to Charixes' full might. I believe Kyrios Krastus is right. We can't trust Charixes to walk away from us without taking a pound of flesh. We may not have expressed displeasure with his rule, but our friendship with Dargos and the bonds we've forged have declared our loyalties loud enough."

Gadnor sat back down, the room spinning and swaying. He prayed his breakfast didn't begin to rise.

Krastus offered him a subtle nod from across the room.

Alypius, however, was unwilling to concede. "Alliances are built on mutual strength. What strength does Dargos provide Golpathia?" The kyrios shot another glare at Dargos. "Charixes has stripped you of your title. You're no more useful to us than a doulos." He swept his gaze around the circle. Several men squirmed in their seats. "Are we willing to risk our future on the assumption his so-called army will even answer his call to arms?"

"My soldiers are armed with vengeance for Tyldan," Dargos growled. "They will answer."

Alypius opened his mouth, but Krastus raised a hand to halt him. Gadnor blinked, shocked as Alypius snapped his jaw closed.

"How would *you* meet this threat, Gadnor?" Krastus said.

Gadnor swallowed the bile rising in his throat, his thoughts and bravery scattering like sparks in the wind. He rubbed his arm, tracing the rough scar with his fingertip. *I have to do this.*

His eyes locked once again on the blue wave above Krastus' head. "I would lead a contingent force through the mountains to Hameth and find out what he's harboring there. Then destroy it."

Kelric turned his head, and Gadnor felt those piercing gray eyes scrutinizing him. Gadnor chanced a glance to glean what he might be thinking. Was he annoyed? Angry? But the expression Kelric wore now wasn't one Gadnor recognized. That was almost worse than the all-too-familiar disapproval.

Silence. Then murmurs. Then Alypius.

"Your spy didn't tell you the nature of this threat?"

Gadnor licked his lips. "No. But a small force will maximize our advantage of remaining unseen."

Alypius laughed. "Hameth is vast, wild, and untamed. Did they even tell you where in Hameth this threat supposedly is?"

Gadnor's ears felt uncomfortably hot.

"So," Alypius continued. Ephastes chuckled beside him. "Having no knowledge of this enemy, the destination, or even if success is achievable, you would lead able-bodied men to their deaths?"

"I will ask no man to follow me who does not wish to," Gadnor announced.

Kelric stared at him, looking neither vehement nor pleased. Gadnor began to sense he had overstepped and waited for Kelric to say so. He didn't.

Ephastes laughed audibly now. "No one wishes to follow *you*, Strategos Gadnor. You are unskilled, inexperienced, and too naive to lead such an important mission as this."

Krastus tilted his head, tapping his fingers methodically on his knee. "Is it true you wrestled a lion with your bare hands, Gadnor?"

Fangs snapped at Gadnor's throat in his mind's eye, and he sank his nails into his arm as an itch exploded beneath the patched-up skin. "Yes."

"Gadnor wrestled *three* lions," Dargos interjected. "I was there, as was Basileus Kelric."

The councilmen whispered and murmured, their eyes scrutinizing the deep scars on Gadnor's arms, shoulders, and cheek. These rumors had been circulating for weeks, but this was the first time Dargos and Kelric had revealed they were eyewitnesses. Perhaps it would be enough to win them over.

"Dumb beasts are not equal to a trained army," Alypius retorted. "If you fail—if you are *caught*—then all hope of negotiating a peace will be forfeit."

Krastus turned his eyes on Kelric. "You have been silent, Basileus. What is your opinion on the fate of your polis?" The delicately worded question fell heavily in the room.

Kelric stiffened, clasping his hands together in his lap—a maneuver their father had done during stressful encounters. "I prefer to hear all opinions before I voice my own. I wouldn't want anyone's candor to be diminished by my influence."

"I believe you have achieved that aim." Krastus tossed an amused glance in Alypius and Ephastes' direction.

Gadnor waited for his brother to meet his gaze, hoping for some confirmation Kelric would agree to his plan and not abandon Dargos. *Trust me.* But even Gadnor wasn't confident—he scarcely remembered what he had said. It would all come back to him later, after he broke free of this room, escaped the stares that shackled his confidence.

Kelric dragged a hand slowly through his hair, refusing to look at Gadnor or give any hints about what he thought. The muscles along his jaw spasmed. Finally, he spoke. "I'm less inclined to cower and beg for mercy than I am to stand and fight. All of you know my skill on the battlefield, and none of you have ever seen me cede ground to an enemy."

More heads nodded. Alypius and Ephastes brooded. Krastus looked thoughtful, and Tryphus tapped his fingers nervously against his thigh.

Kelric puffed out his chest. "I will consider this matter carefully. We will assemble here again in the morning, and I will make my decision."

"And what of Dargos and his kubernao from Tyldan?" Ephastes sneered.

"What of them?" Kelric sighed impatiently.

"What if they flee in the night? If we lose them as leverage, war is all but assured."

Dargos leapt to his feet, eyes flashing, rage pulsing through the veins in his arms. He'd taken a single step across the chamber before Gadnor sprang in front of him, laying a bracing hand against his shoulder.

"Don't rise to his bait." Gadnor's feet had been much faster than his head, and the room spun ever so slightly. Dargos could easily shove him aside if he wanted to.

Blessedly, Dargos settled for glaring over Gadnor's shoulder at Ephastes. He didn't retake his seat.

Kelric growled—the first hint of his usual demeanor. "Dargos is no coward," he snapped. "However, to appease the members of this Council, he will remain under guard at my villa until I decide what course we will take. Tryphus will see to it."

The color drained from Dargos' face, and Gadnor gave his shoulder an encouraging squeeze. He didn't think it helped.

The meeting adjourned, and the kyrioi filed out of the bouleuterion. They clustered outside in small groups of two or three, muttering and whispering.

Gadnor caught Krastus' eye when he emerged. The chief magistrate wore an expression that suggested he wanted to speak, but Gadnor pretended not to notice and quickly left the premises. He avoided the main streets and wandered through the back alleys. The first one he found devoid of humans, he promptly leaned over and retched until his stomach was empty.

CHAPTER 44

LITHANEVA

THE BRONZE MIRROR SHOOK IN Lithaneva's palm. She gritted her teeth and grasped the offending object with both hands to steady it. She scrutinized her neck's reflection in the polished bronze, recalling the fingerprint Helinthia had burned into Gadnor's forehead when she'd caught him spying on them a month ago. Everyone had seen it and made a mockery of him for it. No evidence of Hera's assault lingered around Lithaneva's neck. Only a persistent soreness deep in her throat that neither cold nor warm water could ease, and her tongue felt thick between her teeth.

She laid the mirror face down on her vanity. *Why didn't she kill me?*

Lithaneva had a sinking feeling that she had been transformed into a cat's pre-dinner entertainment. Death would eventually come as the goddess promised, but only after her spirit was torn to shreds, ripped from the very fabric of her soul until she was an unrecognizable clot of human flesh.

I won't let her. She won't break me. She rubbed her temples with shaking fingers. She needed to see Helinthia. Tell her that Hera knew about them, about their plan. Shame squirmed within her as she imagined the look of disappointment on Helinthia's face, her *rage* when she explained how all their carefully kept secrets had spilled from her treacherous mouth like water from a broken cistern.

She had to tell her soon. Helinthia had no idea of the danger haunting her steps.

Will Helinthia murder me?

Hera's revelation that Helinthia had killed her oracle hadn't left Lithaneva's mind, but it hadn't changed her feelings for her beloved goddess. Even if Hera was telling the truth, Helinthia must have had a good reason. It would take more than a corpse to diminish her affection; there would be many feeding Hades' vultures before they were done.

That was the price of war.

A knock at the door made her jump.

"The midday meal is ready, Princess," Torine's muffled voice said on the other side.

Lithaneva sighed in relief. Perfect timing. She could slip out to the garden temple while everyone else ate. *I'll just say I'm ill.* No one would think twice, especially after her mood at breakfast.

"I'll be right there.*"*

Lithaneva frowned. *Why did I say that?* Her palms grew clammy. She was still shaken. What other careless mistakes would she make?

She waited for Torine's footsteps to recede, then slipped out of her room, heart racing, cursing herself for her stupidity. They would come looking for her if she took too long. She stole through the garden and hurried into the temple, stopping before the altar.

Skimming away the ashes of last night's sacrifice with her palm, she searched for live embers, wincing at the burn when she found some. She couldn't do the ritual exactly right this time, but her blood should be enough. It would have to be.

She pulled her dagger from her belt and sliced a finger, letting the droplets fall and sizzle onto the coals, sending steam and smoke upwards.

It seemed like an eternity, but Helinthia finally appeared. Caution guided her eyes around the small chamber. "Lithaneva?" She half crouched behind the altar as though afraid someone would burst in and find her there. Odd behavior, since no one could see the goddess unless she willed it. "Are the cuckoos gone?"

Lithaneva would have laughed if she didn't know the truth.

"Are you all right, Lithie?" Helinthia stepped closer, her brow pinching in concern.

No! She wanted to cry and fling herself in her lover's arms. Where to begin? "You abandoned me here."

Helinthia jolted back, as though she'd been slapped.

Shock reeled through Lithaneva, and then horror seeped in. Something was very wrong. Her response to Torine had been careless, but *this*... Slinging barbs at her anxious lover was nothing short of cruel. And hurling accusations at a goddess was madness.

Helinthia's expression turned defensive, hurt roiling in the depths of her dark eyes. "I left because I knew Hera was watching us— those feral birds are her favorites. Not all of them are her spies, but the way that one looked at me, I was sure it was hers. I panicked. I had to get far away as quickly as possible or Hera would find us. Find *you*."

So that was it. That was why Helinthia had left her, and rightly so. Lithaneva wanted to set her lover at ease, soothe her, assure her that she understood. "Your leaving opened my eyes to the truth."

Her heart began to pound so fiercely it hurt to breathe. *What is happening to me?*

Helinthia's shoulders stiffened. She tilted her head dangerously. "What truth is that?"

Just don't say anything. Just keep your mouth sh— "That you only care about yourself, your own power, your own life. You were willing to sacrifice me without a second thought, without a backward glance."

An urge to grab her head and scream in panic and terror overtook her, but her body refused to heed. A war of wills waged inside of her. She had no idea how to win.

'I curse you, Lithaneva... May you reap the truth of the lies you

sow.'

Never in her life had she been so compromised as now. She wanted to beg Helinthia's forgiveness. Fall on her knees and grovel. Or run, flee before she destroyed the tenderness between them for good. But her knees remained locked. Rigid. Feet rooted to the cold marble tiles.

Helinthia's eyes narrowed. She stepped closer and cupped Lithaneva's face in her hands. "What's happened, Lithie? Did Hera hurt you?" Her eyes flicked to the place where the cuckoo had perched.

Yes! Yes, it's Hera's doing. Please, see through this! "The only one who has hurt me is you."

Helinthia dropped her hands, a wounded flush blooming in her pale cheeks.

No! Lithaneva wanted to shut up. Just stop talking. Stop hurling these cruel things at the one she loved with her whole heart. But the stronger she fought to keep the lies spewing from her lips, the freer her tongue hurled them into existence.

"I no longer wish to be your oracle, your tool to use and abuse whenever you like."

"Lithaneva." Helinthia's tone was sharp. She raised her chin, narrowing her eyes into dangerous slits. "I don't believe you! My mother put you up to this, didn't she?"

Mother? Lithaneva blinked in shock. *Hera is...?* Why had Helinthia never told her that?

Helinthia gripped Lithaneva's shoulders and shook them, gentle, but firm, drawing her attention back. "What has she threatened you with?"

If only it was just a threat. If only Hera had just snapped her neck. This was a far worse punishment than death.

"Lithaneva?"

Branitus' voice calling to her from the garden completed her horror.

"Lithie, who is out here with you?"

No, go away. What lies would her tongue conjure for him?

She tried to keep her mouth closed, but her desperation only fueled the momentum of this conflicting will inside her. "Come to me, my darling." Her voice was sweet and sultry.

Lithaneva wanted to die.

Helinthia's eyes flashed. She shoved herself away, her chest rising and falling rapidly in betrayal and rage.

Lithaneva's heart ached to new depths for her goddess. To be betrayed and sabotaged so callously by her own mother. And now her lover, too. Despair had never gripped Lithaneva so tightly as it did now.

Branitus stepped into the marble temple with a quizzical brow. He scanned the room, his mortal eyes unable to discern the goddess in their midst. "I thought I heard someone in here with you. Are you all right?"

Lithaneva's feet propelled her toward him, to her abject horror. "No one is here but you. Come." Her hands, rebelling against her wishes, slid around his neck and pulled his face down. His beard scratched her lips as she kissed him.

Branitus froze, eyes widening.

Helinthia's enraged gasp pierced her heart.

Branitus pushed her back, bewildered and confused. "Lithie, what has come over you?"

She wanted to scream for help. But to whom? And what would come out if she tried? "I wanted to get you alone. Take me now, right here."

No! No no no no!

"*What?*" Branitus stepped back, renewed concern etched on his brow. He tried to disentangle himself from her arms. "Why?"

Please, gods, I don't want this— "Because I want you. And I want a child." *Helinthia, don't believe it!* Her treacherous hands grabbed at his tunic.

"You said you didn't."

"I changed my mind!" *I haven't. Please!* She grasped his thigh, thrusting her hips against his. His muscles tensed beneath her palm. He leaned back, eyes scanning the marble gods surrounding them.

"Why now? Why *here*?"

Yes, see reason, Branitus. See the madness behind this! "Let all the gods witness it. Why should that matter?"

Her mouth found his again, smothering his response as her hateful tongue pushed between his teeth to swirl against his.

Branitus rested his hands uncertainly on her shoulders. Conflict pinched his brows as he fingered the broaches pinning her chiton. She feared he might succumb. He would have been willing last night, she was sure.

She gasped as his thumbs jabbed painfully beneath her collar bone. He shoved her back and held her at arms' length.

"No."

His brow furrowed over angry brown eyes. "I don't know what's possessed you, but I don't like it. I don't *trust* it. Find me when you have a level head again and we'll have a proper discussion about this. Until then, stay away from me."

Branitus released her, then turned on his heel and stalked away. "Your lunch is cold," he muttered, shooting a backward glance over his shoulder. No doubt to make sure she wasn't running after him.

Lithaneva had never been more grateful for the man her father had forced her to marry. She whirled back around to Helinthia, praying, pleading, that Helinthia was every bit as skeptical as Branitus. *She knows me. She* knows *I would never—*

Despair poured over her like a bucket of icy water.

The goddess was gone.

CHAPTER 45

KELRIC

THE TENSION AROUND THE DINNER table was palpable. Kelric dipped bread infused with garlic and onions and glazed with olive oil into his lentil soup, pretending not to notice the betrayed looks on everyone's faces. Guilt gnawed at him for his behavior at the Council. *Pesky emotion.* An ailment best suited for females. He tried to ignore it, but it festered inside him like a wound wriggling with maggots. Gonivein sat beside him, not speaking. Still angry about the cricket, no doubt, but at least she had shown up to dinner. That was some improvement. Dargos glared at him as he shoveled spoonfuls of soup into his mouth. Forluna was absent, as usual.

Gadnor couldn't lift his eyes off his bowl. For once, Kelric wished to ease his anxiety. Praise him. The plan to go to Hameth was decent, one Kelric himself might have proposed if he were still strategos. It was bold. Too bold for Gadnor. It gave Kelric hope that his influence might finally be rubbing off on his little brother. But he kept his mouth shut. It was best not to invite conversation just now.

It was the scholars' last night in Golpathia, and apparently, they viewed that as an opportunity to proselytize everyone to their radical devotion to philosophy and the gods. Or try to. Under normal circumstances, Kelric would have been pleased to see Dargos' subdued engagement with them, but he knew it wasn't because his brother-in-law was finally coming to his senses about such things.

Euanthe set down a platter of cheese and patted Kelric's arm. He offered her a grateful smile. She was always considerate of the pressure he was constantly under. At least someone was.

Kelric caught Brother Mandus giving them all strange looks every now and again. He answered with a glower when the old man's eyes fell on him. Mandus had always been a bothersome old man. Even at the Library he'd made a habit of nosing into everyone's business. Several times he'd caught Kelric wandering near Gonivein's quarters after dark—nearly caught him sneaking through her window once. Kelric would be glad to be rid of them all in the morning. Dargos exuded too much zealotry as it was, never mind having eight brainless idiots creating a stink this past week.

Much as he disliked them, he had to admit their presence tonight lessened the tension considerably. If it were only Kelric and everyone he had offended, it might come to blows. Dargos and Gadnor would demand answers for his behavior, of that he was sure, and he wasn't ready to give them.

He didn't know what they were yet.

Why hadn't he defended Dargos to his councilmen? He'd fully intended to, but he didn't want the Leirion to leave the meeting believing they knew his next move. Not when he still hadn't decided himself.

The Leirion's claims about Forluna were compelling, but not enough to abandon her. So what if she'd killed the Oracle of Hera? Just like the priestess who'd betrayed the village of Tyldan, perhaps the old bat had deserved death. Still, he didn't need to feel genuine sympathy to take the oath of the Leirion, not when his intent was to cull them from the inside out.

He couldn't tell Dargos or Gadnor. They would insist on helping him, and mess everything up with their stupid morals and honorable ways. Or worse, they would think he planned to join the Leirion in earnest. He wasn't about to take either chance.

Kelric finished eating and left abruptly. Outside, two guards sent by Tryphus stood attentively, waiting for instructions. "Let Basileus Dargos finish eating, then escort him to his apartment or wherever he chooses. Just don't let him out of your sight. His woman can come and go as she pleases. Understood?"

They nodded and stepped into the triklinion, and Kelric headed to his andron.

Helios' chariot pulled Apollo's sun across the sky, shifting the shadows across the ground until they faded into the darkness altogether.

A rustling noise from a dark corner made Kelric's heart race. He tensed, his hand gripping the hilt of the sword he'd laid across his lap. His muscles coiled, waiting for something—or someone—to emerge. Seconds stretched into eternity. The rustling continued, resolving into the sound of some tiny paw scratching against the tiles. Kelric scowled. *Rodents*. He made a mental note to have that idiot doula clean his andron properly tomorrow.

"I thought we had moved past threats of violence, Basileus."

Kelric stiffened, his head jerking to the voice on the other side of the room. Yesterday, he'd been sure the man had hidden behind the tapestry. Now, unease twisted in his gut. Could there be a secret entrance he hadn't discovered?

Kelric glared at him. "Thinking too much will get you killed."

"Have you made your decision?" The man's tone sounded clipped tonight, more impatient. Perhaps his silence had gotten under his skin.

Kelric smirked. "Which one?"

"Let's start with taking the oath of the Leirion brotherhood." He showed no concern for the weapon now within striking distance of him. His audacity was riling.

'No' was on the tip of Kelric's tongue, more for spite than conviction. He didn't like this man's demeanor, didn't like being

startled. But he kept the word in his throat. "What does it get me if I say yes?"

That seemed to be exactly what the man wanted to hear. An eagerness entered his voice. "The loyalty of all Leirion in Golpathia."

"Remind me what good that does me."

The man leaned down and picked up an amphora lying on its side. He shook it, and its contents sloshed. "Golpathia is restless. Hasn't your Archon told you? Or perhaps you've seen it for yourself?"

Kelric recalled the statue covered in shit, but said nothing as the man uncorked the amphora. He sniffed at the spout, then tipped the vessel back for a long swig. This man was too comfortable in his space.

Far too comfortable.

The Leirion wiped his mouth and let out a satisfactory sigh. "This is an excellent vintage. From the vineyards of Critius, I believe."

Kelric narrowed his eyes. He'd always assumed his wine came from their own vineyards. Tetra's meager harvest niggled at his mind.

The familiar feeling of being sneered at burned in his chest.

"Your people are afraid of Charixes, and you have not done much to quell their fears. Take the oath, and the Leirion will help you restore confidence in your leadership. All those miserable people afraid of their own shadow can go back to their villages, assured of their safety. Not to mention the agora will remain well supplied throughout the winter." He sloshed the amphora in his hand again to emphasize his point.

Kelric rubbed his thumb against the soft leather hilt of his sword. *I can set my people at ease without his help.* Perhaps he could ride to every village with Tryphus, or go into the city every day, take stock of complaints, visit the weary. Kiss babies.

It sounded exhausting.

"Why come to me now? I've been basileus for weeks."

The man answered with another sip of wine.

It hit Kelric then. "You knew Charixes was planning an attack, didn't you?" Fury raged hot through his veins. "That's why you've come to me now. You *need* me to placate Charixes."

'A delicate balance, but a necessary one.' His father's death had created a rift in that balance, and Charixes was impatient for the Leirion to fill it. The realization made Kelric smile. He had more control over this arrangement than he could have hoped for. "Charixes would sooner kill you as any Golpathian citizen, wouldn't he? Unless you can produce a new puppet for him."

"I need a *basileus* to swear an oath to the Leirion and obey the anax. It does not need to be *you.*"

I can slit his throat right now, and Golpathia will be better for it. Traitorous leech.

The man set the amphora on the ground and leaned forward with his hands on his knees. The dark cowl hid his face as it neared. Kelric's smile faltered. "Let me tell you what will happen if you say no."

Kelric's arm tensed instinctively to draw his sword, muscles tightening in his legs to lunge.

"If you refuse the oath, we *will* prey on your citizens' fear. Incite a revolt. Golpathia will not be ruled by one who is not of the Leirion. If you will not join us, then we will replace you with someone who will."

Kelric's anger flared. This audacity went too far. "My people may be afraid of Charixes, but they *respect* me. Challenge me and see how far you get."

"I like your tenacity, Basileus." The man's condescending tone reminded him far too much of Mandus' the night he'd caught Kelric outside Gonivein's window. "Will they still respect you when they learn of your patricide? Superstition is a powerful motivator, especially when the *Furies* are involved. I'd wager your father was more beloved than *you.* Don't underestimate how eager your citizens are to assign blame for the growing instability."

A cold chill swept over Kelric. *He has no evidence.* Did he? His mind spun with the details of that night. The dark rooms of the villa, the empty courtyards, vestibules. His father had sent away everyone who could witness him murder Gonivein. And no one who knew Kelric had struck him down—Dargos, Gonivein, Gadnor, Forluna—would have exposed him. Finally, he managed, "You have no proof."

"I don't need proof," the man snapped. "All I need is a rumor in enough influential mouths."

The grin again—the intruder so confident that he grabbed the neck of the amphora and took another swig of wine, tipping the jar up until it fully exposed his throat. Kelric could end it all right now.

But he couldn't make himself react.

His palms grew clammy around the leather binding of his blade.

Kill him now!

What good would it do? Another would come, sooner rather than later, seeking vengeance instead of brotherhood.

The man dropped the empty vessel on the floor with a loud *crack*. "Now that we understand one another, you will tell the Council tomorrow that Dargos and his kubernao will be handed over to Charixes. Deny your brother's silly little plan, and safeguard Golpathia and your position as her basileus indefinitely."

Kelric wanted to end him more than ever.

The spy stood and stared down from the blackness of his hood— like some vengeful wraith of the Underworld. He seemed taller than he had before, towering almost, an otherworldly presence outlined in the rays of the waxing moon.

"I will return after the assembly to hear your oath and take Dargos *and* Pallas into my custody."

Long after the man left, Kelric stared through the doorway at the silvery courtyard outside his andron. Still frozen to his couch.

He had never been one to cower. He'd experienced a great many challenges in his time, from sparring on the training grounds to drawing blood on the battlefield. Always, he'd been the victor. It was how the people of Golpathia knew him. As fierce as the five-headed hydra embroidered on his tunic. It was why they loved him. It was why they would deny these rumors of patricide. He was sure of it.

But for how long?

He saw it playing out in his mind. The whispers, the riots, the angry accusations from all levels of the city, even the military men who had trained and bled alongside him for more than two decades—they would withdraw their support. Eventually, they would all join the call for justice.

What would Gonivein think? He had done it for her, after all. Would she leave him when the truth came to light?

He shut his eyes. Gonivein was already on the cusp of abandoning him. Dargos would be next, with little or no hesitation after the loyalty Kelric had showed him today. Gadnor would stay by his side the longest. Even Euanthe might finally turn away from him, despite her devotion to him.

A mouse stepped onto the threshold. Its beady black gaze fixed on him as though in silent judgment. Its nose twitched, then it slipped outside and scurried off, abandoning Kelric to the darkness.

CHAPTER 46

DARGOS

DARGOS SAT CROSS-LEGGED BEFORE the hearth, elbows on his knees and head resting in his hands as he rubbed his aching temples. The flames warmed his skin, but they weren't enough to quell the chill that gripped him when he'd crossed over the threshold to his apartment and closed his door. The last thing he'd seen was the two guards posted as sentries on either side, barring his escape, obligated to escort him everywhere, even to piss.

Kelric was taking one of his promises seriously, for once.

What is he planning?

Kelric had never been so calm and collected during a Council meeting. Or was it calculating? He must have something tucked into the folds of his tunic. Dargos wished he knew what it was.

Anxiety howled through him. He shot to his feet and began to pace the room. His shadow stretched eerily across the far wall, dancing like an enemy prepared to strike.

He met Forluna's gaze from where she sat on the bed. Her dark, attentive eyes invited him to share his frustrations. He'd told her what had happened, but voicing it aloud had only enraged him.

"Does he want me to try to escape and force the Council's hand?"

He spun on his heel and made another circuit across the room.

"They may claim you abandoned them and advocate for Charixes' mercy even harder," Forluna commented.

Those cowards would do it, too, just to spite him. "So I should stay here and hope Kelric doesn't abandon *me*?"

"Do you think he would do that?" Her tone suggested she thought Kelric more than capable.

That wasn't a good sign.

He stopped pacing and stared at the beams in the ceiling. "I don't know," he said honestly. "Why hasn't he come to explain himself?" Dargos had hoped for a glance, a nod, some subtle gesture of reassurance that Kelric wouldn't hand him over to Charixes.

Forluna picked at the dirt under her nails, artifacts from her patient efforts to revive the laurel on the mountain and grow her herbs. "Perhaps he suspects one of his guards is a spy. Maybe one of those outside the door? One word would discredit him to the Council. They are already a breath away from revolt."

Dargos rubbed his temples and sank onto the edge of the bed next to Forluna. Her warm body leaning into his chased a shiver from his shoulders. "What do I do? Do I trust Kelric has a plan to persuade his men, or do I sneak away and hope they choose battle before beggary?"

Forluna snaked her arm around him and rested her cheek against his shoulder. "What do you *want* to do?"

The answer was on his tongue immediately. "Assemble my army to march. No matter the outcome of tomorrow's assembly, there will be no victory for Shallinath without meeting Charixes in battle. It doesn't matter if we stand alone."

He felt her smile next to him. "Inaction has never been your method. Nor has bowing to another's authority." She elbowed him playfully. "Isn't that why we're in this mess?"

Dargos smiled a little at her tease and raised her hand to his lips, kissing each knuckle before he stood. "Will you come with me?"

A troubled look entered her eyes. He knew before she opened her mouth what she would say. Before she could utter the words that would shatter his heart, he knelt before her and cradled her cheek in his hand. He caught a tear with his thumb as it fell from her lashes.

"Don't. I won't make you choose. Gadnor needs you, and someone has to tell him what I've done, and why. That I'm not abandoning him. And Gonivein, too."

Her hands slid down his arms and cupped his elbows as she leaned forward and rested her forehead against his. A sharp throb in his chest trapped his next words in his throat. He allowed the stillness between them to speak for him. Their soft breath mingled, drawing their lips closer.

Why did this feel like the last kiss they would ever share?

She parted her knees and guided his body between them. Hunger in her eyes.

Blood rushed through him, inciting a flurry of butterflies in his stomach. He smoothed his palms up her back and pressed her body to his. His heart hammered in his breast, as though trying to punch through the layers of bone and flesh and fabric and merge with her heart beating on the other side. It was a space no farther away than a fingernail, but it might as well have been on the other side of the world.

Far too many layers lay between them.

He peeled away as many as he could. Pouring every ounce of passion into this moment, as though the Fates themselves had decreed it would be their last.

For all either of them knew, it was.

He fingered the scar on her thigh where a Leirion bolt had pierced her, then knelt and planted a kiss on the puckered skin. Her body shivered beneath his lips as he moved higher up her leg.

A giggle drew his attention to her face.

Forluna's eyes sparkled. Lips curved into a gleeful, sensuous smile. "That tickles."

Gods, she was beautiful. He ran a finger along her jaw. Down her neck to her breast. Her eyes fluttered closed as he cupped the soft flesh, thumb brushing her hard nipple. He pushed lightly. Dragged his palm across her navel as she reclined. Her body was on fire. His own ached for hers.

He draped her knees over his shoulders and turned his head to continue kissing where he'd left off.

She shuddered with laughter. Until his tongue found the slick heat between her thighs. Her gasp sent pleasure rippling through him, intensifying his ache. But he didn't stop until she was done writhing and lay breathless before him.

Forluna grabbed his arms and pulled him onto the bed. Like a willing supplicant, he let her push him down. Straddle him. Take all of him inside her. He sucked in a breath, craving every thrust of her hips, every electrifying surge of pleasure. Her skin glistened, shimmering in the firelight. Wisps of hair floated around her face like a halo.

How foolish to have wasted so many years worshipping a deity he had never seen. When the only altar deserving of his worship belonged to the goddess on top of him. Around him.

They held each other in silence for what felt like an eternity, and yet it seemed no time at all had passed before they untangled themselves, dressed, and stood.

"I need to get to Pallas," he said.

"I'll distract the guards." She squeezed his hands. "Wait for my signal."

"What signal?"

"You'll know." She raised onto her tiptoes to press her mouth one last time to his. He grabbed her and held her to him, heart shredding at the thought of letting her go.

She broke away from his lips. "Leave through the northern gate." Her eyes lingered on his, and he was one breath away from saying he took it all back, that he wanted to stay here, risk it all for one more night in her arms.

It would be worth it.

Before he could open his mouth again, she squeezed his hands and slipped away. In two fluid steps she was opening the door.

The guards both turned, nodded as she passed, then pulled the door closed behind her.

The latch falling back into its iron cradle reverberated like the gates of Hades thudding closed.

He sank onto the bed, feeling his anxiety pulsing through his veins all the way to his extremities. *Am I doing the right thing?*

Would Gadnor be all right leading Golpathia's armies without him? *I promised I would help him.* Would Gonivein forgive him for leaving? Would Kelric be able to stand his ground before his kyrioi? *If he ever meant to in the first place.*

Dargos wished he could stay angry with his brother-in-law, but he couldn't. He knew Kelric would do whatever it took to protect Gonivein. *Even if it means betraying me.* Dargos didn't blame him for that. In fact, it was oddly comforting knowing his sister would be safe.

And Forluna…

He stood and went to the window. He pushed it open and searched the darkness, waiting for the signal.

A scent of smoke grew heavy in the air. An orange glow flickered in the darkness from somewhere near the gate. It grew brighter as the smell thickened. Dargos' eyes began to sting.

Cries of alarm shattered the stillness.

Dargos cracked open the door just in time to see his guards sprinting across the courtyard toward the gate, where angry flames engulfed the dried foliage and a pile of old rubbish stacked against the wall. The gate guard was slapping at them with his cloak, shouting for help to contain it.

Bold, Forluna.

The ground rumbled.

Leontes and five other horses barreled from the stables across the courtyard in streaks of black and brown, whinnying frantically. The guards shouted incoherent commands to each other. One stumbled toward the gate, hoping to close it, but he couldn't reach it in time before Leontes streaked past with the other steeds in hot pursuit.

By now, apartment doors were opening all over the villa. Bleary-eyed faces peered out, drawn to the smell of destruction and chaos. Gadnor, Tor, and several scholars rushed to help contain the blaze. Confused voices rose into the air as Dargos slipped through the gate and ducked into a dark alley. He clutched his sword tight as he ran to keep it from jangling in its scabbard.

The moon was entering its third quarter now. Still bright enough to make out the path, but only just. Once or twice, Dargos tripped on a loose brick or some rubbish littering the path.

He had to be close to his destination now, located near the large statue of Poseidon that marked the boundary to the lower city. Reaching five meters tall, the bronze god should be easy to spot from the main road.

Dargos chanced stepping out of the alleys to orient himself. The Earthshaker's trident gleamed like a beacon in the moonlight. Dargos was close. He darted back into the shadows.

Guards were stationed outside of Pallas' cousin's house. They had completely abandoned their discipline and sat on the ground on either side of the door. Their helmets and weapons lay carelessly on the dirt beside them. One of the men was definitely asleep, with his back against the wall and his chin on his chest. The other scraped at a piece of wood with a small knife, all his attention on the object before him. No doubt they had decided to take turns staying awake.

Dargos smirked. Not an uncommon arrangement between soldiers, especially this far down in the city where they were unlikely to be disturbed without ample warning.

Dargos slipped around to the back of the house, counting the windows until he was sure he stood outside Pallas' room. He leaned his ear to the crack in the shutters. Pallas' deep snore from within brought a grin to his face. He tapped lightly against the wood.

The snoring stopped.

He tapped again in a deliberate pattern.

For the giant of a man that Pallas was, his footsteps were softer than a mouse, but Dargos knew he was already out of bed and poised on the other side of the thin wood.

"I know you're there, Pallas. It's Dargos," he whispered, keeping the front corner of the house in his sights in case one of the guards overheard.

Pallas opened the window and bent down. "I was wondering when you would come."

Dargos grinned, feeling validated. He hadn't had a chance to speak to Pallas after the Council, and there'd been no opportunity to warn him.

"The guards?" Pallas asked.

"One is asleep, the other distracted."

"Hmph. I'll take the one on the left." Pallas shut the window.

Dargos crept along the side of the house and peered around the edge.

The guards hadn't moved.

The front door swung open. Both men startled, but before either could get their bearings, Pallas grabbed the nearest one by the head and slammed him into the wall. The second guard bolted up, hand reaching for his spear, but Dargos leapt behind him and brought the hilt of his dagger down on his head.

Both men crumpled to the ground.

Pallas clasped Dargos' arm and grinned.

"What of your cousin?" Dargos stared into the dark maw of the open door, half expecting to see the man emerge and sound the alarm.

Pallas quietly closed the door, as though they hadn't just made enough noise to alert everyone inside. "I told him he should stay asleep tonight."

Dargos nodded, satisfied. At least one of them could trust their kin not to betray them.

Pallas looked around expectantly. "The plan?"

"Forluna set Leontes free."

Pallas grunted. "So, he'll be waiting for you, will he?"

Dargos smiled at his friend's skepticism. Leontes was well known in Shallinath for many reasons, one being the long beard that dangled from the steed's chin, another his unmatched speed, and a third the beast's uncanny ability to sense what Dargos needed from him and act accordingly. Few people knew that Leontes came from the Forest of the Shades—the horses of the gods were far superior to those of mortals in both physique *and* intelligence.

Dargos and Pallas made their way to the northern gate of the city and hid in the darkness of the last house on the street.

In the wide-open space between them and the closed gate, two sentries tossed a sheep's bladder back and forth. A few houses down, laughter and the strum of a lyre could be heard from one of the larger abodes. The revelry would provide enough noise to mask their footsteps.

A low whicker drew Dargos' attention to the dark alley beside them, and Leontes' muzzle emerged into the moonlight. The other five horses waggled their ears behind him. There was no sign of the villa guards. No doubt they had given up the chase long ago.

Dargos petted his faithful steed, shooting a triumphant grin at Pallas, who just shook his head and examined the other horses carefully. "Did she release every horse in Kelric's stables?"

Dargos grinned. "Except Inan." He pointed to two of the horses. "Those belong to Kelric and Raleon." Both sired by Leontes, Dargos had presented the foals to Raleon as part of Gonivein's dowry when the engagement had been made. They were the fastest horses in Golpathia.

Dargos pitied the guards Kelric would blame for losing them. Forluna had known exactly what she was doing with this diversion.

"They'll keep pace with Leontes better than yours will."

He saw the conflict in Pallas' eyes as he stroked the snout of his gelding.

Pallas nodded and chose Raleon's horse. He gathered the reins in one hand and slapped the other three animals on the hindquarters with his other. They whinnied in excitement and charged out of the shadows, prancing proudly past the guards and shaking their manes. They seemed to know what was expected of them.

The guards stopped their game and looked at one another in confusion. "That's three month's pay trotting off," one murmured.

"Or a handsome reward. Someone's in for a bad morning," the other said, glancing hesitantly at the gate.

"Best it's not us. Come on, help me corner them before someone from that house sees. No one's worshipping the Huntress at this hour, anyway," the first urged.

Both sprinted off after the beasts, leaving the gate unguarded for Dargos and Pallas.

CHAPTER 47

FORLUNA

"T*O ARTEMIS' TEMPLE,"* FORLUNA HAD whispered to Leontes, and he'd whickered his agreement before bolting into motion like a streak of lightning across the courtyard. The other five steeds had charged after him, moonlight flashing on their hooves like sparks. The only horse left in the stables was her own horse, Inan. She had a different assignment for him.

She stood in the shadows of the stable wall, still unseen, as the members of the villa fought to bring the flames under control. The scholars gawked from the porch steps, seeming far too excited about the imminent danger to their beds. Except for Mandus, who shook his balding head at all of them and disappeared with a slam of his door.

A smile tugged at Forluna's mouth. Mandus had always liked his sleep. His companions shared a good-natured laugh and continued their hushed gossip as the guards finished stamping out the fire. No one except her had noticed Dargos slip away. Her heart ached in his absence.

She would never see him again.

'We're cursed to live with our pain for eternity.'

The words of her kin were like a knife in her heart. Mortality was always going to take Dargos from her arms—she'd known that.

But this?

It felt like every step Dargos took was ripping her soul from her chest.

Kelric barged out of his andron and tore through the side courtyard. He clenched his fists as he rounded the corner, gaping at the chaos and the wide-open gates. "What is going on? Where is Dargos?" Not even the darkness of night could hide the red fury on his face.

The scholars merely shrugged and stepped back to allow him through. Kelric stormed across the grounds to interrogate the sheepish guards, who were covered in sweat and soot.

Forluna felt for them. They'd done their best to protect the villa, though she doubted Kelric would see that. He would only see that they'd abandoned their posts—and now his priceless horses, and Dargos, were on the run.

She turned back to the gathering, scanning for the eighth scholar. She found him standing apart from his companions. Staring in her direction.

A chill crept down her spine. She sucked in a desperate gulp of air and stumbled back into the darkness of the stables. She reached for Inan, ready to fling open his stall door and launch herself onto his back to fly after Leontes. As her blood pulsed in her ears, black encroached on the edges of her vision, threatening to plunge her completely into darkness.

The white stallion nuzzled her palm, the velvety fur of his nose grounding her, reminding her to stay calm. Breathe.

In. Out. Slow.

Her burning lungs filled with air. Tension eased from her shoulders.

"This will never stop, Inan." Her sight cleared again.

Inan flicked an ear.

"Not unless *I* stop it."

She pressed her forehead to his, stroking the stallion's cheeks.

She'd thought the Fates might rethread her destiny if she avoided it long enough. She'd clung to that hope for nearly two decades. Running. Hiding.

There was no more of that now. It was time for the hunted to become the huntress.

It's time to end this war.

"You must help Gadnor." She stared into Inan's black eye and rubbed his ear.

Inan chuffed and nudged her arm.

"You cannot whisk me from my fate any longer. But you can bear Gadnor proudly to his."

Inan pawed the dirt in protest.

"Do it for me?" She felt the knife in her chest twist as her companion's head drooped in sadness. A worse fate would befall Inan if she brought him with her. Charixes would break him, or use him for his own ill purposes.

Inan lipped her shoulder gently.

She scratched under his chin how he liked, combed her fingers through his beard, then stepped away. Inan pressed forward into the stall door and stretched his neck as far over it as he could to reach her.

"Goodbye, old friend." Forluna wiped the tears from her cheeks and turned before her resolve melted.

Kelric was berating the guards, ready to rearrange their faces. Guilt twisted within her, but she brushed it aside. Bruises and wounded pride would heal eventually. Her mission would save lives. Save the heir. Save the man she loved and the island he held dear.

Tor, Klymene, and Euanthe waited on the porch steps. Gadnor, panting and covered in soot, hovered near his brother, ready to intervene. Forluna allowed herself one last long look at the child she'd smuggled out of Ninenarn, at the man he had become. He'd been such a tiny little thing. Now he was grown. A leader with a true heart. She couldn't be more proud of him, and she knew Iptys would feel the same. Her heart ached that she couldn't give him a proper goodbye. Tell him she loved him.

I am not abandoning him. Why, then, did it feel like she was doing exactly that?

Six scholars huddled in the shadows, observing the scene and murmuring to themselves.

Six.

Forluna's hair stood on end. Mandus was in bed. Where was the eighth? Was he sneaking up on her from the shadows? Her eyes roved the scene, skin crawling.

The owl perched on the roof again. Its head twisted toward her. Golden eyes watched, feathered horns rigid in warning. A rustling came from the decaying bushes in the side courtyard, and Xios burst out, scampering and pouncing after a frantic mouse. Tor bent and scooped the rodent into his palm, snatching him away from Xios' claws. Odd. Tor didn't usually interfere between Xios and his prey.

"Go and find out!" Kelric's scream jolted her attention back to the front of the villa, where a guard was tripping from Kelric's rough shove. The poor man scrambled across the grounds toward the stable, flinging gravel and bits of straw as his sandals found purchase.

Forluna ducked out of the moonlight and pressed close to the inner wall. She crept, praying her footsteps were masked by Kelric's own wild pacing and curses.

As she neared the gate, the owl sprang from its perch and glided past the wall and down over the city, drawing everyone's gaze. She seized her chance and slipped out.

Before she'd passed two houses in the Kyrioi Quarter, her ears twitched.

Footsteps. *Many* footsteps.

Her heart thumped against her chest.

Stay calm.

She increased her pace. Her pursuers did, too.

Forluna didn't stop until she had reached the temple of Athena and bounded up the marble steps two at a time. She pushed against the great oak doors as hard as she could, praying the acolytes had not barred it.

The door gave way, and she shouldered inside, her heart beating wildly in her breast. There was so little time. Perhaps no time.

Waiting at the far end of the colonnaded hall was the statue of Athena. She loomed large over the spacious vestibule, the embers on the altar at her feet glowing red on her white cheeks, glinting off the bronze helmet that sat high on her head. She held a long spear in one hand, and her shield was strapped to her other. The gorgon's head in its round center promised death to anyone who defied the might of the war goddess.

'A woman who wins her battles.'

Forluna needed to become that woman now.

Forluna knelt at the goddess' feet, pulling her medicine knife from her boot. She stared at it a moment, her hand shaking. So many herbs had been cut from their stalks with this blade. Herbs to heal and comfort. Linens, too—shredded for bandages. Wounds had been lanced and cauterized. Umbilical cords severed—including Gadnor's. Rocks plucked out of Inan's hooves. She had even shaved Dargos' scruffy face with the blade before he'd decided a distinguished beard suited him better. This knife had only ever aided life.

Now, she vowed, it would take one.

"Athena, goddess of strategy and war, give me courage." Tears pricked her eyes as she lifted them to the marble face of the goddess. "I will be taken from your altar this night, as Cassandra of Troy was taken." She held out her weapon. "Let this dagger heal the wrongs of a past that has chased me for too long across Gaia's flesh. Please, find me worthy. Aid me in my battle."

She sliced her hand, letting the blood coat the sharp bronze. She set it on the pedestal beside the goddess' feet and waited, listening for the creak of the door to signal her doom.

In. Out. Slow.

Any moment now, the hands would seize her. Was this a mistake? Would Athena ignore her? She'd known it was a long shot. Even if the goddess denied her, it changed nothing. Forluna would kill Charixes with or without divine help.

I must.

Athena's *aegis* drew her gaze. It seemed to move, a snaky tendril of the gorgon's head writhing. Her blood chilled in her veins. Would Medusa's eyes open and turn her to stone?

But Medusa's face remained solid bronze as the snake stretched its thin body toward her, wriggling frantically as though stuck. It dropped from the great shield—plucked from the gorgon's scalp—and flopped onto the floor.

Forluna froze, expecting to feel its icy fangs biting into her flesh.

The snake slithered to her. She stiffened, panicked, as it spiraled up her calf, then slipped over the edge of her boot. Its cold scales coiled around her ankle, sending shivers from her leg to her scalp. She slammed her eyes shut, terror paralyzing her. Waiting. But the beast did not strike.

The door creaked.

Her breath hitched. She snatched the blade from the pedestal. Hesitated, remembering the footsteps following her. How many had come? Could she catch them unawares and kill them all?

Calm.

This blade wasn't meant for them. She couldn't let her fear ruin her only chance to end this war. To save Gadnor. Save Dargos. Save everyone. *No more running. No more hiding.* The gorgon's tendril loosened its grip around her leg, allowing her to slide the blade into the soft leather sheath in her boot.

Sandals scuffed lightly, then stopped.

They were waiting. Watching her. Observing her like they would a trapped animal.

She stood, took a deep breath, and turned around.

There, in the dim glow of the torches lining the vestibule to Athena's temple, were three hooded men. Two of them wore leather armor and swords strapped to their belts. Black kerchiefs bearing embroidered white lilies were tied around their forearms.

At their center stood the eighth scholar. His shoulders were stooped more noticeably tonight, but his eyes were sharp. What hair remained on his balding head was gray, his curly beard streaked with white. For the first time, she took her time gazing upon his face. He stepped forward, and there was something familiar about his gait.

The fragments of memory returned, in more detail now. Oracle Eraia splayed on the floor, head twisted unnaturally, misaligned to her body. Iptys pressed to Forluna's side, sobbing in her arms as the porter rushed near and bent over the dead woman.

"Jaxus." A pained expression entered his eyes, as though he had hoped she wouldn't recognize him.

"You haven't aged a day, Forluna." Awe was in his gravelly tone.

"I'm a nymph."

A flicker of fear danced across the wrinkled features before melting into anger. "Then your crimes against the gods are even more grave, for you cannot claim ignorance." He raised a condemning finger at her. "Come quietly, or you will die where you stand."

She raised her chin.

Jaxus shifted uneasily as he spared a glance at the statue behind her. He knew better than to risk the wrath of Athena, whose vengeance had crashed a hundred ships against the cliffs as recompense for the wrongs done to a princess of Troy. "We've searched a long time for you."

She swallowed, and the snake tightened around her ankle, reminding her that she was not alone, that the goddess of wisdom— of war—had answered her. She expected him to ask her about the heir, to confirm he was truly dead. Wasn't that why they still wanted her?

Silence lingered, and confusion rippled through her. Perhaps this wasn't about the heir at all. "Why, Jaxus?"

The wrinkles in Jaxus' forehead deepened in rage. "Justice,

Forluna."

"Justice?" She furrowed her brow. It struck her then—the missing pieces of a two decades long puzzle. "You're the one who killed the soldiers in the palace. You opened the gates!" She'd believed the porter had been killed along with the rest of the palace staff. No doubt that had added to her delayed recognition of him.

Jaxus straightened his stooped shoulders proudly.

"Why? *Why* did you betray us?"

"*Iptys* betrayed us when she chose her own power over her people. I heard the oracle's prophecy. I know what happened."

Forluna's heart stilled. "You're the one who started the rumors that Iptys murdered her."

Jaxus shook his head. "I told the truth! I feared Hera's retribution if Iptys went unpunished, and I was right. Everything Eraia said has come to pass, and worse!" He stepped forward angrily, as though he meant to strike her, then stopped, remembering where they were.

"My only regret is believing she acted alone." He waved the two Leirion forward to seize her. "A mistake I'm glad to remedy to finally restore peace and prosperity to this island."

The Leirion approached, and the familiar flutter of panic came alive in her chest. She swallowed, willing her feet to stay put.

"Be gentle with her." Jaxus flicked a glance at Athena. "Her punishment belongs to Anax Charixes."

Rage and bitterness waged inside her. She wanted to curse him for his betrayal, hurl the truth of Eraia's murder in his face, gloat that his lifelong efforts would amount to nothing. But she bit her tongue. She needed him to believe she was guilty.

Charixes would expect a full confession. She couldn't wait to disappoint him.

The Leirion's fingers dug into her arms like vices as they dragged her from the temple of Athena.

CHAPTER 48

GONIVEIN

THE RUMBLE BENEATH GONIVEIN'S FEET and the shouting outside her door didn't even stir her curiosity. She knew Dargos had gone, and she was glad for it. After learning what had happened at the Council, it was the only course that made sense. The risk that Kelric would turn him over, or be forced to, was too great.

She sat in bed, staring at the door with her back propped against the wall, waiting for Kelric to come and explain everything. Euanthe had sown the tiniest seed of hope in her mind this morning that, underneath his abrasive demeanor and aggression, he had a good heart. She'd believed that once, and she desperately wanted to again.

They hadn't spoken since last night, when he had barred her from leaving their room. She'd seen the hydra lashing out at its allies in her mind as he'd blocked her way. Had the vines already begun their intimidating advance? Then she'd thought of Euanthe's care and compassion for the little grieving boy. Maybe, just maybe, Kelric wasn't hiding his knowledge or complicity with the Leirion. Maybe he was just being overprotective.

A wave of fear rolled through her as she considered just how many interactions with the vines from her vision she might have had today. She'd sold and traded a wealth of gifts. Though, to look at the storeroom, she doubted anyone could tell. But she'd managed to buy enough with her profits—sacks of barley and wheat, amphorae of wine and oil, crates of vegetables, wedges of cheese, and blankets—to fill an entire wagon for the camps. For a city on the cusp of famine, she was surprised at the abundance of goods available, though some stalls were noticeably less stocked than others. The Leirion were at work there, she was sure of it.

The bedroom door creaked open, and Kelric emerged, closing it softly behind him. A pained expression narrowed his gray eyes as he looked at her. Pity stirred in her chest.

Tell me you didn't plan to betray Dargos, she wanted to beg.

He held her stare a moment, then wandered across the room and sank down on the edge of the bed, scrutinizing the broken window in silence.

Before either of them could speak, a knock sounded on the door. Kelric bolted to his feet, drawing his dagger in a quick flash. Gonivein's breath hitched in surprise.

"Kelric."

Gadnor's voice. Urgent. Sharp. Low.

She released her breath as Kelric lowered the weapon and crossed the room, unbolted the door, and cracked it open.

"Ferry it, Gadnor, what do you want?" He shoved his blade back into its sheath with a frustrated sigh.

Gonivein met Gadnor's troubled eyes as he crossed the threshold, and a sinking feeling settled in her gut at his expression. It looked… betrayed.

Fear wormed in her gut. *No.*

Tor followed over the threshold, cradling something in the palm of his hand.

"What is *he* doing here?" Kelric snapped, shooting a glare first at Tor, then to the ground as Xios slipped in. "And why is that abomination in my room?"

Kelric slammed the door. The cub hissed and twined around

Tor's ankles. The boy glanced nervously at Gadnor, ready to flee. Gadnor reassured him with a nod. Whatever they had to say, Kelric wouldn't like it, and everyone in this room knew it.

Gonivein set her feet on the floor and stood, wincing as pain lanced through her hip. She reached for her crutch. She harbored no illusions about her ability to escape any danger, but being on her feet made her feel more prepared.

Gadnor puffed out his chest and squared his shoulders. It was the stance he always took before saying something that would incite Kelric's wrath, as though he were already bracing for the blow. She winced at how many times she'd seen it and done nothing to temper the inevitable response from Kelric.

"Have you been approached by a Leirion?"

The look of panic that crossed Kelric's handsome features was unmistakable.

Her stomach clenched. *No, no, no.*

"Why would you ask me that?" The angry ridges in Kelric's forehead smoothed into a mask of calm. It was unlike him. Ironic how he'd always belittled Gadnor for being a terrible liar, but it seemed they shared that trait.

Gadnor nodded once to Tor, and the boy opened his cupped palms just enough for a tiny gray head to peek through. Its long, whiskery nose twitched, black beady eyes catching the light of the fire in the hearth.

A mouse?

Xios mewled at Tor's ankles, rising on his back legs and swatting at Tor's palm. Even stretched as far as he could go, the lion couldn't reach his quarry.

Kelric's brow furrowed in confusion. Then his expression transformed as realization struck. He sank onto the bed like a withered plant finally succumbing to the heat of the sun. The pride sloughed from his shoulders as he held his head in his hands. His body shook.

Gonivein had never seen Kelric this upset, not since he had

murdered his father. Gadnor shared her open-mouthed expression.

"Kelric, what happened?" Gadnor's tone was soft.

Kelric raked his fingers through his curls as he raised his head, glaring at the mouse. "Don't you already know?"

"I want to hear it from you," Gadnor said.

Gonivein found herself inching closer to Kelric, drawn to this sudden vulnerability. An urge to quell his pain itched at her fingertips. Could he possibly have a good reason? If he did, could she forgive him? She thought of the cricket, its leg twitching, caught in its own smeared guts in the grains of the wood, and Kelric's balled fists as he approached her, face twisted in rage.

She stopped moving. Sank back down on the bed. Waiting. Hoping. Doubting.

"Yes, a Leirion approached me. Threatened to make the people revolt if I didn't meet his demands. Said he would expose my patricide."

The muscles along Gadnor's jaw twitched. "And what were his demands?"

Kelric looked at Gonivein, then lowered his eyes to his hands. "Give Dargos to Charixes in exchange for peace and order you not to go to Hameth."

A silence stretched as everyone processed Kelric's words.

The vines of Gonivein's vision crowded her mind, stretching toward the hydra—toward Kelric—antagonizing, provoking, until the great beast turned on its allies, snapping its fearsome jaws into their flesh. Her rage returned, and with it, a fearlessness she hadn't experienced since she had thrown herself at Tendior in a vain attempt to shove him to his doom. "You were going to betray Dargos."

Her heart thumped wildly as Kelric's eyes met hers. For once, he was speechless. Pain, regret, despair, failure, *fear,* flashed across his face.

"I... I don't know." His honesty pierced through her anger, softened something within her.

Kelric looked at his little brother. "I don't know what I was going to do—what kind of choice was that? It doesn't matter now. Dargos is gone. Forluna, too, it seems. Though her horse is still here."

Tor shifted his feet uncomfortably. He looked like he wanted to say something but was afraid to.

"What is it, Tor?" Gonivein asked.

Kelric's gaze landed heavily on the Oracle of Artemis. Something menacing sparked to life within his eyes, then vanished just as quickly.

Tor looked ready to bolt from the room. "I…"

"Say it," Gonivein urged. This might be the only chance to get everything out in the open. Gods knew that Kelric wouldn't allow himself to fall victim to a situation like this again. Not easily.

"Did the Leirion… demand anything else?" Tor asked.

Gonivein shivered as Kelric's glare turned murderous. Then he sighed. "They wanted me to take their oath and join them."

Beads of sweat rolled down Gonivein's neck. "And did you?" Her tightening throat cinched her voice into a whisper.

Kelric shook his head. "No." He glowered at Tor. "Anything *else* you'd like me to confess?"

Tor dropped his gaze.

Gadnor's brow pinched in thought, his arms folded across his chest. "Why didn't you tell us this?"

"Because they will kill you if they find out." The edge returned to Kelric's voice. Gonivein blanched. "What was I supposed to do, put you all in danger? And for what? What has this accomplished except to do exactly that? Dargos is gone, and I have no leverage to keep the Leirion from making good on their threats." Kelric dragged his hands through his hair with an exasperated growl and stood. "Perhaps they'll just kill us all tomorrow during the Council and save everyone the trouble. We may as well *all* flee."

"Just… wait a minute," Gadnor said, rubbing his temples.

Kelric stood, throwing his hands into the air. "For what, Charixes' assassins to come barging through the door? I don't even know who is with them and who isn't." His eyes captured Gonivein's. "Your vision spoke true. The Leirion's vines have ensnared this city at *every* level. They're always watching. Listening. Choking out anyone who threatens them. There is no escaping them. But gods know I've been trying to find a way."

A chill swept through Gonivein at Kelric's validation of the Leirion's presence.

"Dargos wouldn't flee to save his own skin." Gadnor stared intently at a spot on the floor, deep in thought.

Kelric rolled his eyes and began to pace like a wild animal across the room.

"Crusates has been preparing the Shallinath villages for war since we left the Forest of Shades. Dargos will be here on the spring equinox with his army. I'm certain of it. He's counting on us to prepare Golpathia, too," Gadnor said.

"You assume an awful lot about Dargos," Kelric muttered. "You're just guessing. He left us without warning, without guidance. So did Forluna. You want me to base the future of our polis on a hunch?"

Gonivein's anger bubbled beneath her skin. Surely, Kelric had enough sense to know Gadnor was right.

Kelric plunged his fingers through his frizzing curls. "Dargos abandoned us. How can I maintain peace—"

"Peace?" Gonivein spat, her calm shattering. "Have you forgotten everything Ninenarn has done? To my people, to *me*? Have you even bothered to *see* the fear Charixes has sown in your people? The danger he poses? There's no peace in a world where he rules." She sounded too much like her older brother, but for once, she emphatically agreed with him.

"I know!" Kelric grabbed her hand before she had time to realize he was reaching for it. He grasped it tightly, refusing to let it go despite her efforts to jerk it back. His tone softened. "It's foremost in my mind all the time. And I know what the Leirion are capable of if I'm no longer Basileus of Golpathia. I must maintain peace *here*, between myself and the Council and the rest of my kyrioi. Keeping you safe is *everything* to me."

A lump swelled in Gonivein's throat, tears stinging her eyes at the sincerity in his voice. *'If there's one thing that has never changed, it is how fiercely he protects the ones he loves. He always will.'*

Silence lingered. Kelric didn't release her hand. She stopped trying to pull it back. They stared at one another. Gonivein didn't know what to do. How to feel. The mere fact that Kelric had even considered betraying Dargos burned her. And yet…

'What kind of choice was that?'

"Then take their oath."

Gadnor's words fell heavily on Gonivein's ears. She gaped at him.

"Are you mad?" Kelric tore his gaze away from her. "They'll never believe I'm sincere, not now."

"They will if you convince them you were going to give them Dargos," Gadnor argued. "And they will if you swear to betray me."

Kelric straightened, letting Gonivein's hand slide from his. In two strides he had crossed the floor and grasped Gadnor's tunic. He jerked his brother close. "Are. You. *Mad*?"

Xios hissed, and Tor stepped back from them.

Gonivein half expected them to come to blows.

Gadnor didn't flinch. "Perhaps." Then he offered a lopsided grin. "But I'm also lucky."

As Gadnor explained his idea and Kelric argued against it, Gonivein's mind journeyed back to the first days of trouble, before Ninenarn had captured Shallinath, before they even knew an heir existed. Back then, their plan to overthrow Charixes and restore peace to Helinthia had relied so heavily on Fortune's favor that a part of Gonivein had doubted it would ever come to fruition. It had always just seemed like words. Distant, like a dream or a fantasy.

Until Charixes sent his army to capture her and massacred an entire village of innocent people.

But this?

Gonivein stared at Kelric and Gadnor.

This plan required trust more than Fortune. *Kelric's* trust. Trust that he wouldn't *actually* betray Gadnor, that he wouldn't *actually* conform to the Leirion's views. Trust that he wouldn't *actually* abandon Dargos and Shallinath. Trust that he wouldn't *actually* turn away from everything they had lost. *She* had lost. Suffered. Trust that Kelric wouldn't do any of the things he'd confessed to considering.

Trust that he wouldn't do any of the things he had already done—again.

'He protects the ones he loves.' Euanthe had known Kelric longer than anyone in this room. Wouldn't she know him better than anyone, too? Gonivein studied her husband. Handsome, strong, flawed, hot-tempered. Vulnerable.

The falcon being trampled underfoot sprang into her mind. The vines pushing the beasts to commit a terrible crime against their will.

But what if it was only meant to *look* that way? What if it was just a deception? The gods were known for infusing hidden meanings in their visions and dreams. What if Gadnor's plan for Kelric to 'betray' him was the true meaning all along? Her mind seized in frustration, and she grasped her temples. *Why can't I figure it out? Why can't I just* know *what it means?*

Gadnor and Kelric looked at her, waiting for her input. She stared back, conflicted.

In the end, it was Gadnor's pleading look that convinced her, not Kelric's. This was Gadnor's plan, and he believed it could work. What choice did any of them have?

Gonivein nodded, and a few moments later, Gadnor and Tor left.

Kelric didn't move for a long while. He merely stood still, staring off into oblivion. He seemed to be waiting for her to speak. To invite him back across the room. Order him to leave, perhaps, or turn away and condemn him to another night on the cold floor like a dog.

"I'm sorry," he said finally, stunning her once again. "I let my fears control me, and I treated you harshly. I should have told you everything that first day when I found the kerchief on your pillow. I just… I didn't want you to worry, didn't want you to be scared."

Her blood chilled in her veins. "What kerchief?"

Kelric walked toward her, pulling a black cloth from his pocket. He held it out, and the embroidered white lily weakened her knees. She sank onto the bed, fear blazing beneath her skin.

"The morning after our wedding, I found it right beside your face."

That's why he lashed out at Klymene. He must have thought she was a Leirion sneaking into their chambers. It was a miracle he'd had any restraint at all.

"I don't know how they got so close to you. I was beside you all night. I haven't been able to think about anything else except what they could have done to you. What they could *still* do. That's why I wanted Klymene beside you today. That's why I didn't want you to leave last night. That's why I've been so…" He stared at his hands. "Reckless."

Gonivein's heart clenched in her breast, and before she allowed herself to remember all the ways he had hurt her, she beckoned to him with her hand and crawled into bed.

Kelric's proud shoulders sagged with relief. He clambered onto the bed beside her like a weary man dying of thirst. He threaded their fingers and covered her mouth with his. A hungry, wild kiss. A warm sigh escaped his nostrils, tickling her face.

Desire tingled through her body. *I can trust him. I must.*

She cupped his cheek in her hand and tilted her head, opening her mouth to invite his tongue to explore—an invitation immediately accepted.

Kelric pressed his body against her, heat intensifying between them. He slipped her chiton from her shoulders. She pulled his tunic over his head. Both garments sailed to the tiled floor, leaving them naked and free to tangle themselves in starving passion.

Whatever chaos Gadnor's plan would bring tomorrow, there was unity tonight. And whatever doom awaited them, they would face it together when Dawn arose.

CHAPTER 49

GADNOR

"YOU REALIZE WE MIGHT NOT walk out of here alive, don't you?"

His brother's words made the dark maw of the bouleuterion even more menacing than before. Gadnor swallowed the lump in his throat, then nodded.

Kelric sighed. "I may have agreed, but I still think this plan is mad. No one is going to believe I would betray you."

Gadnor refrained from rolling his eyes. "I think you'll be surprised."

Kelric studied him, confusion contorting his expression. "My entire life has been dedicated to keeping you safe. You have no idea of the pains I've gone through."

Anger swelled in Gadnor's chest. Every belittling comment, bullying action, betrayal, every slap or blow Kelric had ever dealt him flashed through his mind. The worst one—Kelric's arms cinching tight around his waist, hauling him back as Cedrila was dragged off—was a wound that would never heal. "You had a fine way of showing it."

Kelric clamped his mouth shut, a muscle spasming along his jaw. "I won't apologize for doing what I had to do. You're here. Alive and in one piece. I've protected you this far, but once we walk in there, that's over."

There it was. The doubt. The underlying expectation that Gadnor would fail. That he wasn't good enough. Smart enough. Skilled enough to succeed, to survive without his big brother's oversight and protection.

"If we do this, and you go to Hameth, a Leirion *will* accompany you and try to kill you." Kelric drew in a shaking breath. "Even if they accept my oath, there's no guarantee they will tell me who it is. You'll be completely on your own."

"I won't be alone. Tor will be with me."

Kelric scoffed. "Tor is a usel—"

"*Stop!*" The sharpness in his tone surprised himself, but he wouldn't stand by and listen to Kelric's unjustified tirade against his friend. He opened his mouth to say more, but Krastus appeared around the corner with Archon Tryphus by his side.

"Ready, Basileus?" Krastus asked with a charming smile as he passed by and ducked inside the bouleuterion.

Archon Tryphus stopped in front of them, looking nervous as he scanned their surroundings. A few people milled about on the next street over, but otherwise, the clearing in front of the council building was devoid of human activity.

Kelric eyed his archon with a knowing look. "Let me guess, the extra guards I requested haven't reported to their stations?"

Tryphus straightened his shoulders, but his head drooped sheepishly.

"Have you found Dargos and my horses?"

Tryphus shook his head. "My men are scouring the city."

"I'm sure they are." Without waiting for a reply, Kelric marched into the bouleuterion.

Gadnor rubbed the scars on his arm as he followed, trying to stave off the sudden chill that gripped him. The absence of extra guards was a bad sign. Was it lack of discipline, or had the Leirion gotten to them? Perhaps Kelric was right. Perhaps they wouldn't make it out of this meeting alive.

The stone seat was cold, and Gadnor squirmed to find a comfortable position as the councilmen filed into the small room. Greetings were tight-lipped. Most only offered a curt nod. Gadnor fiddled with his clammy hands, trying to ignore the doubts vying for his attention as he built the fire on the altar.

After his brilliant idea had struck him last night, he'd spent the remainder of the evening and the hours before dawn overanalyzing every part of it, contemplating all the ways it could possibly go wrong. The Leirion had decades of experience manipulating and pretending to be friends to their foes. Was it foolish to try and outwit them? What if they had captured Dargos and Forluna? What if Gadnor's friends were hunted down like rabbits and murdered before they could reach Shallinath's armies?

What if Dargos and Forluna had finally realized Gadnor wasn't worthy of their faith, their affection, their allegiance? What if they had no intention of coming back to help defeat Charixes' army at all?

What if I misread everything? He scratched his scars, pushing the intrusive thoughts back into the dark recesses of his mind.

As the last man arrived, all eyes fastened on Kelric.

Kelric splashed the wine unceremoniously over the flames and took his seat. He glowered with unfocused eyes toward the door. Kelric had never *believed* Gadnor was capable of executing even the simplest of plans, never mind one such as this. He would much sooner rely on reckless impulses to dictate his actions and hope the pieces fell to his advantage. Though, Gadnor had to admit those pieces often fell exactly where Kelric wanted them to.

Would he trust Gadnor this one time?

"I'll get straight to the point," Kelric said. "I don't believe Charixes is capable of negotiating a peace. Nor do I believe he would grant us mercy after we've harbored Dargos for weeks. He massacred an entire village for sheltering Gonivein for a single night. His actions have given us no reason to trust him."

Murmurs rippled through the Council, and Alypius' expression darkened. The glance he shared with Ephastes made Gadnor's scars crawl.

"Let our Basileus speak," Krastus scolded, and the room fell silent again.

Kelric studied each face as he formed his response. "We will honor our alliance with Shallinath. My brother will lead a contingent—"

"Where is Dargos?" Alypius flew to his feet.

Gadnor flinched, heart leaping into his throat.

Krastus motioned for Alypius to sit down. "Calm yourself, Alypius, he's not fini—"

"I don't need him to finish to know that our own basileus has placed his personal feelings above the needs of his kyrioi. Everyone in this room knows it. You would sacrifice all of us for *one* man."

Several more men stood in solidarity with Alypius' outrage. Gadnor scratched his arm. So much for a level-headed assembly. The few men who remained seated looked like they wished the floor would open up and swallow them whole.

Kelric shot Gadnor a withering look that said, '*I told you this was madness,*' and stood. Back straight, eyes piercing and menacing, he looked ready to take them all on in hand-to-hand combat.

Gadnor swallowed. That possibility didn't seem so remote.

"Where is the traitor?" Ephastes chimed in, glaring at Kelric.

Archon Tryphus, sitting on the other side of Kelric where Dargos had sat yesterday, waved his arms as though he were herding children across a street. "Everyone, sit down."

He was ignored.

Gadnor rose as Alypius took a step toward Kelric, Ephastes behind him.

Kelric widened his stance, balling his fists. "Do you wish to challenge me, Alypius? I promise I will not be so easily thwarted as my brother."

Everyone was on their feet now. Shouting, goading, arguing. The assembly looked ready to slaughter them all and take matters into their own hands.

Alypius sneered. "Yet your plan for our survival depends on him? Even *you* know he will fail." He stepped closer, turning his murderous gaze on Gadnor.

Gadnor's face was on fire, fingers slipping around the hilt of the dagger at his belt. They were far outnumbered, but he would not be ferried down to Hades without fighting back.

"Why not let the gods decide?" The voice turned everyone's heads to the doorway, where a slight figure shouldered through the throng.

Gadnor's heart pounded as Tor's gaze met his. What was he doing here? He examined the angry councilmen, looking for indications that they would unleash their aggression on the Oracle of Artemis, but they appeared more startled and curious than hostile.

Krastus lifted an eyebrow at Tor. "The memory of those birds surrounding us during the duel will be forever imprinted on my mind. If the gods wish to share their opinion, I welcome it."

The smallest of smiles narrowed Tor's hazel eyes under tousled brown locks. One hand held a rope draped over his shoulder, attached to something behind him. The other hand held a long spear. The bronze point caught the morning sunbeams from one of the windows, illuminating the space with a dazzling brightness that sprouted dark spots in Gadnor's vision.

"Superstition," Alypius muttered.

Tor pressed into the parting crowd, revealing a cart full of shimmering, polished armor. The men surrounding him leaned forward in awe of the treasures.

"What is all this?" Krastus leaned over to examine the contents.

"Please," Kelric grumbled. "Do explain why you've interrupted an official Council meeting, between *councilmen*."

Gadnor couldn't help but note that Kelric's usual vehemence toward Tor was subdued. Was he glad Tor had interrupted? Or was Kelric's usual rage just spread a little thin in this company? Gadnor wasn't sure which explanation, if either, made him feel better. But Tor saving them after Kelric's ridicule of the boy stirred a flutter of satisfaction within him.

After they left Kelric's room last night, Tor had bid him good night without mentioning what he thought of Kelric's confession or Gadnor's plan. They discussed meeting later today to continue their weapons' training, but Tor had said nothing about following them here. This wasn't part of the plan Gadnor had laid out.

The apple in Tor's throat bobbed as he swallowed. "This armor was forged by the gods." His voice became more confident as he continued, never taking his eyes off Gadnor's. "Crafted by Hephaestus himself."

Murmurs rippled around them. Alypius and Ephastes folded their arms across their chests, but didn't turn away.

"How did you come by this?" Krastus asked, the polished bronze reflecting in his wide eyes.

"Artemis delivered it to me this morning," Tor answered.

Ephastes scoffed. "How are we to know you are telling the truth? What distinguishes this armor from any other suit Golpathia has at her disposal?"

It was flashier than any armor Gadnor had ever seen, and he had little doubt Tor spoke the truth. The dubious looks tossed Ephastes' way by others confirmed he wasn't alone.

Tor raised his chin. "This armor will burn the body of any wearer whom the goddess Artemis deems unworthy."

A pit opened in Gadnor's gut. He swallowed.

The hall fell silent. Envy turned to caution. Questioning glances darted around, each daring the others to step forward and be the first to try on the armor, to put their worthiness to the test.

Kelric turned pointedly to Gadnor, not at all amused. "Did you put him up to this?"

Gadnor shook his head. "I know nothing of this." Was this what Tor and Artemis were discussing at Tor's confirmation ceremony? He recalled their unsettling gazes in his direction. How long had Tor been planning this?

Archon Tryphus cleared his throat. "And who does the goddess deem worthy?"

The muscles along Tor's jaw twitched. "The goddess didn't say, Kyrios, but she indicated that I would find such a man among a prestigious gathering." He made a sweeping motion with the spear, sending sunbeams dancing along the walls as the bronze tip flashed. "Such as this one."

Kelric crossed his arms, a sparkle in his eyes. "Since no one seems to trust my little brother with the task of going to Hameth, I have a new proposal. The man the armor deems worthy will lead this mission. Will that please you, Alypius?"

Alypius' lip curled into a snarl. "The man the armor deems worthy will lead this mission *and* be the *strategos*."

Kelric eyed Tor, then Gadnor, searching for the hint that this was part of their deception—theatrics to inspire devotion from the skeptics.

Gadnor waited for the same hint, but Tor didn't give it. In fact, he seemed to be purposely avoiding his gaze. Panic warmed Gadnor's skin beneath his tunic. Maybe it wasn't up to Tor who this armor belonged to. *What if I'm not worthy?*

His family had never inspired such confidence, but something about the way Artemis had spoken to him in the Forest of Shades gave him hope that he *could* be.

Had he come far enough?

He considered everything he'd done since his encounter with the goddess, and what little confidence he had built up within himself withered away. *I'm going to burn in this armor.* He was sure of it.

Tor stared at his feet.

He knows it, too.

Alypius slid his tunic off his shoulders and let it pool around his hips. His broad chest gleamed in the dazzling reflection of the bronze armor. Chiseled muscles glistened from the heat in the crowded room. It wasn't difficult to imagine him, with his god-like physique, leading an army into battle wearing this armor forged by a god. Gadnor had little doubt that the sight of *Alypius* would inspire men to fight for glory and strike fear into the enemy.

Gadnor's scars itched, and he gave in to the impulse to scratch them to distract himself.

Ephastes helped Alypius into the cuirass and greaves, placed the helmet on his head, and fastened the strap under his chin. He reached for the shield and held it aloft.

No sooner did Alypius slide his arm through the straps than his eyes went wide.

"What is it?" Ephastes asked. Immediately, everyone crowded a little closer, craning over the shoulders in front of them to see.

Alypius retracted his arm from the shield and shoved it away, almost knocking Ephastes off balance. "Get this off me!" He tugged at the cuirass first, then yanked the chin strap. Neither piece of armor gave way to his shaking fingers. Panic flashed in his eyes.

"Get it *off!*"

Shock descended on the gathering. Disbelief froze everyone in place, deafened their ears to his strangled pleas.

Until the smell of burning flesh thickened the air.

At once, the assembly sprang to life. Several men scrambled away. A few, including Gadnor, rushed forward to free him.

Krastus managed to loosen the chin strap and pulled the helmet from his head. Gadnor removed his greaves, and Ephastes the cuirass. The bronze pieces clanged loudly as they were flung back into the cart.

Alypius stared down at his chest, now red and raw—a perfect outline of the armor seared into his flesh. The helmet guards had blistered his cheeks, and his long golden hair lay singed and blackened around his scalp.

"Are you all right, Alypius?" Archon Tryphus' tone was awestruck.

Alypius shook, from pain or rage—or both. His gaze lifted from his chest and landed on Gadnor. "I want *you* to put it on. I want to see you burn. And if you do not, I want every priest and physician and herbalist, every sorceress and witch—everyone and anyone who knows anything about poisons to examine this armor and swear on the Styx that there is no trickery in this."

Krastus snapped his fingers at one man near the door. "Fetch a healer."

Alypius collapsed onto a stone bench, gasping for breath.

For all Gadnor despised Alypius, he pitied him. He captured Tor's gaze. Had the oracle known this would happen? Was the armor truly enchanted by the gods? Tor's expression revealed nothing. It took Gadnor a moment to realize everyone was watching him. Waiting for him to put on the armor.

Gadnor would rather fight ten lions than go near that armor. There was no way he was worthy in the eyes of the gods. He would burn alive. Every fiber of his being screamed in panic, muscles tensed to flee from the assembly. Perhaps he wouldn't stop running until he fainted from exhaustion.

Gadnor managed to nod, and something sparked in Tor's stoic expression. Fear, perhaps. Regret. It solidified Gadnor's suspicions that nothing good would come of this. His eyes scanned the faces before him, wondering if they would come to his aid when his flesh began to melt.

Ephastes reached into the cart, cautiously testing the cuirass with a light *tap tap* before lifting it and carrying it forward to wrap around Gadnor's torso.

It felt surprisingly light and didn't suffocate him like his own breastplate. Next came the greaves, which Krastus strapped to his shins. Gadnor closed his eyes, waiting for the sting of burning flesh. The bracers were next, then the sword belt. He opened his eyes to find Tor standing in front of him, shaking out the helmet. Strands of Alypius' burnt hair fluttered to the floor, and Gadnor's stomach flopped.

Tor lifted the death trap and slid it over Gadnor's head. The oracle seemed calm, but for the muscle ticking along his jaw. His gaze met

Gadnor's, a foreboding forest.

Krastus lifted the shield, and Gadnor slid his arm into the straps, wrapping his fingers around the grip. Someone handed him the spear. Then everyone took a few steps back. Staring. Waiting. Holding their breath.

An eternity passed, and Gadnor's arm tingled. Panic lodged in his throat. Was it burning him?

No. Just my scars. His vision danced with purple spots, blurring the faces of the awed councilmen surrounding him.

'Remember to breathe,' Dargos had said. Gadnor drew in a lungful of air. His eyesight cleared and settled on Tor. The oracle's dark, bronze-flecked eyes were bright, and his lips curled upwards in satisfaction.

"Pending examination of the armor for trickery or witchcraft, it seems, Gadnor, son of Raleon, that the gods have found you worthy." Krastus bowed his head.

Kelric observed in silence from a few paces away, eyes narrowed in skepticism, as though waiting for the farce to unravel.

"I volunteer to join your mission to Hameth," Krastus continued. "I may be old, but I can wield a sword better than most men standing here, I'd wager."

Then Alypius stood, his jaw clenched in pain. "I'm coming, too."

Gadnor shared a kindred look with Kelric.

'Rest assured a Leirion will accompany you, and they will try to kill you.' There was little doubt about Alypius' true intentions, but at least Gadnor would be ready for him. He nodded.

Ephastes stepped forward, but Krastus raised his hand before he could open his mouth. "It isn't wise to allow every council member to volunteer for this mission, Basileus. We may not all come back alive, if any of us do. This city still needs her leaders. I suggest the rest of you find suitable replacements to go in your stead."

"Agreed," Kelric announced.

The kyrioi filed out, whispering and murmuring among themselves, tossing final glances over their shoulders.

At last, only Gadnor, Kelric, and Tor remained in the room.

Gadnor sagged against the spear as his breath rushed out of him. "Please." He clawed at the chin strap. "Get this off me."

Tor and Kelric helped him remove the armor and weapons. They carefully returned each item to the cart. Gadnor slumped onto the nearest seat, cradling his head and staring at the glorious pile of bronze before him, panting with anxiety and confusion.

"What is this, Tor? How…? Why…?"

Tor shrugged. "I thought you could use a spectacle."

CHAPTER 50

LITHANEVA

LITHANEVA DRAGGED THE COMB THROUGH her hair for the thousandth time as she sat on her bed, legs dangling off the side. Ripping the tangles from her unruly curls was the one thing she discovered she could do without jeopardizing everything she had accomplished for Helinthia.

After Branitus left her at the temple, Lithaneva rushed to her room and bolted the door. Torine had come to check on her several times. A priest followed when she hadn't shown up for dinner. Branitus sent a physician, and even Larxes had knocked. Lithaneva refused them all entry, too terrified to allow herself another opportunity to speak before she fully understood the rules of Hera's curse. Once she figured them out, she could break them.

Rules could always be broken. She just needed time.

Time she'd wasted wallowing in self-pity and hating herself for hurting her beloved. The pain in Helinthia's vibrant eyes was still vivid and agonizing in Lithaneva's mind. She was repulsed at what she'd tried to do with Branitus. She wanted nothing more than to explain herself, but her tongue refused to form the words.

She'd talked to herself all night and found she couldn't even verbalize what she wanted to say to *herself*. She tried writing, whispering, concentrating so hard on a thought before she spoke it that her head ached. Every new attempt came out twisted and vile, the opposite of what she intended. Her whole body was in revolt against her.

Somehow, this curse *knew* her desires and thwarted them every single time.

It was well past midday now, and she was exhausted. She was beginning to think Hera might have beaten her. After brooding over that thought for far too long, she'd managed to convince herself that she wasn't important to the rebellion. At least, she wasn't as important *anymore*. After all, she'd already accomplished the difficult tasks. The rebels had the heir and were training him, they knew Charixes' plans, and Aden had his instructions on how to aid them in the coming war. There was little else for Lithaneva to do now besides stay out of their way.

And not betray them all with her rebellious tongue.

Helinthia will reclaim her throne without me.

Even better: with Dargos and Kelric's help, the heir would be able to win enough renown to become anax *without* marrying her, especially if he defeated Charixes on the battlefield. The people would demand he be crowned. Lithaneva didn't want to marry the heir, anyway. She'd never liked that part of the plan, and neither had Helinthia. But at the time, it had seemed a necessary bargaining piece with the rebels.

That original plan depended on a long siege of Golpathia—at least two years. That was the required length of time to legally divorce. But her father's whims had ruined everything. He was extremely good at that. Attacking from land *and* sea would almost certainly hasten that timeline. The heir's elevation to the throne by marrying her was out of the question.

Yes. The heir must win the crown on his own merit. Provided he wasn't dead already, as her father had claimed.

She planned to remain tucked away in her room, out of sight, and out of the way of any involvement in politics. Just what her father had always wanted. Ironic that their desires aligned now.

His god had found a way to answer his supplications, it seemed. *And the rebels will find a way to answer Helinthia's.*

The bristles snagged on a tangle, jerking her head downward and ripping strands painfully from her scalp. "Ergh!" She threw the brush across the room as hard as she could. It hit the wall, tearing out a chunk of plaster and sending dust and debris scattering to the floor.

She panted, tears of pain and frustration clouding her vision. She held her aching head, fighting to keep hope alive. When Helinthia won her island back, would Hera be forced to release Lithaneva from this curse? The thought of the Anassa of Heaven losing despite all her spiteful hard work and hateful tricks was almost sweeter than Helinthia's kiss.

Almost.

A new pang twisted in her gut. How could Helinthia's own mother be so vile as to want her daughter to lose control of her island? To torment and humiliate her like this in front of all the gods? Lithaneva loved Helinthia so much more knowing they shared such deep parental betrayal. *Why did you never tell me that, my love?*

There was a tap at the door, breaking her from her musings. She lifted her head. *Dinner?*

She settled her weight into her feet and stood, her stomach cramping in discomfort. She hadn't felt like eating lunch, so she didn't open the door when Torine came with the tray. The food was left outside to harden in the cold. She'd heard Torine come and collect it a while later, accompanied by a worried sigh as she walked away.

Lithaneva's rekindled hope for Helinthia's victory had teased her appetite. She walked to the door, not daring to open her mouth and blurt out the opposite of what she truly wanted. And she *wanted* to eat dinner.

But the knock didn't sound again.

Lithaneva got down on her hands and knees and lowered her

cheek to the freezing floor. She peered under the crack, expecting to see Torine's feet, hoping to see a wooden tray with savory smells wafting through to tickle her nose.

Instead, she saw a bare threshold, except for the dust. She frowned, making a mental note to tell Torine to sweep the villa. Although, if she tried to tell her now, it would probably come out as a command to dump manure everywhere.

Despite everything, that thought brought a smile to her face. How Branitus and Larxes' noses would wrinkle at the smell of the beautiful villa covered in cow feces.

She stood and shook the dust from her dress, stomach growling with disappointment. Something crunched behind her, and a potent floral scent singed her nostrils. *Hera!* She spun.

"Princess."

Her breath hitched. Before her stood Aden, lifting his sandal from her crushed alabaster jar of incense that had found a new home on the floor during one of her outbursts.

Her eyes darted to the window. The shutters were open. She swore she had closed and bolted them to block the spying eyes of the cuckoos, dull their infernal warbling. She wished she could wrap her bare hands around their necks and snap their vertebrae between her fingers.

Aden slid a metal hook into a pouch at his waist, revealing everything that had transpired while her back had been turned.

He'd shown her his skills at lock picking and bolt sliding at the Library Critius more than once. He used to open her window after dark so she could sneak out and spend the night hours poring over forbidden scrolls with him.

"That smells very expensive. Sorry." He threw her a sheepish grimace before scanning the destroyed room. Worry creased his brow. "What happened here?"

Lithaneva clamped her mouth shut. Closed her eyes. *Say nothing.*

"Princess?"

She detected concern deepening his tone, and her panic flared.

Why was he here instead of rallying the troops in the villages?

"Branitus said you were ill and wouldn't see anyone, but I didn't believe him. Did he lock you in here?"

Please leave!

Aden's hands slid around her shoulders. "What's happened? Did he hurt you? I'll kill him."

Lithaneva opened her eyes, surprised by the emotion in his tone. How she wished she could tell him everything that had happened. But she didn't dare try.

Aden dropped his hands, scrutinizing her with narrowed eyes. "Why aren't you saying anything? Is there something wrong with your voice?"

If only she could answer that question truthfully. "I'm fine."

She would sew her lips together with a bone needle and horsehair if she could.

Aden nodded slowly. He knew her well enough to trust that she would say what she needed to. He needn't probe. Now that he'd seen her, alive and well, and reporting nothing with which to concern himself, he would leave.

But he didn't move.

Her breath shortened in panic.

"The kubernao of Argeas has agreed to inflate his numbers, so have the kubernai of Pacar, Tarakus, and Kormu. I will visit Straxon tomorrow. Everything is going to plan, just as you said." He smiled, and victory bloomed within her at his report.

Yes! "The plan has changed."

No!

Aden's smile dissolved. "What do you mean?"

Lithaneva's tongue flicked in rebellion, and try as she might, she could not clamp her teeth tight enough to keep the words from spilling out. "We're sending all one thousand men to the battlefield, and you will make sure they fight for Charixes."

Aden narrowed his eyes. "Why the sudden change?"

Shut up, shut up!

Lithaneva tried to lift her hands to her mouth, but they remained limp at her sides. "I was wrong to trust the rebels."

Then, as if her cursed tongue knew exactly what to say to convince the man before her, she said, "I don't believe they will take our men as prisoners. They will kill them all to weaken our polis."

A muscle ticked along Aden's jaw. A spark of hope glimmered within her that maybe, just *maybe*, he would defy her. Proceed with the plan anyway.

Aden bowed his head. "I will trust your judgment, Princess. It will be as you say."

He turned to go, and her spiteful mouth opened again. "One more thing."

He paused. His hand gripped the windowpane, but he didn't look at her.

"Send a message to Charixes." Her heart plunged into despair. "Tell him I have information about the rebels."

A sharp nod, then he slipped out as stealthily as he'd come.

Lithaneva's knees gave out. She sank to the floor and stared hopelessly at the trees through the open window.

Blood pulsed in her ears. Her heart hammered against her chest. It was over. She would reveal everything to her father, and the rebels would fall beneath the combined armies of Ninenarn and Thellshun. The casualties would leave every polis in dire straits.

Unless…

I have to break this curse. Somehow. While there was still time. But how?

CHAPTER 51

KELRIC

THE SIGHT OF THE LEIRION in his andron before the sun had set startled Kelric. He froze on the threshold, propping the door open with one hand and instinctively grasping the hilt of his dagger with the other. The man sat on the couch, positioning himself with his back to the window to block any light to his face. His sword laid casually across his lap, an unmistakable parallel to Kelric yesterday.

Kelric had expected a visit tonight, of course, but in daylight? That was bold. Too bold. He already despised Gadnor's plan. It left him with too little control. And now this? This intruder had walked right past his guards, which indicated they were either loyal to the man or vulnerable to his leverage. Either way, no one would be coming to help him. *Damn you, Gadnor, for putting me in this position.* He'd always known his little brother would be the death of him.

"I thought we had moved past threats of violence," Kelric said.

He felt the familiar smile from beneath the hood. "I thought I made myself clear what would happen if you let Dargos go and sanctioned this little escapade of your brother's."

"I didn't let Dargos go," Kelric snapped. "He escaped."

The man tilted his head, unconvinced.

"I told Gadnor my intention to hand him over, expecting his support as my strategos. Instead, he went behind my back and warned Dargos to force my hand."

The man chuckled. "You can come up with a better lie than that, Basileus. At least *try*. Your brother isn't capable of such a bold move."

"He *wasn't*, but Gadnor has let this 'favored by the gods' nonsense go to his head. The Oracle of Artemis never leaves his side and constantly fills him with grandiose ideas. The birds only emboldened him. And now this armor…" Anger pulsed down his arms.

This meeting was supposed to be full of carefully crafted lies, but that last part had been true. Gadnor followed Tor around like a dog on a leash, and Kelric was sick of it. Tor was a selfish coward who would leave Gadnor to the wolves at the first sign of danger to himself or the feline abomination always trotting at his heels. If Gadnor planned to rule the island one day, he needed to think for himself, not grovel around Tor and worry over the opinions of petty gods. "He is focused on his own glory now, no matter what danger it puts Golpathia in." *Or me.*

The Leirion tapped a finger lightly on the hilt of his sword.

Kelric stepped the rest of the way into the room and let the door close behind him. "It seems I have no one I can trust. My own guards are willing to let an assassin stroll right through my gates."

The smile again.

Kelric narrowed his eyes at the shadowy cowl, allowing the tension to build. "I will take your oath."

The tapping stopped. "The time for our oath is over, Kelric. You have broken our terms."

Kelric's fingers tightened around the hilt of his dagger. The Leirion's answer suited him just fine. He'd rather kill the man and be free of Gadnor's schemes.

"Unless…"

Kelric waited, annoyed.

"Give me the name of your spy, and I may reconsider."

"I don't know their name."

The man laughed. "Do you think we're fools?"

"My brother met the spy in Thellshun at the wedding feast of Branitus. I wasn't there. But I'm sure you can acquire the guest list and narrow your suspects."

"Surely he told you?" The disbelief was evident.

"I didn't entertain the truth of it, at the time. I thought he made it up to make himself seem important. What spy would approach *Gadnor* with their secrets?" Kelric couldn't keep the chuckle out of his tone. He was still amazed that the story was true, and still skeptical of Lithaneva's loyalty. "Now, he refuses to tell me. It's the one tiny thing he controls."

"You expect me to believe that?"

"I expect an all-knowing brotherhood of spies to recognize when a person wants more power than he's owed," Kelric snapped. "If you can't do that, then perhaps your boasts of usefulness are as baseless as my brother's."

"I don't believe you, but it's no matter. We will find out for ourselves. We are already close. The question remains. What can you offer us?"

"Gadnor."

The finger began tapping again.

"I will tell you his route, and you can set an ambush for him." Kelric sat on the couch across from the assassin. The blade remained in the man's hand, but Kelric no longer worried he would use it. He'd captured the man's attention.

"I do not need to know his route to set an ambush."

"The Oracle of Artemis is going with him. Any assassin you try to hide within his contingent will be discovered by some critter or other—the boy can talk to animals, you know. Even insects."

The tapping stopped.

So, he didn't know that. Kelric's lip curled in satisfaction.

"You would have your brother slaughtered like some sacrificial bull?" The man chuckled. "My. You really do hate him."

'I think you'll be surprised.' The validation of Gadnor's prediction stung Kelric. Had he really been such a terrible brother?

"I have Golpathia to look out for now, and Gadnor has proven that he is willing to sacrifice the entire city for his own renown. He's a liability." Kelric shifted his jaw. "I don't *want* to betray my brother. I didn't *want* to betray my brother-*in-law* either, if only for my wife's sake. But my father trusted me to protect this city and all her inhabitants. If their lives are the price I must pay to fulfill my duty, then I will pay it. I am Basileus of Golpathia, and I'm not giving that up so Dargos can drink his fill of blood, or so my brother can prance around in a flashy suit of armor like he's some ancient hero on the shores of Troy."

Kelric clenched his jaw, wondering if his speech was entirely deception. He suddenly realized that taking the oath of the Leirion was the only real option he'd ever had, even before Gadnor barged into his room with Tor on his heels—*the snake*—and that silly little mouse. Before Dargos had abandoned them all.

But at least now Gadnor and Gonivein couldn't hate him for it. They were complicit.

A silence lingered between them. The Leirion's fingers remained still.

Kelric's stomach began to twist with anxiety. "Well, are you going to try and slit my throat, or give me the oath?"

The smile again.

"There is far too much at stake. I'm afraid taking the oath is still not enough without additional assurances of your loyalty. You wouldn't be the first to try and feign your allegiance to save your own skin or reputation. And I promise, you would not be the first to die in the attempt."

Unease crept along Kelric's spine. "I've already offered you my brother. What else do you want?"

"Ridding yourself of Gadnor was already in your best interests.

That's hardly a sacrifice."

Confusion sprouted within Kelric. "Then what? Do you want money? Power? Position?"

"Sacrifices require blood. Kill someone you love. That will suffice."

Fury ignited in Kelric's chest. He'd known this was a stupid, useless plan. "There's no one else I *love* except Gonivein, and I will burn this city to the ground before you lay a hand on her."

The Leirion chuckled, his shoulders shaking with amusement. "Not the Oracle of Apollo. It would not further our cause to so boldly provoke *his* wrath. Agamemnon learned that lesson for all of us."

"Yet Apollo *and* his sister are already against you." Kelric was growing impatient and angry. This man was a lunatic. *Who could I possibly love besides Gonivein?*

"That is only half the truth." The Leirion shifted his weight on the seat and leaned forward, as if sharing a secret. "There are more powerful gods than *them*—gods who are well acquainted with *our* sacrifices." He settled back again, exuding confidence.

Kelric brooded in silence. He needed no lesson on worship from this man. He'd had enough of that from Dargos to last a lifetime.

"What about your cook? What is her name? Euanthe?" The Leirion twisted the knife between his hands.

Kelric's rage guttered out, and a chill ran through his limbs. Euanthe was an old woman. Just a doula. She didn't matter to him. It was Gadnor who fawned over douloi.

And yet, the thought of Euanthe's magnanimous presence—her infectious smile, her constant doting, her delicious spice cakes, her motherly affection—being gone, *taken* from him, made him feel sick. The villa would never be the same without her. She was the one person who remembered his mother. Euanthe had tried so hard to emulate her for him. As much as a doula could.

Horror wormed inside of him. He did love her. Very much. It shamed him that he'd never realized it until now.

"Don't worry, I'm sure you will have no trouble finding a replacement. There are hundreds of young doulai eager to serve their basileus." The Leirion sneered. "In more ways than one, I'd wager. Perhaps that little wedding gift of Gonivein's?"

Kelric's heart pounded in his chest. He wanted nothing more than to shove his dagger down this man's pompous throat. He considered revealing Lithaneva, but then the Leirion would know he'd intended to deceive him. Desperation rooted in his mind. He grasped at the one thing he had left.

"I know who Iptys' companion is."

"So do we."

Kelric's breath hitched.

The man leaned forward. This time, Kelric caught a glimpse of the flashing white teeth. "We've already taken care of Dargos' whore. No more secrets, Basileus. No more games."

They have Forluna. That explained why Inan was still here. In offering her up, he'd hoped she would be far away from here with Dargos by now. Knowing she was at their mercy sickened him.

He truly had nothing left to bargain with.

He rubbed his temples. *I should have given Dargos to the Council the very first day.* Euanthe meant much more to him than Dargos ever had. *Damn you, Dargos. And damn you too, Gadnor.* Even with Dargos gone, if Gadnor hadn't made Kelric agree to this stupid plan, he would kill this man and see where the pieces fell.

For a moment, he considered ending this man's existence anyway. To Hades with the plan.

But then Gadnor would be killed, and Gonivein…

What misery will they force on her? At least this way, Kelric would remain the leader of Golpathia, Gadnor *might* survive, and Gonivein would remain safe by Kelric's side.

"Fine. Kill Euanthe."

"Oh no, not me, not any of the Leirion. *You* must kill her."

CHAPTER 52

GADNOR

GADNOR FOUND WORDS HARDER TO form than usual as he stood inside the entrance of Golpathia's palaistra His head still spun with everything Tor had done for him, so he had no idea what to say about the new item glittering in Tor's hands.

The oracle held a bow made of ivory, from some magical creature, surely. Gold and lapis inlays reinforced the handle grip in decorative spirals, and a sheet of bronze was hammered to the back for extra support. It looked like it belonged in a sealed treasure vault rather than in the hands of someone destined for a bloody battlefield.

A crooked smile stretched across Tor's boyish face as he held the bow out to Gadnor. "Go on. It's yours. There's no test with this one, I promise. It's a gift."

Gadnor gulped, feeling the heat creep into his face. He gripped the handle, testing the comfort, and ran a finger along one lapis inlay. He stood in awe of its beauty. "From the gods?" He already knew the answer.

"From Artemis. She really believes in you."

Tears stung Gadnor's eyes at the high praise. He had no idea why the goddess bothered with him, and he was terrified of losing whatever favor he carried. One day, that armor would burn him alive. He only hoped this rebellion was over before that time came.

"You've already given me everything I need for the battlefield. This should be yours." Gadnor tried to hand it back, but Tor raised his hands and stepped away.

"You gave me my life, Gadnor."

The words transported him back to the rundown shack in the Ordan—Kelric sneering down at Tor, his new doulos. The weapon in Gadnor's hands suddenly felt as heavy as the sack of gold he'd thrown at Kelric's feet to buy Tor and free him. He hadn't thought twice about his decision since, and he'd never expected Tor to devote himself like this in recompense. Gadnor wished he knew how to feel about this privilege, but 'worthy' was not it.

Gadnor just stared.

Tor's cheeks reddened under the scrutiny. He dropped his gaze, attempting to smooth a curl away from his forehead. "The armor is to help you become who you need to be. But this…" He reached out and lightly flicked the string of the bow, sending a vibration thrumming into Gadnor's palm. "This is to remind you of who you *are*."

Gadnor wanted to say something grateful, hug him even. He didn't deserve Tor's friendship, and he found himself terrified to lose it. "This mission will be dangerous. If you want to remain here and keep Xios safe, I won't hold it against you."

Tor chuckled, shaking his head. "If you're leading those men into battle, then you're going to need someone watching your back who doesn't want to put a sword through it. I'm coming with you."

Gadnor's mind scrambled to find something adequate to convey the feelings welling up inside him, but the screech of a predator bird interrupted his thoughts. He'd come here early for a reason, and it wasn't only because he enjoyed Tor's company.

He slung the bow over his shoulder and fished in his pocket to pull out the tiny scroll. He had very little talent with poetry, but he'd done his best to follow Lithaneva's example and convey his message in cryptic verse. He cleared his throat, dislodging the emotions trapped there. "Can you ask the hawk to send this to Lithaneva?"

Tor nodded. It took only a moment for him to wrap his cloak around his arm and call the bird down. The great creature dove with lightning speed. Gadnor stepped back instinctively as it neared. Yellow toes outstretched, it opened its wings to catch the air and slow its descent. The wicked talons curled around Tor's arm with a graceful flutter.

At Tor's amused grin, Gadnor closed his hanging jaw.

Gadnor gulped. He'd done this before, but that experience hadn't eased his fear of the hawk in the slightest. He leaned cautiously forward. The bird merely looked at him, then flapped his wings as though urging Gadnor to hurry it up. He moved a little faster, but carefully, and tied the message securely around the scaly leg with a leather thong.

Tor lowered his arm and thrust it upwards, launching the bird into flight. Both of them watched in silence as it sped toward Thellshun, growing smaller and smaller in the sky until it disappeared into the vast expanse of clear blue.

"I spoke to Inan."

Gadnor raised an eyebrow, tearing his gaze from the sky. "Forluna's horse?"

"He says Forluna asked him to bear you proudly to your fate."

Gadnor's breath caught in his throat. His eyes stung. He'd known Forluna hadn't abandoned him, but hearing the confirmation flooded him with relief and gratitude. He was about to ask more, but the sounds of voices, footsteps, and Xios' hiss alerted them to others approaching. He turned, shielding his eyes against the sun.

Krastus and Alypius emerged under the palaistra entrance, leading twelve men. Alypius' face was red where the helmet had touched his skin, and around his neck and shoulders where the chest plate had rested. He wore his tunic over both shoulders, which hid most of the damage. His hair was freshly combed and cut short, erasing most of evidence it had been singed. He glowered at Gadnor and Tor.

The subdued aggression threw Gadnor off balance. "Kyrioi." He nodded to them.

"Your contingent force." Krastus gestured to the men with a sweep of his hand. His eye flickered to the bow over Gadnor's shoulder before his brow raised curiously at Tor. "Another gift from our goddess?"

"Yes," Tor said.

Alypius scoffed and folded his arms across his chest.

Gadnor swung the bow from his shoulder and held it out as Krastus stepped closer.

"Incredible." The older man ogled the fine craftsmanship before studying Gadnor. For just a moment, Gadnor saw his unworthiness to hold such a weapon reflected in the magistrate's dark eyes. Krastus was every bit as puzzled over the goddess' favor as Gadnor was.

Gadnor straightened his shoulders. *Time to change that.* He directed his attention to the men standing behind Krastus. "This is everyone who's agreed to follow me?"

Krastus nodded. "Indeed, Strategos, by personal invitation from each councilman. Do you require more?" The question was sincere.

Gadnor shook his head. "Fifteen of us can move with stealth. Any more and we risk detection."

Krastus nodded approvingly, then beckoned to the men behind him with a flick of his wrist. "Come forward."

The men obeyed, their tall frames casting long shadows across the ground from the afternoon sun. Almost all of them looked older than Gadnor by at least ten years, with full beards, broad shoulders, and sculpted muscles. Many bore scars or bent noses, suggesting they had seen battle already. Gadnor didn't recognize any of them from the army's ranks, but that wasn't too strange. His father had restricted his training to the grounds at the villa. Kelric would know these men, though.

As Krastus introduced each volunteer, they bowed their heads, expressions devoid of emotion. Underneath the blank stares, Gadnor could sense their skepticism.

His heart sank, though he couldn't fault them. They had no reason to trust him. For all they knew, he would lead them straight to their deaths. And perhaps he would.

Something else itched at his skull.

He addressed the one closest to him: "Which weapon are you most comfortable with, Pernias?"

Pernias cut a glance at Krastus before lowering his eyes to the ground. "I… suppose I would prefer a sword, Strategos."

That was a strange response. His inflection suggested a question rather than an answer. Gadnor shoved down the gnawing anxiety and moved on to the next man. "And you, Clymicus?"

Again, there was a shifty glance at Krastus before answering. Gadnor began to sense they were afraid to say the wrong thing for fear of reprisal. But from who? He continued down the line, all displaying the same nervous behavior before responding.

Introductions and weapons' assignments noted, he decided to ask about their experience. He had no doubt he would be conducting his training much differently than these men were used to. Most commanders assigned duties based on the needs of the unit rather than individual skill set. But he was on a tighter deadline. The spring equinox was two months away. Gadnor needed to leverage every existing skill as much as possible to shorten their time to readiness. "How many of you have seen combat?"

Only the crickets answered him, chirping at the base of the colonnade edging the palaistra grounds. Gadnor shared a confused look with Tor. Alypius was smirking.

Warmth flooded his face as he realized. This was a setup. A trick to discredit him. He should have seen something like this coming. He'd let his guard down with Krastus. A mistake he hadn't even realized he'd made.

He looked squarely at the chief magistrate, mustering all the calm he could to keep his expression stoic and his voice even. He wouldn't give either of them the satisfaction of knowing they had riled him. "What am I missing, Kyrios?"

Krastus shifted his jaw thoughtfully, as if trying to form words.

Alypius' smirk devolved into a chuckle. "These men aren't trained to wield weapons, and *none* of them have seen combat."

Gadnor's brow furrowed. That's when it struck him.

These weren't soldiers the councilmen asked to volunteer. These were douloi.

His anger flared. "I asked for willing men, Krastus." His voice edged on cracking. Why couldn't his fury manifest as confidence like other men? Why did his body seize up and his voice become squeaky instead? He tightened his grip on Artemis' bow, frustrated at himself.

'She really believes in you.' So did Forluna. So did Dargos.

The thought calmed him.

Krastus didn't seem to notice his outburst. "The Council *willingly*, and graciously, provided their douloi to accompany you in their stead. Is there a problem?"

"Yes," Gadnor snapped.

The douloi shared apprehensive glances between themselves.

Alypius laughed again. "These men are willing enough for your purposes. They know their family's well-being depends on their success."

Tor's hand on his shoulder was the only thing keeping him grounded now.

"Are you concerned you do not have time to train them?" Krastus' tone sounded deceitfully innocent. "Two months is a reasonable amount of time for a strategos to train a small contingent. Besides, these men are quick learners, and you can see for yourself that they are all strong enough to wield any weapon you give them with speed and precision."

Gadnor lifted his gaze to the douloi. Their faces revealed nothing, but Gadnor sensed a deep resentment in their rigid stances. He eyed the scars on Pernias' shoulders. Not made by a sharpened blade from an enemy, but by a whip from a kyrios. He felt sick. And angry.

Tor gave his shoulder a squeeze, bringing Gadnor back to the palaistra and the awkward, infuriating position he found himself in. "It's not about the time or the training, Krastus." Gadnor drew in a deep breath. An idea bloomed.

He stepped closer to the douloi so Krastus and Alypius were no longer an obstacle between them. All eyes settled on him, waiting. If the councilmen wanted to undermine him and flaunt their power, then he would repay them in kind.

"This is a dangerous mission." He thumbed the raised edge of the bow's handle, focusing his thoughts. "I don't know what awaits us at our destination—how many men, the terrain, what our odds of success are in completing the mission with our lives, but I swear to you, the spoils we collect are *yours*. Not your kyrios', *yours*. You fight for them, you bleed for them, you keep them."

The eyes of the douloi widened in surprise, and a throat cleared behind him. Gadnor turned.

"You overstep your authority, Strategos." The magistrate smiled as though schooling a wayward child. "These douloi are here at the behest of their kyrios. Therefore, whatever they acquire in performing this service belongs to their kyrios by right. I admire your charisma, but unfortunately, the law does not permit you to make decisions or promises regarding property that does not belong to you."

Gadnor smirked, bitterness on his tongue. "I am the strategos, and it is *my* right to set the rules for this campaign, and I say every man who kills the enemy has a right to their loot, doulos or no. Any man who interferes will answer to me. If the council members wish for riches, they are *free* to switch places with their douloi and take the loot by their own merit."

Krastus' smile faded.

Alypius spat. "What use does a doulos have for spoil? What has he to buy, and where will he put it? He has no home of his own, no place in which to admire treasure."

It was Gadnor's turn to smile. "He can buy his freedom if he chooses, his family's freedom, and whatever else he damn well pleases. Isn't that the law, Krastus? Any man may buy his freedom if he has acquired the coin to do so?"

Alypius took a step toward Gadnor. "You've always been a foolish coward with an unnatural affection for those beneath you. When will you learn your lesson?"

"It is the right of the strategos, Alypius, as he has said." Krastus stroked his beard. "Be warned, Gadnor, if you commit to this, you will win no favors with the kyrioi of Golpathia or anywhere else in Helinthia."

'You should not be ashamed to disagree with them, or people like them.'

I'm not ashamed, Goddess. Gadnor turned back to the douloi, mind made up. He raised the bow, holding it out in front of him. "I swear on this bow, gifted to me by the goddess Artemis, that if you fight for me, I will fight for your freedom."

The smallest of smiles lifted the corners of Pernias' and Clymicus' lips, fire lighting behind their eyes.

"You can't do th—"

Krastus interrupted Alypius with a raised hand. "A bold promise, Strategos. Are you sure you can keep it?"

Adrenaline surged through Gadnor's veins. He'd never been more sure of anything. "Until my dying breath."

An unsettling grin twisted Krastus' mouth.

Tor turned so only Gadnor could see his pale face. He was hardly breathing. "If they weren't planning to put a sword through your back before, they certainly are now," he whispered through blue-tinged lips. "What are you doing?"

Gadnor gazed at the faces of the douloi. They still maintained their bearing, but an eagerness swirled behind their eyes now. He vowed this would be the last time their fate was not of their choosing. He smiled at Tor. "I'm surrounding myself with lions."

CHAPTER 53

KELRIC

KELRIC PACED. CHARIXES' SPY WAS long gone, and Helios' journey was done. Kelric's hair was frizzy from raking his hands through the curls too many times, and he'd missed dinner.

Gods. Dinner.

His last opportunity to eat a meal from the loving old woman he was about to murder. She'd knocked on his door when he hadn't showed. It was rare that he missed one of her meals, but he'd sent her away without even opening it. Shame ran hot through his veins. He couldn't bear to look her in the face and lie about why he was in such an emotional state, a state she would immediately try to remedy because she cared for him.

His stomach growled, though not from hunger. He doubled over and retched, but there was nothing to purge.

He sat back on his rump and leaned against the couch, staring up at the dark ceiling. *I'm doing this for Gonivein, for Gadnor, for my city. Lives are lost in exchange for much less every day.*

But the tightness in his chest didn't subside. He growled in rage. *No, I'm doing this because Dargos left me no choice, because Gadnor wants to play hero. They've tied my hands.*

Dread swelled within him. Dazed, he pulled himself back to his feet and crept out into the night. His footfalls through the vacant, decaying courtyard sounded too loud. Anxiety writhed within him, tightening his lungs. What if someone saw him?

So what if they do? This is my villa.

He rounded the corner of the house and climbed the porch steps. Pausing at the top, he scanned the shadows along the inner wall, scrutinizing the dark corners where dead foliage still clung to a past life of prosperity. Was a Leirion watching him? Waiting to see if he would go through with it?

At the far end of the front courtyard stood the gate guard, both hands wrapped around his spear, diligent at his post this time. Even in the dark and from a distance, Kelric could see his swollen eye—not punishment enough for abandoning his post. The brazier beside him burned with too much enthusiasm for such a cold, desolate night as this. The only glow to be seen anywhere on the villa grounds. Everyone else was asleep in their beds. Even the moon had hidden her face behind a cloud.

Kelric had to make sure his deed was noiseless, otherwise he would alert the guard. That wouldn't do.

He ducked into the atrium and emerged into the center of the villa. Again, he scrutinized the shadows for movement under the peristyle. He eyed his bedroom straight ahead on the other side of the fountain and house altar. The door was closed, and a faint orange line flickered under the door. Gonivein was waiting for him. His heart pinched. He still hadn't quite forgiven her betrayal with Apollo, but their union last night had tempered the raging storm between them. She would never approve of what he was doing now, would think he was a monster, which meant he'd have to lie. How short-lived, the honesty between them. Blissful. Fleeting.

Like all good things he'd known in his life.

Kelric turned his feet toward the triklinion and carefully opened the door, stopping just before it creaked. He squeezed through the gap. His eyes strained against the pitch-blackness before him, but he didn't need light. He knew every inch of this room and could walk it blindfolded. He tiptoed to the door that led into the kitchen and followed the same procedure, opening it until just before the hinges screeched, then slipped inside.

The kitchen still smelled of the dinner Euanthe had prepared—meat and bread and spices, thyme and rosemary and pepper. His mouth watered. Embers burned in the hearth, but the kettle was empty. The table inside the door already had items laid out for tomorrow's breakfast: dried fruits, eggs, and barley.

Scattered images of memories spent in this room as a boy, as a youth, as a man, flashed through his mind. He couldn't recall a single bad memory of Euanthe. She always had a smile for him, and something delicious to eat.

His eyes stung and he drew his hands up to rub them. He'd killed many people in battle, but no one in cold blood. He was no stranger to wanting to, however. Tor and Genia, the priestess of Tyldan, came to mind. He would have gloried in their warm blood staining his sword and pooling around his sandals. Their pleas for mercy feeding his lust to end their existence. Even Klymene, if he'd slit her throat, his only regret would have been Gonivein's outrage.

He'd never had a problem taking a life before. Why was this one so hard?

She's just a doula. She has no purpose but the one I give her.

The thoughts brought him no comfort. A sacrifice, the Leirion had called her. Sacrifices were useless, especially those given to the gods. Just a way for men to justify gorging themselves on roasted meat more often than they should. Killing Euanthe was even more senseless and misguided.

Euanthe's room sat at the back of the kitchen. Kelric stared at it, numbness worming through him. Sometimes she would visit her nephew in the lower city. Maybe…

A glow underneath the door dashed those hopes. A fire in the hearth, or a candle? He leaned forward, listening for noises. There was nothing. He focused his attention on the rest of the villa. A rush of wind from outside and the distant crash of waves on the rocks far below their plateau. No voices. No footsteps.

He slid his fingers around the cold iron bar of the latch and lifted it. A realization struck him as the door slid open—a critical oversight. He'd forgotten to plan how he would kill her.

His heart lurched into his throat.

Euanthe was sitting up on her modest cot, eyes wide and staring straight at him.

His muscles seized with sudden panic even as hers seemed to relax, her familiar and warm smile stretching across her face. Her gnarled hands clutched a cloth and needle. She was mending something. A cloak. *His* cloak.

"Basileus." Her tone was soft and quiet, but it seemed louder than a scream to his frazzled nerves.

He stepped the rest of the way in and closed the door behind him, praying no one had heard her.

Euanthe's smile waned and her brow furrowed as she set aside her mending. "Oh, your hair is all fluffy. What's troubling you, child?" She started to rise, trying to push off the bed with her hands. Her knees shook with the effort. She was so frail. He'd never noticed that before. He rested a hand on her shoulder to stop her.

"Don't get up, I just…" His tongue stuck in his throat. His insides churned, screaming for escape.

Her big eyes peered up at him, crinkling at the edges in concern. "Let me get you some dinner. I saved some for you."

His hand stayed firm on her shoulder. Had he ever come to her room before? Even as a child, he couldn't remember needing anything bad enough to encroach on her like this.

"Basileus?"

"I…"

Was there a point to talking? What good would it do besides prolong the inevitable? Or frighten her. What if she screamed?

He shoved her down on the bed—it was easy, almost no resistance from her feeble arms—and grabbed her pillow. Her wide, surprised expression disappeared underneath it as he pressed it over her face faster than either of them could think about what was happening.

No going back now. Perhaps if she'd been asleep, he could have talked himself out of this and walked away. Just backed out and closed the door behind him. Found some other way to deal with the Leirion. But not now.

She thrashed under him. Her hands flailed at his wrists before swinging toward her vanity, reaching for some weapon. There was a candlestick there, but her frantic movements toppled it to the tiled floor with a *clang*.

Kelric hissed as hot wax splashed across his sandal, burning his skin. His heart pounded in his ears as he cursed and threatened every god. She squirmed for what seemed like an eternity, her muffled screams warming his palms through the linen and down. He leaned his weight onto her. His father pressing the pillow over Gonivein replayed again and again in his mind. The images were vivid. He glanced behind to see if someone was about to stab him in the neck. There was no one.

Kelric's eyes stung, conflict waged in his chest, roiling and threatening to burst through it. A sob caught in his throat. Finally, she stilled, but he didn't dare move. Not yet. She could be feigning death. She was wise and experienced—she would think of something like that.

He'd been there so long, the arm holding the pillow had gone numb from his elbow down. Surely, it was over now. He pushed himself up and stared at the pillow for a long breath. He couldn't bear to remove it, to see the betrayal in her dead eyes. But he knew he couldn't leave her like this. It had to look like a natural death. She was old. Who would suspect murder?

Everyone would if they found her this way.

He raked his hands through his hair, then stared at them, hating them. He swallowed the acid climbing up his throat.

He arranged her in the bed, tucked the pillow beneath her head, and drew the covers up around her chin. A basket beside her vanity containing bolts of thread and scraps of linen caught his eye. He wadded up her mending and stuffed it on top. He would never wear that cloak again. Ever.

Kelric closed Euanthe's eyes, his own stinging, then picked up the candlestick. "I'm sorry," he whispered. The irreversible weight of what he'd done constricted his lungs. Maybe he would wake up in a couple hours and all of this would just be a nightmare.

But the feeling of murdering someone he loved was too familiar, and he knew better than to believe such wishful lies.

Something moved from the corner of his eye. Something small. Dark. With a long ropey tail.

Tor.

The mouse scurried along the edge of the wall toward the door. It ducked behind a basket of herbs, poking its whiskery nose out on the other side. Its beady black eyes gazed up at him.

Both of them seemed to understand the stakes.

It darted out, streaking across the open floor to the crack under the door.

Adrenaline surged into Kelric's sluggish limbs. He stomped. Missed. Stomped again. Then a third time. Tiny bones crunched beneath his sandal.

It didn't even squeal.

Kelric picked the creature up by the tail and glared at the crushed corpse, then threw it onto the dying fire. Tor would not ambush him this time. Nor ever again.

Damn you, Tor. None of this would have happened if Tor hadn't intervened with the first mouse, sowing mistrust, stealing Gadnor away. If Tor had kept his sniveling nose out of it, then Kelric could have handled the Leirion *his* way, and Euanthe would still be here.

The mouse's fur began to smoke, wafting a stench into the air. Kelric crinkled his nose. What did Gadnor see in Tor, anyway? Was it obvious to no one else that Tor was trying to manipulate him? Ever since they'd found him in the Ordan, Gadnor had shown Kelric nothing but contempt. How could his brother think so little of him after Kelric had devoted his life to keeping him safe?

'You have a fine way of showing it,' Gadnor had said. But the fact remained that Kelric *had* shown it. More than Tor ever had. Gadnor would never learn who to trust. Kelric needed to stop waiting for a day that would never come.

Kelric glanced back at Euanthe. Her lips were blue, her eyes and cheeks sunken without the lift of her smile. Hardly recognizable. This was Gadnor's doing as much as Tor's. It was *his* plan for Kelric to take the Leirion's oath, his idea that drove Kelric to this horrific deed. Gadnor had inflicted a wound that would not easily heal.

Kelric was done playing nursemaid. Whatever lay in store for Gadnor now, he'd brought it on himself. Kelric had a wife, a city, a duty. Gadnor could play hero on his own, but Kelric would not lose anyone else to his little brother's misguided whims or Tor's manipulative tricks.

Let the gods have him.

CHAPTER 54

LITHANEVA

L ITHIE, IF YOU DON'T OPEN this door, I will bust it down!"
Branitus' fist beating against the door threatened to sever Lithaneva's last thread of self-control.

She didn't dare trust her voice to answer him. She grabbed her brush from the floor and hurled it at the door, hoping the loud *clack* would be enough to satisfy him.

"What was that? Are you hurt? Do you need help?" Branitus pounded again.

She growled and rolled off the bed.

"I'm not leaving until I see you're well with my own eyes. Nothing more." His voice sounded strained.

A longing stirred to set him at ease, not because she loved him, but because she appreciated that he cared, despite the annoyance of it. Her father would never have bothered seeking her out. He certainly would not have insisted on setting eyes on her to prove she was well. And Helinthia? Well, their encounters were fire and lust and passion.

Lithaneva slid the bolt free, drew in a deep breath, and opened the door.

Branitus stepped back. He wore an awkward, scared expression, as though he thought she might try to seduce him again. She was just as frightened of the same.

She smiled sweetly at him, swept her arm down the length of her body to guide his gaze to her good health, spun around once, and then promptly slammed the door. She slid the bolt back into the latch. Her chest heaved, immeasurable relief rushing through her.

"Thank you, Lithie." The door creaked as he leaned against it on the other side. "I don't hate you, if that's what this is about. I… I just don't want you to hate *me*."

Lithaneva's eyes blurred with tears. She sagged to the floor, feeling drained.

Branitus stayed a moment longer, then she heard him leave. Her chest ached even more with his absence.

She turned to go back to her bed and froze.

In the open window was the hawk, examining her with a golden eye. The creature fluffed its feathers and repositioned its talons on the sill. Lithaneva's gaze fell on the yellow leg, where a tiny scroll was bound.

Her heart leapt. Another message from Gadnor? She stepped carefully through the mess on the floor. It wouldn't do to make a racket. Despite their previous, subdued encounter, Lithaneva knew a wild beast was reliably unpredictable, and it would be just her luck for the bird to gouge her eyes out with the slightest provocation. As she neared the window, she wondered if her curse might prevent this interaction. Her heart fluttered with excitement as she extended her hand unimpeded.

The hawk scrutinized her fingers as she worked to loosen the bindings. As soon as the scroll was in her possession, the creature turned around and launched into the air.

She stared after it. Shocked. Eager. She unraveled the scroll. Breathless.

To Hameth's shores the acolyte goes
To find the Earthshaker, and learn what he knows.

Lithaneva's fingers curled around the paper. Relief swept through her. She sank onto the bed. The acolyte had to mean the heir. *He's alive!* Her father had lied, or perhaps his information was wrong. She was thrilled her ode had been interpreted correctly.

A sob of joy caught in her throat.

Then her happiness evaporated. Aden was on his way to undo all the carefully laid plans they'd crafted to aid the rebellion. Worse, he was going to tell her father to come to Thellshun. To *her.* She stared at the paper in horror. She would be forced to tell her father everything. The heir would be walking into a trap.

She stretched out on the bed, spiraling into a familiar despair. She stuffed the paper into her mouth and chewed. Best to destroy as much evidence as possible. For whatever it was worth. She grimaced, tasting dirt and the distinct flavor of unwashed animal as she swallowed.

'Got you, got you.'

The cuckoo's warbling whined in Lithaneva's skull, scattering her thoughts. She didn't know how much more she could take. Anger simmered. *I should have realized Hera was using the birds.* The species was migratory, and with the coming of winter, those birds should have been gone long before now. Hera must have commanded the little beasts to stay and torment her.

'Got you, got you.'

She rolled onto her stomach and buried her head under her pillow, pressing the sides to her ears. It dulled their mocking racket, but not enough.

'Got you, got you.'

'Beautiful creatures, aren't they? Loyal creatures.' There had been such affection in Hera's voice.

Lithaneva bolted upright, flinging the pillow as hard as she could across the room. It slapped into the wall and landed on her messy floor with a *plop.*

"I'm going to *kill* those little beasts!"

She wanted to pop their little heads off their bodies and fling their corpses on the altar of her beloved. Breathe the scent of burning feathers into her lungs and revel in the knowledge that she'd taken something precious from the Anassa of Heaven.

Hera might decide to return and murder her for it. But what did that matter? She was a liability to everything and everyone she cared about. Better that she was dead before Charixes arrived. The dead, at least, kept their secrets.

A smile spread across her face. *Death by a goddess.* Even better that her last act would be holding sweet revenge in the palm of her hand—what little of it she could grasp.

She stood and marched across the room, flinging the door open so hard it banged against the wall. She stormed out of the villa and galloped down the porch steps.

"Princess!" Larxes' surprised voice from where he sat at the edge of the fountain didn't slow her down.

She whirled and gazed at the eaves, shielding the blinding sun with her hand. She circled the building twice, like a bloodthirsty wolf. A concentrated gathering of bird droppings streaking a wall in the back garden finally caught her eye. Fury burned in her as a little gray head peered out from under the fluted terracotta shingles. Just one.

By now, Larxes had abandoned his music and joined her. "What are you looking for?"

She didn't dare answer. Gods only knew what would come flying out.

How was she going to get to the bird? If she came close, it would fly away. She could destroy its nest, perhaps. But that wasn't enough. She tapped her foot, letting the *tap tap* of her sandal against the gravel calm the rhythm of her heart.

Gravel. She examined the ground, then stooped to sort through her missile options. She selected a large one—this would stun it for sure.

"Princess, what are you doing?"

Lithaneva ignored him and held the rock in front of her, aiming. She reeled back her arm and threw it as hard as she could. It crashed into the tiles above the nest. A shard plummeted to the earth. The cuckoo startled out of the nest with a ruffle of feathers and perched on the edge of the woven grasses.

Larxes stepped back.

"Princess!"

Ferry it, she seethed, snatching another stone. She doubted she would have a third chance. The bird warbled as it stared at her. This time, it seemed to say, *'Uh oh, uh oh.'* It tensed to fly.

Lithaneva unleashed her stone. It smacked into the nest. Bird and sanctuary plummeted to the ground. She thought she'd missed the cuckoo entirely and it would leap into the air as soon as its legs found purchase to push off. But as it flopped and squeaked in the gravel, she realized she'd injured it. A wing or a foot, perhaps. It was off balance, slapping at the air to stay upright.

Lithaneva pounced. It leapt away, but she was quicker. She seized the little beast, trapping its wings to its body with one hand and curling her fingers around its neck with her other. She was ready to wring it as she'd seen Torine do to the chickens and geese.

A sudden surge of pity stayed her hand. She clenched her teeth, gazing into the shiny black eye. This poor creature was a victim of Hera's schemes every bit as much as she was.

Larxes' hands covered his face. He cracked a finger open, revealing a wide eye that darted from her face down to the bird and back again. He released a breath, slowly letting his arms drop. "What are you…?"

Lithaneva didn't answer. She held the bird close to her chest and marched past him. Up the porch steps and back to her room, shouldering past a bewildered Branitus.

"Lithie…?"

She kicked the door closed behind her and shoved the bolt into the lock with her elbow before raising the cuckoo up close to her mouth. "Can you hear me, Hera? Are you watching through this pathetic creature's eyes?" She was a little confused that her words were coming out how she wanted them to. Or… were they? "I'm going to murder it."

Was that still true? She hadn't thought so a moment ago, but she hardly knew what was fact or fiction anymore. She considered saying more, but decided she better not tempt Fortune to abandon her.

She righted an overturned basket with her toe. Bolts of thread tumbled out of it. She set the bird inside. It limped on the woven reeds, fluttering its wings awkwardly. She could clearly see where she'd wounded it. Several feathers were bent and sticking out at odd angles, and it seemed to be favoring one leg. It looked up at her from the darkness, tilting its head curiously. Wisely quiet.

Lithaneva placed the lid on the basket and sat on the bed.

And waited for Hera.

CHAPTER 55

FORLUNA

THE LAST TIME FORLUNA BEHELD the city of Ninenarn, the white marble and limestone temples, houses, baths, and fountains had been blanketed in dark smoke. Where the bronze statue of Helinthia stretched her elegant arms toward the sky just inside the gate, orange flames licking the stars had outshone her brilliance.

As Forluna and Jaxus drew nearer, sounds of life met her ears—though her mind wanted to conjure screams of the dying and anguished.

The city's walls had been repainted with images of Ordanus, son of Apollo, and his heroic journey across the waves, interspersed with diving falcons and olive trees in bloom. Perhaps to most people coming and going, the city appeared tranquil and glorious, but Forluna knew its dark history. She could still smell ash and iron in the breeze, discern traces of flames lingering in the cracks of the mortar. Black stains that neither wind nor rain could erase.

A queue formed at the entrance to the city. Forluna craned above the shoulders of those in front of her, spotting four guards ahead. They were stopping everyone, searching carts and sacks, inspecting papers. *At least they aren't running them through with swords and spears.*

Jaxus cursed beside her, shifting his feet impatiently. He leaned toward her ear. "Don't even think about trying to beg sympathy with these guards. They won't listen, not when they see who I am."

Forluna leaned away from his foul breath. *Before this day ends, it will be you begging sympathy from the guards.* She almost pitied him.

Almost.

Finally, they reached the front of the line. The waiting guard looked bored and hungry as he swept his eyes over them. He seemed to half-listen as Jaxus began explaining why he and his companions were leading a bound woman into the city. Forluna longed to plop down, pull her feet free of her boots, and rub her aching soles. Even if Jaxus would have let her do such a thing, she dared not. Medusa's tendril still snaked around her ankle.

Something bumped into her boot. The snake startled, coiling tighter inside. Forluna froze, expecting fangs, then looked down to find a bolt of red thread against her ankle. She followed the unraveled string to the other side of the gate, where two guards had unstrapped several bags from a donkey and were rummaging through them. One sack had fallen over, unleashing a rainbow of threads in every direction. A woman with light brown hair streaked with silver was hurriedly trying to gather them all before they were trampled and ruined.

Just as Jaxus cleared their entry with the guard, the woman spotted the bolt of red, then Forluna's bound wrists. Her gaze continued upwards. Recognition flashed between them as their eyes met. A young girl bringing lunch to a palace guard, perhaps a father or uncle, sprang into Forluna's mind. She'd known she might recognize someone in Ninenarn. Yet part of her was convinced that every face she remembered belonged to a rotting corpse. Or an enemy.

The woman stepped forward. Her mouth opened to speak, but before she could utter a sound, Jaxus yanked on the rope, tugging

Forluna after him like a beast.

Not a stone was out of place in the buildings or roofs along the main route. Though the slight discoloration where new bricks and tiles had repaired holes and gouges was noticeable, at least to her. The street teemed with citizens and douloi, not screaming or running in terror, but hurrying with a determined calm.

Jaxus pulled her along, snapping at people to move aside. Several times she felt a brush against her arm. Her heart beat frantically, urging her to panic. The noise was disorienting, dizzying. Everywhere she looked, she saw more faces resembling people she knew—people she'd seen slaughtered like rats. Their family members, perhaps? Or was her mind simply playing tricks?

They passed a fountain burbling with crimson water. Splatters of blood marred its limestone base. She froze in horror. Jaxus jerked on her wrists and she stumbled forward. She looked again, blinking. Clean and clear water gushed forth from an amphora carried by the goddess Hebe. Forluna's lungs burned.

In. Out. Slow.

Perhaps she should keep her eyes on the ground until she was standing before Charixes.

Cobblestones turned to tiles beneath her boots, large at first, then tiny, multi-colored, and patterned. A mosaic of a grand atrium. The noise of the city gave way to the solitary echoes of their feet. They were in the palace, but she couldn't bear to look up. Too many ghosts wandered these halls. If she met their eyes, they would see the coward who'd fled.

She couldn't face them. Not yet. Not until their vengeance stained her hands. Not until the ones who'd survived—Gadnor, the woman at the gate, the families she'd glimpsed in the crowded streets— could finally sleep without fear, wake without dread for what dangers Dawn might bring in her rosy fingers.

"The anax is busy now. Come back later."

Panic fluttered at the base of her throat at the deep, stern voice.

Charixes. Despite all her resolve, she shivered. What if she couldn't stop him? What if she couldn't bring herself to kill him? *Give me courage, Athena.*

The gorgon's tendril stirred inside her boot.

"There's no business that would keep the anax from seeing me. Tell him Jaxus has returned with all that was promised."

"I'm not interrupting him. Come back *later.*"

Forluna allowed herself to glance up. Her eyes focused on a figure carved into the door behind the porter. Ordanus, the son of Apollo, stared right at her. He wasn't as intimidating as she remembered. In fact, he almost seemed inviting, as if he were welcoming her home.

Jaxus planted his hands on his hips, his patience disintegrating. "He's been waiting for my arrival for *years.*"

The porter laughed. "Then what's another hour? The emissary with him has far more pressing news, I assure you."

Jaxus growled and tore something from the purse on his belt. He thrust it toward the guard, who flinched away with a scowl. The object fluttered to the ground and landed beside Forluna's foot. A black kerchief with a white lily. She bit back a scowl. She was sick of seeing that emblem.

"Tell him I have the oracle-slayer."

Forluna felt the guard's eyes fall on her. She didn't look up. She had to appear defeated. Broken. She was too close to victory to fail because of a glance.

The snake slid slowly up her calf.

"This woman? Doesn't look old enough."

Jaxus leaned closer to the man's ear, hissing, "This *nymph* was Iptys' companion."

Her dear friend's name on Jaxus' foul lips made Forluna seethe.

His bony fingers, like talons, dug into her shoulder and wrenched her forward. Pain exploded across her scalp as he yanked a fistful of her hair back, exposing her long, cat-like ear.

She stifled a sharp gasp, her eyes meeting the guard's shocked expression just before he opened the door and disappeared inside the throne room. The handle jangled as the great oak slab slammed behind him.

Jaxus shoved her away. She glared at his back as he bounced from foot to foot. Why was he nervous? This was his moment of triumph. She expected him to be thrilled. Instead, he seemed more terrified than she felt.

The porter reappeared and held the door, ushering them in wordlessly.

Jaxus straightened his shoulders smugly and pulled Forluna inside. His two men followed, silent and menacing.

"The gods have blessed me today." Charixes' voice boomed across the hall, slamming into Forluna like a tidal wave.

Her breath lodged in her throat and her legs rooted to the throne room tiles. The sight of him standing there, with one sandaled foot elevated on the throne steps, elbow lazily resting on the arm of Iptys' chair, was enough to scatter her thoughts to the wind. Sucked out by the draft of the door slamming behind her. Locking her in. With *him.*

Charixes had aged. Gray streaked his hair and beard, but he remained muscular, shoulders straight, back unbent—*unburdened*—by the grief he'd inflicted on others. On *her.*

Loathing bubbled within her, pushing the air out of her throat and letting her lungs fill again with renewed purpose. Adrenaline tingled through her, reinvigorating aching muscles. The snake moved higher up her leg.

Jaxus bowed at the waist. "Anax, I have found the murderess of Oracle Eraia, as I promised."

Charixes sniffed and stepped off the dais.

His footsteps synced with the thundering of Forluna's heart as he drew near. Her ears rang with blood and heat. Her whole body was on fire.

"Twenty years too late."

Jaxus' ears reddened. "I did not give up, unlike the rest of the Order."

Charixes glowered at him. "The rest of the Order did not promise to find her.”

Jaxus averted his gaze, frustration twitching along his jaw.

Charixes turned to another man Forluna hadn't even noticed. Blond hair fell over his dust-covered cloak. A white stallion embroidered his dark tunic.

Thellshun.

“Tell my daughter I will visit by the new moon.” His voice dropped to a threatening tone. “Tell her I'm eager to hear what she's discovered. I'd better not be disappointed.”

Princess Lithaneva. What game is Helinthia playing now? Urgency jolted through her. Something terrible had happened, or was about to. Charixes could not leave this room alive.

The Thellshun man straightened crisply and bowed, then strode out, tossing a curious glance at her as he passed.

Everything and everyone around Forluna dissolved, except for Charixes. Her chest ached with the pain of his betrayal and all the agony it had wrought, and would continue to wreak, upon Helinthia if she let him walk away. This was why she was here, to stop him. To save the ones she loved. To deliver vengeance. *For Iptys. For Gadnor. For* me.

She was here to win her battle.

Charixes nodded to one of the men beside her. Gruff hands grasped her shoulders, pushing her down.

She collapsed to one knee, barely managing to fold her body so her leg with the knife remained upright instead of under her. Her chiton fell over the lip of her boot just as the Gorgon's tendril flicked its forked tongue out. She gritted her teeth, straining at the bindings around her wrists. She would have to be quick when she grabbed her knife, otherwise she would draw too much attention.

Charixes padded nearer, and the men holding her down stepped back to give him room. “Never thought you would bow to me, did you, Forluna?”

She squirmed in discomfort, exaggerating her movements just enough to slide her hands under her skirt without notice. The snake dropped onto her wrists and coiled itself around them, resting its head over her knuckles. She could feel the flutter of its tongue on her skin, though her skirt hid it from view. Forluna drew strength from the creature. She would only have one chance to strike. Either the serpent would kill her, or Charixes would.

Charixes' oiled sandals entered her line of sight. "Did you think I would just let you go?" He *tsked* and leaned down, hooking her chin gruffly in a vice and jerking her face up to his. His lips twisted into a cruel, triumphant smile. "*Murderess.*"

Rage coursed through her. She grasped the hilt of her dagger and wrenched it from her boot. She sprang. Driving the knife toward his chest.

Charixes had been Iptys' greatest warrior. A crown had not changed his nature. He reeled back. Twisted sideways, swinging his arm to knock hers away. Blood splattered as her blade sliced into his shoulder.

No!

She careened to the cold floor and immediately pushed herself up again, determined to drive her blade into his heart.

Charixes seized her bound wrists, holding her at arms' length while Jaxus' men restrained her.

The serpent hissed. It struck, fangs burying deep between the tiny bones in Charixes' hand.

Charixes roared and shoved Forluna back. A Leirion caught her, hooking his arms through her elbows as she fell against him. The other guard plunged his fist into her gut.

The wind rushed out of her. Her knees buckled and she sagged, shoulders wrenching as her body hung limp. Her bindings cut into her wrists under the strain. The serpent plopped to the ground just before another blow fell. Her vision grew dark as she fought to breathe.

A moment later, the Leirion dropped her. She fell hard, coughing and spluttering. The two men swatted at their ankles. Could they see the gorgon's tendril as it struck at them, or merely feel its sting?

Jaxus stared, open-mouthed at everyone flailing around him. The gorgon's tendril sank its fangs into his calf. He stumbled back, yelping in surprise and pain.

Through the darkening haze clouding Forluna's vision, she saw the creature's tail as it slithered out of sight.

"You will pay dearly for that."

She shut her eyes at the hateful voice. Charixes was alive.

I failed.

Pain roiled through her as his foot collided with her ribs. Her body scraped across the floor. Rough edges of the tiny mosaic tiles cut into her arms. He kicked the knife from her feeble grasp. It skittered across the floor and slammed into the far wall so hard it ricocheted away.

Forluna's lids fluttered open just in time to see Charixes' sword sear slowly into her shoulder, laying it open to the bone. Hot, burning pain convulsed through her. She screamed, shaking in agony.

"I always wondered if nymphs could bleed. But that won't kill you, will it?"

She fought against her darkening vision. Helping her body remember how to survive.

In. Out. Slow.

The burning in her chest abated just a little.

In. Out. Slow.

A wheezing Leirion hauled her onto her knees and yanked her head back by her hair, forcing her to look at Charixes.

Charixes had sheathed his sword and now sat on his throne. His tunic had been removed, revealing rivulets of blood running down his chest and side. An attendant stood beside him, dabbing at the wound.

"You came here to kill me." Charixes' feral eyes glowered at her.

Jaxus' gaze flickered anxiously between them. No doubt worried what the penalty was for bringing an armed assassin before the anax.

Between dabs of the attendant's cloth, Forluna could see the wound was deep. Charixes tried hard to hide his pain behind his rage, but she saw it. He seemed to sense that she did, because his scowl deepened.

"Do you know how to kill a nymph?" His tone sounded too calculating, too... *pleased.*

What remaining strength she had dissolved.

"You are forest creatures. You thrive in mist and earth and trees. The forest made you, so it is said." He tilted his head. "Do you remember your birth?"

She didn't. Not exactly. Her first memory was of being amongst the trees, drawing energy from the mossy ground beneath her feet, the bark under her hands. The mist had settled on her skin like an embrace. Forluna closed her eyes, recalling how her spirit sang with the birds in the treetops, like a rush of pure joy.

Another attendant hurried into the room, carrying medical supplies and bandages. Charixes winced as they crowded him, and he had to push one aside to maintain his line of sight on Forluna.

"To kill a nymph, you must remove her from where she draws life. No earth. No mist. No trees. No living creatures. And slowly, like a shrub whose roots are torn asunder, or a tree whose trunk is felled to rot on the landscape, a nymph will wither and die."

The blood drained from Forluna's face at the very idea of such a desolate place. Did it even exist?

Charixes leered in triumph, and she knew that it did.

CHAPTER 56

LITHANEVA

THE SCENT OF OLIVE BLOSSOMS alerted Lithaneva to Hera's presence in the shadows of her room. She fidgeted on the edge of the bed, gripping the fabric of her chiton to steady her hands. Hera glided toward her, eyes focused on the basket still on the floor. The cuckoo warbled from inside.

'*Thank you, thank you,*' it seemed to coo, shaking its cage with excited hops.

Hera's shoulders visibly relaxed, and she directed her attention to Lithaneva.

Lithaneva stood on shaking legs. She bowed on instinct.

The goddess' coldness from before was gone. In its place was something unreadable and unsettling. Calculating. She waved a delicate, deadly hand. "I'm here."

Lithaneva willed her tongue to speak, but she couldn't get her lips to move. Was this the curse at work, or terror?

Hera inclined her head. "You cannot lie to me, so don't try."

Lithaneva swallowed. It was terror, then. She shoved it down, reminding herself that death was an acceptable outcome. "I want you to release me from this curse."

The boom of Hera's laugh made her jump. "You honestly think

427

you can threaten me, threaten my darlings, then ask for my *favor*?"

Indignation flared within Lithaneva. *You threatened* my *darling.* But she kept the thought to herself as Hera clasped her hands in a gesture of disbelief.

"The Titans whine about their woes and punishments, but the Fates have the greatest burden of all. You petty mortals think you deserve everything just because you draw breath." Hera's eyes flashed. "You're not worth one stitch of their toil and thread."

The truth in those words stung. Lithaneva swallowed, feeling smaller than an ant. She wished she was one so she could more easily disappear. What a terrible idea this had been. Poorly thought out, horrifically executed. Helinthia would be ashamed of her.

Hera raised her hand, pressing the pads of her thumb and second finger together. "I could have my husband's thunderbolt in my grasp with a single snap and show you just how insignificant you are."

Lithaneva shivered, fighting the urge to cower and throw her arms over her face. But she did not drop her gaze, nor fall to her knees in penance. It wasn't in her. Even now.

"I see why Helinthia chose you." Hera's eyes roved down Lithaneva's frame, her scowl softening with something that looked a little like surprise, or intrigue. "Your boldness could rival a god's. Pity you don't have the power to make it work to your advantage. What you could achieve if you were one of us."

Lithaneva's chest swelled. It was the highest compliment, coming from Hera, but the sentiment echoed her father's too closely to squash the flare of resentment. Not born a boy. Not born a goddess. Would nothing at her core ever be acceptable?

Hera crossed her long, graceful arms over her chest, bracelets flashing. "If you were a silly girl, I might be persuaded to take pity on you. But you're not a silly girl. There is no admiration that could convince me to loosen your tongue from my curse."

The cuckoo warbled in the basket.

Hera side-eyed Lithaneva. "Unless…"

Hope sprouted at the tiny word. The goddess stepped close, and

Lithaneva raised her chin to keep her gaze aligned with Hera's—she barely met the goddess' chest in height.

Hera's smile crinkled her eyes. "Unless you become *my* oracle."

Lithaneva's breath became a stone in her throat.

"Devote your talents to my glory. Forget Helinthia, as she has forgotten you. I will give you your father's throne, shower you in glory so that all will know you are my favorite. None of this secretive, undignified devotion. Your name will be uttered in awe and reverence, not scorn and pity."

Lithaneva's knees were knocking together now, and she felt a growing urge to empty her stomach. "But my father… isn't he your champion?" Her mind spun. She didn't really care about the answer to this question, but she needed the extra time to think.

Hera merely shrugged. "Champions win renown, then fade away. His deeds will live on. As will yours, if you accept my offer."

Lithaneva cradled her head in her hands, blocking the edges of her vision as though that would somehow help her focus on the right answer. *Become Hera's oracle?*

What would Helinthia think? Was there a worse betrayal than that?

She'll never forgive me. I can't do this to her.

And yet...

Her racing heart stilled as her mind delved deeper, past the terror, the horror, the grief, the regret for the pain she would inflict on Helinthia twisting in her gut. She reached down to where her resilience, her ambition, still thrived deep in her soul.

She'd never accepted the idea of death. She'd never accepted defeat, even when her own body was driven to her destruction. She glanced down at the basket, and the realization of why she hadn't wanted to kill the cuckoo slowly set in. She'd wanted Hera's attention. Now she had it.

"The last time I offered a mortal this gift, an entire civilization burned to the ground for his insolence." Hera lifted her chin, eyes flashing angrily. "Do yourself—and the world—a favor, and think beyond your sexual impulses before you open your mouth."

Lithaneva's face flamed with embarrassment. She knew of whom Hera spoke. Paris, the man who'd chosen a woman over power—power he could have wielded to claim, conquer, or seduce any lover he wanted. He had been a fool.

She would not make the same mistake.

She raised her head from her hands and straightened her shoulders, refocusing her gaze on Hera. The cuckoo was out of the basket and in Hera's palm now. The wing feathers were smoothed, and the creature had nestled down and closed its eyes as though the goddess' hand was its nest. Its sanctuary.

"The curse will be lifted?"

"Of course. I can't have you spilling *my* secrets to fools, now can I?" Hera didn't even bother looking up from her precious bird as she stroked its back with her long fingers.

Lithaneva smoothed clammy hands down the skirt of her chiton. She had lost Helinthia. Taking a thunderbolt through the heart would not win her lover back. But with control of her tongue returned and her will freed from this curse, there was a chance, minuscule but real... *I can still secure her victory.*

That was enough.

Lithaneva swallowed. "I accept."

Hera lifted her head from her pet. Her brow furrowed in surprise, or was it... revulsion? Before Lithaneva could sort it out, the goddess' expression turned murderous. "Try to cross me, and I will ensure a miserable eternity for you in Tartarus. I'll think of something far more creative than pushing a rock up a hill."

Lithaneva nodded, her mouth dry.

Hera frowned down at the cuckoo, as though the creature had offended her. She seemed disappointed, annoyed even.

Why wasn't she beaming in triumph for stealing her enemy's oracle?

"Summon the scholars at the Library," Hera commanded. "You will be a *proper* oracle this time. The entire island will know you are *mine*."

ACKNOWLEDGEMENTS

To list everyone who supported and encouraged me to keep writing would be another novel, but I want to especially thank a few who dedicated considerable time, patience, and feedback along my journey.

First, my husband Eric, whose acceptance and support of the exorbitant amount of hours I spent at the keyboard is something most people only experience in fiction novels.

Elana Mugdan, my partner in crime for author events and depressive/obsessive episodes that boosted my motivation in ways I can't even fathom, and for her amazing editing skills.

Laura and Katie, veterans of my Augusta Writer's Critique Group, whose honesty and genuine desire to help me succeed destroyed many of my best plots and arcs and enabled me to build them back better.

My beta readers, Silja, Xtian, Anna, and Laura. I really thought this story was done until your insightful feedback and suggestions pointed out critical opportunities I'd missed to make this story not just good, but GREAT.

To my illustrators, Sadie and Marina, whose skill, patience, and professionalism through my very meticulous requirements for the covers and character drawings breathed new life into the world of Helinthia and its heroes.

My final note of gratitude goes to you, Dear Reader. I hope you have enjoyed book 2 of the *Epic of Helinthia* series. Please consider leaving a review and sharing your experience so other readers can find *Epic of Helinthia* and *Oracle of Helinthia*, too. Your words mean everything to me.

ABOUT THE AUTHOR

MJ Pankey is an author, editor, and host of the Augusta Writer's Critique Group. She has been writing fiction since she was 12 and has published several short stories. Her muse is most inspired by ancient mythology and the intricacies of human psychology and behavior.

An Air Force veteran, she lives in Augusta, Georgia with her husband, Eric; three children, Dante, Athena, and Artemis; and furry writing companion, Petey.

Oracle of Helinthia is the second in a series of four novels. Join her newsletter and learn more about her at the link or QR code below:

https://linktr.ee/mjpankey

CONTENT WARNINGS

Oracle of Helinthia contains the following adult themes and situations:

Suicidal ideation
Self-abuse
Severe depression and PTSD
Psychological and emotional Abuse
Gaslighting
Domestic manipulation
Murder
Slavery
Gore and violence
Animal cruelty and death

WAR OF
HELINTHIA
MJ PANKEY

PROLOGUE

HELINTHIA

In the first year of the reign of Anassa Iptys

THE GOLDEN GATES OF Olympus loomed high on the mountain peak. Wisps of clouds curled around the marble frieze depicting gods and titans locked in battle. The scent of olive blossoms, lavender, and honeysuckle mingled with a tang of wine on the breeze. The air was clear. Crisp. Tame.

Unlike the wild, primal atmosphere of Helinthia's beloved shores, where the wind carried the essence of salt spray, dewy petrichor, and arid sand. Even here, so high above the earth, Helinthia could almost smell the pine smoke and spices of mountain herbs burning over an altar dedicated to her.

Pride bloomed in her chest. For the last five centuries, Helinthia had nurtured her island. She had *become* her island. And it was everything she'd dreamed it would be. She'd given life to the laurels, creating nymphs to be her companions; and she'd guided Apollo's son, Ordanus, and his heirs in building a nation.

Olympus's gilded doors opened as she neared, the great golden handles pulled by Hephaestus's minions. The soulless giants stood tall and straight as she passed through the archway between them.

Joyful notes of lyres and the Muses singing grew louder as she sauntered through the grand *atrium*. Laughter echoed and goblets clinked. Breathless sounds of abandon escaped from several shadowy doorways.

The *symposium* was in full swing.

She stopped on the threshold of the grand hall and scanned the room. Apollo strummed his lyre beside the Muses, head bobbing with the melody. His hand stilled when he saw Helinthia, and a wide grin spread across his handsome face. He motioned to the Muses to continue without him and glided toward her, a sparkle in his cerulean eyes.

"Little sister! Where have you been?"

Helinthia grinned. "My island, of course. I almost couldn't bear to leave it."

Apollo's eyebrows waggled mischievously. "My descendants are learning to behave themselves, then?"

Helinthia feigned an exasperated sigh. "Yes, finally!"

The half-century after Ordanus and his scraggly band of refugees landed on her shores had been full of excitement, exploration, and development—a honeymoon period between mortals and their new goddess.

But when Ordanus died and left a daughter as ruler, a squabble over which *basileus* would wed her erupted into a decades' long war that reverberated through the next four centuries. She shook her head as she recalled her frequent headaches during that period.

Humans were a resentful, stubborn species—but they were also curious, passionate, and resilient. That thought returned the smile to her lips. She could watch humans for an eternity and never be bored. And she planned to.

"Mortals are petty and easily provoked to violence." Apollo shrugged.

A secretive smile twitched at the corners of Helinthia's mouth. "My mortals *were* petty and easily provoked. Not anymore."

Apollo quirked an eyebrow. "You can't change human nature, Little Sister. You may have peace for now, but it won't last."

Poseidon strode past with his wife, Amphitrite, on his arm. He glanced over his shoulder, tossing a wink at Helinthia before disappearing into the crowd of deities. He'd overheard them. His gesture was small but encouraging.

Emboldened, she lifted her chin at Apollo. "We'll see."

Apollo eyed Poseidon's disappearing form warily and lowered his voice. "I wouldn't say that again in this company. You know how jealous our family can be."

A spark of annoyance ignited in Helinthia's chest. "They're *your* mortals I'm looking after. You should be happy I want to boast about them rather than destroy them."

Apollo's gaze softened. "I am happy. That's why I want you to be careful. Trust me. Don't mention your island more than you have to."

Helinthia looked away, her excitement dulled. Her island was her passion, her purpose. Suppressing pride in her mortals was akin to suppressing her own goddesshood.

Resentment surged beneath her skin. Why did her family always have to make everything about themselves? Why couldn't they just be happy for someone else?

Apollo squeezed her arm, jolting her from her angry thoughts. "Come. Father has been waiting on you to start the feast."

Helinthia pulled away. "You go ahead."

She tried, but failed to keep the sharpness from her tone.

Apollo sighed and walked off.

Helinthia glared after him as she fixed her clothes and rearranged the bangles on her arms.

Zeus was waiting on her, was he? *I should just leave and let them all starve.*

She hated leaving her island unattended, anyway. Especially now.

A recent plague had elevated a new anassa to the throne: Iptys.

She was strong-willed and cunning, but also young and inexperienced. Helinthia had tasked a nymph with mentoring her, but in truth, it wasn't the girl Helinthia was worried about.

Despite her boast to Apollo, Helinthia had yet to see her mortals honor a woman as a ruler and not simply a bride for the next anax. Iptys had shown little desire to entertain the latter, which was bound to bruise the egos of her male subjects and stir unnecessary chaos. Accepting that a woman was just as capable as–if not more than–a man when it came to leadership remained a virtue beyond their reach.

Why am I not there?

Nothing was more important than her island. Certainly not a stupid, frivolous feast. Mind made up, she turned to leave. Before she could take two steps, Artemis entered the atrium, blocking her escape.

"Hel." Her older sister stopped before her. The dazzling smile on her lips faded as she took in Helinthia's expression.

"Oh, what happened?"

"Your brother," Helinthia muttered, and Artemis raised her brows.

"*Our* brother? What's he done this time? Not dropped another bastard on your beach, I hope?"

"Quite the opposite. He doesn't want me to talk about my island or my mortals. Says our family won't like it."

"Ah." Artemis fell silent for a moment, then nudged her playfully. "Well. He's probably right."

Anger surged through Helinthia. "Everyone else gloats and boasts. Why can't I do the same?"

"No one will stop you," Artemis said slowly. "But don't expect applause from this jealous lot."

Helinthia folded her arms across her chest. "I hate it here. I'm going back to my island."

Her sister giggled and looped her arm through Helinthia's. "Come on, let's at least enjoy the food. Hmm?"

Artemis clearly didn't think she was serious. As she opened her mouth to protest, Poseidon's gaze found her from across a sea of faces and elaborate crowns. He smiled as their eyes met.

Apollo's warning thrummed through her for a moment before her resentment washed it away like a wave. She smiled back. Perhaps she could stay a while. She did owe her uncle a conversation; after all, he *had* raised her island from the depths of the sea.

Artemis guided her in between the guests. Gods, titans, and nymphs from all over the world stared at her as she brushed past them. Their less than friendly—or perhaps just indifferent—looks stirred her ire.

She started to pull away from Artemis. Poseidon's sudden appearance stopped her.

"Niece." He beamed down at her, the long strands of his curly beard waving as he spoke. Ironically, it reminded her of seaweed.

"Uncle." She dipped her head.

"Sit next to me. I want to hear what you've done with my island."

'My island.' She bristled and opened her mouth to correct him, but his playful wink stopped her.

"I've claimed her company tonight, Uncle," Artemis said, squeezing Helinthia's arm protectively.

"Then sit on her other side," Poseidon declared, placing a hand on Helinthia's back and ushering her forward before either goddess could argue. He guided her to one of the couches surrounding a huge table piled high with meats, fruits, and cheeses.

As soon as Helinthia sat, a serving nymph handed her a plate of food and a goblet of wine. Artemis sat on her other side, as suggested, but it was clear Poseidon intended to dominate the conversation. She was forced to angle away from Artemis as he began speaking.

"Are your mortals warring?" he asked, eyes eager as he chomped into a slice of meat.

"No," she answered, the familiar pride fluttering in her stomach.

He stopped chewing and lifted his brows. "No? Not at all?"

Helinthia picked at the crispy skin on her goose leg.

'You know how jealous our family can be.'

"There was plenty of war at the beginning," she corrected, "but not anymore."

"Really?"

Helinthia bit into the roasted meat and made a show of chewing to buy herself time to respond. Something menacing hid beneath Poseidon's smooth, innocent tone. She couldn't quite place it, but she wished she hadn't let Artemis convince her to stay. Her brother had been right to advise caution.

Helinthia caught her mother staring at them from her throne atop a marble staircase veined with gold. Hera leaned over to murmur in Zeus's ear. She did not look happy.

Is she angry with me? But why?

"This peace fascinates me." Poseidon said more, but his words were lost on Helinthia as Hera stood and descended the steps. She pressed into the crowd, making her way toward them.

Gaia, she looks even angrier than a moment ago. Helinthia swallowed, the half-chewed food scraping down her throat. She reached for her wine to wash it down.

Hera stopped before them and clasped her hands in front of her. "What have you to say to my daughter, Poseidon?"

His eyes sparkled as he popped a grape into his mouth and crushed it. Drops of juice squirted out, landing on Helinthia's hand.

She grimaced and wiped it on the couch.

"She's telling me how much better her mortals are than everyone else's. Isn't that right?"

Helinthia furrowed her brow. "I never said that."

"No? Did you not attest that your mortals were no longer petty or easily provoked to violence?"

Oh no. This was a trap. Her eyes scanned the crowd, landing on Apollo. He was watching them, irritation in his furrowed brow.

Everyone was watching them.

Helinthia's tongue felt thick in her mouth, sluggish.

"I heard you say it," Poseidon continued. "Are you accusing me of lying?"

"Of course not, Uncle," Helinthia said quickly, trying hard to keep the venom from her tone. "I did say that earlier. To my *brother*."

Hera's lips pinched into a thin line.

"So, you attest that your mortals are superior to other mortals?" Poseidon pressed.

Helinthia's blood hammered in her ears. It was unbearably hot. Where were the nymphs with the *rhipes*? Artemis squeezed her arm. Helinthia knew the gesture was meant to encourage her, but it felt like a manacle closing around her wrist.

"That's not what I said."

"But that's what you *meant*." Poseidon's friendly-uncle facade was gone.

Oh, how she wished she hadn't taken offense to Apollo's warning. She had played right into her uncle's scheme.

Helinthia poked at a grape as she considered denying his accusation. She could declare her words were a joke, but the storms in her uncle's gaze promised he'd contest her honesty. She would be forced to drink the water of the Styx to prove it.

And she would fail.

What would become of her island while she wandered the earth for a year, witless, waiting for the effects of her lie to wear off?

She shuddered.

"Daughter?" Hera said, her tone much softer than Helinthia expected.

"Yes, that is what I meant," Helinthia admitted. She raised her eyes to the crowd gathered around them. Zeus, Hermes, Athena, Apollo, Aphrodite, Ares, Demeter, Hestia. Even Hephaestus had wandered over in curiosity. They watched with bated breath, like hounds waiting for the killing blow before sinking their own teeth into the prey.

Poseidon had caught her in his snare, but he would not take her pride.

Helinthia lifted her chin. "My mortals are reverent and benevolent, generous with their offerings, and loyal to me as their goddess. Under my patronage, the mortals and nymphs of my island have become worthy to take their place among the greatest heroes of Greece."

"Heroes are forged in battle," Ares chimed in.

Helinthia's fingers tightened around the goose leg. Juices dripped over her knuckles as she glowered at her brother. Had he ever said an intelligent thing in all his existence? *Jealous brat. Always trying to sound smart and inserting himself where no one asked him to.*

Poseidon glared up at Hera. "Indeed. A shame your daughter doesn't know this. How have you allowed her to become so arrogant and disrespectful? I gave her an island, and this is how she shows her gratitude?"

Hera drew in a breath to reply, but Helinthia didn't give her mother the chance. "What do you want from me, Uncle?" she snapped, earning a few scattered gasps.

Athena quirked a brow at her—the smallest hint of admiration in the gesture. Few dared to put Poseidon in his place. Helinthia had no idea why. He was a coward. How many times had Athena single-handedly proven that?

Hermes groaned. "Can we *please* not do this again?"

"Do what, Brother?" Ares' mischievous smirk stirred Helinthia's ire even more.

Poseidon's lips twisted into a malicious grin. "Mortal warfare."

Fluttering in her stomach turned to a frantic buzz. "What do you mean?"

"My 'inferior' mortals against yours. Victor controls the island and all its inhabitants."

Hermes groaned again and tapped his cup at Ganymede, who pressed through the deities to reach him with an *amphora* of wine. "The last time you decided to measure each other's egos, I didn't stop ferrying souls to Hades for twenty years. Every time you squabble amongst yourselves, I'm saddled with the consequences."

Helinthia's nerves burst into a thousand sharp knives as images of her mortals, slain and mutilated, flashed into her mind. *No.* She couldn't lose her island, her humans, her friends. She'd worked so hard for them.

Why is Poseidon doing this to me?

'You know how jealous our family can be.'

Was that it, then? Did Poseidon see her success and want it for himself? Or were his feelings deeper than that?

She looked to her father. She'd always believed Poseidon had gifted her an island willingly, but Zeus's sympathetic stare and the lack of surprise in his features revealed a different story.

How could you? she wanted to scream. Zeus could have warned her Poseidon harbored resentment. Her eyes flickered over the other gods, and the wound of betrayal deepened in her gut as she read their expressions. They *all* knew.

"You're right, Poseidon."

Her mother's words hit her like a slap. Helinthia stared, breath catching in her throat. Of all the immortals here, Hera had the most experience being baited and trampled on by other gods. Surely, she wouldn't let this happen to her own flesh and *ichor.*

I'm your daughter, Helinthia pleaded with her eyes.

Zeus's gaze turned wary, as though wondering what scheme his wife was planning now.

"If it is depravity you seek to prove in Helinthia's mortals, you won't accomplish that with an attacking force. That will only strengthen their virtue. Immortalize it."

Poseidon narrowed his eyes. "Do you have a better idea?"

Hera cast him a withering look. "Of course."

A spark of hope bloomed within Helinthia. *Please, Mother…*

Hera faced Helinthia. She towered over her, and though Helinthia hoped for rescue, she couldn't help but feel more like she was about to be scolded.

"Daughter, Ordanus's heirs have ruled your island from its

inception, have they not?"

Helinthia nodded slowly.

"Why them?"

"They are loyal to me." She answered without hesitation.

"Why do the other mortals not challenge their power?"

Helinthia swallowed the lump in her throat. "I have promised the island favor through their rule."

Poseidon scoffed. "So their 'superior nature' is the result of divine bribery? How..." He smirked. "*Mortal* of them."

Helinthia shot her uncle a menacing glare, but worry tightened in her stomach.

Hera raised her hand at Poseidon to silence him, irritation flashing in her furrowed brow. "Heroes are not forged by *battle*" — she cut her eyes at Ares— "but by their willingness to sacrifice everything for truth, bravery, and loyalty."

A chill ran down Helinthia's spine. Poseidon met her gaze, her wariness mirrored in his turquoise eyes. Where was her mother going with this?

Hera played with a tassel on her veil. She was enjoying the attention—the control—far too much. "Daughter, do you attest that Ordanus's heir will remain loyal to you at any cost?"

"If you're planning to kill them—"

"*Willingness*, Helinthia," Hera interrupted.

Helinthia clamped her jaw shut. There was a trap in this questioning, but what choice did she have? "Yes."

"And will the other mortals remain true to your chosen sovereign, even when your favor is in doubt?"

"My favor is not in d—"

Hera raised her hand again.

Rage boiled in her chest. Helinthia drew in a deep breath. It would not do to lose her temper with the Anassa of Heaven. She didn't want to answer this question—she was less sure of her answer, but she couldn't back down now. "Yes."

Hera smiled. "I will issue a test." She surveyed the nosy gods with an authoritative stare. "The test is for *mortals*. If anyone feels inclined to meddle, you may do so only through your oracles. There will be *no* divine interference outside of this, or there will be severe consequences."

Helinthia's lungs tightened. What did that mean? Could she no longer speak with Iptys? Counsel her? Warn her? All Helinthia's questions jumbled in her head, refusing to form into words.

Poseidon waved a dismissive hand. "Fine. When her mortals fail, I get my island back."

Horror twisted in Helinthia's gut.

No!

Hera's eyes were cold, unflinching. "Agreed."

In the eighteenth year of the reign of Anax Charixes

Angry tears streamed down Helinthia's face like the falling leaves of the laurel trees around her. The memory of Hera's betrayal felt as fresh now as it had the moment she'd taken Poseidon's side.

Helinthia reached the marble platform where the giant statue of a titaness had fallen over and lay covered in vines. Gaia, she was sure.

Great-Grandmother. She choked down a sob as she slumped against the stone face.

This was the place Helinthia had come that fateful day— heartbroken, angry, vengeful, desperate. She'd always found comfort resting against the statue's smooth, vacant features. Like a gentle touch from beyond the ages. This was the place where she had devised her grand plan to intercept Hera's oracle, Eraia. To bend the outcome of this nonsensical challenge to her advantage.

If only she had trusted Iptys to remain loyal. Instead, Helinthia had doubted her anassa's ability to lead: the very same offense she had worried her mortals would make.

Now a madman ruled her island.

What would have happened if Helinthia had not interfered? If Hera had not thrown her full support behind Charixes as punishment?

There was no doubt in Helinthia's mind that he'd always meant to claim the throne. Iptys had known it, too—she had seen the monster hiding beneath the gallant gestures and handsome flattery.

Charixes would have failed, and Helinthia would have her island.

Helinthia's grand—stupid—plan had crumbled into dust like the bones of the oracle she had silenced.

Hera had taken her final revenge.

The image of Lithaneva with her lips on Branitus, begging him to defile her, flashed hatefully over and over in Helinthia's mind.

Lithaneva would not betray me so utterly and completely without Hera's meddling. Helinthia was sure of it.

Hera, the anassa of lies and deceit, had broken her own rule and interfered. She must have threatened Lithaneva. Tortured her. Twisted her somehow.

But the fact remained that Lithaneva *had* betrayed her.

Utterly and completely.

Another victory notch in her mother's quest to prove that Helinthia's mortals were depraved, gutless, and traitorous. No more superior than worms mindlessly wriggling toward the closest beam of warmth.

A sharp stab in Helinthia's chest nearly took her breath away. *Lithaneva...*

So many times, Helinthia might have given up if it hadn't been for Lithaneva. The mortal princess had grounded her, emboldened her, kept her faith in humanity strong.

"This is not over!" Helinthia ground out, clenching a fistful of tangled vines. Her voice carried through the Forest of the Shades, startling a few birds from the branches.

Helinthia had tried so hard to keep her lover safe. All the nights Helinthia had abstained from the warmth of Lithaneva's touch—the cold, lonely, restless nights—tore at her. She could almost feel her lover's smooth skin on her fingertips, the soft tickle of her dark curls floating across her body.

Helinthia yanked at the vines, ripping the tendrils from the stone and revealing the statue's curved mouth.

It was all for nothing!

Helinthia tore another vine free. Then another, screaming in rage until the bindings lay in a heap on the ground and the stone titaness gazed at her through lidless eyes.

Why was Hera so bent on destroying her? She didn't have to side with Poseidon. If it was a fight she'd wanted, she could have fought beside her daughter. Fought *for* her daughter.

Hera had loved much—and lost even more—since Zeus had freed her from Cronos's belly. Was she beyond wanting a better Fate for her daughter?

'You know how jealous our family can be.'

Did Helinthia's happiness burn Hera so much that spite suppressed all her motherly instincts?

Whatever Hera's motives, Helinthia had given up trying to understand them.

But she would never give up without a fight. No god of the ocean or goddess of heaven was going to take Helinthia's island from her. Ordanus's line was pure and heroic. She had made sure of it, nurtured every ruler with patience and love.

They would prove themselves again.

The branches of the laurel trees sent another cascade of leaves and petals downward, disturbing the thick mist in chaotic swirls. A sweet fragrance filled her nostrils—a reminder of all she held dear. Of all she still fought for.

Lithaneva was lost to her. But Helinthia still had Dargos, the man she had healed to become her champion. She still had Gadnor, the hero who would usher in a new age of peace and prosperity. Together, they would prove to all the gods that her mortals were superior.

She smiled through her tears.

They will not fail me.

MORE FROM MJ PANKEY

When a madman seizes the throne, the gods on Olympus fall silent, and the isle of Helinthia descends into decay…

Anassa Iptys' glorious city burns. Forluna escapes with the rightful heir, a descendent of Apollo, and hides him away. But the new Anax, Charixes, is relentless. He will not rest until his hands are drenched in their blood.

Under Charixes' rule, the gods abandon the island, and a devastating famine ravages the population. Desperate to win divine favor and end Charixes' cruelty, Dargos persuades Kelric and Gadnor to join him in rebellion. They embark on a quest to rally support for war, leaving Dargos' sister, Gonivein, safe behind the walls of Shallinath.

But the Anax' spies have been watching, waiting for the right opportunity to strike. Capturing Gonivein is the devastating blow Charixes needs to crush all opposition to his tyranny.

To defeat him, they need the gods on their side. The heir of Apollo can bring them back.

There's just one problem: only Forluna knows where he is, and she has vowed to take her secret with her to the Underworld.

Read the first installment of the *Epic of Helinthia* series. Available everywhere you buy books.

450

MORE FROM MJ PANKEY

"Before Gods" in *Muses of the Muses*, published by <u>Brigids Gate Press</u>.

Listen to the Muses, as they sing aloud…HER story.

Musings of the Muses, 65 stories and poems based on Greek myths, is an anthology of monsters, heroines, and goddesses, ranging from ancient Greece to modern day America. They, like the myths themselves, cast long shadows of horror, fantasy, love, betrayal, vengeance, and redemption. This anthology revisits those old tales and presents them anew, from her point of view.

Available everywhere you buy books.

MORE FROM MJ PANKEY

A Greek mythology inspired early reader chapter book series!

Meet Iris. She lives with her parents beside the ocean. Every day, she waters the clouds to make it rain so the plants will grow.

When a boy arrives from Olympus, Iris is tasked with helping him solve a mystery: Zeus's daughters have accused each other of lying, but each argues they are telling the truth. Their friendship is in peril and the tension is causing mayhem on Olympus!

Iris must find a magical river and bring some of its water back to Olympus. This water will make anyone who drinks it tell the truth.

There's just *one* problem. Iris must go to the Underworld—a dark, terrifying place filled with dangerous monsters—to find it.
Can Iris face her fears and uncover the truth?

COMING DECEMBER 2025!